SHADES
of
FORTUNE

BOOKS BY STEPHEN BIRMINGHAM

Young Mr. Keefe
Barbara Greer
The Towers of Love
Those Harper Women
Fast Start, Fast Finish
"Our Crowd"
The Right People
Heart Troubles
The Grandees
The Late John Marquand
The Right Places
Real Lace
Certain People
The Golden Dream
Jacqueline Bouvier Kennedy Onassis
Life at the Dakota
California Rich
Duchess
The Grandes Dames
The Auerbach Will
"The Rest of Us"
The Lebaron Secret
America's Secret Aristocracy
Shades of Fortune

SHADES
of
FORTUNE

A NOVEL BY

Stephen Birmingham

LITTLE, BROWN AND COMPANY

BOSTON   TORONTO   LONDON

Publisher's Note: This work is one of fiction, but does contain characters
who exist in real life and companies that exist outside of this novel. None of
the personal activities or corporate actions in which the novel depicts these
persons as being involved did in fact occur.

*Published simultaneously in Canada
by Little, Brown & Company (Canada) Limited*

PRINTED IN THE UNITED STATES OF AMERICA

SHADES
of
FORTUNE

Part One

A FAMILY ALBUM

"*I*F YOU WANT to make a good impression on people," my father used to say, "be a listener, not a talker. It's known as drawing people out, and it's not hard to do. Most people enjoy talking about themselves, and when they find someone who'll listen to them, they're happy as clams at high tide. They'll like you right away."

Most people pay little attention to parental advice, but this one small piece stuck with me. And after a lifetime of listening to people talk, and making notes of some of it, I have developed a habit, which has become something of a private hobby, and that is imagining what people are talking about when I could not possibly be around to hear their conversations. That was what I began doing when I saw that extraordinary-looking young couple step out of a taxi in front of Mimi Myerson's building at 1107 Fifth Avenue that late-August evening in 1987, while I sat on a bench on the park side of the avenue filling out, in a desultory sort of way, the squares of the crossword puzzle in that afternoon's *Post.*

Though I had not yet met this couple, I knew immediately who they were, and knew they were also going to Mimi's dinner party.

I envisioned the girl entering the gilt-and-walnut elevator cab and immediately addressing the mirrored panel at the cab's rear, intently scrutinizing her face, applying the business end of a rat-tail comb to a wayward wisp of dark hair, and saying to her companion, "What's she like, I wonder. I hear she's a real bitch."

The young man, who appeared more poised and certainly more worldly-wise, says, "Didn't you have an *interview?* I had an *interview.*"

"I was chosen from my composite," the girl replies, still studying her image in the glass. "Out of a hundred finalists. Do I have too much eye makeup on? Tell me the truth."

"Rule number one," the young man says, "is that if you have to ask *whether* you have too much eye makeup on, you *do*."

"You're the one who's the bitch," the girl says.

Their names were Sherrill Shearson and Dirk Gordon, known by certain of his friends as "Flash" Gordon. His name was real, while hers was the invention of the Ford Modeling Agency. Sherrill Shearson was born Irene Godowsky. That much I knew about them, and I could imagine Buddy, the elevator man, whom I'd already gotten to know quite well, listening impassively to this exchange while pretending not to, as he guided his passengers upward to Mimi's apartment entrance on the fourteenth floor.

Eleven-oh-seven is one of the few buildings left in New York City where the two elevators are still manned by a pair of uniformed operators who wear gold epaulets and white gloves. It is a building whose entrance lobby is secured not only by a doorman but also by a concierge who sits all day long at a desk inside the entrance, behind a sign that reads, ALL VISITORS TO 1107 FIFTH AVENUE MUST BE ANNOUNCED. It is a grand old building, put up in the twenties when cost was no object, and its splendid old Otises rise slowly, majestically, almost noiselessly. It is the kind of building that, as Mimi Myerson herself has said humorously, "If you live here, you become instant old money." No one was surprised, a while back, when Ralph Lauren bought the duplex just two floors below Mimi's. The people who live here, many of them, are the kind of people who the people in Ralph Lauren's ads pretend to be. If you had seen Sherrill Shearson and Dirk Gordon entering Mimi's building that evening, being announced, and being ushered to the north elevator, you might have imagined them stepping out of a Ralph Lauren ad, but with a difference. Their faces were less jaded, fresher, younger.

The reason I happened to be sitting on a park bench across the street, working the *Post*'s crossword, was that I was early for Mimi's dinner. Traffic up from the Village had been lighter than I'd anticipated. At the time, I didn't know Mimi as well as I later got to know her—hadn't fallen in love with her as, in an odd way, I later did. But I did know her reputation as a fastidious hostess, a perfectionist in every detail of entertaining, and I knew that at the last minute before any party there were always small, last-minute details to attend to—an anthurium with a browning pistil to be plucked out of a centerpiece, for instance. I also happened to know that it wouldn't matter if Dirk Gordon and Sherrill Shearson were a full ten minutes early.

For they were, essentially, no more than a part of Mimi's decor, not much more important than one of her flower arrangements.

But that's not quite fair. From a business standpoint, they were important to her, though their importance was not of the sort that they appeared to attach to themselves. Watching their entrance into the building, one might have supposed that these two were principals in some sort of currently unfolding national, or even international, drama. For one thing, there was a certain studied exquisiteness about this pair, an insouciance—he in that impeccably fitted dinner jacket, she in a lipstick-red Scaasi, which, knowing who she was and where she came from, I suspected had been borrowed from a more affluent roommate. Then there was that moment when, after alighting from the taxi, they both paused almost haughtily beneath the building's marquee, looking first up the avenue, then down, as though they expected flashbulbs to start popping and videotapes to start rolling and were giving the cameramen time to adjust their shutters and set their lights. "Where is *Women's Wear?*" they seemed to be demanding. "Where are the people from NBC's *Nightly News?*" Of course there were no cameras. And yet in just a few weeks' time—or at least this was Mimi's plan—these two were to become the focus of just that sort of national attention. Fame and recognition were part of Mimi's plan for them, and I knew that Mimi Myerson was a woman who always had a plan.

The plan was to make Sherrill Shearson's face as famous as Brooke Shields's and Dirk Gordon's as recognizable as Robert Redford's as, in the next few weeks, they began seductively addressing Americans from their television screens and the glossy pages of the fashion magazines as the Mireille Woman and the Mireille Man.

If the campaign was successful, before it was over each would have earned something in the neighborhood of two million dollars.

And then what? Though these beautiful two did not know it yet, once this costly advertising campaign had run its course, both might find themselves virtually unemployable. It is one of the glum ironies of this business. For this is a business in which intense celebrity can be followed by an even more intense oblivion. It is called overexposure. A few years from now, I thought, unless they were very careful, she might be going back to modeling shoes on Seventh Avenue, and he might become a dance instructor at Arthur Murray's.

But who knew at that point? Tonight they were nobodies about to be, however briefly, Somebodies—she, a raven-haired girl of nineteen who, with her eye makeup and in her Scaasi, managed to look two or three years older, and he, a young man of twenty-five who, for career purposes, said he was twenty-two, with hair the color of canary feathers.

"I want a blond male and a brunet female," Mimi had said. These were they. It didn't matter that they loathed each other.

And their importance to the story is that Mimi's dinner party was where it all began, and these two were the first to arrive.

As they ascended in the elevator, I imagined her saying, not to him, but to her reflection in the mirror, "So. If you've met her, what's she like?"

And his superior reply, "You'll see, love."

And her turning now to Buddy to demand imperiously: "So you work here. So what's this broad like?"

And Buddy, not approving of this sort of talk in his car, saying politely but reproachfully, "You'll find that Mrs. Moore is a very great lady, ma'am."

Now they are at the fourteenth floor, and Buddy's white-gloved hand slides the door open for them, and they step out, and the door glides closed behind them.

"Never talk about your hostess in front of her elevator man," the young man says. "Bad form, love. Rule number two. It'll get back to her that you said you heard she was a bitch."

The elevator foyer of Mimi's apartment is a small, oval room, with walls covered in pale yellow silk and with a pair of Regency commodes flanking the front door, and above each commode hangs an oval mirror in a silver frame. I saw the young woman immediately go to one of these, lipstick in hand.

"And what's this Mrs. Moore shit?" the girl says, pouting at the mirror. "I thought her name was Mimi Myerson."

"Rule number three," the young man says. "When you're in her office, she's Miss Myerson. When you're in her house, she's Mrs. Bradford Moore."

"This isn't a house. It's an apartment, asshole."

"On Fifth Avenue, an apartment is called a house, even if it's an apartment. That's rule number—what? Four, I think."

"Fuck you and your rules," the girl says.

The young man leans languidly against the door frame, plucks an invisible fleck of lint from the sleeve of his dinner jacket, and says, "Oh, my, what a foul little tongue we have in that pretty head. That pretty, empty head. When you've finished with your face, let me know, and I'll ring the doorbell. Meanwhile, knowing a few rules of correct behavior might explain why I get five hundred an hour, and you've never made more than two-fifty."

"Not anymore that's all I get, faggot," she says.

"Try charm," he says. "Try it tonight. Who knows—if you tried a little bit of charm, you might even have a future, love. It would certainly be worth a try."

"I got this contract, didn't I?"

"This woman could always change her mind, you know," he says. "She's been known to do that in the past."

From the mirror, she gives him a brief, frightened look—in that moment she looks about thirteen—and he touches the doorbell with the tip of his index finger, as though testing a soufflé for doneness.

Downstairs, from across the street, and imagining this typically unpleasant exchange between two unknowns—"I want unknowns," Mimi said. "I want two brand-new faces, faces that will belong exclusively to me"—I looked up at Mimi's apartment through the leafy shade of the trees and saw the lights coming on in room after room. Then, in a sudden oblique shaft of afternoon sunlight against an open window of what I knew was her bedroom, I was amazed to see, even from fourteen floors below, her unmistakable silhouette, and for a moment I imagined I heard her special, ripply laugh. Then I saw the figure of a man approaching her, and saw her quickly turn her back to him. The man bent over her, and I realized that he was zipping her into a white dress, and that this man was not Brad Moore, her husband. Brad, I knew, had been detained at his office and would be fifteen or twenty minutes late. I saw that the man helping her with her zipper was Felix, Mimi's major domo.

There was nothing unusual about this. But then I saw something that astonished me. I saw Felix's tall shape bend lower and kiss her bare shoulder. There was no mistaking this. He had kissed her. Then both shadows moved away from the window, he presumably to answer the doorbell, and she to start down the curved staircase to greet her first guests.

I was mystified by the kiss. Mimi Myerson Moore did not strike me as a woman who would have a love affair with her butler. It was incongruous. It simply did not fit. In the aftermath of that accidental invasion of her privacy, I kept trying to turn the man's shape into that of Brad Moore. But I knew that Brad had said he would be late, that I was early, and that since my arrival no one had entered the building except the Mireille Man and the Mireille Woman. Also, Brad's was a shorter, stockier, more athletic frame. This man had been taller, thinner, slightly stooped, unquestionably Felix. And somehow the kiss on the shoulder conveyed a more heightened degree of intimacy and tenderness than even a kiss full on the lips would have done. I was nonplussed by it.

Later, I would learn the significance of that kiss. In time, I, too, would be asked to kiss her in just that fashion. But, at the time, I was stunned by what I'd just seen. And I was left with the decidedly unpleasant feeling that, by looking up at her windows just then, I had inadvertently and unintentionally been wrenched from my accustomed role as a listener and become something I have never been, nor ever wanted to be: a voyeur.

* * *

Meanwhile, from other parts of town, other guests are making their way to Mimi's dinner party. Mr. Edwin Myerson's limousine left his house on Sutton Square punctually at seven-fifteen, heading westward. Edwin Myerson, whom everyone in the family has always called "Edwee," is Mimi Myerson's uncle, her father's younger brother. Edwee, as some of you may know, has never had anything to do with the Miray Corporation and is, instead, an art historian and critic of some note, as well as a gourmet cook. His recipes sometimes make their way into the pages of magazines like *Vogue* and *Town & Country*, and his art criticism, which is often harder to follow than his directions for preparing a *galantine*, is published from time to time in *Art & Antiques* and *Connoisseur*, where even his editors are sometimes not sure what Edwee is trying to say. ("The coy caprices of Poussin, so underestimated, are qualified only in the quantum and are introspective by virtue of their quixotic relationship to the later fauves and pointillists. . . .") Edwee is a fop, a dandy, a bon vivant, and pleased that his full head of hair, cut rather long, is greying in all the right places. He is fifty-five, and his trademark is the red carnation he always wears in his buttonhole. He is a pet friend of Nancy Reagan's and has sported his signature *boutonnière* at White House family dinners.

With Edwee in his car is his wife of just six months, a young woman with peach-colored hair named Gloria. Marriage is a new experiment for Edwee Myerson, and he is finding it both novel and reasonably pleasant. "You look like a faustian rose," he has just said to his bride in the back seat of the car, for she is wearing a dress, of the same sherbet color as her hair, that he picked out for her in a little shop on Madison, which, thus far, only he and Mrs. Reagan know about.

"*What* kind of a rose?" And then, "What's this dinner party all about, anyway?"

"One of M-M-Mimi's little whimsies, I fancy." Edwee Myerson has a little stammer and has particular trouble with his *m*'s and his *b*'s. In the back seat, Gloria reaches out and tickles Edwee's crotch with her lacquered fingertips. "Naughty little pussycat," he whispers.

At 200 East 66th Street, Edwee and Gloria's limousine makes its first stop, which is to collect Naomi Myerson, Edwee's older sister and Mimi's aunt Nonie, along with her escort for the evening, a somewhat younger man named Roger Williams, whom Edwee has not met before. Edwee's greeting to this Williams is of the customary chilliness he reserves for all strangers whose names are not familiar from the press and, in particular, for male friends of Nonie's. Nonie, after all, despite her fame as a great beauty in her youth (the forties and fifties), has had notably poor luck with men, both as husbands and as lovers, and even as casual acquaintances.

"Darlings," Nonie murmurs as Edwee's driver helps her into the car and as she immediately fills the interior of the vehicle with waves of some violent and passionate and dangerous new perfume. "Darlings, I want you to meet my *brilliant* new friend, Roger Williams," she says as they settle into the car. "Roger, these are my brother, Edwee, and his wife, Gloria."

"Hello," says Edwee, extending his hand halfway.

"Pleased to meet you, I'm sure," says Gloria.

The car moves northward into the traffic.

In the flattering evening light, and within the tinted-glass interior of Edwee's car, Naomi Myerson, whom everybody in the family calls Nonie, is almost beautiful again. Nonie is not young, but few people in the family can do more than guess at her exact age, and she has lied about it for so long that even she, if she suddenly decided to be truthful, would probably be unable to give you the figure. Only her mother could tell you the date of her birth, and her mother would never dare to do this, knowing how Nonie feels about this subject. Not even Edwee knows his older sister's age, though by the time he was ten years old Nonie had already been married and divorced. You do the arithmetic.

Nonie's age is a secret she will carry with her to her grave. She has never been required to reveal it. By the time she was old enough to drive a car, her father could afford a chauffeur, and so Nonie has never owned a driver's license. The birthdate on her passport is off by a mile. Though she has worked—oh, Nonie has worked at a number of different enterprises and enthusiasms—she has never needed to apply for Social Security. If you are rich enough, there are some things you never have to do. If one is rich enough, too, one can occasionally find oneself in certain financial straits, which has been one of Nonie's recurring problems, but more of that later.

Suffice to say that Nonie Myerson (through all her marriages she has always kept Myerson as her "professional" name) looks younger than she is. She takes good care of herself. She is always dieting, and she is proud of her slim legs and slender ankles, and of being a perfect size four. Tiny, almost invisible scars behind her hairline have replaced wrinkles that might have appeared. In the past, pregnancies have been terminated before they could threaten her with stretch marks. Her hair is still the glossy auburn shade that it always was, and thanks to the ministrations of a clever hairdresser on East 69th Street, it still bounces like a teenager's when she walks. Tonight, in a short black Dior, which flatters her, with a simple strand of pearls at her throat, pearl-and-diamond earrings, and a single diamond solitaire on her ring finger, she looks, as her friends sometimes say about her, "remarkably well-preserved." Needless to say, they do not say this to her face.

She has a habit of sitting with her chin tilted upward, as though balancing something very small and light—a feather, perhaps—on the tip of her perfectly sculpted nose. In the car, she sits this way now.

"So what's this dinner party all *about?*" her new sister-in-law, Gloria, asks again, this time of Nonie.

"I expect little Mimi has some sort of *announcement* to make," Nonie says. "Something about the company. She said it was going to be mostly family, but there would be one or two surprise guests. Don't you detest surprises?"

"What a wretched business," Edwee says. "How does poor Mimi stand it, dealing with that class of people?"

"I haven't seen you tearing up your dividend checks, Edwee dear," Nonie says, still balancing whatever it is on the tip of her nose.

"I mean so vulgar. The cosmetics business. Not much better than the rag business, is it? So Jewish."

"Well, Edwee dear, we *are* Jewish," Nonie says.

Gloria lets out a little squeal. "Edwee?" she cries. "Are we *Jewish?* You never told me that!"

He pats her knee. "Just a little bit Jewish," he says. "Don't worry your little head about it, pussycat."

"But I think I should of told my mother about that, if I was going to marry somebody Jewish, I mean."

"Doesn't Mumsy like Jewish people, pussycat?"

"I just don't think she's ever *known* any."

"Well, now she knows me," he says.

"Does that make *me* Jewish?"

Edwee, changing the subject, turns to his sister, who has been ignoring all this, still gazing upward at the ceiling of the car, and says, "Mostly family. Does that mean poor Alice will be there?"

"Yes, I believe so."

"Then I predict a debacle," Edwee says.

"Not necessarily. Alice's been behaving herself lately. The Betty Ford Center, you know."

"But how long will *that* last? How long have all of Alice's other treatments lasted?"

"I think we should try to show Alice that she has our support," Nonie says.

"Until the next fiasco," Edwee sighs.

"Who is Alice?" the young man named Roger Williams asks in a pleasant voice.

"Ah," says Edwee, settling back in his seat and carefully lighting his pipe. "A very good question, Mr. Windsor. Who is Alice?"

"It's Williams."

"Mr. Williams, then. Who *is* Alice? How would you answer that, Nonie dear?" Without waiting for her reply, he continues, "Alice is Fair Alicia, no relation of ours whatsoever, except by a little fluke of circumstance called marriage. Alice is dear Mimi's mother. She is our tragic sister-in-law, in tragic decline, the widow of our tragic brother Henry, who was Mimi's father. Alice is *La Dame aux camélias*. She is Alice of the haunted past."

"I see," Williams says drily. "Now I know all I need to know about Alice."

"Alice is of little consequence to this family, other than the fact that from her loins sprang Mimi, like Athena, full-b-b-blown, from the head of Zeus. There are some Williamses in Cincinnati. A very fine old family. Are they your people?"

"I'm afraid not."

"I thought not," Edwee says, dismissing this elegant young roughneck with a gesture of his pipe.

The car has one more stop to make before heading toward its final destination at 1107 Fifth Avenue. This is at the Carlyle, to pick up Fleurette Guggenheim Myerson, Edwee and Nonie's mother, Mimi's grandmother, and the widow of the great Adolph Myerson, who started everything. As the long black limousine approaches the Carlyle, the doorman recognizes it and steps into the lobby to assist Mrs. Myerson through the door.

Fleurette Myerson, whom Mimi and the younger members of the family call Granny Flo, is eighty-nine now, and a little frail, and nearly blind, but she still manages to get around a bit. To be certain that she will not be late when her son's car comes for her, this tiny lady has been sitting in the Carlyle's lobby for the better part of the past hour. As the car pulls up, Fleurette Myerson emerges from the hotel entrance, one hand tucked into a bellman's elbow, the other gripping a Lucite cane, while the doorman holds the door open for them. Edwee's chauffeur leaps out of the car with unusual speed, for it will take the three men to steer Mrs. Myerson safely into the back seat without mishap, see that she is settled there, her cane within her reach, a karakul robe spread across her lap. Now, with her reticule perched on her knees, she sits securely throned under a soft coronet of pale purple hair.

"Thank you, Harry," she says to the bellman as these small feats are accomplished. "That one's called Harry," she says to the others in the car. "He's on nights. He's a good boy. He finds Lawrence Welk for me on the TV." Now her small gloved hands flutter about the interior of the car, touching the others, identifying them by the feel of a kneecap, a shoulder, a wrist. "There's someone else in here!" she cries in a fluty voice. "I recognize

Edwee, I recognize Edwee's sweetie, I recognize Nonie—but who's this other one?"

"This is my friend Roger Williams, Mother," Nonie says, guiding her mother's outstretched hand toward his. "Remember I told you about him? How brilliant he is?"

"I'm not Edwee's sweetie anymore, honey," Gloria says with a giggle. "I'm Edwee's wife, remember?"

"Oh, yes. I did know that."

"You sent us that silver candle thing. Remember?"

"An epergne," Edwee corrects.

"Oh, yes, yes."

"How are you, Mother?" Nonie asks, brushing her lips against her mother's cheek.

"Well, actually, I'm upset," her mother says as the car moves forward again. "Yes, you could really say I'm upset. You remember Mrs. Perlman who lived in fourteen-C when I lived at Thirty Park Avenue? Used to play mah-jongg, had arthritis? She was married to Norman Perlman who turned grey overnight, you know who I mean, he took his mother's death so bad he turned absolutely snow-white grey overnight! Family had jewelry stores, and didn't Rose Perlman have the jewels! Oh, my! He got them wholesale for her on Forty-seventh Street. He was so good to her, and why they never had children I'll never know. He died of a broken heart. Anyway, she called me today, and can you imagine what? Someone in her building poisoned her little dog, Fluffy, and she thinks she knows who. She thinks someone put poison on the carpet outside her front door because she saw Fluffy sniffing and licking at something. Two hours later Fluffy was in convulsions and died in her arms! It must have been poison. Mrs. Perlman is beside herself, just beside herself. 'Fluffy was the only joy left in my life,' she said to me. 'The *only joy!*' Isn't that an awful thing, to poison a little dog that's never harmed anyone? Oh," she says, dabbing at her eyelids with a gloved fingertip, "just look how upset it's made me—I'm crying myself. Oh . . . what a cruel thing. Do you think anybody would try to poison my Itty-Bitty?"

Nonie pats her mother's hand. "No, I don't think anyone would poison Itty-Bitty, Mother," she says.

"What's the world coming to, I ask myself. Do you ever ask yourself that, Nonie? Edwee?"

"I ask myself that *constantly*," Edwee says.

"Where are we going?" Fleurette Myerson asks suddenly. "I've forgotten."

"To Mimi's for dinner," Nonie says. "A family dinner, remember?"

"It promises to be breathtakingly boring," Edwee says.

"Really, Edwee? Then why are we going?" Then she laughs. "Oh,

Edwee, you're just making one of your little jokes, aren't you. I'm always forgetting how you like to make little jokes. Ha-ha. That's a funny one. Still, I don't know how I'll have any appetite for anything, thinking about poor Mrs. Perlman and her poor little dog, Fifi."

"You said Fluffy."

"It was a poodle. An adorable little poodle. White, I think, not black like Itty-Bitty. What's the world coming to?"

There is a brief silence, and the car stops for a red light. Then Nonie's friend Williams says, "Edwee—that's an unusual name. How did you get it?"

Edwee gives him a frosty look. "It attached itself to me in boarding school," he says. "Groton."

"Why, Edwee, that's not *true*," his mother says. "I gave you that name when you were a tiny baby! When they first handed you to me in the delivery room of Mount Sinai Hospital, I took one look at you and I said, 'He's so *wee!* He's so *wee!* His name is Edwin, but he's my little Ed*wee!*' And that's funny, because Mr. Monticello asked me that same question this afternoon."

"Who is Mr. Monticello, Mother?"

"From the museum. He came by to see my collection. I said to him, 'Edwee may not like what I'm going to do, but I'm going to do it anyway.' That's when he asked me how you got your name."

"What is it that you're going to do that I may not like?" Edwee asks as the car moves forward again, and there is a trace of tension in his voice.

"I'm thinking of giving my paintings to the Metropolitan Museum. Or at least some of them. Or maybe letting them take their pick. Mr. Monticello seemed very interested."

"Are you speaking of Philippe de Montebello?"

"Yes. I was going to tell you later, but now you've forced it out of me by wanting to know why we called you Edwee."

"Mother, this is a very foolish thing you're thinking of," Edwee says. "Have you talked to the lawyers, M-M-M-Mother? Your collection is p-p-p-priceless, it's—"

"See? I told you you wouldn't like it, Edwee. But why shouldn't I? I used to think of those paintings as my friends. I used to talk to them. But now I can't see them anymore, what good are they to me? Let somebody else enjoy them."

"Not the Cézannes . . . not the B-B-Bentons . . . not the *Goya* . . ."

"Stop stammering, Edwee. It makes me nervous. You didn't use to stammer. Anyway, I think Mr. Monticello wants them all."

"I forbid you to do this, Mother, without consulting—"

"Consulting who?"

"M-m-*me!*"

"I should think you'd offer them to the Guggenheim first," Nonie says soothingly. "Under the circumstances."

"I never liked Uncle Sol. He high-hatted me, and he high-hatted your father. And he had other women. That's one good thing I can say about your father. He never had other women. At least that I knew about. Uncle Sol's wife knew about his. She died of a broken heart."

"Mother, m-m-must I be the first one to tell you? That you are *senile?*" Edwee almost shouts.

"Just like poor Mrs. Perlman's husband. Oh, I keep thinking about that poor little dog—poisoned by someone putting poison on a rug. *That's* what breaks *my* heart. The only joy of her life."

"I'm going to have you probated. I'm going to have you declared incompetent! Incompetent to handle—"

The car pulls up, now, in front of 1107 Fifth Avenue, and the doorman strides forward. "Where are we going?" Fleurette Myerson asks again. "Is it to Mimi's? Is that what you said? Are we at Mimi's house now?"

"Yes, Mother," Nonie murmurs.

Fleurette Myerson sits very still, her hands in her lap, as though sitting for a portrait to decorate a box of old-fashioned chocolate candies. But when she speaks to Edwee now, her high-pitched voice has a steely edge to it. "We are not going to quarrel in front of Mimi," she says. "Do you hear me? Mimi won't have it and neither will I. Don't forget that there are a few things I know about you, Edwee Myerson, that you would not like to see in headlines in the morning papers. Shall I mention the name of Collier? Shall I mention Florida?" She rearranges her knees, hitches herself forward, and prepares to be assisted from the car.

Another limousine is also making its way to Mimi's dinner party, this one hired by Mimi herself and containing only one passenger, Alice Bloch Myerson, Mimi's mother and the other daughter-in-law of Granny Flo. Alice did not want to go to tonight's party.

"*Must* I go, Mimi?" She had begged her daughter on the phone. "Please don't make me go."

"Oh, Mother, please. I want you here. This is a company, but it's also a *family*. I want all the family here."

"I'm just not ready for it," Alice said. "I'm not up to it yet."

"Of course you are."

"I'm not ready for *them* yet, Mimi. You know how they treat me. They treat me—Nonie, Edwee, Flo—as though they were candling an egg. That's exactly the way they treat me, as though they were holding me up against a candle, peering through my shell, looking for blood spots."

"That's silly, Mother."

"It isn't, Mimi. That's the way they've always made me feel. Like an outsider. I'm not a real member of that family, Mimi."

"You're my mother, aren't you?"

"But that doesn't make me a real Myerson. You're one, but I'm not. I'm just a Myerson by marriage. That's the way they think of me. That's the way they make me feel. That's the way they've always made me feel. An outcast, a trespasser."

"Besides, I want to show you off," Mimi said. "I want them to see the new you. I'm so proud of you."

"But the new me is so new yet," she said. "I'm not sure yet who this new me is! Besides, there've been so many new me's over the years that I can't tell them apart anymore. I'm still living with the old ones."

"The old ones are ghosts now, Mother. Gone with the past."

"Ghosts, yes. But not gone. I live with them every day. I'm the ghost," she said.

"Mother, you'll make me very unhappy if you don't come to dinner next Thursday night."

Alice had hesitated. "Well, if you put it that way, of course I'll have to come. I wouldn't do anything to make you unhappy, Mimi."

"I'm putting it that way."

"After all you've done for me."

"I'll send a car for you."

And so, reluctantly, Alice had dressed for the evening, choosing a simple dress of eggshell crepe, a dress that Nonie wouldn't consider too competitive and that Flo wouldn't think too flashy, and the car had picked her up at her house in Turtle Bay, where she lives alone, and now she, too, is moving northward up Third Avenue through the traffic.

Just before leaving her house, Alice swallowed a valium. It is beginning to calm her a little.

One other passenger is also heading northward, not many blocks behind Alice's car, this one in a taxi snaking its way uptown through the Lower Park Avenue tunnel and up the ramps that make narrow, right-angled turns around Grand Central and through the Pan Am and Helmsley buildings. This is not a guest but the party's host, Bradford Moore, Jr., Mimi's husband. Brad Moore is unhappy, too, but not about returning home to his wife's dinner party. Brad Moore is comfortable with dinner parties. He has been going to them and giving them since Harvard days, and handling himself at black-tie dinners is second nature now—a little to drink, but not too much, an ability to sniff and taste the wine to see whether or not it is corked, the polite and interested conversation about news events, pleasant gossip picked up on The Street or at the Downtown Club, revealed with lawyerly discretion, tact, and poise. *Poised* is a word often used to describe Bradford Moore, Jr., when, on occasion, his advice is sought or his opinion is asked by reporters from *U.S. News & World Report* or *Barron's* or *Business Week.* And when he sees himself described as "poised" or "polished," he smiles, remembering a small black volume his mother placed on the night-stand by his bed as a boy, titled *Poise and How to Attain It.*

But he is not smiling now. He is unhappy because he is ashamed of the place he has just come from, and ashamed of the lie he has told his wife. "Whenever you are worried or depressed," his mother used to tell him, "remember who you are. Remember that you are both a Moore *and* a Bradford of Boston. The Bradfords and the Moores were not put together with flour-and-water paste. Clement Clarke Moore did more than write 'The Night Before Christmas.' He was a distinguished linguist, historian, and lexicographer, who compiled the first Hebrew-to-English dictionary in America. And don't forget *him,* either," and she would point to the portrait of William Bradford, *Mayflower* passenger and the second governor of the Plymouth colony.

But all the family portraits gazing sternly down at him from their heavy frames in his parents' house on Beacon Hill could not erase the feelings of unworthiness that consume him now over the place he has just come from, and the lie.

As the taxi passes the Waldorf, Brad Moore suddenly sees a familiar face in the street. It is none other than his own twenty-six-year-old son, Brad Moore III: handsome, eager-looking, a little windblown, his black tie still loose and his collar unbuttoned, cheerily trying to hail a taxi for himself. Immediately, his father sinks back deep in his seat and averts his head lest his son recognize him.

What a thing to do! How to explain this? Why would a father spot his own son on the street and not immediately order his driver to stop and give him a lift? Badger, his father knows, is also heading for 1107 Fifth Avenue. In just a few minutes, he and Badger will be pumping each other's hands and throwing mock punches at each other's shoulders like the friends they are, father and son. Why not stop the cab, throw open the door, call out to Badger, and tell him to hop in? What kind of father would *not* do this? What is wrong with a father who is ashamed to have his son find him heading homeward in a perfectly ordinary Yellow Cab? But while all these thoughts are racing through his head, the opportunity—to stop the cab, call out, "Hey! Badger! It's me! Hop in, kid!"—has passed. The taxi is blocks beyond the Waldorf, and Badger is out of sight.

It is because of where Bradford Moore, Jr., has just come from. He can hear his son, hopping in beside him, saying, "Hey, Pop—what's with the taxi? I thought you always took the subway uptown. Don't tell me you're finally starting to live like a rich person!"

But then the taxi meter would tell the story. He could not have come all the way from Wall Street for three dollars. It would mean another lie.

"And so that's who'll be here," Mimi is telling her first-arrived guests, Sherrill Shearson and Dirk Gordon. "My sweeet mother, my aunt Nonie and my uncle Edwee, my dear little old grandmother who's almost blind and"—she taps her forehead—"just a *little* bit dotty. Sometimes. Other times, she can be sharp as a tack. And my husband, Brad, of course, who'll be a little late, and my son, who's also Brad, but whom everybody calls Badger. We're big on nicknames in this family, as you can see. Most of them were handed out by my Granny Flo. Badger's still not married, and I know he'll flip for you, Sherrill—may I call you Sherrill? He wanted you for the Mireille Woman the minute he saw your composite. And, let's see . . . who else? Oh, there's a man Aunt Nonie's bringing whom I haven't met named Williams, and there's Uncle Edwee's brand-new wife, whose name is Gloria. Does that make twelve of us?" She counts on her fingers. "Oh, I nearly forgot. There's a young man named Jim Greenway whom we all must be *especially* nice to. He's a writer for *Fortune*, and he's writing a piece on the company and the Myerson family. I thought this would be a good way for him to meet everybody in the family and get a feel for our business all at once. You see, I always say the Miray corporation isn't just a business. It's also a family, and the two of you are going to be a part of the Miray family —at least for the next few months. But don't worry about this Mr. Greenway—I doubt he'll ask you many questions. Oh, he may ask you what it's like to be working for me, or something like that, and just be absolutely truthful. I've always found, when dealing with journalists, that it's best to be truthful. If you start playing games with them, they'll start playing games with you. So, if you think I'm going to be a demanding bitch to work with, just say so. . . ."

Dirk Gordon gives Sherrill a small sideways look.

"This sure is a nice place you have here, Mrs. Moore," Sherrill says.

"Well, thank you," Mimi says. "And please call me Mimi. Everyone does." She thrusts her hands deep into the pockets of her white silk dress and, in the same motion, turns on one heel toward Felix, who stands at the library door, his silver tray in one hand. "Now, what can Felix get you from the bar?" she says.

"I'd like a tequila sunrise," Sherrill says.

"A tequila . . . sunrise. Oh, dear. I wonder if we . . ."

Dirk Gordon clears his throat conspicuously. "We're not in a Mexican restaurant, love," he says. "Maybe you could settle for something a bit less

. . . exotic? I'll have a Perrier with lime," he adds, with a slight nod in Felix's direction.

"Oh," Sherrill says, looking abashed. "Well, uh—"

"Oh, but you know what Felix *can* make," Mimi says brightly, stepping in to save the moment. "He makes an absolutely smashing banana daiquiri—in the blender, using both light and dark rum. Felix's banana daiquiris are practically world famous. Why not let him fix one of those for you?"

"Uh . . . okay," the young woman says.

"And you know what I want, Felix," Mimi says.

This is the Mimi Myerson you have read about in *Vogue* and *Harper's Bazaar* and *Town & Country*, and also in the *Wall Street Journal*.

A great deal has been written about her beauty, which is arresting, about her fair hair, which tonight is caught back in a simple ponytail secured with a small, white satin bow, and about her luminous skin, which, even at forty-nine, seems to need very little of her own products in terms of makeup. She is one of those fortunate women who can wear any color, and tonight her color is white, a pale chiffon off-the-shoulder sheath by Jimmy Galanos that is almost Grecian in the way its gathered folds swirl about her body. She is also one of those rare women who are not necessarily improved by jewelry, and tonight her only adornment consists of a pair of small diamond earclips and the ruby and diamond ring her husband Brad gave her when they became engaged in 1958.

Mimi has always been the sort of woman who, if you saw her on the street, possessed the sort of quality—is it her posture? her sense of style?—that would make you pause and take a second look. She is the sort of woman who, if you saw her at a party, and did not know who she was, would cause you to turn to a companion and say, "That tall blonde over there—who is she?" There is a certain aura about her that conveys a certain mystery, which has nothing to do with her beauty. But, to me, her eyes are her most striking feature. They are large and, some captious critic might insist, a touch too far apart, but they are of an extraordinary pale grey color. She sometimes makes jokes about "my beige eyes," but the word *beige* does not really do them justice. A friend of hers once said that her eyes had the color and luster "of fine old silver when it's polished every day," and that describes them better. Then there is her laugh, which is deep and throaty, but with a soft ripple to it, rather suggesting water flowing over smooth, round pebbles in a stream. Or am I getting carried away with metaphors? She is laughing that pebbly, throaty laugh now, over something Dirk Gordon has just said about their taxi driver thinking that 1107 Fifth Avenue was in Harlem, when any fool would know that this is one of the four best addresses in Manhattan, the other three being 825 and 834 Fifth Avenue, and

River House. Mr. Gordon is obviously the sort of young man who, coming from out of town, would know such things.

A lot of adjectives have been used to describe Mimi, and a lot of qualities have been ascribed to her to account for her extraordinary success over the past twenty-five years at steering, almost single-handedly, this company from the brink of bankruptcy—where it was at the time of her father's tragic death—to where it is today, among the *Fortune* 500. She has been called a visionary. She has been called an organizational genius. She has been called a workaholic, and much more. She has been called a stainless-steel butterfly, an Iron Maiden in silk pajamas, the Mata Hari of Mascara, the Dragon Lady of Lip Gloss, and a number of other, less flattering things, for this is a business where the competition is both articulate and ruthless, and makes no bones about it.

But none of these descriptions quite sums her up. She is, among other things, essentially a gambler, possessed of what the men who work the tables at Las Vegas call "heart." What riskier business is there than the beauty business? Where are the stakes higher, the odds against success more staggering? Even tonight's dinner party is the opening move of another huge gamble on Mimi's part: millions of dollars from Mimi's advertising budget have already been spent to launch her first venture into the fragrance market with a new scent called Mireille, and a companion *eau de toilette* for men called Mireille Man. Though the first ads and television commercials will not appear until after Labor Day, to run with increasing frequency through the fall in hopes of capturing a share of the Christmas market, all the others in the industry—Lauder, Revlon, Arden, and the rest—are aware of what she is up to and are betting, and devoutly hoping, that she will fail. Mimi is betting that she will not. Her last two product launches were successes. She is shooting for three in a row. So she is also overdue for a flop. Ladies and gentlemen, no more bets, please. . . .

She is also a talented showperson. For what is the beauty industry but a kind of show biz? As in show biz, a lot depends on the appeal of the stars, and as her stars Mimi has deliberately cast two unknowns: Sherrill and Dirk. Aside from their obvious beauty, will they also reveal themselves to have that mysterious star quality that will cause audiences to line up, three deep, at the box office? Both possess a kind of soigné, sophisticated look. That may go over with the New York crowd, but will it play in the nabes, will it play in Peoria? No one has the answers to these questions yet.

Even tonight's dinner has been planned as a kind of drama, as a theatrical event. At a certain point, when all the guests have gathered, concealed jets, installed behind the bookcases of her library, will release an invisible mist of the new Mireille fragrance into the air. At each place setting in her dining room, a generous sample bottle has been placed—Mireille Man for the gentlemen, Mireille perfume for the women—as a party favor. Even Mimi's apartment has been decorated—quite deliberately, she would admit this—as a kind of stage setting for what she does. In the library, where the guests are gathering, the woodwork has been painted with Tiger Lily, one of her most successful nail lacquer shades. The books on the mirrored bookshelves are all identically bound in matching leather. Behind the books, small invisible lights create a mysterious glow, like footlights glowing across an act curtain beneath a stage proscenium.

But it is Mimi's dining room, at the end of the central gallery, that is perhaps the most dramatic room in the apartment. Its strié walls are painted in a dusky-rose blush to match one of her Miray face powders, and, incredibly, in late August, Mimi has found fresh tulips to match the blush exactly. These fill three George I epergnes arranged across the length of the rosewood dining room table. In this room, too, are Mimi's famous set of Louis XIV chairs, an even dozen of them, signed "Boulle," their backs inlaid with tortoiseshell and yellow and gold metal in scrolls and cartouches, their seats covered with a deep pink Fortuny fabric. This same fabric has been used to treat the three tall, park-facing windows. A splendid pair of eight-paneled coromandel screens flank the fireplace, and its mantel displays a pair of eighteenth-century Sèvres vases—in the same pink as the Fortuny, an unusual color for Sèvres, which is more commonly blue, the color called *sang du roi*—and these are filled with more dusky-rose tulips, baby's breath, and thin strands of bear grass.

This is the room where, when she entertains, Mimi likes to use pieces from the collection of *motif* French and English china dinner and dessert plates that she and Brad have been building over the years. She now has plates to match almost any course she chooses to serve. If, for instance, a main course is to consist of baby lamb chops, Mimi has a set of Wedgwood plates painted with a pastoral scene of sheep grazing in an English meadow. Tonight's dessert, poached fresh pears in *crème fraîche*, will be presented on plates decorated with pears, pear leaves, and blossoms. She also has plates decorated with grapes, strawberries, plums and apples, and on and on. For years, for Christmas, anniversaries, and birthdays, Mimi and Brad have given each other sets of *motif* plates to add to the collection, and a favorite pastime on Saturday afternoons for Brad and Mimi has been exploring the antiques shops along Second and York avenues, looking for plates with food motifs, no matter how whimsical the design. No one in New York has a collection quite like theirs.

Mimi has been called a perfectionist. But look more closely. That Sèvres vase on the left has been broken, and repaired. When Badger Moore was nine, he and his friend Alex Brokaw came home from St. Bernard's and, in an unsupervised moment, decided to construct a pair of forts in the apartment. The boys used sofa cushions from the living room and library, over-turned ottomans and Boulle chairs, and, in a stroke of military inventive-ness, decided that the pair of vases would serve admirably as cannons. The vase on the left was one of the first casualties of that battle.

"Your mother is going to be *furious!*" Felix roared when he heard the crash and came running from the kitchen. "Your mother is going to *kill you!*"

But of course it wasn't quite as bad as that.

"Get rid of them both, darling," the famous decorator Billy Baxter told Mimi when he noticed the maze of tiny lines where the Sèvres vase had been pieced together. "As a matched pair, they have no value now, since one of them's been broken. Get rid of them, and replace them with some-thing of museum quality."

But Mimi demurred. Whether they are broken and restored or not, she still loves those vases. Besides, who else owns a piece of pre-Revolutionary French porcelain that was once mustered into service as a cannon?

Yes, as the young model commented, it is a nice place that Mimi and Brad Moore have here, and it works, both as a showcase for Mimi's consid-erable talents and as a home. It works as a home because so much of what it contains has a story like that of the Sèvres vase. Cole Porter, Noël Coward, and Richard Rodgers have all played that Bösendorfer piano in the living room, and when, in the middle of a particularly spirited arpeggio, Sir Noël managed to fracture the ivory of the highest C, Mimi refused to let him worry about the split key. "It will always remind us," she told him, "that we had the fun of listening to you play in this room." And when Andy Warhol's cigarette rolled out of an ashtray and burned a hole in a *faux marbre* table-top, and he offered to have the top refinished for her, Mimi said, "Never! That's a *Warhol* burn."

And the apartment works as a showcase on nights like tonight when, dressed for a party, filled with off-season flowers, lit with recessed lighting behind cornices and within bookcases, glowing with candles that have been artfully placed to catch the return gleam of mirrors, the whole apartment, room after room, full of shimmer and shadows, seems to float on some powder-puff cloud high above the Central Park lake, a theatrical artifice on invisible wires.

And of course, as a final touch of theatre, there is Mimi's plan to surprise her family—and fellow stockholders—by introducing them not only to her new scent but also to the pretty young models, her stars, who will sell her product, and so the evening will have something of the quality of a backers' audition. This in itself of course is a gamble, which is where we started off describing Mimi. This tactic may fall flat on its face. The young woman seems dull-witted, and the young man seems like a snot. But we shall see.

"Is that a real oil painting?" Sherrill Shearson asks.

"Yes. That's my grandfather, Adolph Myerson, who started the company."

"He looks . . . ooh, sort of mean!"

"He does look a little, well, *dour*, doesn't he? But he took this business very seriously. I was always terrified of him. I just can't take the business *quite* that seriously. To me, it's a business that's all about fantasies—hopes, wishes, dreams. Dreams of looking better, younger, healthier, happier, richer —and perhaps even feeling better about yourself if you can dream that you look that way. Wouldn't you agree?"

"Well, I never really thought about it all that much, actually," the girl says. And then, "Hey, isn't that painting kind of . . . lopsided?"

"You mean the subject doesn't occupy the center of the frame. Yes, and there's a story behind that which I don't have time to go into now."

Now Mimi must mingle with her other guests, and she moves away.

"I didn't appreciate that crack about Mexican restaurants," the girl says. "If this is supposed to be polite society, I call that effing rude."

"You're about to lose an earring, love," the young man says. "No, the other one."

"All the books here are the same *color*. How do you tell which book is which?"

"By reading the *titles*, love. You *can* read, can't you?"

"Asshole."

2

*A*S HER OTHER GUESTS arrive, Mimi greets them one by one at
the library door and leads them to be introduced to the Mireille Couple,
who stand in front of the mirrored bookcases in an impromptu receiving
line, rather like a bride and groom, smiling, now, their soon-to-be-famously-
seductive Mireille smiles. No one would ever believe that the word *asshole*
had been spat moments earlier from Sherrill's carefully parted lips. These, of
course, are tutored smiles, carefully practiced in front of mirrors and Polar-
oid cameras, improved upon by dentists and modeling coaches. A word
should be inserted here about Mimi's own smile, which is quite different. It,
too, has evolved as a result of a certain amount of practice—we all should
practice our smiles from time to time—but Mimi's smile is a curiously
intimate smile, a communicative smile, a smile that seems to have words in
it. When Mimi smiles at you, her smile seems to take all of you in, saying, in
the process, that you have never looked better, healthier, prouder, more sure
of who you are and where you came from; that you, this perfect new you,
impeccably put together as you have always wanted to see yourself, are the
only person living in the world whom Mimi has ever wanted to see or talk
to. Naturally, there is also a reverse effect. When Mimi turns this smile
away from you, as she must, you feel that you have been left floating in some
limbo, without a friend left in the world. The patroness of that smile has
fallen in love with someone else.

"Aunt Nonie," Mimi says, "I want you to meet our special guests of
honor, Sherrill Shearson and Dirk Gordon. I'll tell you why they're going to
be so special to us as soon as everybody's here. . . . Oh, and here's Jim

Greenway, who's also special. Jim's going to write about us in *Fortune* magazine and so, of course, you're all under strictest orders to say nothing but the
nicest things about us. Mr. Greenway isn't interested in family skeletons."

"Not true. I like family skeletons," Jim Greenway says.

"Ah," Mimi says with a look of mock disappointment. "Then you're in
for a letdown, I'm afraid. This family doesn't have any skeletons."

"Oh, but we *do!* We *do!*" cries Granny Flo in her piping voice.

"Well," Mimi says with that rich and easy laugh of hers, "if anyone
knows which closets they're hiding in . . ." Turning from Greenway, she
says, "And you must be Mr. Williams, Aunt Nonie's friend."

"Business associate," he says.

"How exciting! Later, you must tell us all about it."

Felix moves among the guests, taking drink orders, and a maid in a black
uniform appears with a tray of canapés.

"What's *that?*" Sherrill whispers to Dirk.

"It appears to be artichoke bottoms stuffed with caviar."

"Ooh, *caviar!*" She helps herself to one and takes a tentative bite. "Oooh,
it's *salty.*"

"Yes, I rather expect it *would* be."

Speaking to whomever might happen to be within earshot, and gazing
straight ahead of her with dead, dull eyes, Granny Flo says, "My daughter's
real name is Naomi, after Naomi in the Bible, but everybody has always
called her Nonie. When she was a little girl, she was such a stubborn little
thing, and I was always saying to her, 'No, Naomi, no, no, no, no, *no.*' And
after a while, before she did anything, she'd look at me and say, 'May I do
that, Mama, or is that a nonie?' And I'd say, 'No, that's not a nonie,' or,
'Yes, that's a nonie,' whichever thing it was she wanted to do, and that's
when I decided to call her Nonie. My husband, Adolph Myerson, used to
say I was good at naming things. My newest daughter is only two years old.
Her name is Itty-Bitty. That's right, I'm eighty-nine, and I have a daughter
who's just two years old! She's my little Yorkie, and she's as itty-bitty as they
come. She weighs just two and a half pounds. She follows me around,
wherever I go, and because I've lost my eyesight I have to be careful not to
step on her, but she seems to understand because she stays just behind me,
making little sounds for me to tell me where she is—*whiff-whiff-whiff.* I
thought of naming her Whiffy, but I didn't. I named her Itty-Bitty. I used
to live in a big place, but now I live in a hotel. Itty-Bitty is the only dog
who's allowed to live at the Carlyle. Now my friend, poor Mrs. Perlman, on
the other hand. . . ."

"Mother, do shut *up!*" Edwee says.

Now everyone is here except Brad Moore and Badger, and small conversational groupings have developed in the room. Except for Alice, who stands

alone, looking nervous and a little frightened, waiting for her valium to give her a boost of chemical courage, enough to join a conversation. Mimi notices her mother's discomfort and starts to move toward her, then decides against it. One of the tenets of the Betty Ford Center is that people like her mother should learn to cope with situations on their own. So she settles for a smile of reassurance in her mother's direction from across the room. Her mother's response is a hunted look.

"Yellow tulips!" Granny Flo exclaims, her eyes fixed on empty space in front of her. "Mimi? Where did you find yellow tulips in *August*, Mimi?"

"Your eyesight must be improving, Mother," Nonie says. "How did you know these were yellow tulips?"

"I've learned to see with my nose," her mother says. "When you lose your eyesight, your other senses get better. I've lost my eyesight, but I can see with my nose! I smelled tulips, and I smelled yellow."

"I didn't realize tulips had any odor at all."

"You see, Nonie? That's where you're wrong."

Mimi takes all this in. Another remarkable thing about Mimi is her ability, even at a distance, to follow the drift of a number of different conversations at the same time, to filter them out, as it were, and to discern their implications, even in a much more crowded room than this one. At her dinner parties, she is able to observe, and hear, all her guests at once and, whenever situations seem to be approaching rocky or dangerous shoals, to avert unpleasantnesses with a swift, bright change of topic.

In one corner of the room, Nonie's young escort, Roger Williams, has pulled Nonie aside and is saying to her, "What was all that business in the car about? Between your mother and your brother?"

"Mother and Edwee have been going at each other like that for years," she says. "It doesn't mean a thing."

"Your brother doesn't like me."

"Makes no difference. Edwee's not the least bit important to our plans. As I told you, the only person you need to make a good impression on is Mother."

"I gather your mother has an important art collection?"

"I suppose so. It's sort of a mishmash. She's got some Thomas Hart Bentons, a few Impressionists—a couple of Cézannes, an Utrillo, some Monets, a Goya portrait of some Spanish countess. She got a lot of things in the Depression when they were dirt cheap. She got her four Picassos at a time when Picasso would give you a painting if you bought him dinner."

He whistles softly. "It sounds as though some of those might be pretty valuable today."

She shrugs. "Maybe so. Art is the one thing I don't know much about."

He nods, frowning slightly, having noted that art is "the one thing" she knows little about.

"Anyway," she whispers, "I slipped into the dining room a few minutes ago and changed the place cards. Mimi won't notice. I placed you next to Mother, so you can work on her. The way we discussed."

He nods again.

"Even though she's blind, she's a pushover for younger men."

In another part of the room, Jim Greenway is saying to Mimi, "One thing that interests me is what caused the famous rift between your grandfather, Adolph Myerson, and his brother, Leopold, and what caused Leopold to leave the company in nineteen forty-one, never to return. What was it, do you know?"

"I really don't. It all started before I was born, and in nineteen forty-one I was only three years old. I have only the dimmest recollection of Uncle Leo. There are cousins, of course—Uncle Leo's children and grandchildren—and some of them are still Miray stockholders. But I've never met them. The rift, as you call it, was that complete. Sad, but whatever it was left us a divided family."

"Where's Nonie?" her grandmother suddenly cries, though no one is standing in her immediate vicinity. "Someone take me over to my daughter, Nonie. I want to talk more to that young man she brought. Is she having an affair with him, or what? Does anybody know?"

In the little silence that follows, Mimi says brightly, "Quick, everybody: come to the window and look at the lake. It's covered with seagulls. That means there's a storm out at sea. Whenever there's a storm on the Atlantic, the seagulls fly in and settle on the lake. Isn't it wonderful?"

There is a general movement toward the library window, and a great deal of ooh-ing and ah-ing over the sight of the lake afloat with birds. "Isn't it nice to have reminders that, after all, we live in a seaport?" Mimi says.

Edwee moves toward his sister. "Well, *that* was a charming outburst from our mother, wasn't it?" he says. "And, speaking of affairs, are you ready for a bit of *on dit?*"

"What's that?" she says.

"Note that the master of the house has not appeared yet. Well, it seems that Brad Moore has some woman on the West Side."

"Has some woman?" she asks, looking puzzled.

"Is keeping a woman. In her twenties, I'd say. Certainly younger than Mimi. Not *bad*-looking, in a cheap way."

"How do you know this, Edwee?"

"I was lunching the other day at Le Cirque with Nancy Reagan and Betsey Bloomingdale and another friend, and who should I spot in the farthest, darkest corner of the restaurant? Brad Moore. In very *serious* conversation with this woman. Their heads were bent together. His hand was on top of hers. She was obviously unhappy. She was weeping. Well, what do you think of that?"

"How do you know she's from the West Side?"

He makes a vague gesture with his right hand. "She had that West Side *look*. You know—bangs."

"Bangs."

"A déclassé look. So. Who should be the first to tell our dear little Mimi what's going on, you or I?"

"Well, I—"

Edwee suddenly presses his index finger to his lips. "Ssh!" he says. "He just walked in."

Sure enough, Brad Moore has just arrived and greeted his wife with a kiss, and is moving around the room shaking the hands of the male guests and kissing the cheeks of his female in-laws. He is followed very shortly by his son, Badger, who looks, as always, happy and alert and is tugging at the sleeves of his dinner jacket as though he had just tossed it on in the elevator.

Her guest list complete, Mimi makes a small signal with her hand to Felix, who touches a small button beside the library door. Mimi waits for a few moments to let the scent penetrate the room and is grateful that no one is smoking. Soon the Mireille fragrance will fill the air, and Mimi, ever the practiced impresario, moves toward the center of the room to make her announcement.

Edwee is still whispering to his sister. "Can you get rid of your young man when this is over?" he says. "I need to talk to you. Alone. As soon as possible. Can you drop by my house for a few minutes after we leave here?"

"Yes, I suppose so."

Now Mimi is about to make her little speech, and she begins, "Family, friends . . ."

But her grandmother beats her to the punch. "I smell something!" she says loudly. "What is it? It's perfume. Who's wearing it?"

Mimi laughs and claps her hands. "Good for you, Granny," she says. "Family, friends . . . the fragrance you may be noticing in the air means that the Miray Corporation is about to embark on an exciting new venture. We're about to launch our first perfume, and you are the first people outside our boardroom to be exposed to it. You are my special guinea pigs. Sample bottles are at each of your places at the dinner table, but this is the premiere. Now I need you to tell me, honestly, what you think."

All noses now are poised in the air to catch the scent.

"Woodsy," someone says.

"Yes, piney."

"No, more floral, I'd say."

"Beautiful."

There is more ooh-ing and ah-ing, and then, led by Mimi's husband, there is a loud round of applause followed by congratulatory noises.

"What's in it?" someone asks.

"Oh, a bit of vetiver, a touch of clove, verbena, some lemon. But I'm not going to give you the complete formula. That's a secret, locked in the boardroom safe."

"I think it's more exciting than Giorgio!"

"Do you? Well, that's one of the big guns out there that we're hoping to take on."

"What are you going to call it, Mimi?"

"We experimented with literally hundreds of different names. And in the end we ended up deciding to call it . . . Mireille."

"Lovely!"

"That's her real name, you know, Mireille," Granny Flo says to no one in particular. "Mireille Myerson. She was named after my husband's company. Miray—Mireille. Get it? I gave her the nickname Mimi when she was a tiny baby because she made a little sound that was like *mi-mi-mi-mi-mi!*"

"Now that's not true, Granny," Mimi says. "I renamed myself Mimi when I was fourteen, after seeing a performance of *La Bohème*."

"She's lying," Granny Flo says cheerfully. "I named her because she was always going '*mi-mi-mi-mi-mi.*'"

"Well, it doesn't matter, does it?" Mimi says. "What matters is that we —you, me, all of us who are stockholders—are going to be in the fragrance business for the first time. And Dirk and Sherrill, who are our special guests tonight, are going to be the Mireille Woman and the Mireille Man in all our print advertising and television commercials."

There are more congratulatory sounds.

"Frankly, it smells a little *cheap*, if you ask me," Edwee whispers to his sister.

"But knowing Mimi, it'll have a fancy price tag."

"Oh, we can be sure of *that*."

Now the conversation becomes general again, with much emphasis on analyzing the new scent.

"I smell the lemon in it."

"And cinnamon, too, I suspect."

"Rose oil, too."

Mimi finds her mother, who has been standing alone and somewhat apart from the others, and says, "Now, aren't you glad you came, Mother? Isn't this turning out to be a nice sort of family reunion?"

"I hate all sorts of family reunions," Alice says. "I hate this one no less than all the others. No less and no more."

The reporter, Jim Greenway, turns to Mimi and touches his glass to hers. "I wish you luck—no, not luck, success—with your new fragrance," he says.

"Thank you, Mr. Greenway."

"Please call me Jim. And tell me, when you took over the company twenty-five years ago, after your father's death, did you ever think you'd be so successful?"

"Never. I was terrified. Just as I'm terrified now."

He laughs. "Then terror is the secret of your success?"

"Absolutely. Terror is the secret of every success. The opposite of terror is complacency, and complacency is the secret of every failure."

"I like that," he says.

"And you may quote me," she says, touching his elbow and laughing the pebbly laugh.

From the doorway, Felix announces, "Dinner is served, madam."

Entering the dining room, Mimi immediately notices that the place cards have been changed, and she also knows immediately who must have done it. But she decides to let the seating remain as it is, though she can't refrain from a slight feeling of annoyance at Aunt Nonie. Nonie is always creating mischief like this. Let it pass, she thinks. She will not let it disrupt the planned flow of her evening. Now, in the dining room, fingering their Mireille samples, everyone is exclaiming over the packaging.

"Elegant."

"Lovely."

"Sophisticated. I love the colors. Black and gold."

"And the bottle. A perfect teardrop shape."

"Look—the bottle is by Baccarat!"

"It certainly *looks* expensive," Edwee says.

"Thank you, Uncle Edwee."

"Suggested retail is a hundred and eighty dollars an ounce," young Brad says.

"I'd pay that."

The soup course is served, and Felix moves around the table, pouring the wine. From the head of the table, Bradford Moore turns to his mother-in-law, who is seated on his right, and says, "It's wonderful to see you, Alice. You're looking positively radiant tonight."

Alice, who actually still looks a bit uncomfortable, despite her valium, covers her wineglass with two fingers of her right hand before Felix can fill it and says, "Why do people keep telling me how wonderful I look, Brad? Is it to remind me of how awful I looked before?"

"I didn't mean it that way at all, Alice," he says. "You always look wonderful."

"No, I don't. You know I always don't."

"Alice is so *sensitive*," Granny Flo says to the table at large. "That's always been Alice's problem."

Hearing this, from the other end of the table Mimi says brightly to everyone, "Once we'd settled on the black-and-gold color scheme for our packaging, we wanted the perfect models—one dark, one fair. And voilà! Sherrill and Dirk!" She lifts her wineglass. "I'd like to propose a toast: to the Mireille Woman and the Mireille Man!"

"Hear, hear."

And, half-rising, young Brad says, "And I'd like to propose another: to my brilliant, beautiful, and sexy mother. Here's to you, Mom!"

"Hear, hear."

"Thank you, Badger."

In Nonie's new arrangement of the seating, her young friend Williams is now placed at Granny Flo's right, to take advantage of her good ear. "It's such an honor to be seated next to you, Mrs. Myerson," he says. "I've heard so much about you."

"You have? What have you heard?"

"How charming you are, how gracious—"

"Did my daughter tell you that?"

"She. And others."

"Whenever Naomi Myerson starts talking like that, it means she wants something. Money, usually." She turns to her other dinner partner and says, "Who are you?"

"My name is Jim Greenway, Mrs. Myerson," he says. "I'm researching a story on the Myerson family, for *Fortune*."

"There wasn't any fortune. Didn't you know that? When my husband died, it turned out he'd spent it all. I had to sell everything—everything except my paintings. Did I tell you about my friend Mrs. Perlman's little dog?"

Sherrill Shearson is now on Edwee Myerson's right, and turning to her somewhat loftily, aware that she is a member of a lower social order, he says to her, "You certainly make a handsome couple. Are you two married?"

She giggles. "Are you *kidding*? Dirk's bisexual."

Nodding, Edwee takes this information in, and his eyes travel across the table to where Dirk Gordon sits, carefully spooning his soup, and he gives the younger man a long, appraising look. "Really. How interesting," he says.

From across the table, too, Edwee's wife catches this look of calculating appraisal. "Edwee," she mouths. "You promised!"

His answer is an almost indiscernible wink.

"One thing I'm interested in knowing about," Jim Greenway is saying to Granny Flo, the sad saga of Mrs. Perlman's pet having come to an end, "is what caused the rift between your late husband and his brother, Leopold, years ago. Can you tell me anything about that?"

"Why, it was perfectly simple," Granny says. "My husband was jealous of Leo. Leo was tall and dark and handsome and always got the girls. My husband was short and fat and ugly. Do you still have your grandpa's portrait in your library, Mimi? You could see in the portrait how ugly he was. No girl would look at Adolph, except me."

"There must have been more to it than that, Granny," Mimi says.

"That was the gist of it. I'd have much rather married Leo than Adolph, but Leo was already married to someone else, so I had to settle for Adolph. 'Settle for Adolph,' my father said. My father was Morris Guggenheim, in case you didn't know. When he was born, he was called the world's richest baby."

"Interesting," Jim Greenway says.

"But he wasn't the world's richest baby. That's the point. So don't put that in your story."

Nonie's friend Roger Williams is still trying to draw Granny's attention away from her other dinner partner. "Nonie and I are about to launch an exciting new business venture of our own, Mrs. Myerson," he says.

"Oh? What's that?"

"Spot foreign exchange. You see—"

"Foreigners," she says. "That reminds me of President Hoover, when my husband and I were invited to the White House. President Hoover was fat, and so was his wife. She was named Lou—Lou—Hoover. And they were both fat. Not too tall, either, but fat. Isn't that funny that both would be fat? My husband used to call them Tweedledum and Tweedledee; isn't that funny? He could be funny, my husband. But I remember we talked about all the foreigners. President Hoover said there were too many foreigners coming into the country. He wanted them stopped, and I think he was working on some sort of way to stop them. How much does Nonie want from me this time?"

"Well, if you were interested in coming in as an investor, Mrs. Myerson, we'd certainly be most happy to—"

"Nothing to do with foreigners! There are too many of them. President Hoover said so, and he ought to know."

"Mother," Nonie begins, "what Roger is trying to explain is—"

But at that moment, Felix steps into the dining room and whispers something in the senior Bradford Moore's ear. Brad Moore frowns slightly, places his napkin beside his plate, rises, and says, "Excuse me—a business call."

In his absence, Edwee turns to Alice, who is on his left. "Well, isn't *that* interesting?" he whispers to her.

"Isn't what interesting?"

"Brad has a woman on the West Side. But wouldn't you think she'd know better than to call him at home—while he's at dinner?"

"What makes you think that, Edwee?"

"I know what I know, Alice."

"I don't believe any of this!"

"I've seen the woman. I've seen them together, holding hands. So, who is going to tell Mimi that her husband has another woman? Shall you, or shall I? Obviously, she's got to be told."

"I told you I don't believe you."

"What are you two whispering about?" Mimi says from the far end of the table. "Whisper-whisper-whisper. Won't you let the rest of us in on whatever gossip it is?"

"We were just talking about the West Side," Edwee says easily. "How it's changed. All the shops on Columbus Avenue, and all the cheap merchandise one finds there."

"This rift with his brother Leopold," Jim Greenway is saying. "Was it sudden, when Leo left the company in nineteen forty-one, or was it a disagreement that had been building over the years?"

"Over the years. Yes, over the years. My husband kept a diary, you know, over the years. It was all in his diary—everything."

"Really?" he says eagerly. "A diary? Do you still have it? I'd love to see that."

"Oh, no," she says sadly. "It's gone. Disappeared. Destroyed, perhaps. Gone, all gone, but it was all in there, the whole thing."

"Really, Granny?" Mimi says. "I never knew that Grandpa kept a diary."

"Oh, yes. Wrote in it every day. Put everything in. Sometimes he'd read it to me."

"It would certainly be helpful to Mr. Greenway in his research, Granny, if we could locate Grandpa's diary."

"But it's gone. Vanished. Gone."

Speaking up in full voice for the first time now, Alice Myerson says, "I certainly never heard that my father-in-law kept a diary. If he had, certainly Henry would have mentioned it to me."

"But he did. He did."

"I don't believe you, Flo!"

From across the table, Granny Flo gazes steadily at her daughter-in-law. Then, turning to Jim Greenway, and nodding in Alice's direction, Granny Flo says, "She killed a man once, you know. It was all in Adolph's diary." She pauses for a moment to let this sink in. Then she says, "I have to go to the toilet. Will someone lead me?"

Brad, returning from his telephone call, steps to her chair. "I'll show you the way, Flo," he says, taking her hand.

Felix, in the silence that follows, clears the soup bowls, one by one, and serves the salad course.

"This is my cook's famous Niçoise salad," Mimi says brightly, breaking the silence. "Instead of tuna, she uses smoked Scotch salmon, and she's found a little shop where we get *fresh* pimentos!"

"Mr. Greenway," Nonie says when her mother is out of earshot, "I must apologize for my mother. It's—well, it's Alzheimer's disease, I'm afraid. She forgets things. She loses track. She imagines things. In other words, you really must not pay any attention at all to anything she says."

But, across from her at the table, Alice Myerson's eyes are very wide and very bright, and two pink spots have appeared on her cheeks. "*What—did —she—say?*" she demands. "What did she say about me?" She flings her napkin on the table. "Why does everyone in this family hate me? Why is everyone trying to hurt me?"

"Mother," Mimi murmurs. "Mother, dear—"

"She's saying that I'm to blame for your father's suicide, isn't she? Well, it wasn't me! It wasn't me who put that bullet through his head! If anyone's to blame, *she* is! She, and Adolph, and Leo, and all the others! Put that in your story, Mr. Greenway: that evil old woman killed my husband, killed her own son, just as surely as if she'd been in the room when he pulled the trigger! Yes, put that in!" There are tears in her eyes now, and she pushes her chair back from the table.

"Mother, please—"

"Please! Please! I'm the one who should be crying 'please.' Please, leave me alone, all of you! All of you, in this family of hating and hurting and destroying people. Where can I go now, what can I do? When will you all have had enough of me, and let me die in peace? Never, that's when! Not till I die in my tracks from exhaustion, from the exhaustion of trying to fight back against this family that's destroyed everything . . . my husband . . . everything I ever loved. You didn't see it, Mimi, you were too young, but I saw it happening, happening every day, day after day, as she and his father destroyed him to the point where he was desperate, lost, with no one left to help him, not even I, nothing he could trust but his poor . . . little . . . service revolver. Oh!" she sobs. "I didn't want to come here tonight; I knew something like this would happen. Oh, just let me go home, Mimi. Let me go home, away from the cruelty . . . home . . ." She jumps from her chair and runs sobbing from the room.

After a pause, Mimi says quietly, "I'm sorry. My mother is . . . my mother is recovering from an illness. I thought she was . . . sufficiently recovered to . . . but apparently not. I'm sorry." Turning to Sherrill and Dirk, she says, "What else can I say?"

"She got hysterical," Sherrill Shearson says, as though this provided an explanation for everything.

Edwee whispers to Nonie. "What did I predict? A debacle. I knew something like this would happen if poor Alice were here."

Returning to the table with his wife's grandmother on his arm, Brad Moore asks innocently, "What became of your mother?"

"Mother . . . had to leave," Mimi says.

"Good riddance," Granny mutters. "Little tramp."

And so, I ask you, how do you rescue a formal dinner party from a disaster like this one? When the *Titanic* struck an iceberg, the passengers turned it into a romp and tossed handfuls of slivered ice at one another. In this case, there is a salad course, a main course of *noisettes de veau* and tiny green peas, a dessert course, and coffee to get through before the lifeboats can be lowered and the hapless prisoners at 1107 Fifth Avenue can be released to the salvation of their homes and cool beds. The answer is, you do your best to rescue a foundering evening with artifice, with showmanship, with bright and inconsequential chatter: the day's headlines, Bernhard Goetz, subway violence, will this extraordinary bull market ever end? Brad Moore works on Wall Street, what do his banker friends say? Outside, there is the quality of the sunset to be discussed, how, across the park, the setting sun turns the glass and concrete canyons of the West Side into ribbons of fire. Questions, questions. Mimi has questions to ask of everyone, keeping the evening afloat, keeping the conversation going, the dinner partners turning from one side to another, as the courses proceed, one after another. No one ever said that this sort of thing is easy, but Mimi does her best to carry it off, even going so far as to express her concern and shock and caring over the fate of Mrs. Perlman's little dog. "Oh, what a terrible thing, Granny."

The show must go on! It is one of those occasions where Mimi must remind herself that a business is not just a family, and that a family is not just a business but a shared heritage of old wounds that have not yet turned to scars, of hurts that cannot be forgiven, of seething memories that refuse to simmer down. It is the old story of love gone uncollected, and of luck, which is love's opposite, walking off with all the winnings, and a smirk on its face.

Mimi's husband is the first to excuse himself. "Some work to catch up on at the office," he says. "The Sturtevant case . . . pretrial discovery phase . . . depositions to take in the morning. . . ."

"Of course," Mimi says, offering her cheek again. "Don't be too late, darling."

Edwee rolls his eyes significantly in Nonie's direction, and of course Mimi, who notices everything, pretends not to notice this.

The remaining guests move into Mimi's all-white living room, where candles are lighted, and where Felix serves coffee.

Perhaps, I thought, she had worn white tonight just for this all-white room, for her dress was of the same oyster shade as the linen fabric that covered the walls. It was part of her sense of personal theatre. Later, of course, I would wonder if this room was an echo—an unconscious one, perhaps—of another all-white room that had once had a certain meaning in her life. But tonight this room was predominantly white and crystal, Baccarat obelisks and spheres and cubes, all sending refractions of colored light from low, glass-topped tables against the oversized white sofas and ottomans and low-backed chairs. In this white room, tonight, she even placed white cymbidium orchids in white Chinese vases. But there were also bright splashes of color from the walls: a huge blue-and-white Jack Youngerman, a varicolored Morris Louis waterfall cascading behind a sofa. "Is this a Jasper Johns?" I heard Dirk Gordon ask her as he admired the paintings.

"Yes, it is."

"And this: Imari?" as he pointed to a green and orange goldfish plate.

"Kutani, actually. But you're close. You know a lot about porcelain, Dirk?"

"A bit." Mr. Dirk Gordon clearly did his homework on Brad and Mimi Moore.

"My husband and I are passionate collectors."

"And this must be V'soske carpet."

"Why, yes, in fact, it is."

"The most expensive, and the best," he said, a young man who would make it his business to know such things, and then, "Whoever was your designer did a marvelous job." Mimi laughed her special laugh, and said, "Thank you," though I knew that no room in this apartment had ever known the banality of an interior decorator. Everything in this room, right down to the little cluster of Steuben glass mushrooms that had been "planted" in sphagnum moss in an antique ironstone tureen, had been selected by Brad and Mimi themselves, for Brad also has good taste. At least he appreciates fine things.

"But her rooms don't *track*," the designer Billy Baxter once complained, a trifle pettishly perhaps, since he had nothing to do with their design. By this he meant that the rooms—the white living room, the Tiger Lily library, the French dining room—seemed at odds with one another. Today's designers tend to pick two or three fashionable colors—at the moment, persimmon and pomegranate are two of these—and use them, with varying degrees of emphasis, throughout a house. (Remember when every smart living room had to be painted a deep mint green?) But Mimi prefers to let each room create its own experience. "After all," she argues sensibly enough, "a person can't be in more than one room at a time." This approach gives her house a certain sense of quirkiness and playfulness.

Mimi moves around her sparkling living room now, trying to sparkle herself. But, of course, her mother's little explosion has left the evening with a taut edge, and the sparkle can't help but feel a little forced. And so, one by one, after a polite enough interval has passed, Mimi's guests begin their thank-yous, their good-byes, and leave.

"Stay and have a quick nightcap with me, Badger," Mimi says to her son. And, when all the others have gone, she leads him back into the library, where Felix has set out a decanter of Armagnac and thimble-shaped glasses.

"Yes, a brandy," she says to young Brad's offer, and she flings herself in her long white sheath deep into a green leather sofa. Only then does she permit herself to unwind, let down her guard, and let the angry tears come. "Oh, shit, shit, *shit!*" she says through clenched teeth, making tight fists of her hands and pounding the sofa cushions with them. "Shits! *All of them!* Why did I even bother?" Badger hands her her glass, and she downs the contents with a gulp, then holds out the glass to be refilled.

"Just . . . *shits!*" she cries. Tears stream down her cheeks, but there are no sobs.

"Okay, Mom," her son says pleasantly. "Let it all out."

In a business noted for temperamental characters, Mimi Myerson is not known for emotional outbursts. During her years in the industry, she has been exposed to various of its titans: the volatile Helena Rubinstein, who, hearing news she did not wish to hear on the telephone, would often rip the cord from the wall and hurl the offending instrument across the room; the imperious Elizabeth Arden, who enjoyed making surprise visits of inspection to her salons where, finding nothing to her liking, she would sweep through her selling floors crying, "Fools! Knaves! Nincompoops!" while salesgirls cowered behind their counters in her wake; and the notoriously foul-mouthed Charles Revson, whose favorite tactic was to leap from his desk and shout, "You're fucking *fired!* Get the fuck out of here!" Mimi has never found temperament to be an effective business tool and has always practiced a more coolheaded, evenhanded executive style, having discovered that more can be accomplished with honey than with vinegar or vitriol. But now, of course, in the privacy of her own home, and alone with her own son, it is a different matter altogether.

"That shit Nonie!" she says now. "She changed all my placecards. Did you know that? To put her used-car-salesman-type greasy boyfriend next to Granny, so he could talk up some new hare-brained scheme of Nonie's. And then Edwee and Nonie, whispering together like two old maids and refusing to join the conversation. And *wretched* old Granny! Wouldn't you think, after all these years, she could let up on Mother? But she *never* lets up! And poor Mother—who didn't want to come anyway, but whom I *made* come. And those stupid-ass models: did you ever encounter such a pair of airheads? The whole thing, the whole evening, was a stupid idea to begin with. Why didn't you tell me, Badger, that this whole evening was a stupid idea?"

He spreads his hands. "*Mea culpa,*" he says. "It was all my fault."

"Of course it wasn't. It was *my* stupid idea. Even your father wasn't a lot of help, was he? Sneaking out on some trumped-up excuse, and leaving me to sweep up the wreckage."

"He said the Sturtevant case. I know it's been on his mind—"

"Ha! You don't live with a man for twenty-nine years and not know when he's fibbing. If he's working on the Sturtevant case right now, I'm the Virgin Mary!"

"Come to think of it," Badger says, "there is a certain resemblance. But in letting off all this steam, your halo's gotten a little crooked."

"Oh, shut up," she says, only half-crossly. "It's just . . . it's just that I wanted everything to be so . . . perfect . . . with the whole family . . . just once . . . to celebrate . . ."

He moves across the room now, sits beside her on the green sofa, and circles her shoulders with his left arm. "It wasn't your fault, Mom," he says. "Sometimes things just go wrong. The best-laid plans of mice and men . . ."

"And my beautiful dinner—people just played with their food. And Mr. Greenway here from *Fortune*. I'd worked so hard."

"No more self-pity, Mimi Myerson. Nothing old Greenway writes about us can hurt us. The old farts who read *Fortune* don't buy Mireille perfume. Besides, maybe you work *too* hard, Mom. Ever think of that?"

She looks quickly at him. "Is that it, Badger? Have I been working so hard with this company that I've let the rest of my family fall apart all around me?"

"Why not give me more to do? I'll take a promotion any old day."

"Oh, Badger. You're the best. You're the best thing that's happened to this family, *and* this company. Ever. I couldn't run it without you."

"Well, I do have some interesting news for you," he says, "if we can get back to business for a minute."

"Oh? What's that?" The tears and the anger are gone now, and she sits up straight.

"Naturally, I didn't want to mention this at dinner. But I've found out who's been buying up our Miray stock in big units, forcing the price up."

"Who is it?"

"It's not one of the funds, as we thought. It's an individual."

"Who, Badger?"

"Mr. Michael Horowitz. Himself."

She stiffens slightly. "You're sure."

"Found out this afternoon. One of his partners plays squash at the Racquet Club. He just casually mentioned it—as though he assumed I knew. I don't envy that partner's future with Horowitz if Horowitz learns he let the cat out of the bag."

"No. Don't tell anyone. I don't even want to know your friend's name."

"He's got over four percent of us already."

"At five percent—"

"Right. SEC regulations require that he make a public announcement. But what puzzles me is why? Why would a real estate guy who's got hotels and co-ops and casinos in Atlantic City want to get into the cosmetics business? Is it the old greenmail, do you think? Driving the price of our stock up to the point where we'll have to pay his price to get it back? Or do I detect a not-so-friendly takeover attempt in the making? Or what?"

"Michael Horowitz," she says. "Again. I should have guessed."

"What do you mean, 'again'?"

"First it was Grandpa's Florida house he wanted. Now it's this."

"The house was a perfectly friendly sale. This isn't. This is back-door stuff. This is sneaky."

"He seems to want to buy up whatever belongs to the Myersons. Isn't that pretty clear?"

"But why, I wonder?"

At first she doesn't answer him. Then she says, "Personal reasons. Jealousy, perhaps."

"*Jealousy?*"

"Maybe he sees us as old Jewish money. He's new Jewish money. His father was a caterer in Queens. Something like that." She laughs briefly. "Isn't it silly? My Grandpa Adolph started out as a housepainter in the Bronx!"

"How well do you know this guy, Mom?"

"Know him? Well, I know him. Everybody knows Michael Horowitz if they've spent five minutes in New York."

"Then why not call him, Mom? Set up a meeting. See what's on his mind. Confront the guy with what we know. You're always at your best at a high-noon shoot-out."

She shudders. "Oh, please," she says. "Haven't we had enough talk tonight about shooting—about guns and killing?"

"Sorry," he says easily. "Unfortunate metaphor. But I do think this guy Horowitz is becoming a threat that our company is going to have to face."

"Yes," she says. "Yes, I'll call him."

"They say he's tough."

"*I'm* tough," she says.

He laughs. "Good girl! Your halo's back in place."

She is silent for a moment. Then she says quietly, "This means it's even more important for the perfume to be a success, doesn't it."

"Of course. If we're going to fight a takeover, we'll need to fight from strength."

"Suddenly, the future of this company—your future, my future—and your future is even more important than mine—all depends on the success of a, a silly little fragrance!"

"Not a silly little fragrance. A fifty-million-dollar fragrance. A very important fragrance."

"Well, it got off to a pretty rocky start tonight, didn't it?"

"Tonight was just family."

"Oh, Badger," she says, "it *will* succeed, won't it? It *can't* fail, can it?"

"Of course it can't," he says.

But they both know that this is a business where there is never any guarantee of success, never any insurance against failure.

The two sit quietly on the green sofa, sipping their brandies. Outside, the seagulls are slowly lifting from the lake and circling back to sea, a signal that the Atlantic storm has passed. Elsewhere in the apartment, Felix moves from room to room on silently slippered feet, turning out all unnecessary lights, leaving lighted only those that will guide his master and his mistress to their respective bedrooms at their respective hours. In the library, the portrait of Adolph Myerson scowls down upon his only granddaughter and his only great-grandson from under his museum lamp.

Is the room talking?

"Practice your curtsy, Mimi," she hears her mother's voice say. "Lower your body a little more, bend your right knee a little deeper, and the left foot a little further back. That's better. Now hold out your right hand for balance, and say—"

"Good afternoon, Grandpa, sir. Good afternoon, dear Granny Flo."

"*Much* better. Now try it again: back straight, with your chin a little lower, but with your eyes looking directly into Grandpa's."

"Why is Papa unhappy, Mama?"

"Your Papa is unhappy because your Grandpa is unhappy. But if you and I can make your Grandpa happy, and your Grandma happy, your Papa will be happy, and everyone will be happy—happy as happy can be. Now practice the curtsy, chin down, eyes up . . ."

But from where he glares down at them from her library wall, her grandfather's face fails to register even the slightest trace of happiness, or pleasure, or approval, at all.

3

AT NUMBER 3 Sutton Square, Edwee Myerson opens the front door of his house using four different sets of keys—one for the main lock, one for the deadbolt, one for the chain, and one for the heavy Fox lock that braces the big door from within (New York is no longer the safe place it once was) —and lets the three of them in: himself, his wife, and his sister, Nonie. His servants have all retired for the night, and the house is very still. He leads the two women down the dimly lit entrance gallery with its Oriental rugs and its dark walnut-paneled walls from which his famous collection of Greek amphorae are suspended from wrought-iron brackets, turning on lamps as he goes, toward his office in the southeast corner of the house.

Edwee's office, like the other rooms in the house, is arranged more like a private museum than a workspace. The office overlooks the East River and the city skyline and bridges to the south, as well as a more intimate view of Edwee's small city garden, with its fruit trees and boxwood hedges as well as its raised centerpiece, which is Edwee's herb garden, where he grows the fresh herbs for his second career as a gourmet cook. Within the office itself are displayed more of Edwee's collections. Bookcases along one wall contain his collection of over two thousand cookbooks, some of them quite old and rare. More cases contain his even larger collection of art books, and against the wall between the two French doors that lead out into the garden are displayed his collections of antique dolls and miniature dollhouse furniture, including complete living room and dining room sets signed by the Master Thomas Chippendale himself—the only such sets the Master is known to have executed, and which the Smithsonian has been after for years. Illuminated cases display his collections of coin-silver spoons and early American pewter serving pieces. There is much, much more. One table displays his collection of silver and crystal inkwells; another, a collection of millefleur paperweights; still another, a collection of old snuffboxes. Tucked between the books on the bookshelves are specimen pieces of Chinese Export porcelain, and an almost-complete edition of Dorothy Doughty birds, risen incomparably in value since the artist's death. A bronze umbrella stand holds a valuable assortment of antique gold- and silver-handled walking sticks. Another stand, fashioned from an elephant's foot and lined with rosewood, holds swords, sabers, and fencing foils with variously carved and jeweled hafts, and above the door through which one enters the room hangs a collection of antique pistols. Flanking Edwee's big partners' desk, which is made of cherry and burled walnut, are six-foot-high floor lamps whose bases are an identical pair of twisted ivory narwhal tusks. One could go on and on describing the contents of this extraordinary room. Next door, for instance, is a fully-equipped kitchen, Edwee's personal domain where he tests his recipes, which has nothing to do with the main kitchen of the house.

Edwee hardly ever sets foot in this other kitchen, which he calls "the service kitchen." And, conversely, no servant is permitted in Edwee's personal kitchen except, of course, for cleanup. Every imaginable cooking vessel and utensil is stored here: the zinc-lined copper roasting pans, the silver chafing dishes, the crockery serving dishes, the pots and pans of glass and stainless steel, the wooden spoons. Because, as any fool would know (and as Edwee will explain), certain foods demand certain materials for proper preparation. Who would dream of preparing a bouillabaisse in anything but copper, for example, or of stirring it with anything but a wooden spoon? What sort of idiot would plank a turbot on anything but a board of bleached ash? (Pine or maple "rapes" the flavor, Edwee points out.) Is there another way to serve wild asparagus than on bone china so thin that you could see a finch's foot through it, and with ivory tongs? (Yes, you could use ivory chopsticks.) Also, with the exception of the twelve-burner range and the four ovens, nothing in this kitchen is electric. Edwee makes his butter in a wooden churn, the only way. Edwee even has a candling device for candling his eggs, which come from upstate, where they are laid by free-range chickens. His servants complain about his refusal to buy a dishwasher, but that is their problem.

One could go on and on, and then add that all the other rooms in Edwee's house are furnished in a similar artfully eccentric fashion. From time to time, if the cause is sufficiently worthy, which is to say sufficiently fashionable, Edwee Myerson will allow his house to be toured for charity, but this is a nuisance since a brace of security guards must be positioned in each room to keep an eye on their costly contents.

At the door to his office now, Edwee says to his wife, "Don't you need to powder your nose or something, pussyface? My sister and I have important family m-m-m-matters to discuss."

Gloria pouts. "Well, don't be too long," she says. "Your little baby's toesies get cold in bed if she doesn't have her daddy to snuggle up to."

"I won't," he says, and kisses her on the forehead. She leaves, and he closes the door behind her and stands for a moment with a dreamy smile on his face. He sighs softly and says, "Isn't she simply . . . wonderful?"

"You seem so *domesticated,* Edwee, dear. Given up your old ways?"

"Oh, yes. Oh, yes." He moves to his chair behind the partners' desk, and his sister arranges herself in the Queen Anne armchair opposite him. "You see, she introduced me to oral sex. She sits on my face, and I sit on hers. All those years of impotence are suddenly over! No more problems with getting an erection, no more p.e.—premature ejaculation—no more miserable masturbation, no more using the vacuum cleaner—"

"The *vacuum* cleaner!" Nonie cries. "What are you talking about, Edwee?"

"I used to use the rubber end of the vacuum cleaner hose to try to arouse myself. All at once, with Gloria, those days are gone forever."

"Really, Edwee," Nonie says. "*Really.* It must be that female Jungian you've been going to."

"I'll say this, Nonie: forty-two years of analysis have finally begun to pay off. You see, I've finally learned to be honest with myself, and to act out my fantasies. Thanks to Dr. Ida Katz—and Gloria."

"Well," she says, tapping the tips of her fingernails on his desktop, "I'm sure you didn't drag me back here to talk about your sex life, which I'm really not interested in—"

"And we videotape each other," he says. "*That* was Dr. Katz's idea. We videotape each other while we're having sex, and then, while we're having sex the next time, we play the videotapes back. We even have videotapes of ourselves making videotapes. Oh, it's quite wild and, as you say, quite wonderful."

Nonie says nothing, looking up at the ceiling, once more as though balancing something small and invisible on the tip of her nose.

"But, back to less pleasant matters," he says. "We really have a pretty kettle of fish on our hands, don't we?"

"You mean Brad and his alleged lady friend? I thought he and Mimi seemed perfectly relaxed and normal tonight. I don't think we should get involved in it, Edwee. If they're having any problems, that's their business. After all, all she is to us is our niece."

"Oh, I'm not talking about *that,*" he says. "I agree that's a very minor matter. Interesting, but m-m-m-minor." He fumbles in the pocket of his dinner jacket for his pipe, finds it, extracts it, and lights it carefully. "I'm talking about our mother, Nonie. I'm talking about *Maman*. It's perfectly clear to me that she's finally gone around the bend. She's going to have to be put away, and it's going to have to be our unhappy task—yours and mine —to do it."

"You mean her outburst at Alice tonight? I agree that was . . . unfortunate. But it was Alice's fault. Alice shouldn't have contradicted her. Mother doesn't like to be contradicted. She's always been like that."

"No, no, *no*," Edwee says, gesturing in the air with his pipe. "I'm not even talking about that, though that was more of her craziness—saying that Alice had killed a man, for God's sake, when we all know that poor Henry's death was a tragic accident, and Alice was hundreds of miles away in Saratoga when it happened. And saying that our father kept some sort of diary, which we know he didn't, and getting that young reporter all excited. I'm not talking about any of that. Besides, poor tragic Alicia was drunk as a lord."

"I don't think she was, Edwee. I saw her refuse wine at the dinner table, and I heard her ask Felix for ginger ale during cocktails."

"Anyway, I'm not talking about any of that. I'm talking about *Maman*. You may call it Alzheimer's disease, but I call it senility—senility in its most advanced, irreversible stage."

"I only mentioned Alzheimer's because I didn't want that reporter to take that outburst of hers too seriously. She's not—" He rises slowly from his chair, carrying his pipe, and moves toward the French doors. "A poor old woman, nearly ninety," he says, "now completely incompetent to handle her own affairs. Probably incontinent, too. Did you notice the many trips to the bathroom?"

"I only noticed one."

"Living alone, totally blind—"

"I'm not even sure about that, Edwee. I think she sees better than she lets on. She noticed yellow tulips. She said she could smell they were yellow. Did you ever hear of such a thing? I never have!"

"No," he says, "the real point is that she can no longer manage her own affairs. She needs special care. I hate to say this, Nonie, but she must be placed in a nursing home. And not a moment too soon. We should probably start making arrangements the first thing in the morning."

"A *nursing* home! But she's perfectly happy at the Carlyle. She has room service, maid service, her linens changed every day. They love her there, and treat her like a—"

"I've already located a place in Great Barrington that sounds quite ideal for her. She'd have her own little room. People her own age for company—"

"But she has plenty of company, Edwee. People drop in on her all the time, she spends half her day on the telephone talking to people like Mrs. Perlman. The hotel staff is in and out—"

"And Great Barrington's far enough away so that she'll understand why you and I won't be able to come and see her as often as we might like. No pets, of course."

"You'd make her give up Itty-Bitty? That would *kill* her, Edwee!"

"Well, it's got to be done," he says. "I know it's sad, but it's got to be done."

"But *why*, Edwee? Mother is . . . Mother. She's always been the way she is. After all, I'm a few—well, a couple of years older than you, and Mother has been the way she is for as long as I can remember. What we saw tonight was just . . . Mother!"

He hesitates. "I'll tell you something, Nonie," he says. "Something you may not know. Before our Papa died, he said to me, 'Edwee, I want you to take care of your mother. And if ever the time comes, I want you to see that she is given the proper care. I want you to promise me that, if the time should come when you feel that she needs to be institutionalized, you will see that it's done. P-p-p-promise me that.' I promised him. It was a death-bed promise, Nonie."

"But Edwee, Papa died in his sleep in a San Francisco hotel. You were in Paris, remember?"

"Nevertheless, that was my promise, and it's my sad duty to honor that promise now. I'll call my lawyers at Dewey, Ballantine tomorrow, have the legal paperwork done. Have her declared incompetent, incapable of handling her own affairs. You and I can do it, because we're her only remaining living issue. We'll just sign whatever papers are necessary to declare her—"

"Oh, Edwee, no!"

"*What do you mean, no?*" His voice is angry now.

"Because she's *not* incompetent! No more than she ever was, I mean, which was never very—"

"Damn it, she *is*. Do I have to draw pictures for you? Didn't you hear what she said in the car? About giving away the art collection—just *giving it away!* Do you call that competent? That collection is p-priceless! The Goya, the Bentons—the Goya alone! She's already seen Philippe de Montebello, Nonie! God knows what de Montebello may have gotten her to sign! Well, if she's signed anything, we'll have it declared null and void, based on her incompetence. That collection is part of our inheritance, Nonie. It's ours."

"Well, it really isn't, Edwee. It's hers, and hers to do with as she wishes, it seems to me."

"Do you mean to say you *approve* of this insanity—just giving away this priceless collection of paintings?"

"I've never cared all that much about art," she says.

"Well, *I* do," he says. "I care."

"Just because she wants to give away her collection doesn't seem to me reason enough to have her shipped off to a nursing home," she says. "It just doesn't."

"One of us will have to be appointed her conservator," he says. "I think that should be you. You've always gotten along with her better than I have. Besides, you don't have anything else to do."

"What do you *mean*, I don't have anything else to do?"

"It's just a legal technicality," he says. "How much work could be involved in taking care of somebody who's a vegetable?"

"Edwee, this is our *mother* you're talking about!"

"Well, can you think of a single reason why we'd want to keep that old hag around any longer, that old hag that does nothing but cause us trouble? Unless . . ." He hesitates, and his eyes narrow slightly. "Unless . . . unless—"

"Unless what, Edwee?"

"Unless," he says, "*you* have some *personal* agenda that involves keeping her around. Is that it, Nonie? Have you got some new scheme up your sleeve that involves Mother?"

"Well," she begins guardedly, "I do have a life to live, and . . ." She falls silent. She knows from experience that it is unwise to divulge too much of her plans to her brother. He cannot be trusted.

"That's it, isn't it? And it probably involves that young thug you brought to Mimi's tonight, doesn't it?"

The house is silent now, except for the oddly soothing rumble of the traffic that passes, unceasingly, along the FDR Drive and through the Sutton Place Tunnel beneath the foundation of the house. All the houses on Edwee's little mews experience this steady rumble, and it is Edwee's opinion that this small, steady vibration has a salubrious effect on the growth of plants. His herb garden, he claims, benefits from this effect, and he has even expounded on this theory in an article for *House & Garden*, which an unfortunate change in editorial direction caused an inexperienced new editor to reject. The vibrations from the FDR Drive as it passes through the tunnel, he wrote, has the effect of "massaging" the roots of his specimen herbs, an effect that he likened to "subterranean petting—petting to climax."

"Of course," he says finally, "I should have known all along. You have some new scheme up your sleeve. That's why you oppose having Mother put away. What is it this time, Nonie?"

"I really don't see that it's any of your—"

"How many others have there been, Nonie? How many other money-losing schemes? Let's see: there was the dress shop on M-M-Madison Avenue. There was the little restaurant. There was the jewelry boutique. There was the p-p-p-pathetic attempt to start a new fashion magazine. All of these required the financial backing of *M-M-Maman,* of course. Who else would back such obvious losing schemes?"

"Certainly not you!" Nonie cries. "I've learned long ago that it's useless for anyone to turn to *you* and ask for help."

"You've always been so money-grubbing, Nonie. Why is that? Why are you so money-grubbing? Money bores me."

"Money bores *you* because you're rich! I'm not. I'm the poor relation. I was shorted out of Papa's will, remember?"

"You were shorted out of Papa's will because he didn't consider you *responsible.* He considered Henry and me responsible."

She reaches for her bag and gloves to go. "You're not telling me anything I haven't known for years," she says. "I was shorted out of Papa's will because I was a girl, and Papa had no use for girls. He only wanted sons. I was a disappointment to him from the moment I was born."

"No, I think it was later, as you grew older, that he began to actively dislike you."

She stands up, facing him, and slowly his eyes withdraw from hers. "But what ambitions he had for his two sons," she says. "Do you remember? Henry was to run the company, and look what happened to him. You were to become the first Jewish President of the United States, remember that? 'Edwin will be the first Jew in the White House,' he used to say. Well, now you've become Nancy Reagan's little pet, and I suppose that's close enough —being Nancy Reagan's walker."

His right hand, holding the pipe, jerks visibly upward, as though about to strike her, but he manages to restrain himself, and the hand falls downward.

"Good night, Edwee," she says. "Have fun sitting on your wife's face." Then she is gone.

Alone in his office, among his crowded collection, Edwee Myerson returns to the chair behind his big desk and relights his pipe. The pipe is ordinarily just a prop. He uses it mainly just for effect, pointing its stem at a conversational partner to emphasize an argument or to drive home one of his well-thought-out opinions. But now he puffs on it fiercely, inhaling deeply, as though the pipe and its tobacco were an uncontrollable addiction.

His eyes travel upward to one section of walnut-paneled wall that, miraculously, considering the well-planned clutter of the room, is unaccountably bare of ornamentation or garniture. This space has been reserved, always, for his mother's Goya.

There are two possessions of his mother's that he has always been determined one day to own. One is her large square-cut emerald solitaire with its girdle of diamonds. The other is the Goya. He would not want to wear his mother's emerald ring, of course. But he would like to hold it, fondle it, rub the emerald's facets with his fingertips, to possess the ring as one would possess a lover. His passion for the Goya is just as powerful, just as sensual, just as erotic. Someday, he has always known, he must possess just those two things. The absence of those two things has created a hole in his life that nothing else can fill, a well of longing, a black hollow of desire, as achingly empty as that waiting square of walnut wall.

He has always known that it would be futile, sheer folly, to ask his mother for those two objects. He knows her too well to do a thing like that. She is an accomplished player, a pro, at turning down requests, at deflecting solicitations, at ignoring panhandlers, and at being both blind and deaf to beggars. At denying the needs of others, his mother should be given a Lifetime Achievement Award. Except, of course, for her soft spot, which is Nonie. He has, however, tried to suggest to her obliquely that there are a couple of things of hers that he rather fancies. He has said, for instance, of the emerald, "If I owned that ring, I'd display it, in a lighted jar, suspended on the thinnest platinum chain." And as for the Goya, when in her presence—when she still had her eyesight, that is—he would try to send signals to her subconscious by simply standing for long periods in front of the painting, gazing at it worshipfully. Now, it is clear, these mental messages never reached whatever remains of her cerebrum, for she is thinking of giving his Goya away.

His eyes wander to the collection of firearms and flintlocks displayed above the door, and to the collection of lethal blades in the elephant's foot. Is there a way to murder his mother? Is there a way to snuff out the life of the conniving Philippe de Montebello?

Dimly, the vague shape of a plan begins to float into his mind, and he lets its scattered pieces fall into place. At first, the pieces do not fit. He shuffles them, re-sorts them, rearranges the elements of the plan, first this way, then that. The first thing he must do, he decides, is to make sure that he is on the best of terms with Mimi. A letter is required.

From the center drawer of his desk, he removes a sheet of his heavily crested ivory letter paper, with the serifs of his monogram—E.R.M.—twisted and curled around and within each other like royal blue liana vines. He takes his antique quill pen, the one he uses when setting down his essays, dips it in a silver inkwell, and begins to write. "My dearest Mimi," he begins.

Thank you for your truly quite splendid dinner, and you were a jewel to include me. Your food, flowers, and decor were, as always, perfection, and I thought to myself as I watched you from my end of the table: "Has Mimi ever looked lovelier? No! Never! Jamais dans sa vie!"

Second only to your beauty, I decided, was your new fragrance, which you named so aptly—nay, brilliantly!—Mireille. I have just now dabbed a bit of the men's cologne on myself, and the scent is positively thrilling— luxurious, thrilling, utterly captivating, and quite different from anything else I have ever sampled in men's toiletries. I know you are going to have a brilliant success with this, Mimi, and that Mireille will provide just an- other bright feather in your already well-feathered cap.

May I also say this, dear Mimi? Your dear father would be so very proud of you!

A very clever touch, Edwee thinks. He envisions Mimi dabbing at her eyes over this evocation of her dead father.

Of course I must also apologize for the unspeakable *behaviour of poor, dear* Maman. *I know it must have upset you, but brave*

He gropes for the right noun. Brave girl? No, girls don't like to be called girls anymore. Brave woman? Brave little soldier? Brave little trouper?

creature that you are, you did not let the upset show. I must say that after Maman's *behaviour*

He always spells it "behaviour," the English way.

tonight, I am convinced, sadly, that she is now completely ga-ga, no longer responsible for either her words or actions. Indeed, tonight, your aunt Nonie and I had a long meeting to discuss the advisability and possibility of a

The words *nursing home* have an unpleasant connotation. What else can one call it? He writes:

an alternative care facility.

Thank you, dear Mimi, and I don't need to wish you success with Mireille because I can "smell" success in the sample you gave me. Con- gratulations in advance!

Fondly, your
Uncle Edwee

He puts down his pen, and there is a buzz on the house intercom. He picks up the telephone and says, "Yes, Pussyface?"

"Aren't you *ever* coming to bed, Daddy? It's almost one o'clock!"

"Just finishing up," he says. "I've an *Art & Antiques* deadline. You know deadlines! You know the creative process!"

"I've got the poppers out and *every*thing."

"Five more minutes, Pussy."

He now adds a hasty postscript.

P.S. Incidentally, that

Now he rummages in his mind for the proper adjective. Charming? Delightful? Pleasant? Attractive? Interesting? Sexy hunk? He settles on something bland and noncommittal.

nice young chap who's to be your model for your advertising mentioned that he had some recipes that I might like to try. When she has a moment —no hurry—ask your secretary if she'd drop his name and address and home phone number in the mail for me. Thanks much!
E.

He folds the letter (it ran to three pages), places it in an envelope, addresses it, licks the tip of the envelope, and seals it.

Outside, the private security guard that the residents of Sutton Square employ is making his hourly rounds, quietly testing doorknobs, and Edwee makes his way upstairs and to Gloria, turning out lights as he goes.

Alone in her bedroom, Mimi sits at her dressing table removing her makeup, using many tissues, and then creams her face. Appraising her reflection in the glass, she says: Not bad. No, not bad at all for forty-nine. I'll give this face at least five more years before I begin to worry about it. In this business, your face is part of your overhead. Look at her face, people say. It must be her cleansing creams and toners and moisturizers that do it, and they remember this as they browse the cosmetics counters at Bergdorf's and Saks and Bloomingdale's, picking up the little jars and bottles, trying the samples, and see the name Mireille, and remind themselves that there is a woman, and a face, behind that name. A name behind the face. A face. The face that launched a thousand little jars of night cream by Mireille, for a thousand women who dream of looking only a little better, a little younger, when their husbands or their lovers turn to them at night and say, you look so young, you feel so young.

"I love your face," someone had once said to her. "Your fah-nee, fah-nee face." He had also said he loved the color of her eyes. She had always thought of her eyes as her worst feature. Too grey, too pale. She studies her eyes in the mirror now. Nowadays, with cosmetics, with tinted contact lenses, one can even change the color of one's eyes, but she had never changed hers. "Her wide, snapping black eyes," she had read of the heroine in some novel long ago, and she had used to wish that her eyes were snapping black. Eyes that snapped. Noisy eyes. Eyes that yipped and snarled like one of Granny's little dogs. Try as she might, her eyes would never snap. But he had said he liked her eyes. "Silver," he said. "Like George the First antique silver that's been polished every day. They go just right with your fah-nee, fah-nee face." Who had said that in the movie? Oh, yes, Fred Astaire, in *Funny Face.*

Facts to face. Fact one. He is, I know he is, of course he is, there's nothing to be gained by denying it, by gainsaying it, so say it: he is. Who is she? I don't want to know. There's nothing to be gained by knowing her name, she doesn't need to have a name, she doesn't even need to have a face. Does he turn to her in sleep and call her by my name? That would be nice. Oh, yes, old Brad, old boy, old pal, old friend, you can't keep that from me, no sir, no siree. We used to say we were like one soul, we knew each other's thoughts. The words of a song would be going through my brain, and you'd start whistling it. About time for him to call, I'd think, and the telephone would ring. Must clean out the garage in that summer place we rented at the Cape in '74, I'd think, and I'd go out and find you doing it. I need to wash my tennis shorts, you'd say, and I'd say, they're already in the dryer, and feel holy. On the beach at St.-Jean-de-Luz, you buried my feet in the sand because you knew that was what I wanted you to do. That's how close we were, that's how young we were.

You won't find Bradford to be a very *demonstrative* young man, your mother said. None of us Moores or Bradfords are. It's the New England in us. Why should I want him to be demonstrative? I asked her. She looked so uncomfortable, poor dear. She said, I mean . . . I mean . . . I guess what I'm trying to say is that the Jewish people I've known, my Jewish friends, seem to be such *demonstrative* people. Hugging. Kissing. Things like that. We're just not quite that way. Poor thing. That's how little she knew you, that's how little she knew the Jews, the so-called passionate people. Oh, she'd have much preferred it if you'd married someone else named Moore or Bradford, she made that quite clear, but she didn't disapprove of me, she didn't try to stop us. An ancestor of ours compiled the first Hebrew-to-English dictionary, she told me proudly, as though that proved the family's long history of religious tolerance. She touched my elbow when she said that, to show she liked me. Demonstrative.

Oh, it wasn't really passion, was it? No, because *passion* comes from the Latin word for suffering. I looked it up once. No, because passion comes to an end and so, in the end, does suffering. It was more like affection, friendship, caring, pleasing one another, delighting in each other's pleasure and the pleasure of each other's company, collecting things together, the things that endure, that don't come to an end. These are the things that last, that can make a marriage last for twenty-nine years. Or so I thought.

I suppose he finds her sexually exciting, whoever she is, this nameless, faceless woman. That's all right. Or is it? It is a new thought for me, something I never thought about before, something I never had to think about, because this is the first time it has happened to me, though I am hardly the first woman in the world who has had this happen to her. It has happened to googooflex women—googooflex: in school we used to say this was the highest number in the world. I am not alone, so join the club, old girl, and here's your membership card.

But I'll tell you one thing, old Brad, old chum, old pal, she isn't making you happy, this whoever she is. I can see it in your eyes. I see new worry lines around your eyes, I saw them tonight. I suppose she's the type who'll say no, not until you divorce your wife. The ultimatum type. But men don't like those types, the ultimatum types, those old-tomato types. Particularly you don't like those types. And particularly you aren't the type who would divorce his wife, not you, not now, not after all these—or are you? Why am I suddenly not so sure? Why am I suddenly not so sure I know you as well as I thought I did? Do I know you at all? I just don't know.

Is it because you've finally grown tired of the jokes? We used to joke about it, you and I. The introductions at the business parties: And this is Mimi Myerson's husband, Bradford Moore. We made a joke of it, of you being Mr. Mimi Myerson with my business people. We were just another two-career couple, you used to say, with two different names for business purposes, with separate listings in *Who's Who*. But has the joke worn thin after all these years? Has it become stale and overworked, and when you hear that sort of thing now, does it stick in the craw, sourly, like a poorly digested meal? Is that what she offers you, this person whom I do not know—a male identity at last, an opportunity to be something more than someone else's husband? "Now I know what Prince Philip must feel like," you said once at some Miray function. "Always having to walk that required one pace behind the queen." A joke? Haven't I let you enjoy your sovereign malehood, your princely individuality? Haven't I offered that to you, too? Haven't I tried? Come back, Brad, come back to Mama, and I'll try harder. Come back, and you'll see how hard I'll try.

I will not say the word *forgive*. I am in no position to offer you such a flashy gift as forgiveness. Let she who is without sin cast the first stone, they say, and I am not without sin. I did it, too, to you, and what's more I did it first. It was long ago, but that makes no difference because time does not create an alibi for disloyalty, for cheating. If I could sit here and look into my mirror and say I never cheated on our marriage, without lowering my eyes, remembering everything, that would be one thing, but I can't. Even though you never knew about it, never suspected, that doesn't mean it didn't happen, because it happened. I knew what I was doing, as they say, and I did it. Only with one person, perhaps, but one was enough to draw the line between a woman who cheated and a woman who can say she never cheated. Or perhaps you did know, perhaps you did suspect. Is that it? What's good for the goose is good for the gander. Tit for tat. Serves you right, old girl. Try a taste of your own medicine. See how you like it.

That time there was passion—*passionare*, to suffer.

And there've been other times I could have done it. Your law partner, Harry Walters—he wanted to. Your very own law partner, the man whom you play tennis with on Thursday nights, your dear friend, he asked me to. Are you getting it good enough from Brad in the sack? he asked me. I've seen him in the shower, and he looks kind of small in that department. I laughed in his face, and never told you. And there was the buyer at Bendel's who suggested that he'd buy our products if I'd check into the St. Regis with him, and for two years no one could understand why Bendel's wouldn't buy us. I could go on. I could compile quite a little list of men who wanted to—even a woman who wanted to—but the list of people I've said no to doesn't turn me into a woman who's never cheated on her husband, does it? No way, old girl. No way, José.

Dear Brad, she writes to him in her mind, dictating to herself the way she dictates those long and chatty office memos she likes to write. Dear Brad. Brad darling. Darling Brad, dearest one, dear heart, dearest husband, dear Brad. Has the trouble always been that you don't really approve of the business I'm in, is that it? I mean, I know at the time you supported me when I wanted to do it, you were the only one who thought I had a chance, but perhaps, way back then, you had no idea that I would be so successful, that this little business of mine would become so big, that it would consume so much of my time and my life. Perhaps you thought it would be like the painter Ingres and his violin, a pastime, a hobby, an avocation, like our Saturday strolls around antique shops, looking for unusual plates. But now I've become a Cosmetics Queen—they call me that—and I've made all this money, richer, probably, than Grandpa ever was, and perhaps, years ago, you never really expected that. Do I earn more money than you? Yes, probably, but we've never discussed that, thank God; we've never had to, thank God.

And then there are the kinds of people I have to deal with, the retailers and merchandise managers and buyers, the tough-talking Charlie Revson types, the spike-heeled fashion editors in their turbans, the New York types, the media salesmen and the ad agency reps; they're really not your types, are they? They probably bore you, and you probably even find them a little vulgar. They don't have names like Wickersham and Hollister and Cadwallader and Stettinius and Lord, the names you lunch with at the Downtown Club. They have names like Bernstein and Lifschitz and Goldbogen and Livingston that used to be Lowenstein and Robbins that used to be Rubin. I'm not saying you're a snob, but these aren't the people you're used to, that you really feel comfortable with, at ease with. I picture you in your office sometimes, all tweedy carpet and chocolate-colored leather chairs, good *cracked* leather, old leather, lamps with parchment shades, and a view of Trinity Church and the Stock Exchange and Alexander Hamilton's statue guarding the U.S. Treasury Building, Old New York, so different from mine. In Old New York, the lawyers come and go, talking of *Paine* vs. *Bigelow*. I know what your secret ambition is, or used to be. It was to be appointed a United States Supreme Court Justice. But has there ever been a United States Supreme Court Justice whose wife was a Cosmetics Queen? Will there ever be? Is that the trouble? Has my success collided with your ambition? I wanted you to be proud of me, I guess, but instead of pride I've brought you disappointment.

Perhaps if we'd had another child. But then . . .

Your goal was prestige. Mine is . . . perfume.

I can't sit here all night thinking thoughts like these. We have an advertising meeting in the morning. He'll come home, eventually. At least he always has before.

In her bedroom, Mimi's maid has turned down the covers, drawn the curtains closed, and placed a small plate of fruit on her bedside table: an apple, a banana, and a plum, red, white, and blue. With the fruit knife, she slices a wedge from the apple and places it in her mouth. Then she slides between the sheets and arranges many small lace-edged Porthault pillows around her head and neck and shoulders. Then she turns off the bedside lamp. Close your eyes and think happy thoughts, her mother used to say, and you'll be sure to have a good night's sleep.

But, instead of happy thoughts, omens and portents swirl around her in the darkness. Tonight was supposed to have been the special family preview of her new Mireille fragrance, and that little preview did not go well. Does that bode ill for the future of the fragrance? Mimi tries to remind herself that she does not believe in omens and portents. Hers is a business, after all, that is based on superstitions, hunches, guesswork, instinct, gut reactions.

Elizabeth Arden would not make a business decision without first consulting her horoscope. Charlie Revson consulted regularly with a palmist and would not do business with a man whose license plate had the number thirteen in it. Even Mimi's building believes in witchcraft. There is no thirteenth floor. If you go looking for evil omens, you can find them everywhere. From beneath a pillow, Mimi reaches for her sleep mask. The sleep mask has the effect of pressing her wakeful eyelids closed.

Much later, she has the dream. It is a dream she has had before, though not lately, and it is a dream that, even as she dreams it, she knows is only a dream, and she knows that she will awaken from it, and always at the same point. In it, she is a little girl again, and in a car somewhere, and suddenly there is a terrible screeching of brakes, and a loud crash, and a large dark object flying up across the sky, and people screaming everywhere, and then there are only her mother's screams and sobs. This is where she invariably awakens, with her mother's screams, never finding out what the screams mean, or what has happened.

Awake, she realizes that the sound that awoke her was the sound of her husband's bedroom door closing across the hall. From the digital clock at her bedside, she sees that it is ten minutes of three, and she realizes that he has not come into her room to kiss her good night, the way he usually does.

On the beach at St.-Jean-de-Luz, you covered my feet with sand, and then my legs, and then my belly, and then my arms, and then my breasts, until I was covered with sand all the way up to my neck, and all that was sticking out of me was the head. And you said that now I had a figure just like Mae West's, and then you kissed me on the lips and said that even if I got to be as old and fat and bloated-looking as Mae West, you'd still love me.

Mimi told me all of this, much later.

4

*I*T IS NOW TEN O'CLOCK the following morning, and Mimi and her advertising director, Mark Segal, sit in the small conference room of the Miray offices at 666 Fifth Avenue. Mimi is perched on one end of the conference table, and Mark sits at the other, and between them, spread out across the table, are the pasteups for the print advertising and the story-boards for the television commercials for the new Mireille campaign. Seated a short distance away from them, trying to be unobtrusive, is Jim Greenway, whom Mimi has invited to follow her about during a somewhat atypical business day. It is atypical because it is not every day that the final details are worked out for a fifty-million-dollar campaign that will spell either success or failure for a brand-new range of products in a notoriously fickle marketplace.

There is tension in the air as Segal, an athletic-looking young redhead with a fiery beard, in jeans and shirtsleeves, holds up one after another of the ads and storyboards for Mimi's inspection. At first, no one speaks. All the ads, which feature the Mireille Couple in various romantic locales and situa-tions, are signed with the line, which is Mark Segal's, "Mireille . . . at last the miracle fragrance." The television commercials, which are designed to expand on the situations depicted in the print ads, also close with this signature line. Watching Mimi's reactions closely, Segal nervously flexes the biceps of his right arm.

Finally, he says, "Something's bothering you—I can tell. What is it?"

Mimi continues to study the photographs of the two models. Then she says, "She's lovely, there's no doubt about it. Lovely. She's got just the look I want. Of course, you'd hope that with looks like that would go just a little *glimmer* of intelligence, but in her case there just isn't any. It doesn't seem fair, does it—that a girl who can sparkle like that in front of a camera should be such a dim bulb in real life? But it doesn't matter. She looks . . . simply wonderful. I wouldn't change a thing about her."

"Fortunately, only Sherrill's friends will get to see her in real life," Mark says.

"If we decide to use her live in any in-store promotions, just make sure she's not allowed to open her mouth. They were both at my house for dinner last night, and you should have seen her trying to figure out which fork to use. It's sad, isn't it? You'd want a girl like that to have *every*thing, wouldn't you? But all she is is a gorgeous face."

"That's about all you can say about most of these girls," he says.

"Well, maybe the exposure we'll give her will help her wise up—go to charm school, or something. But it's not her I'm worried about, Mark. It's *him*. Why does he seem too . . ."

"Pretty?"

"Yes. That's it, exactly. Here's the case of a boy who, when you see him in the flesh, looks nice and wholesome—rugged, outdoorsy, like he belongs on a ski slope, or on top of a diving board, or sculling with the Yale crew. But in front of a camera, he seems to go all . . . soft, somehow."

"Effeminate, you mean?"

"Not effeminate, exactly. Just . . . soft. Do you see what I mean, Mark?"

"Yes, I'm afraid I do."

"Can we screen the first commercial again, Mark?"

"Sure," he says. He dims the lights, the screen descends from its recess in the conference room ceiling, and the video projector begins to roll.

The scene is the dock in front of the Seawanhaka Yacht Club in Oyster Bay, a balmy summer afternoon; sunlight on the blue water of Long Island Sound refracts the camera's eye with diamond flashes. Through these flashes, we see a snappy yawl-rigged sailboat move into view, the Mireille Man at the tiller, in dark blue jeans, bare to the waist. There is a bright sting of music. The camera then moves to pick up:

The Girl, standing on the dock, waving to him, all in white, her skirts blowing in the breeze.

THE GIRL: You're late!

THE BOY: Tricky winds!

We see the boy maneuver the sailboat expertly to the dock and throw a line, which she catches and lashes around an upright pier. Then we watch as he holds up both arms, as she steps into them, and as he lifts her lightly down to the deck. He nuzzles her shoulder. Then, in close-up:

THE BOY: Hey! What's that you're wearing? You smell brand-new!

THE GIRL: It is brand-new! It's Mireille—by Miray!

We watch him as, nostrils flared, he nuzzles her some more, drinking in her scent with obvious pleasure and excitement; nuzzles her shoulder, her cheekbones, her ear lobe, and finally brushes her lips with his. There is another musical sting, a clear, high, bright electronic chord.

THE BOY: You smell . . . miraculous!

Once more the screen fills up with diamondlike flashes of sunlight refracted on water as, simultaneously, the legend travels across the screen: *Mireille . . . at last the miracle fragrance.*

The screen goes blank, and the lights come up again.

"Do you see what I mean?" Mimi says after a moment. "A soft look. What can we do, Mark, to make him have a harder edge?"

He says nothing.

"His face has no *corners* to it. Do you agree?"

He nods, frowning, looking unhappy, and flexes his biceps several more times.

Suddenly Mimi picks up a grease pencil from the table, and, pulling out the storyboard for the commercial they have just screened, she makes a mark across the face of Dirk Gordon. "I think I have it," she says.

"What is it?"

"What if we gave him a scar, Mark?"

"A scar?"

"Yes—like a dueling scar. Across one cheek. It would break up that dumb *symmetry.* And it would give him a history, like—"

"Like the Hathaway man with the eyepatch?"

"*Exactly,*" Mimi says. "Only this would be more exciting than an eyepatch. How did that good-looking man get that ugly scar? the viewer will wonder. In some barroom brawl? Defending some maiden's honor? In some nasty accident? Or on the lacrosse field in some really rugged play? Smashed in the face by a hockey puck? See what I mean?"

Mark Segal scratches his red beard thoughtfully. "I see what you mean, but—"

"But what?"

"I don't know how little Dirkie-boy will feel about us turning him into Scarface," he says.

"Well," she says with a little laugh, "we do have him under contract, don't we? It's really up to us how we decide to make him look, Mark."

"That's true, but—"

"Again, but what?"

"You're talking about reshooting the entire campaign, Mimi."

"Look," she says, "maybe for the print ads we can airbrush in the scar. If that doesn't work—"

"Then what?"

"Then, I guess we reshoot. It's not the first time we've had to do that."

"You're also talking about reshooting three thirty-second television commercials. You can't airbrush TV film. Do you know how much that's going to cost?"

"Of course I do. But Mark, I honestly think that the scar could make all the difference—between an excellent campaign and one that's *spectacular*. I think we've got to try it, Mark, don't you?"

He is scowling now. "Well . . ."

"Really, Mark. Because this is the most important product launch we've ever done."

"The most important *ever?* How come?"

"It just is. All at once it is—for reasons I can't go into right now. Just take my word for it. This campaign can't just be successful. It's got to be *sensationally* successful."

He shrugs. "If you say so," he says.

"Let's try it with the airbrush first. Give the head shots of Dirk to the art department, and have them experiment with scars. Have them try different kinds of scars. Tell them I want some real tough-looking scars. Once we see the airbrushing, then we'll decide—"

The door to the conference room opens, and it is Mimi's secretary, Mrs. Hanna. "Mr. Michael Horowitz, Miss Myerson," she says. "Returning your call."

"Oh, yes," Mimi says, hopping off the edge of the table. "I want to talk to him." To Segal, she says, "We'll decide when we see what the art department comes up with," and blows him a kiss.

Segal, still scowling, begins gathering up the layouts and pasteups and storyboards from the conference table. Before immediately following Mimi back to her office, Jim Greenway steps over to him and says, "What do you think of this scar idea, anyway?"

At first, Mark Segal merely grunts. Then he mutters, "Brilliant. As usual. Fucking brilliant. Simply fucking brilliant, is all I can say."

It all began, needless to say, with one of her famous "Mimi Memos" more than two years ago, in the spring of 1985.

MIRAY CORPORATION
Interoffice Memorandum

TO: All employees
FROM: MM

(Over the years, her employees have learned that whenever they see that double *M* on an interoffice memo, something important is on the boss's mind. But that the subject of this memo should have now gained the importance that it has, they could not have guessed.)

SUBJECT: Perfume

The perfumer's art is at least 10,000 years old, and the earliest perfumes were in the form of incense. Indeed, the word derives from the Latin *per* and *fumus*, literally "through smoke."

Ancient man, believing that the greatest offering to his gods could only be one of his most precious possessions, offered in sacrifice a domestic beast—or another human. The earliest perfumes were resinous gums such as frankincense, myrrh, cassia, and spikenard, which were sprinkled on an animal (or human) corpse before it was burned, in order to mask the stench of burning flesh. In the Bible, Noah, having survived the Flood, offered burnt animal sacrifices in gratitude, and "the Lord smelled the sweet odor"—of incense. Gradually, the burning of these resins alone replaced the sacrifices, and the burning of incense survives today in the ritual of the Catholic Church.

The logical next step was for men and women to anoint their bodies with these fragrant resins, and by 3000 B.C. the Sumerians in Mesopotamia and the Egyptians in the Nile Valley were literally bathing themselves in oils and alcohols of jasmine, iris, hyacinth, and honeysuckle.

Cleopatra believed in using different scents for different parts of her body. She scented her hands with an oil of roses, crocuses, and violets, and her feet with a lotion made of almond oil, honey, cinnamon, orange blossoms, and henna.

In ancient Greece, men spurned facial cosmetics but used perfumes liberally, scenting their arms with mint, their chests with cinnamon, their hands and feet with almond oil, and their hair and eyebrows with extract of marjoram. In fact, in Greece the perfumed male became a symbol of decadence, and the Athenian statesman Solon enacted a law forbidding the sale of fragrant oils to Athenian men. The law was routinely flouted and soon went off the books.

From Greece, male scents traveled to Rome, and a Roman soldier was considered unfit for battle unless he was anointed with scent. As the Roman Empire grew, new scents appeared from conquered lands: wisteria, lilac, carnation, and vanilla. From the Far and Middle East came fragrances of cedar, pine, ginger, and mimosa.

Perfume trivia corner: The Emperor Nero spent the equivalent of

$160,000 for rose oils, rose water, and rose petals for himself and his guests for a single evening's entertainment. For the funeral of his wife Poppaea, more perfume was splashed or sprayed over the proceedings than the entire country of Arabia could produce in a year. (Even the mules in the funeral cortege were scented.)

From the East, 11th-century Crusaders brought "attar of roses," still one of the costliest of scents. (It takes 200 pounds of damask-rose petals to produce a single ounce of attar.)

The Crusaders also brought back other perfume ingredients that had been theretofore unknown in the Western world: animal oils. These are sexual and glandular secretions, and there are essentially four of these:

Musk: A sexual secretion from the abdomen of the musk deer of western China.

Ambergris: A waxy substance from the stomach of the sperm whale.

Civet: A genital secretion from both the male and female civet cat of Africa and the Far East, it can be collected regularly from captive cats without harm to the animal. On its own, it smells simply ghastly, but when blended with other essences it miraculously takes on a most agreeable odor and is an important "fixative" in fine perfumes—the fixative is what makes the scent last longer when worn.

Castor: A secretion from the stomachs of Russian and Canadian beavers. Again, castor is a scent-extending fixative. The reason why these animal essences work as fixatives, chemists tell us, is because of their heavy molecular weight. The heavy molecules serve to "anchor" the scent, preventing it from rising too quickly above the surface of the liquid and evaporating into the air. The varying strengths of these anchors, or fixatives, are what give a particular fragrance its "note," or distinctive quality.

A note to animal lovers: Musk deer, beaver, and even—in some parts of the world—sperm whales are still hunted for their oils. Certain European perfumers still speak of using "legal ambergris," since ambergris is a calculus formed in the intestines of certain diseased animals and is sometimes discharged naturally and drawn up by fishermen in their nets. (The largest piece ever found this way weighed 248 pounds and brought the lucky sailor who found it the equivalent of $50,000.) But in the United States, all use of natural ambergris is against the law. Meanwhile, musk, castor, and ambergris can now all be chemically synthesized.

On to more appetizing matters. All the above floral, herbal, fruit, and animal oils and essences, or their chemical equivalents, are used in the making of fine fragrances today, and they can be mixed in a literally infinite number of permutations and combinations.

But yesterday a jobber came to my office and offered me a sample of a floral essence that I can only describe as magical. It is called *Bulgarian rose absolute,* and it is distilled from rose petals that are gathered—at dawn—on certain slopes of the Balkan Mountains that must face *east.* When I rubbed a drop or two on my wrist, I'm not exaggerating when I say I could smell not only Bulgarian roses but also Bulgarian morning dew! It is very expensive, roughly $6,000 a pound wholesale, for you can imagine how many thousands of pounds of dawn-developing rose petals a Bulgarian peasant must have to gather to distill just an ounce of the absolute. I immediately began to think of ways we might use this fragrance in our products, either now or in something *new.*

And by now you have all doubtless guessed the purpose of this memo. It is to announce that I have asked the chemists in our labs, using this or something equally extraordinary, to come up with the most exciting new fragrance in the world—for us.

Back in her corner office, with its spectacular view of the twin spires of St. Patrick's Cathedral, Mimi picks up the telephone and says, "Michael?"

"Miss Myerson?"

"Yes."

"One moment, please, for Mr. Horowitz."

To Jim Greenway, standing just outside her door, she makes a beckoning gesture, and he steps inside, closing the door behind him. With her left hand covering the mouthpiece of the phone, Mimi says, "We're playing musical secretaries. It's always a contest to see which one can get to put the other one's boss on hold. This time, I lost." Then, speaking into the phone, she says, "Michael. How *are* you? . . . Oh, I'm very well, but it's been ages since I've seen you. . . . All I do is read about you in the papers, while you try to tell Ed Koch how to run the city of New York. . . . Michael, I think we need to talk, you and I. I'm sure you know what's on my mind. . . . You don't? Well, I'll tell you when I see you. When can you have lunch? . . . Next Thursday? Let me see." She flips the pages of her calendar. "Yes, that would be perfect. Let's make it one o'clock at Le Cirque. . . . My secretary will make the reservation. . . . Good, Michael. I'll see you then." She replaces the telephone carefully in its cradle.

Mimi sits at her desk, her polished-silver eyes focused on some invisible point in the middle distance. On her desk, in silver frames, are a formal Bachrach portrait of her husband, Bradford Moore, and another color photograph of her son, Badger, grinning in his tennis whites, wearing a braided wristband, a racquet in his hand, looking as though he had just aced a serve. The corner office is large and airy, and Mimi has decorated it in light, bright colors, with a cheery mix of fabrics (flowered chintzes and plaids on the chairs and sofas), contemporary paintings on the walls (including Andy Warhol's silk-screen multiple portrait of herself combing her hair), and greenery (a tall ficus tree in one corner, and windowboxes filled with flowering plants that are changed with the seasons). The office colors often inspire her with the buoyant names for some of her lipsticks and nail polishes: "Dappled Sunlight," "Winter Fire," "Russet Apple," and the rest.

But the expression on Mimi's face is far from buoyant now. Instead, her look is pensive, even troubled, and for a moment or two she seems to have forgotten that she has a visitor. Usually so poised, self-possessed, slightly amused—even self-mocking—there is no self-mockery in her expression now. For a moment, she seems to repress a small shudder, almost of revulsion. She brushes a loose strand of pale hair away from her face. Then she sighs and says, "That was Michael Horowitz. An old friend. And an old enemy."

"With supposedly the biggest ego in New York."

"That ego is his Achilles heel." She sighs again. "I'm not looking forward to that lunch." Then, collecting herself, she says, "Well, I have a few minutes. Is there anything in particular you'd like to talk about?"

Jim Greenway seats himself in front of her desk and removes a ballpoint pen and notebook from his briefcase. "Let's start at the beginning," he suggests. "Let's start with your grandfather. Tell me everything you remember about him."

"Oh, dear," she says, shaking her head as though loosening all the scattered memories of Adolph Myerson from her brain. "Oh, dear. It would fill a whole book to tell you everything I remember about him."

"Let's begin, anyway."

"Well, I was named Mireille, after his Miray Corporation, as my grandmother told you last night. It was my parents' pathetic attempt to curry a little bit of favor out of him. Of course it didn't work. . . ."

Meanwhile, not that many city blocks away, in her apartment at the Carlyle, Adolph Myerson's widow is spending her morning, as she customarily does, on the telephone, and as New York women of leisure have done since the year 1900 when residential telephone service became widely available in the city. Right now, Granny Flo is talking, again, with her friend Mrs. Norman Perlman. "You know, Rose," she is saying, "the more I think about it, the more I just can't believe your neighbor deliberately poisoned your little Fluffy. I just can't believe that anybody could be that *mean*. And in your nice building. What I think must have happened is that little Fluffy got into something when your doorman was out walking him. You know how little doggies are, always sniffing and snuffing around at things they smell on the ground, licking at things they really shouldn't with their little tongues.

Anymore, there's so much litter in New York! Filthy city! And then the garbage men go on strike! What for? More money so they can raise our taxes? Sometimes I thank God I'm blind so I can't see the trash anymore, Rose. I mean it, sometimes I thank God I'm blind. Anyway, I'm sure that little Fluffy must have licked at something on the street that was bad, like a —like a stale potato chip that had gone rancid. Yes, like a rancid potato chip. That would do it. Their little constitutions are so weak, these little doggies; a rancid potato chip would have been enough to make him go into a convulsion. I'm sure that was what it was. Hold on, Rose. My other phone is ringing. Hello? Who is it? Oh, Nonie, I can't talk now. I'm on another important call. I'll call you back. Rose? That was my daughter. Nonie wants something, I can always tell. She thinks I'm a bottomless pit. But I'm *not* a bottomless pit. I'm an old woman, living on a fixed income, like you. But anyway, where were we? Oh, yes, little Fluffy. I've decided what you must do, Rose. You must replace little Fluffy right away. I know, a replacement is never the same as the thing you've lost. Nothing you really love can ever be replaced, but you've got to try, Rose. A new puppy will fill up the gap. I've lost things I loved, and I know how it is. You know how Adolph was always buying me jewelry. Jewelry I never wanted, but he bought it to impress my family. But there was one diamond ring I really loved. It wasn't a big diamond—maybe half a carat—but I loved it because, because when he gave it to me it was when I thought he really loved me, and wasn't doing it just to impress my family. And one day, years ago, when we still had that big place in Maine, I was out walking in the garden and I suddenly noticed that that diamond had fallen out of its setting. I felt it fall! It fell in the grass. I searched and searched, but I couldn't find it. Adolph said, 'Don't worry, we'll replace it,' but I said, 'No, no, I want that particular diamond,' and for weeks and weeks I hunted in the grass for that little diamond, up and down, back and forth, in that little piece of grass where I'd felt it fall out of my ring. No luck at all. Then, one day, it was early in the morning near the end of summer—soon it would be time for us all to go back to New York again— I was out in the garden for one last look. 'If I don't find it today,' I told myself, 'I never will.' And just then I saw a little brightly shining, sparkly thing in the grass: my diamond, at last! But when I reached down to pick it up, the little brightly shining, sparkly thing just dissolved between my fingers. Because you know what it was, Rose? It was just a tiny drop of dew! And I burst into tears, Rose, just sat down in the grass and sobbed." Granny Flo is weeping now at the memory of this experience. "Because, Rose, that was when I knew I'd never see my precious little diamond again, that it had turned into just a little drop of dew. . . . Oh, Rose, if I'd let him replace it, would anything have been any different? It's too late now. . . ."

Part Two

IN THE BEGINNING

❧

5

*A*dolph *Myerson* was a man who started with nothing more than a dream. But it was a beautiful dream, and it was a dream of beauty."

So begins the "official" biography of the founder of the Miray Corporation in the corporate history that was published by the company in 1946.

"The bright, ambitious young man's dream," this history continues, "was essentially a simple one. Without concern for personal power or pelf, the youthful Myerson dreamt of creating, for the American woman, a new sense of pride and self-esteem and self-worth through the gift of lovelier lips and fingertips. The American woman, the farsighted young man foresaw, could perceive herself more fully, and fulfill herself more wholly, were it possible for her to feel better about herself through presenting to the world a more beautiful appearance and a more radiant allure. Years ahead of his time, the young man decided that he, and he alone, would create a spectrum of beauty products that would help American women to become the most beautiful, the most envied women in the twentieth-century world. A true *non pareil*, young Myerson. . . ."

"It's mostly a lot of hogwash," Mimi Myerson says to Jim Greenway when she gives him the corporate history to read. "Most of the dates are correct, but remember that this was written by Grandpa's P.R. man, with Grandpa standing over his shoulder and telling him what to write."

In fact, as Mimi explains it, if her grandfather had any sort of dream at all in 1912, the year that his little company was founded—and who is to say that no man lacks some kind of dream?—he was dreaming of the Bronx. Also, Mimi points out, despite his anonymous biographer's frequent use of

such adjectives as "young," and "youthful," Adolph Myerson was not exactly a teenager in 1912. That was the year that saw Adolph Myerson
celebrate—if that is the proper term for it—his forty-second birthday.

"The Bronx!" he wrote to a young female cousin in Germany, whom he
was still in the process of trying to persuade to come to America to marry
him. "You must see this place to believe it, Lizetteleine! This is the true city
of the future! All that is finest in America is being constructed here. Picture
it, Lizette, my little one, if you can. First, there is a great broad avenue
being built running from north to south across this greatest county of the
greatest city in the world—broader than the Champs Élysées in Paris,
grander than Unter den Linden. It is to be called the Grand Concourse, and
it is at this point very nearly finished. Stately trees will line its length, and
gardens will grace its central boulevard, for this will be known as a 'Garden
Suburb.' A Great Hotel, larger and grander than any hotel ever built, to be
called the Concourse Plaza, is going up before my eyes, bigger and more
splendid than any Kaiser's palace. Huge and towering blocks of flats (here
called apartment houses) are being erected of gleaming sandstone and marble and yellow brick, and each of these buildings will contain spacious living
quarters with all of the most modern of conveniences, including kitchens of
electricity and central heating, dumbwaiters and lifts (here called elevators).
Soon will come the Underground (here, subways) to whisk the businessman
in minutes from the noise and bustle of the city into the clear, clean air of
the Bronx countryside. It goes without saying that I am 'proud as Punch,' as
they say here, to be a part of all this grand construction. Come to the Land
of Golden Opportunity, dear Lizette, this *goldene medinah,* and let me take
you to this earthly paradise, this Garden of Eden, the Bronx. . . ."

Apparently, Adolph's entreaties fell on deaf ears, for Cousin Lizette remained in Germany, and how this letter survived is something of a mystery.
It was discovered among a small packet of papers after Adolph's death in
1959. Perhaps it was never sent. Or perhaps Lizette returned her letters to
him after she married someone else. It has been determined that Lizette
and her family died at Auschwitz in 1943.

"He had a certain journalistic flair," Jim Greenway says to Mimi after
reading this letter. "Are you sure there were no diaries?"

"I'd never heard of any until the other night," Mimi says. "Granny Flo is
often confused these days. As Nonie said, you mustn't give too much weight
to what she claims to remember."

From Adolph's rapturous description of the "Garden Suburb" that, in
those innocent prewar days, the Bronx was designed to become, and from
his talk of pride in having "a part" of this development, it is possible to

suppose that Adolph Myerson was the developer himself. He was not. He was a housepainter, and on that fateful day in April 1912—the day that would change the fortunes of the family forever—Adolph and his five-years-younger brother, Leopold, were engaged in painting the kitchen of one Mrs. Spitzberg, in her new apartment at 3124 Grand Concourse in the Bronx.

And if Adolph had been able to persuade his Lizette to join him in America, he would have been able to do no more than to take her on the streetcar to look at, and admire, the Bronx and the rising buildings along the new Grand Concourse. He could not have afforded to bring her there to live, for the Bronx was the choice of address for the newly affluent, and Adolph Myerson was not one of these. Every poor Jewish immigrant, even those who had at that point made it out of the ghetto of the Lower East Side and into the less crowded reaches of Brooklyn or Harlem, dreamed of one day moving to the Bronx. The Bronx was a beacon that was at once both economic and psychological, for by crossing the Harlem River it was possible to feel that one was entering the mainstream of American life. For immigrants such as Adolph's parents, who had begun the long journey to America in 1879, when Adolph was nine, the trip had entailed going from island to island—from Hamburg to England, from England to Ellis Island, and from Ellis Island to Manhattan. But if one could attain the Bronx, the only borough of New York City that is not surrounded on all sides by water, one was at last setting foot on the mainland.

But Adolph and Leopold's father, Herman Myerson, had not been so fortunate. Arriving in New York, he had found work as a housepainter. When back troubles had made him no longer able to scale a ladder, and forced him into retirement in 1888, when Adolph was eighteen and Leopold was thirteen, his two sons had followed him into the trade. By 1912, the families of prosperous lawyers, doctors, dentists, pharmacists, and accountants, who had put themselves through City College, were moving into splendid apartments in the Bronx. But Adolph was still living with his parents in a railroad flat on Henry Street, and Leopold, who had by then married and had a young son of his own, lived not far away in a similar flat on Pell Street, still on the Lower East Side.

As for what actually happened on that life-changing day in 1912, while painting Mrs. Spitzberg's kitchen, we are forced to rely on accounts that Adolph gave verbally to his family, since no living witnesses to the event remain. As Adolph later told it, the brothers had been bickering, as they often did, on the job. The two had never met Mrs. Spitzberg, but Leopold had decided that Mrs. Spitzberg was wrongheaded, if not downright crazy. She had decreed that her kitchen be painted fire-engine red.

"This is craziness, this is *narischkeit*," Leopold kept muttering (according to Adolph). "Why does a woman want her kitchen painted the color of a fire engine? A kitchen should be white, or maybe yellow. Not like a fire engine!"

"This is a rich woman, Leo," his brother had counseled. "A rich woman wants her kitchen painted like a fire engine, so she gets a fire engine. A good tailor cuts the cloth to suit the customer. Our job is to give Mrs. Spitzberg what she wants."

"She won't like it when it's done, wait and see," Leopold predicted. "When she sees all this red, like the bedroom of a whore, she's going to make us do it over. Wait and see. And how many coats of white paint will it take to cover up all this red? Three? Four? Maybe five?"

"Mrs. Spitzberg is the boss."

And it was while the brothers argued, back and forth, over Mrs. Spitzberg's color scheme, mixing a five-gallon drum of paint to the exact hue of an N.Y.F.D. truck, that Leopold accidentally poured an extra quart of the chemical toluene into the mixture. At least that was the way Adolph told it. It could easily have been the other way around and could have been Adolph who supplied the accidental overdose of toluene. But Adolph invariably blamed every careless act on his younger, clumsy brother, and so the story would go down through the family for seventy-five years that the extra toluene had been Leopold's misstep, and that it was Adolph's ingenuity that had managed to save the day.

The chemical toluene is a thickening agent, which, added to a paint, causes it to cling more evenly to the brush and also to dry more quickly. But, with as much as a whole quart of toluene added to a drum of paint, the paint becomes too viscous to use, hardens within seconds after exposure to the air. If the brothers had attempted to apply such a mixture to Mrs. Spitzberg's kitchen walls, the result would have been a sagging, gummy mess.

We can be sure that Adolph Myerson spent some time berating his brother for his clumsiness. After all, nearly two dollars' worth of ingredients —two dollars that had come out of the brothers' pockets—had been wasted. Leo had been able, according to Adolph, to come up with no solution other than to throw the mixture out, swallow the loss, and start mixing another drum of paint. But then Adolph—and, again, we have only Adolph's word for this—came up with his inspiration.

Women had been painting their fingernails for years, though usually with clear lacquer or a pale pink shade. Only in the theatre did actresses paint their nails bright red. But fashions were already moving toward a more liberated era, which would come to a climax in the Roaring Twenties, and the painted-lady image, no longer confined to actresses on Broadway, was being taken up by fashionable women on Fifth Avenue who were appearing with crimson-painted nails. The only trouble with nail lacquers of the day was that they dried slowly, and a woman often had to sit immobilized for twenty minutes or longer, with her fingers outstretched, while she waited for her nails to dry, unable to perform any other task without risk of smearing her polish. Adolph's brainstorm was to peddle his fire-engine-red housepaint, which his brother had considered ruined, as a new kind of quick-drying nail lacquer. Dipping a fingertip into the drum of paint, Adolph showed his brother how quickly it dried hard and lustrous and smooth.

"We'll sell it as nail polish," he said to Leo. Or so he always claimed.

In any case, Adolph moved quickly at that point. He immediately sealed the drum of red paint tightly, before exposure to the air caused its surface to form a thick "skin." That very day, he was able to buy a wholesaler's over-stock of small bottles with tiny brushes affixed to their caps, for a total cost of ten dollars. With the paint transferred to the little bottles, he began peddling his new quick-drying nail polish door-to-door, concentrating, for his customers, on the newly rich Jewish ladies who were moving to the Grand Concourse. From a five-gallon drum of spoiled housepaint that had cost him less than two dollars, he was able to create thirteen hundred bottles of half an ounce each, which he sold for ten cents apiece. Thus, for a total investment of twelve dollars, Adolph's return was one hundred and thirty dollars—a profit of more than a thousand percent, and no businessman could possibly complain of figures like these! What was more, Adolph's customers were delighted with his product. News of it spread by word of mouth. New orders and reorders poured in, and Adolph and Leopold Myerson were on their way. Within a year, the brothers were able to place their nail polishes in five-and-ten-cent stores, and to begin advertising with the slogan, "Dries in just seconds' time!" . . . and with the brand name Miray, which Adolph came up with by rearranging the various letters in his name.

By the time Adolph Myerson was rich enough to move to the Bronx, he was too rich to want to live there.

And the Battle of the Brothers was well under way. Which one deserved more credit for their success? The brother who had had the lucky accident, or the one who had had enough wit to turn it into profit?

"My first memory of him?" Mimi says. "Oh, I must have been six or seven, so that would have been nineteen forty-four or 'forty-five. My grand-parents lived in a big ugly house on Madison Avenue and Sixty-first Street. It's gone now, but it took up half a block, and the other half of the block belonged to August Belmont. Granny, of course, was a Guggenheim, and her money helped, and how she and Grandpa met is a whole other story; they were not from the same sort of background at *all*. The house had great, wide marble steps leading up to the front door, which was on Madison, and I remember my mother leading me by the hand up those steps and making

me practice my curtsy on each step as we went up. I had to have my curtsy
perfect before she would ring the bell. I remember how humiliated I felt,
curtsying and curtsying, going up those steps, a little girl curtsying in front
of a huge, blank, closed front door! People passing by on the street must
have looked at that little girl, dipping down in deep curtsies in front of a
door, again and again, bobbing up and down like a marionette, and thought
that there must be something terribly the matter with her. There was a girl
in my class at Hewitt who was a spastic. It was probably multiple sclerosis, or
something like that, but in those days it was explained to us that Eileen
McKensie was a spastic—she had this terrible, lurching gait. I was sure that
everybody on the street was watching me, and was thinking I was a spastic,
just like Eileen McKensie. . . ."

   "One more time, Mireille," her mother said. "Just one more time before
we ring Grandpa's doorbell."
   "Oh, Mama, *please*," she begged, trying to squeeze back the tears.
   "Just once. Ah. *There*. You see? That was *much* better. Now remember
everything I've told you. Curtsy to Grandpapa first, then to Grandmama.
Say, 'Good afternoon, Grandpa, sir,' and then 'Good afternoon, Grandma,
dear.' Then don't say another word until one of them speaks to you. Then
don't forget always to call Grandpapa 'sir,' and Grandma 'ma'am.' Don't
remove your gloves until tea is served, and then remove only the right one,
to hold the teacup with, and place the right glove in your left hand. When
the tea sandwiches are passed, never take more than one at a time, and
never eat more than two sandwiches altogether. It isn't ladylike to appear to
be hungry, so if the sandwiches are passed a third time, just shake your head
politely. It isn't necessary to speak to the maid. Oh, and—my God, I almost
forgot! If you have to go to the toilet, just excuse yourself politely, and
always remember to put the lid of the toilet seat down after you've finished.
And another thing: *never* use one of Grandmama's little linen guest towels!
After you've washed your hands, dry them on a piece of toilet paper, throw
that in the toilet bowl, and flush *again*. And then put the lid of the toilet
seat *down again*. Can you remember all that, Mireille?"
   "Why is there so much to remember, Mama?"
   "Because we want your Grandpapa to think you are a perfect lady, don't
we? Your Grandpapa would be very upset with us if he didn't think you a
perfect lady." With a gloved fingertip, her mother reached out to press the
doorbell.
   Her grandparents' butler opened the door and, bowing, admitted them
wordlessly into the house.
   The entrance gallery she remembered was all red damask and gilt, red cut
velvet and velours. The walls were covered with damask, and the doorways

leading from it were swagged with heavy red damask portieres fringed with gold. Large, heavy, and uncomfortable-looking chairs, covered with more cut velvet, lined the hall, and, from the walls, gilt-framed portraits slung from velvet-covered chains (later she would learn that these portraits had no bearing whatever on her family) gazed menacingly down upon her. The butler led Mimi and her mother down the red-carpeted entrance hall to the double staircase that ascended upward to the parlor floor, and Mimi remembered that the banisters were upholstered with more red velvet and that, where the double curves of the staircase met at the landing, the newel posts were surmounted by identical bronze statues of a winged Mercury, one foot lofted in the air, each holding up an electrically lighted flame-shaped torch. Mimi remembers reaching out to touch one of Mercury's bare heels, and her mother's harsh whisper: "Don't touch!"

At the top of the stairs, the butler led them to the closed double doors of the drawing room, tapped lightly on the door, and then stood aside to let them enter as he opened it.

"Mrs. Henry Myerson, and Miss Mireille Myerson," the butler announced.

Her grandparents sat at the opposite end of the long, dark, formal room in a kind of five-sided bay window, its panes of green and purple and red stained glass, at either end of an extraordinary semicircular sofa unlike any piece of furniture Mimi can remember seeing before or since. It was covered in purple toy plush, tufted and buttoned in a diamond pattern. Its legs were in the shape of eagles' talons clutching golden balls. But the most astonishing thing about it was that midway in its half-circle it seemed to change its mind and become a jardiniere, for mounted in its frame was an Oriental-looking vase, planted with a tall palm tree. Later, Mimi learned that her grandfather had had this multipurpose piece specially designed for this window alcove of his house, and Mimi remembers thinking that from where her grandparents sat they could not possibly see one another through the vase and the thick palm fronds. As mother and daughter moved toward the seated couple, her grandfather rose in a maroon velvet smoking jacket, and her grandmother remained seated, a square of needlepoint-work in her lap.

Now it was time for the curtsies. "Good afternoon, Grandpapa, sir. Good afternoon, Grandmama, dear."

Her grandfather motioned them to two chairs opposite the curved sofa, and Mimi remembers seating herself carefully, as her mother had told her to do, arranging her skirts carefully beneath her, her legs crossed at the ankle, and her white-gloved hands folded in her lap.

Her grandfather returned to his seat on one end of the curved sofa, and then for the longest time—an eternity, as Mimi remembers it—no one said anything at all.

Finally her grandfather spoke. "You are in school, Mireille," he said, putting it as a statement, not a question.

"Yes, Grandpapa, sir."

"And are your grades exemplary?"

Mimi had not understood this word but, inferring that an affirmative reply was expected, she said, "Yes, Grandpapa, sir."

"Oh, she's doing just wonderfully, Father!" her mother had said a trifle too quickly and loudly. "Her teachers send home the most glowing reports!"

Mimi remembers her grandfather giving her mother a long, somewhat baleful look, and there was silence again. Her grandmother had resumed her needlework.

From out of some dark corner of this cavernous room a maid appeared in a black uniform with a white lacy collar and cuffs, wearing a small lacy cap, wheeling a huge silver tea service on a lace-draped cart. The maid wheeled the cart in front of Mimi's grandmother, who inspected its contents—a large silver urn and its accompanying vessels: teacups and saucers and other smaller silver bowls and pitchers for hot water, for milk, and for sugar. As her grandmother began to pour from the great silver urn, Mimi noticed that she was wearing little black lace wrist-length gloves that had no fingers! Her grandmother poured for her husband first, then for Mimi's mother, and the maid transported each person's cup to each. Knowing that her turn would be next, Mimi removed the white glove from her right hand, removing it finger by finger, starting with the pinky, as her mother had taught her, and placed it in her left hand.

"One lump or two, Mireille?" her grandmother said. It was the first time she had spoken.

In a panic, Mimi had looked quickly at her mother. They had not rehearsed this part of the ritual.

From where her hands lay in her lap, her mother raised one gloved fingertip.

"One lump, please, Grandmama, ma'am," Mimi said.

One lump of sugar was tonged into her cup, and the cup was delivered to Mimi, who accepted it with her ungloved right hand. Then there was silence again, and, in another panic, Mimi began to realize that she did want to go to the toilet but had no idea where the bathroom was in this vast house. She squeezed her legs tightly together.

They sipped their tea. The maid reappeared with a silver tray arranged with tiny sandwiches. Mimi accepted one. It was made of the thinnest white bread she had ever seen, and inside it there was a tiny sliver of cucumber, which, as Mimi remembers it, had absolutely no taste at all. She heard her mother whisper, "Sit up straight, dear."

Finally, her grandfather put down his teacup, rose, and crossed the room to some dim and distant corner of it. When he returned, he was carrying a small, leather-bound book. "This will interest you," he said and, sitting down again, opened the book to a page marked by a leather bookmark.

"Tomorrow morning, a Monday, the third," he began, "I have a marketing meeting at ten o'clock. I can devote no more than half an hour to that, because at ten-thirty I must telephone Paris and reach them before their offices close at five. Now that the war is over, Revson is going to try to beat us into the European market, but we're not going to let him. At eleven-thirty, I have an appointment with my dentist. At twelve-thirty, I am lunching with Andrew Goodman at the Plaza. Bergdorf's has not been displaying our products to the best advantage, and I intend to correct that situation with Andrew himself. At two-thirty, I have a . . ."

He was reading to her from the pages of his engagement calendar. He continued reading until he had recited every appointment on his calendar for the entire week that was to follow. Then he closed the book after Friday's last meeting of the day, and it was time to go.

Rising, Mimi's grandfather turned to her mother and said, "We shall do this again next Sunday, Alice. Four o'clock, for tea. Here."

As they left the house, Mimi's mother ran down the marble steps, clutching Mimi's hand in hers. "He's invited us *back!*" she cried. "Do you know what this *means?* It means he *likes* us, darling, because he's invited us back!" She waved excitedly for a taxi in the street.

In the taxi, Alice Myerson said, "Isn't this *exciting!* Oh, your father will be so pleased. I can't wait to tell him! He'll be so pleased with you! So pleased with me!" From her reticule where she kept it, her mother removed a small flask, uncapped it, lifted it to her lips, and took a long swallow. "My medicine," she said.

But from her seat in the taxi beside her mother, Mimi, though her legs were squeezed together as tightly as she could squeeze them, could no longer control herself. She felt the first warm drops. Then it all came.

Her eyes brimming with tears of shame, she whispered to her mother what had happened, but her mother seemed totally unconcerned. "It doesn't matter," she laughed. "We did it. He's asked us back! Do you see what this means, my darling? It means that everything's going to be all right!"

Of course, at the time, Mimi had no idea what her mother was talking about.

"And so that," Mimi says to Jim Greenway, "is what my mother and I did from that day on—until I was twelve years old and went away to boarding school. Every Sunday afternoon, we'd get dressed up and go to have tea at my grandparents' house, four o'clock on the dot. It was always the same:

the same little tasteless cucumber sandwiches, my grandmother with her needlework, saying nothing. It wasn't until after he died that she began to get garrulous. I think that when he was around she was too frightened of him to open her trap! And it always ended with Grandpa reading from his appointment book—everything he was doing the following week, the lunches with captains of industry, the dinners with senators, the weekly sales meetings, the appointments with his proctologist—*everything.* You see, I think that's where Granny is confused when she talks about a diary. It wasn't a diary, it was just an appointment book. . . . Needless to say, I finally found out where the bathroom was. And do I need to add that it had a toilet disguised as an antique wicker chair?

"What was the point of it all? Afterward, we'd go home to our miserable little dark apartment on Ninety-seventh Street, and the more of these teas I went to, the more confused I became. Obviously my grandparents were rich, but why weren't we? I couldn't understand it. I knew my father worked for my grandfather's company and had a title of vice-president in charge of something or other, but no money seemed to go with it. We had no butler, no cook, no maids—nothing but an old black lady who came once a week for a couple of hours and ran a dustrag around the place. My mother did her own cooking, her own ironing and mending, everything. It was terribly confusing to me. My uncle Edwee, Daddy's brother, was rich—and he didn't even work! So was my aunt Nonie. But we weren't. There was never enough money in our house, and there were always arguments, terrible arguments, about it. All I was able to conclude was that Grandpa gave Daddy a job, and that Daddy was lucky to have that, and he gave him a fancy title but no money to go with it. And I began to realize that these Sunday visits, these high teas, had something to do with trying to get Grandpa to give more money to Daddy, but no more money ever came.

"I was right about this, in a way, but I was also wrong. Years later, when Grandpa was an old man, he said something to me about 'how hard your grandmother and I worked to try to get your mother to control her drinking.' I thought at the time: What is he talking about? What had they ever done to try to control my mother's drinking? Then I realized that as far as *they* were concerned, that was what all those high teas were for! They thought they were trying to control my mother's drinking by giving her high tea on Sunday afternoons! What horseshit! What utter horseshit! She'd start drinking as soon as we'd get into the cab, with a belt of Scotch—'My medicine,' she called it. . . .

"You see, my mother is an alcoholic—a recovering alcoholic, as they say. Recover*ing,* not recovered, because they tell you that alcoholism is a disease from which you never recover. My mother has been through the program at the Betty Ford Center, and maybe, perhaps, we'll see . . ." She crosses her fingers and closes her eyes, making a wish. "That outburst of hers at my house the other night wasn't a drunken outburst, it was an outburst of sobriety. Which is worse, I sometimes wonder, drunkenness or sobriety? At least when my mother was drinking, she could be gay—sometimes. Not always, of course. But at least she was never . . . boring."

Mimi runs her fingers through her fine hair and says, "Why am I telling you all this, Jim Greenway? Why am I suddenly being so frank with you? Usually, I don't trust journalists. On television, if you make a horse's ass of yourself, it's your own fault: you did that, you said that, and you sounded like a horse's ass. But with a journalist, you have no control. A journalist, if he doesn't like you, if he *thinks* you're a horse's ass, can rearrange the quotes, add what's called 'analysis and interpretation,' and turn you into a horse's ass on his word processor. I'm usually never as candid with journalists as I'm being with you. Why?"

"Perhaps because you can tell I like you and don't think you're a horse's ass. And perhaps because you can tell that I admire honest people and try to be one myself."

"Am I like old Diogenes, then, wandering through the streets of Athens, with my lantern, searching for an honest man?"

"I think you've already found several honest men."

"Really? Who?"

"Your husband. Your son. Mark Segal, your ad director. And, I hope, me."

"You think so?"

"I think so," I said.

Because there is really no point in keeping up the pretense any longer that Jim Greenway and I are not the same person. It has become a dumb pretense at this point, though giving it up goes against all the journalistic principles I was taught in school. "Be careful to distance yourself from your subject," I was taught. "Never become involved with the people you write about. Depersonalize yourself from your subject matter. Beware of the first-person pronoun." I even had one professor who said, in all seriousness, "A good journalist should not have friends."

And so, in dropping the pretense, am I admitting that I am not a good journalist?

It was not that, in the short time I had known her, I had become "involved" with Mimi, in the romantic sense that the word *involvement* implies. It was more that I was developing an attachment to her, an attraction to her that made me want to be her friend, and to keep her as a friend.

There was something about her that made me keep wanting to know more. When she spoke of her grandfather, for instance, that same pensive,

troubled look would strike her face that I had seen after her talk with
Michael Horowitz. It was a haunted look that would streak across her eyes.
This woman, I sensed, was haunted by ghosts from the past: her grandfather, her father, her mother's drinking. For all her jauntiness—the way her
skirts swung, her hands deep in her pockets, as she strolled through the
offices of her company, the swing of her hair, the set of her shoulders, the
cocky tilt of her chin—for all her apparent self-possession, her self-deprecat-
ing humor, even her occasional outbursts of mild vulgarity, I sensed that
beneath all this lay a little girl too afraid to ask where the bathroom was and
who, overcome by fear, would finally find herself having to pee in a taxi.
From the look in her eyes, that hunted and haunted look when she spoke of
her grandfather, I suspected that she was still frightened of a man who had
been dead for nearly thirty years.

Isn't it interesting, I thought, the way a human life can become polarized
around one particular event, or person, in the past? Polarized.

Later, of course, I would discover that the polar point, that center of
gravity of Mimi Myerson's life, was someone altogether different.

6

*A*DOLPH MYERSON'S first great ambition, once he realized he was becoming a rich man, too rich to bother with the new Jewish bourgeoisie that was moving into the Bronx (I learned all this later from my conversations with Granny Flo), was to become a member of the congregation of Temple Emanu-El.

In those days, membership at Emanu-El was probably the greatest Jewish status symbol in the city of New York. From humble beginnings in a dreary railroad flat on the Lower East Side, and with a starting treasury of about eleven dollars, the congregation and its congregants had grown and prospered to the point where, in less than two generations' time, Temple Emanu-El occupied a splendid edifice right on Fifth Avenue, where it stood cheek by jowl with the great churches and cathedrals of the Christian faiths —a symbol of a degree of assimilation that Jews, nowhere in their history, had ever known before. It was a symbol of the triumph of the Reform Movement, of reason and rationality over Old World barbarism and provincialism. It was also a symbol of the triumphs of the American capitalist system, for the German Jews who founded it and whose families still ran it had nearly all arrived penniless from Europe in pursuit of the American Dream. Here they had pursued it and, in a remarkably short space of time, captured it, through successful careers in commerce, banking, and industry. The very splendor of the temple itself—its magnificent stained-glass windows, its hand-laid mosaic walls, its vaulting ceilings, its cascading chandeliers—announced proudly to the world that for some, at least—those willing

to work hard, lead upright lives, give honest weight, and be a little lucky—
America was indeed the Land of Golden Opportunity.

Attendance at a Sabbath service at Temple Emanu-El was free and open
to all, to Jews and Christians alike. After all, no house of worship in America
can legally close its doors to any orderly person. But membership in Temple
Emanu-El was something else again. It was a little like being taken into a
private club. The temple was governed by a board of trustees, all of whom
were members of what had by then become New York's uptown German-
Jewish establishment, and among the trustees' duties was the assignment of
certain pews to certain families. Needless to say, the best pews in the sanctuary—those in front, closest to the pulpit, and those along the west wall—
had long been rented by Loebs, Lehmans, and Lewisohns, who were all
related to each other, and by other Loebs, Schiffs, and Warburgs, who were
also related to each other, as well as by Seligmans, who were related by
marriage to everybody else. The rentals of these principal pews were passed
along from one family generation to the next.

By 1915, however, Joseph Seligman—the patriarch of the Seligman family—had become much drawn to the ideas of Felix Adler, a German rabbi's
son who advanced theories of a society based on ethics rather than religious
piety, and Seligman was turning away from Judaism toward Adler's Ethical
Culture Society. Thus it was that an excellently placed Seligman pew suddenly became available that year. And Adolph Myerson, applying for membership in Emanu-El, and pointing out that he was in a position to contrib-
ute handsomely to the temple's coffers, was not only accepted but was given
occupancy of the Seligman pew. It was located directly behind the Guggenheim family pew.

The Guggenheims occupied a somewhat ambiguous position in New
York's Jewish society at the time. They were a part of it, and yet not a part.
For one thing, the Guggenheims were not properly German but had originally emigrated from German-speaking Switzerland. For another, they owed
their fortune not to hard work and building a reputation as men of honor, as
the others did, but rather to a lucky accident—not unlike the one that had
befallen Leopold Myerson and his brother. Meyer Guggenheim had spent
most of his life as an unsuccessful peddler of laundry soaps and stove polishes until one day in the 1880s when, in settlement of a bad debt he had
been trying to collect, he was handed some shares in an abandoned mine in
Leadville, Colorado. Journeying to Colorado to have a look at what he
owned, he had discovered a mine shaft filled with water. But when he had
the shaft pumped out, he found one of the richest veins of copper ore in the
world. Out of this came the American Smelting and Refining Company, the
Anaconda Copper Company, and a good deal more. By the early 1900s, the
Guggenheims were among the richest families in America, their companies

worth even more, some said, than the oil-refining companies controlled by John D. Rockefeller. New York's German-Jewish upper crust would have preferred to snub these upstarts, but the Guggenheims had become too rich to ignore—a situation in which Adolph Myerson would soon be pleased to find himself.

From his pew just behind the Guggenheims, at Sabbath services and on the High Holy Days, Adolph Myerson could not help but notice, and be attracted to, the pretty Fleurette Guggenheim, a dainty creature with wide blue eyes and golden ringlets. Adolph Myerson was able to make his presence known to Fleurette in little ways. Once, when Fleurette dropped her prayer book during the service, Adolph reached down to the floor beneath her seat and handed it back to her, for which her eyes fluttered a thank-you. On another occasion, when Fleurette appeared to have forgotten the words to a blessing, Adolph leaned across her shoulder and whispered the words in her ear.

But the only trouble was that little Fleurette was surrounded in her pew by a number of burly and protective brothers, by an even greater number of heavyset uncles, and by her formidable father, Morris Guggenheim, one of Meyer Guggenheim's many sons, and a man whom, when he was born, the press had dubbed "the world's richest baby." These little attentions of Adolph's to Fleurette did not go unnoticed by the menfolk in her family, and after one of these, a council of war was called by the Guggenheim family at the family's summer mansion on the New Jersey shore. Fleurette's father stated the problem bluntly. "That nail polish man," as he always referred to Adolph, "has been sniffing around Fleurette."

The pros and cons of the situation were weighed carefully. On the one hand, there was no questioning the fact that the nail polish man was a successful entrepreneur who would be able to care for little Fleurette and provide for her in the manner to which she was accustomed. On the other hand, there was the marked difference in their ages. Adolph was by then forty-five, and Fleurette was only seventeen.

At the same time, there was a special problem in terms of Fleurette. Within the family, it had been decided that Fleurette was "simple."

"Little Fleurette is a sweet child," her third-grade teacher at the Brearley School had written home to her parents. "She has a gentle, giving nature, and we on the faculty are all very fond of her, but the fact is that she simply cannot do the work at our School. At the third-grade level, when she should be doing her multiplication tables, she still cannot do simple sums. Nor have her reading or writing skills improved at all, and she even has trouble reciting the alphabet. We are terribly sorry, but we do not feel that holding Fleurette back, and asking her to repeat another grade, will provide a solution to her learning problems. It is our advice that Fleurette be withdrawn from Brearley, and that you consider the possibility of further education through the use of private tutors in the home. . . ."

A later generation of therapists might have diagnosed Fleurette's problem as dyslexia. But, in those days, the word did not exist, and Fleurette was taken out of school and tutored at home in music and art appreciation, home management, and needlework.

"The nail polish man doesn't know Fleurette that well yet," her uncle Ben pointed out. "So he hasn't noticed anything. This may be just the man we're looking for."

"She's too sweet and pretty to grow up a spinster," her aunt Hattie said. "But who would ever want to marry her?"

"The nail polish man."

"Opportunity knocks but once, Morris," said Aunt Hattie.

"The nail polish man, then," Fleurette's father agreed.

"And the sooner the better, Morris. Before he has a chance to . . . find out."

And so it was that the Guggenheims proposed Fleurette's hand in marriage to Adolph Myerson, and not the other way around. At the time, Adolph was almost dizzy with happiness over his good fortune.

With Fleurette went a dowry of one million dollars.

Now, more than seventy years later, Fleurette Guggenheim Myerson sits in her apartment at the Carlyle with her second-born child, and only daughter, Naomi, on a quiet Monday afternoon. The apartment is not small, considering that it has but a single occupant. There is a thirty-foot living room, a fair-sized dining room, a "service" kitchen, a small library dominated by a giant remote-controlled television screen, and two bedrooms and baths, the second of which is called "the guest room," though to anyone's knowledge it has never housed a guest. From its location on the twentieth floor, Granny Flo's apartment commands a view of Central Park, not unlike Mimi's view a few blocks to the north, and from Granny's bedroom windows there is even a view of the East River and, beyond it, of Queens and the rising and descending planes at La Guardia Airport—all views, of course, that Granny is no longer able to enjoy.

Still, though not small, the apartment seems that way because it is so crowded with furniture—pieces from the big house on Madison Avenue, as well as from two other houses in Maine and Palm Beach, that Granny has been unwilling to part with. Even a fully sighted person, one might think, would have difficulty picking her way between the nested stacks of little tables, the chairs and ottomans and benches and the floor lamps that are assembled here. But, Granny insists, she has memorized the narrow, twisting passageways that lead between the furniture from one room to the next and can navigate them even in total blindness by reaching out to touch the back of an armchair here, the fringe of a lampshade there. Adding to the sense of crowdedness in the apartment is her art collection, which covers every vacant space of wall from floor to ceiling in every room, two rather unremarkable Bentons having been given just as much prominence as the extraordinary Goya upon which Philippe de Montebello of the Metropolitan Museum gazed so long and thoughtfully the other day.

Granny is seated in one of the many armchairs now, with Nonie opposite her, and with her tiny black Yorkshire terrier, Itty-Bitty, nestled in her lap. Itty-Bitty's chin rests on her mistress's knee, and her buttony round, black eyes gaze intently, even suspiciously, at Nonie, while her mistress's eyes are blank, unfocused. Granny Flo is trying to explain once more to her daughter that Nonie's father did not resent her simply because she was a girl.

"Your papa loved you just as much as he loved the boys," she says. "What you forget is that when you were growing up he was busy building his business. There wasn't as much time for fathering as he'd have liked."

"Still, he shortchanged me in his will."

"His will was to give the boys enough to carry on the business."

"And I was left with virtually nothing. Nothing to build a life on at all."

"I'm not a bottomless pit, Nonie," her mother says again.

"Just five million, Mother. That's all it would take. Five million is *nothing* to you."

"Five *million?* Nothing? You talk as if five million dollars was no more than the cost of a streetcar ride!"

"Surely one of your Guggenheim trusts. Each of your uncles left you—"

"A trust is a trust! I don't know what a trust is, Nonie, but I know that much. Mr. What's-his-name at the bank explained it all to me. I get the income from those trusts, but I don't get the whatchamacallit until after I die. Then it goes to you and Henry and Edwee and Mimi, in a trust. It's all invested in different things."

"Henry's dead, Mother," Nonie says.

Her mother hesitates. "He is?" she says. "When did Henry die? Why didn't anybody tell me?"

"Years ago, Mother. Anyway—"

Thoughtfully, her mother scratches Itty-Bitty's topknot, which is secured with a tiny yellow grosgrain bow, and the little dog closes its eyes and squirms with obvious pleasure, nestling itself deeper into its mistress's lap. Which Itty-Bitty is this one? Nonie tries to remember. It is at least number three, if not number four. There have been many Itty-Bittys over the years.

"Anyway, couldn't you borrow against one of those trusts, Mother? Enough to give me just a short-term loan? Because I could pay you back in just a few months' time—maybe even less."

"But I don't understand what you want it *for*, Nonie," her mother says. "I know your young man said it had something to do with foreigners, and I told him that President Hoover was against the foreigners. He seemed quite impressed at how well I know the Hoovers."

Nonie sighs. "Mother, Hoover has been dead longer than Henry has," she says. "And this has nothing to do with foreigners. It's called spot currency exchange. And if you'll just try to listen to me, Mother, I'll try to explain to you again how it works."

"Yes. Explain it to me, Nonie."

"I'll try. Now please try to follow me closely, Mother. It works like this. The dollar fluctuates from day to day, from minute to minute, against the Japanese yen, the Swiss franc, the German mark, even the Canadian dollar. There's money to be made whichever way the dollar goes, up or down, it doesn't matter. And my friend Roger is an expert—an ace, an absolute ace —on these trades. I mean, it's as though he wrote the book on the subject, Mother."

"You see? I was right. Foreign money."

"Please listen, Mother. There's nothing illegal about it. The biggest banks in the country do this sort of thing, and it's so easy! Listen. He gave me a demonstration the other day, right in my apartment, of how it works. He telephoned Zurich, right from my apartment, and said he was interested in buying five million U.S. dollars. He was quoted the prevailing rate, which was seven million, six hundred and fifty-five Swiss francs. I know this, Mother, because I heard the quote. Roger had me listen to his calls on an extension. One minute later—one minute, Mother—the rate had crept up fifteen hundredths of a Swiss centime, and the moment that happened Roger made another call to a bank in Chicago, offering to *sell* five million dollars. If he had, his profit from the trade would have been twelve thousand, five hundred francs—or about eight thousand dollars. That's eight thousand dollars a *minute*, Mother! Hypothetically, of course, because Roger was just demonstrating how it worked to me. But that's what the profit *would* have been if an actual trade had been made. Think of it, Mother! Eight thousand dollars a minute, and Roger can make hundreds of these trades a day. Isn't it exciting? I knew you'd think so."

Her mother says nothing. The little dog hops now from her mistress's lap and settles on the floor beside her feet. "Where's Itty-Bitty going now?" her mother asks. "Oh, there you are, sweetheart," she says, nudging the animal with her toe.

"Our plan is to start small," Nonie continues, "right in my apartment. Of course, we'd have to install lots of extra telephone lines, because this business involves being on the telephone, all over the world, all day long, and even into the night with some markets, handling many different calls at once. Eventually, of course, we'll hire a staff and move into an office—probably in the Wall Street area, where the action is. But we'll be making hundreds of thousands a day right from *day one*, Mother. And you'd be paid back in no time. If it's to be a loan, we'll pay you back with interest. Or, if you decide to buy stock in our company, you'll get income from dividends. You can't lose, Mother, either way!"

Once more, her mother says nothing. Then she says, "If this man is so smart, why isn't he rich?"

"He needs seed money, Mother. It's called seed money. He needs a sponsor, a patron. Every genius needs a patron." She looks up at her mother's art-crowded walls and has an inspiration, a small one, but an appropriate one. "Even Michelangelo couldn't have painted the things he did if he hadn't had a patron!"

"And so you're to be his patron. Or rather, I am."

"Just to get us started, Mother. And for such a little amount of money. Would you like me to bring him by and have him demonstrate to you how simply it all works?"

"Frankly, I didn't like his looks, Nonie," her mother says.

"You didn't like his *looks?* But how can you tell what he *looked* like, Mother, when you can't—"

"I can smell a man's looks," her mother says quickly.

"If you smelled anything about him, it was Mimi's new cologne! I saw him splash some on his hands before he sat down to dinner."

"I smelled him *before* he splashed the cologne on," her mother says firmly. "He had an oily smell. He smelled like a greaser. That's what your father would have called a man like that—a greaser."

"But he's *not!* He's a graduate of the Harvard Business School."

"Is he? I wonder. He didn't talk like a Harvard man. Edwee's a Harvard man, and Edwee doesn't talk like that. I don't even believe that Roger Williams is his real name. It sounds like a made-up name to me. Roger Williams sounds like the name of some hotel."

"But it *is* his name."

Once again, her mother says nothing, gazing emptily into space, and stroking Itty-Bitty's back with the tip of her toe.

"This is my one big chance, Mother."

Softly, her mother begins, "How many other big chances have I given you money for, Nonie? The dress shop, the restaurant, the—what was it?—oh, yes, the fashion magazine. All of them cost me money, these big chances of yours. I am not a bottomless pit."

"Those were . . . bad luck, I admit. It was bad luck, bad advice, untrustworthy partners. But don't you think I've learned something from my mistakes?"

"Have you?"

"Oh, yes! I have! I've learned to be much tougher. I've learned to be . . . like Mimi, and look what she's done! Oh, Mother, please—give me one last chance! Edwee's been given the money to do what he wants. Even Henry was given a chance! Oh, Mother, I'm not getting any younger. Please give me one last chance to become somebody, the person I deserve to be!" In a sudden gesture that she knows would displease her mother if she could see her, Nonie flings herself to her knees on the floor in front of her mother's chair and stretches her arms across her mother's lap, which is still warm from Itty-Bitty. "Mother, do you see what I am doing? I am begging you. I am begging you for one last chance. I am begging you on bended knee!"

"Stand up, Nonie," her mother says quietly. "That's undignified. It's unladylike. Are you sleeping with this man?"

"No!"

"Then stand up. Stop acting like a child."

Rising, Nonie sobs, "It's just that I want this . . . I want it . . . so much . . ."

"Why don't you ask Edwee for the money? He's rich. Or Mimi? She's rich, too."

"I couldn't . . . humiliate myself like that. To ask Mimi for money. She's my *niece*. And Edwee—I don't trust Edwee. Edwee is a sneak."

Her mother nods. "You're right about that," she says. "I hate to say that about my own son, but you're right. Edwee is a sneak. Sneakiness has always been Edwee's problem."

"Then who else? Who else can I turn to?" She extracts a hanky from her Hermès bag and blows her nose noisily into it, aware that the sound is harsh and unpleasant.

Her mother's eyes gaze vacantly into space. When she speaks now her normally fluty voice is hard and even. "How much have I given you over the years, Nonie, for your various enterprises? Thirty million? Would that be a good ballpark figure? Thirty million, over the years, and that's not counting what it cost me to bail you out of three marriages. People used to say I was no good with figures, but when figures like that come out of my pocketbook, I keep track. Did it ever occur to you that is more than either Edwee or Henry inherited from your father in Miray stock? And yet you say you were shortchanged. That is why I am saying to you today that I am not a bottomless pit."

Nonie, dabbing at her eyes, at first says nothing. Then she says, "If you can't afford five million, Mother, then how much could you lend me? As you can see, I'm desperate."

"Five thousand."

"Five *thousand!* That's an insult, Mother! I can't do anything with five thousand dollars. I need—"

"And let me ask you another question. Where's my jade elephant?"

Nonie gasps. "What are you talking about?"

"My jade elephant. Han Dynasty, first century."

"I—I don't know anything about a jade elephant!"

"It used to sit over there," her mother points, "on that piecrust table. It was there the last time you came to see me, in July. After you left, it was gone. No one else was in this apartment. Have you taken to pinching things from me, Nonie, as well as from other people?"

"Why—why—what a perfectly dreadful thing to accuse me of, Mother! Your own daughter, your own daughter who—"

"Are you sure you didn't just drop it into your purse, Nonie, as you were walking out?"

"Of course not! Obviously, one of the hotel staff—"

"I've lived at this hotel for fifteen years, Nonie, and I know all the staff. Nothing has ever been missing before."

"A waiter, or a—"

"My waiter is always Eric. They always send up Eric, because they know I like him. And Eric hadn't even been in that day. I'd lunched out."

"What a perfectly despicable, contemptible thing to accuse me of, Mother!"

"Let me just say one thing, Nonie. It's one thing when you come to me asking me for money. But when you start pinching my things, it's another."

"I can't believe I'm sitting here listening to this sort of thing! I—"

Her mother sighs. "Well," she says, "if you decide to sell it, don't take it to some Third Avenue pawnshop. Take it to John Marion at Sotheby's. It should fetch quite a nice price. If John Marion has any questions about it, refer him to me. I'll tell him I gave it to you." Then she says, "What time is it?"

Hesitantly, dabbing at her nose, Nonie sniffles, "Four-thirty."

"Then I'm going to have to send you on your way, Nonie. That Mr. Greenway is coming by at five to interview me. He says I'm a living link with the past. What do you think of that? A living link with the past!"

"You're sending me on my way on a perfectly horrid note like that? Accusing me of stealing—"

"Edwee may be sneaky, but at least he's never stolen anything from me."

Suddenly Nonie leans forward, close to her mother's face, and says, "And speaking of darling Edwee, I don't suppose you've heard what darling Edwee is planning to do with *you.*"

Her mother's eyes snap immediately into focus. "*What?*"

"He's planning to ship you off to a nursing home. In Massachusetts. He's going to have you legally probated. He's going to have you declared incompetent. He's collecting witnesses to say that you're senile and incapable of handling your own affairs. You'll live in a tiny cell. You'll have to give up your apartment and all your things. You'll have to give up Itty-Bitty."

Her mother's hand flies to her throat. Then she reaches quickly down and scoops up her little dog and clutches it protectively against her bosom. "What?" she cries. "He can't do that, can he? He can't take Itty-Bitty away from me!"

"Who knows what he can do? He's the oldest surviving son, and he's working on it already. He's got the nursing home all picked out; your room's reserved."

"You wouldn't let him do this to me, Nonie!"

"What can I do? He's the oldest surviving son, and he's got all these lawyers at Dewey, Ballantine working on it. He can afford to hire forty lawyers at Dewey, Ballantine to have you put away. I can't afford that sort of thing to fight him."

"Mimi won't let him! Mimi's the boss of the company now, isn't she? She wouldn't let him do this sort of thing to me, would she?"

"*Mimi!*" Nonie cries. "Don't you know that Mimi *hates* you, Mother? Hates you—because of the way you treat her mother. Like the other night, at her dinner party."

"What are you talking about?"

"The other night. At Mimi's dinner party. The way you lashed out at Alice."

Her mother blinks. "I've been to no dinner parties at Mimi's," she says. "I haven't set foot in Mimi's house for at least two years!"

"Now, Mother. This was last Thursday night. Surely you remember. That was when you met my friend Roger Williams, remember? That was when you suddenly lashed out at poor Alice. I wish you could have seen the expression on Mimi's face when you said what you said. It was an expression of . . . sheer horror, Mother. No, I don't think Mimi feels very charitable toward you—particularly right now. Mimi's not going to do anything to help *you*, Mother."

"Well, if she hates me so, why did she ask me to dinner?"

"She probably thought you'd behave yourself. So you *do* remember the dinner."

Her mother says nothing, still clutching her little dog. "Well, perhaps," she says at last. "Perhaps I do remember. But Alice—Alice's trouble is ingratitude. Alice has never learned the art of being grateful. Gratitude is an art she's just never learned, that's all. If you only knew what your father and I did, what we went through, to try to help Alice, and help Henry. Not even

Mimi knows. And never so much as a word of thanks! I've never understood
how a person could be so ungrateful!"

"Still, Alice is Mimi's mother. And the things you said to her were not
nice. Did you ever call Mimi to apologize? I'm sure not."

"Oh, Nonie!" her mother cries suddenly. "You've got to help me! Will
you help me, Nonie?"

Nonie dabs the last tears from her eyes with her handkerchief and replaces the handkerchief in her clutch bag. Suddenly the expression on her
face is one of regained self-confidence. Gently, she reaches out and touches
her mother's knee. "What I'm suggesting," she says almost tenderly, "is
that I could try to help you, and you could try to help me. We could help
each other, Mother."

The little dog in her mother's arms reaches down and, with its rough pink
tongue, begins licking the gold bracelets that tumble from the sleeve of
Nonie's black silk suit.

The delivery men from F.A.O. Schwartz could barely maneuver the huge
shipping carton through the front door of Mimi's parents' apartment on
East 97th Street, and their job was even more ticklish since the carton was
affixed with big red FRAGILE stickers. At last they had the box wedged into
the narrow entrance hall, and, their job completed, they presented Mimi's
mother with the receipt form to sign.

It was Mimi's tenth birthday, and inside the big box was a card that read,
"Happy Birthday, dear Mireille, from your adoring Grandmama and Grandpapa." Then came the chore of removing the contents of the box from
many layers of white tissue paper.

It was the biggest and most beautiful dollhouse she had ever seen, and it
was nearly as tall as she was. It was white with green shutters, in a Palladian
style, and its front opened outward on hinges to reveal the rooms within. On
the first floor was an entrance hall with a curving, carpeted staircase. On one
side of this was the parlor, completely furnished with tiny sofas, chairs,
tables, and lamps, all very formal. Across the hall was the dining room, with
table, chairs, a pair of Victorian sideboards, a crystal chandelier, even dishes,
silverware, and candlesticks to set the table with. Pictures the size of postage
stamps hung from the walls. Next to this was the kitchen, with a miniature
old-fashioned cookstove, an icebox that opened to reveal tiny bottles of milk,
a little china loaf of bread, a cake with pink icing, a trussed chicken ready to
pop into the oven. Tiny pots and pans and cooking utensils hung from hooks
along the walls, and cabinets opened up to display more dishes, cups, saucers, and a larder filled with canned goods. A cookpot no bigger than a
thimble stood on the kitchen stove, and on the kitchen table rested the
smallest possible rolling pin beside a bowl of rising dough. Upstairs, there

were three formal bedrooms, a bathroom with an old-fashioned tub and bowl, and a child's nursery filled with dolls, stuffed animals, and a rocking horse, all fashioned to scale. On the third floor, under the gabled and dormered roof, were the prim and Spartan servants' rooms with their little iron beds and plain wooden chests of drawers.

The dollhouse was too large to fit into Mimi's bedroom, and so it had to be set up in a corner of the dining room. Mimi can remember sitting on the dining-room floor, introducing her two favorite dolls, Matilda and Miss Emily, to their new house, while her mother screamed at her father in the kitchen next door.

"How much do you suppose that thing *cost?*" her mother cried. "From *Schwartz's?* Two thousand? Three thousand? Why don't they give her something she can *use?* Why don't they give us money? What did they give her last year? An ermine jacket with a matching muff and hat! *Ermine!* I don't even own a decent winter wool coat! Why don't they send us money? Why don't they help us pay for her education so that we're not always applying for scholarships? Why is there never any money, Henry? What's wrong with them? *What's wrong with you?*"

"Do you want a divorce, Alice?" she heard her father ask.

At that point, she heard the word *divorce* so often that it had lost its power to terrify her. She tried not to listen to their shouting and to concentrate instead on Matilda and Miss Emily, who were seated now at their new dining table, preparing for an evening meal.

"Will you serve the soup, Matilda?" Miss Emily said.

"Certainly, Miss Emily." The dolls were always very formal and polite with one another.

"Is that it, Alice? Do you want a divorce? Because if that's what you want, you can have it!"

"Divorce!" her mother sobbed. "Then where will I be? What will become of me? What will become of the child?"

Mimi remembers thinking that, whenever her parents quarreled, she was always just "the child." When they were like this, she had no name at all.

"This soup is delicious, Matilda!" Miss Emily said.

"Thank you, Miss Emily. It is made from larks' tongues and quails' eggs, of tiny golden apples from sunny Spain, of spices grown in the Fairy Islands, of herbs cultivated in far Cathay, of honey and hibiscus blossom and raspberry flowers, and salted with Mother's tears. . . ."

"You see, Mr. Greenway," Granny Flo is saying, "the thing that distinguished my husband from his brother, Leo, was that my husband came up with the idea of giving his colors *names*. I mean, he named his colors. He was the first one to do that. Before that, if a nail polish was pink, it was called pink. If it was red, it said 'red' on the label, and if it was clear, it said 'clear.' But Adolph was clever. I think I told you that his first color was from a paint that was supposed to be the color of a fire engine. So what did Adolph decide to call it? He called it 'Three Alarm.' Wasn't that clever? Three Alarm caught on right away. Women liked it, and they liked the name. All those others who came later, Revlon, Arden, Rubinstein, and the rest, with their fancy names for colors—they just copied Adolph. He was the first, with Three Alarm." Granny Flo spreads her fingers. "I remember the first time he painted *my* nails with Three Alarm; I thought it was so pretty. Adolph used to say that I had pretty hands, and he loved to have me wear his polishes. He liked me to wear the kind of little lace gloves that have the fingers cut out, so that I could display my fingers—and his polishes, of course! You may notice that I no longer wear nail polish. That's not out of disloyalty to my husband. It's because I can no longer see my fingernails, and my pretty hands, so what's the point?"

"Your granddaughter mentioned that your husband used to read from an appointment book, Mrs. Myerson."

"Oh, yes. His appointment book. Every Sunday afternoon."

"Was that what you meant when you mentioned a diary the other night?"

"Oh, no. The appointment book was an appointment book. The diary was a diary. He put everything in the diary, the good things and the bad. He read the appointment book to us to remind us of how busy he was, of how hard he had to work, and also to help him memorize all the appointments he had in the week to come. It was a loose-leaf thing. At the end of each week, he threw all the used pages out. But the diaries he kept. Eventually, there was a stack of them"—she holds out her hand—"there was a stack this high. He used to read aloud to me from them. I was never much of a reader, but I liked to listen to Adolph read to me from his diaries. He never read to anyone else from these because, well, frankly, Mr. Greenway, because there were a lot of things in there that were confidential. Family matters. Not for publication."

"And the diaries are gone now?"

"Gone, yes. Disappeared. If you ask me, Leo took them, but I can't prove that. Leo's dead now, and there's no way of proving that. Leo was a crook."

"A crook?"

She holds up her hand. "No. Don't put that in. Don't put it in that I said Leo was a crook. Leo is dead, and speak no ill of the dead is what I always say. Just say that Adolph and Leo had . . . different business philosophies. Yes, that sounds good. Different business philosophies. And my husband was smarter, what with coming up with the idea of names."

"Can you remember any details from the diaries, Mrs. Myerson?"

"Ha!" she says. "I might choose to remember some of the good things,

Mr. Greenway. But you won't get me to remember the bad things. You heard what Mimi said Thursday night at her party: 'Say only nice things about the company to Mr. Greenway.' I was thinking before you arrived that there are some not-so-nice things I could say about my son Edwee— things even my daughter doesn't know—but I'm not going to say them. They're not for publication—not yet, anyway. We'll see. Besides, most of the bad things are dead things now. They died with my husband, with Leo . . . and with poor Henry, I suppose. But where was I? Oh, the good things, the good things . . ."

"What are the good things, Mrs. Myerson?"

"The good things are that we're the recognized leader in the American cosmetics industry today!" she says triumphantly. "And you can quote me! *That's* for publication. The Magnificent Myersons—that's what they called us back in the thirties. That was the headline of the article about us in *Town & Country*. I could probably dig the article out for you, if you'd like. They called us magnificent then. Then there were some hard times. But now we're magnificent again, and you must give Mimi all the credit for that."

Now, as I set this material down, I notice that a strange thing has begun to happen. Though I have been working on this story for less than four weeks, it is as though each member of the Myerson family is trying to adopt me, for his or her personal reasons. It is as though I am to serve as a kind of private messenger, a bearer of personal sentiments between them. There are only seven members of the immediate family (I am not counting Edwee's wife, Gloria, as an immediate family member), so this doesn't present much of a chore. But it's as if, even in a family as small as this one, lines of communication between the individuals are often jammed. And I have been assigned the task of unjamming them, passing along the little dispatches from one to another. I feel a bit like Jodie, who is the traffic manager in Mimi's office, a formidable Irishwoman whose formidable responsibility it is to see that each new job is carried out from initial concept to finished product ready to be shipped.

For instance, when I was interviewing Brad Moore in his Wall Street office yesterday about the problems—or rewards—of a two-career household, he said a strange thing. I see Brad as a decent, intelligent, and somewhat shy man who, as a lawyer, doesn't want his own feelings to be revealed too much. Behind the obvious polish and poise of the man, there is a certain dignified reserve, and it is easy to see why, in considering various New Yorkers to fill the late Armitage Miller's unexpired term in the U.S. Senate, the name of Bradford Moore, Jr., has been brought up several times. But occasionally there are breaks in that reserve. And yesterday he suddenly said to me, "You know, Jim, you must make it clear in whatever you write about us that my wife is the most important person in the world to me. Not just the most important woman. The most important *person*. Whatever you hear in this very gossipy business she's in, no matter what you may hear the gossips say, she is the most important person in the world to me."

I thought: Fair enough. Then I thought, "My wife." Not "Mimi." And, question: If he wishes to convey the message that his wife is the most important person in the world to him, why does he tell me? Does he want me to pass that word along to her? Has he ever told her that himself?

7

IT IS WEDNESDAY NIGHT, and Mimi and Brad Moore are having dinner at home alone at 1107 Fifth Avenue. "This will be a rare pleasure, sir!" she said to him cheerfully on the phone when he called to say that, for a change, he would not be working late tonight.

"A rare pleasure?"

"It seems like ages since you and I have had dinner together at the usual time and place."

"Only three and a half weeks."

"Anyway, we can have a good talk, darling. I've got loads to tell you about." And she thought: Interesting, that he has been keeping count of the days and weeks as well. But counting them, perhaps, for a different reason.

She has been telling him about her idea for applying a scar to the face of the male model, but he has seemed only mildly interested. "Anyway," she says, "who knows whether it'll work? I hope I'm not boring you with this."

"It's not that," he says, spooning his fresh raspberry dessert from a rasp-berry-decorated dessert plate. "It's just that I don't have a pictorial sort of mind, I guess. It's hard for me to visualize what differences it would make."

"Do I have a pictorial sort of mind? Maybe I do. You, being a lawyer, have a mind trained to deal with facts, which is why you're so good at what you do. Me, in the beauty business, I deal all day with fantasy—artifice. Women's fantasies, for the most part, not hard, male facts."

"Are facts exclusively male?"

"I think, for the most part, yes. Don't you think women fantasize more than men do?"

"I've never really thought about it," he says.

"You see? There you are. The difference."

They sit catercorner at one end of the long candlelit table, and she thinks: Is she blackmailing you, my darling, this nameless, faceless woman? Surely you, the brilliant lawyer, would know how to deal with a blackmailer. But I do know this: if she is blackmailing you, then I do hate her, this other woman whom I would love to hate. She says, "Is something on your mind, darling? You seem . . . preoccupied. Is it the Sturtevant case still?"

He touches his lips with his napkin. "Well, yes, I suppose so. It's still going on. It's all over money, of course. Sturtevant *père* versus Sturtevant *fils*. I had to spend an hour this afternoon listening to Sturtevant *père* tell me what an asshole his son is. Can you imagine it? A father and his son fighting over money?"

She laughs softly. "Yes, as a matter of fact, I can," she says.

"Oops. Sorry. I forgot about that."

"And it's not that *much* money, is it?"

"Lousy thirty thousand dollars. By the way, I met Leonard Lauder today."

"Ah. My stiffest competition."

"Somebody brought him over to my table at lunch and introduced him. He said, 'I know who you are—you're Mimi Myerson's husband.' "

"Honestly. I'd have thought Leonard could have come up with a snappier opening line than *that.*" And she thinks: So, my midnight guess was correct. It *does* bother him, this sort of thing. It's gone on for years, but it's finally begun to get under his skin, and who can blame him? She says, "And so what did *you* say?"

"I said, 'And I bet you're one of Estée Lauder's kids.' "

"Ah!" she cries. "Good for you, Brad. Wonderful. I can just see the expression on Leonard's big, dopey face!"

"He did look a bit, well, crestfallen, I guess."

"Does that sort of thing bother you, Brad? Tell me the truth. I mean, I get it too. At that Statue of Liberty party, for instance, when your firm hired that party boat, and it was all lawyers. And all the men, and their wives, came up to me and said, 'You must be Brad Moore's wife.' Most of them had never heard of Mimi Myerson."

"Hell, I'm used to it by now," he says.

"But it isn't always Leonard Lauder who does it—and you get the chance to zap him the way you did. Congratulations, darling."

"Well, I must say I thought I was pretty quick on my feet today." His craggy, homely-handsome Yankee face is smiling now, recalling it, and Mimi thinks: Ah, the ice is beginning to break a little bit.

And why, she asks herself, do I always think of his as a Yankee face?

Because of the prominent nose, of course. Why are the Jews often thought of as a big-nosed people? Mimi's own nose is small. So is her mother's, and her grandmother's. So have been the noses of everyone she has known in her family. Yet the noses of old New England families like the Moores—big, rawboned outdoorsmen, descended from Highlanders and Gaels and Celts —were inevitably large, with flaring nostrils. Looking at her husband now, she is pleased to see that Brad, at fifty-one, has not lost his rugged good looks, not lost his hair, which is going grey in all the right places, and, perhaps best of all, not lost his figure. You are a fine figure of a man, she tells him wordlessly. I can see what she sees in you, whoever she is, wherever she lives, whatever she does for you. For that, I can sympathize with her.

The maid appears to clear the dessert plates and says, "Would you like me to serve coffee here, or in the library, Mrs. Moore?"

"We'll have it here, I think, Edna. It's easier." To Brad she says, "Really, the only reason why I use the name Myerson in the business is because a lot of our customers still associate Miray products with Grandpa. I actually overheard a salesgirl at Magnin's in Chicago saying to a customer, 'You know, there really is a Mireille Myerson who makes this night cream; she's the granddaughter of the founder.' I think it gives our customers a good feeling to know that there's an actual person behind the name."

"Of course. Makes damn good sense." Their coffee arrives.

"It doesn't bother you that much, then."

"It wouldn't bother me at all, if every time it could be Leonard Lauder."

"Do you know that we're the only company in the industry that's kept a member of the family at its head into the third generation? All the others— Revlon, Rubinstein, Arden, all of them—got gobbled up by conglomerates the minute the founder died. Which reminds me. I got the silliest letter from Uncle Edwee today."

"Really? What's he want?"

"Well, among a lot of other silly stuff—really, Uncle Edwee has got to be the silliest man on two feet—he wants me to give him the home telephone number of—are you ready for this, darling?—of our new male model."

Brad Moore appears to choke slightly on the first swallow of his coffee. "My God," he says. "I thought Edwee had stopped chasing after the little boys. I thought that was what Gloria was for."

"Actually, it worries me a little bit. If there was any kind of scandal— even any kind of backlot talk—about our supposedly virile young male model and Uncle Edwee, it could knock our campaign into a cocked hat, if you see what I mean."

"Don't you have a morals clause in the kid's contract?"

"Oh, we do. But that doesn't stop the titillating little rumors from circulating through the industry. Rumors alone could sour the whole campaign, if not sink it altogether."

"What about little Gloria?"

"Exactly. If Gloria suspected some sort of hanky-panky was going on, there's no telling what sort of fuss she might kick up. Suddenly, Gloria's become a loose cannon in all this. Stupid Uncle Edwee!"

"Gloria's a bimbo."

"And a dumb one, to boot. I can deal with smart people easily enough. It's the dumb ones you have to watch out for."

He is smiling again. "Which category do I fall into?" he says.

She laughs. "I've been dealing with you all these years, haven't I?"

"So I take it you're not going to supply Edwee with the young man's number."

"Let's say I'm not running a dating service. If he keeps after me—and he may—I'll say I have no idea what his number is. I'll suggest that he call the agency, who won't give out telephone numbers, either."

"Would it help if I had a word with Edwee?"

"What would you say to him, Brad?"

"I'd just say that I'm aware of this, ah, interest of his, and I'd suggest that he'd be playing with fire if he decides to pursue this interest. Just a word or two from me might be enough to scare him off."

"Well, let's wait and see if we hear anything more from him. Maybe it was just a . . . passing fancy, though I wish I didn't suspect that that casual little postscript of his was the whole point of his letter. But sometimes, if you ignore a problem—"

"It gets bigger. I think I should have a word with Edwee."

"All right. Yes, do that, Brad." Suddenly she reaches out and covers his hand with her own. "Have I told you lately, darling," she says, "how wonderful you are to put up with my crazy family? My crazy family, and this crazy business we seem to be in?"

"It's certainly never dull, is it."

"Neither is life in a lunatic asylum. Tomorrow, for instance, I'm having lunch with Michael Horowitz."

His eyes flicker with interest. "Oh?" he says. "What's that to be about?"

"I'm not sure yet. But have you noticed how Miray stock has been behaving? For most of this year it's hovered between fifty-two and fifty-five. Today, it closed at sixty-seven and five eighths."

"Rumors about the new fragrance, maybe?"

"We thought perhaps it was institutional buying. But Badger's found out that it's not an institution. It's Michael himself."

"What for, I wonder? His game is real estate, not the beauty biz."

"That's what I intend to find out. Badger and I think he may be attempting some sort of takeover."

"Again, what for? He's always been a kind of family friend, hasn't he?"

"Well, yes, in a funny way I guess you could say that. He seems to have a peculiar interest in anything to do with the Myersons. First, after Grandpa died, and there didn't seem to be any money left anywhere, Michael appeared on the doorstep to help Granny sell the Madison Avenue house. Then he helped her sell and subdivide the place in Bar Harbor."

"Those were good deals, weren't they?"

"Oh, yes—at the time. Very. Good deals for Granny, as the seller, and for him as the developer. Then, for a while, we didn't hear much from him. Then, two years ago, he suddenly bought Grandpa's Palm Beach house and moved into it."

"That was a good deal, too, wasn't it? The place was a white elephant nobody else wanted. Granny Flo couldn't even give it away."

"Well, he made us our best offer—after letting the place sit on the market for years, begging for buyers, until it began to look like a distress sale."

"Better than paying taxes on it for another twenty years."

"And now this. Do you see a pattern emerging, Brad? I do."

He hesitates. Then he says, "Wasn't he an old beau of yours, Mimi?"

"Oh, I guess, sort of. Once upon a time, years ago."

"Well, maybe that's it," he says.

"Oh, no," she says. "That's silly. In any case, he's not behaving like an old beau now. He's been buying our stock very secretly and underhandedly, through dozens of different brokerage accounts. This seems definitely hostile. Badger thinks so, too."

"Know something? I bet he's still in love with you."

"Oh, no," she says, perhaps too quickly. "It's not that. He was—oh, it was so long ago I don't even remember it. Anyway, what I wanted to ask you was, if it begins to look as though we're heading into a takeover fight, would McSwain, Moore and Hollowell represent us? Or would that be a conflict of interest?"

He is thoughtful for a moment and then says, "No, I don't think that would be any problem. I'd have to discuss it with the other partners, of course. But I think we could handle it. After all, one of our young guys got Bob Hollowell his divorce."

Divorce, she thinks. Why does his mind fly to divorce, when we have been discussing takeovers and acquisitions, which, after all, are his specialty? She says brightly, "I might as well hire the best law firm in town if I'm going to lock horns with someone like Michael Horowitz."

"Compliment noted," he says.

"Because," she says, "I don't want this company just for myself. I want it for Badger, and we both know that it's what he wants, too. I don't intend to hang on here for too many years. In a few more years, I'm going to turn it over to Badger; he'll be ready. After all, we are unique in this industry. I'm the third generation, and Badger will be the fourth, and then—"

"And then what will *you* do?"

She laughs. "I'm going to become a lazy, contented housewife, flopping around the house in my horrible bedroom slippers and coffee-stained wrapper, watching the daytime soaps."

"Somehow," he says, "I can't quite picture you in that role." Then he says, "I would, too, you know."

"You would what? Flop around watching the soaps?"

"Carry the torch for you. After all these years."

"Why, darling! That's the sweetest thing to say!"

"Somehow, it just popped out."

They are silent now, sitting catercorner at the dining room table, the candles in their silver candlesticks guttering in the slight, late-summer breeze that blows in from Central Park, billowing the glass curtains into the room. If one had looked in on them just then, one might have taken them for two conspirators, a two-party cabal, plotting intrigue on a summer night.

There was another summer evening. She had begun to come out of the anaesthetic at New York Hospital, and when she opened her eyes she could not understand what Brad was doing lying on an identical hospital bed beside her, his shirtsleeve rolled up, with a small bandage on his right arm. The baby had begun to come three weeks earlier than Dr. Ornstein had said it was due. She had been rushed to the hospital, and after nineteen hours of labor, the doctor had said to her, "We're facing a breech delivery, Mimi. I'm going to do a section." She had merely nodded. "Don't worry," he said. "Caesarian babies are beautiful babies. They don't have to be squeezed out. You'll be fine." That, of course, was the last thing she remembered.

Some pelvic flaw, it seemed—inherited, perhaps, from her mother, who had a similar problem giving birth to her—had caused the trouble. The operation had gone well enough, and the baby had been taken, but soon afterward she had begun to hemorrhage. All this she learned later, but now, still groggy from the anaesthetic, and cross with the way she felt, it annoyed her to see her husband lying in the next bed. "What are you doing here?" she said angrily. "What the hell are you doing here?"

"Hush," he said. "Don't move. Lie still."

"What's going on here, anyway?" she said, trying to raise herself up on her elbows in the bed.

"Don't move, I said. You needed blood. I just gave three pints. I'm feeling a little weak, too. That's my blood that's going into you right now."

"Your blood is going into me?"

"My blood is in you now. And it's in our little son. It cements us, doesn't it."

"A son," she said sleepily. And then, instead of that irrational anger she had felt upon first waking up, she was suddenly suffused with an almost delirious feeling of happiness. In her drugged half-sleep, she let this feeling gather and fold itself around her like a warm blanket. Details of the room floated lazily in and out of focus, and she lay in this blissful, drowsy dream. "A son," she said again. "I want to name him after you. I want to name him after you . . . after you . . . Mi—"

"Don't try to talk. Just rest," Brad interrupted.

"What are you thinking about?" he says now.

"Thinking? Funny, but I was thinking about the beach at St.-Jean-de-Luz," she lies. "The day you buried me in the sand."

"I made you look like Mae West, remember? You were always too damned skinny."

" 'Bradford is not a very demonstrative man,' your mother said."

"She was always saying that. 'We Moores are not a very demonstrative family.' She seemed to think demonstrativeness was in violation of the Scriptures. Sort of naughty."

She smiles, turning away from him toward the window. "But you were able to demonstrate some things to me that afternoon in Athens. Remember that? The view of the Parthenon from your room?"

"My, weren't we naughty then."

"And I'm thinking about something Jim Greenway said to me today. He asked me if I thought of you as a father figure."

"And what did you say to that?"

"I said no, I thought of you as a husband figure."

"I have some news for you," he says.

"What's that?"

"I think I may be picked to fill out Arm Miller's unexpired term."

"Really, darling? How exciting!"

"That's the word from Albany. But would you like that, Mimi? Living that kind of a fishbowl life in Washington as a Senate wife? What about your business here?"

"I'd commute on the shuttle, like lots of other people do."

"We could live in Washington during the week, and come back up here for weekends—for our Saturday shopping sprees."

"We haven't been on one of those in ages."

"We've both been busy."

"Yes."

There is a silence. Then he says, "There's something else we haven't done in quite a while."

"Which is?"

"Why don't we fill our wineglasses and go upstairs and be demonstrative for a little while?"

"Why, Brad, what a lovely idea!"

"Promise not to tell my mother."

"Promise."

She rises first, and he follows. On the stairs, she says, putting her lips close to his ear, "Tonight, I think I'd like to do the thing you like best. Remember? In Athens? What you said you liked the best? After all, I've never made love to a United States Senator before."

He takes her hand and they run up the stairs together, like the guilty children they once were thirty years ago. All's right with the world, Mimi thinks, at least for now.

"The Magnificent Myersons!" declared the headline of the picture story on the family that was published in the November 1939 issue of *Town & Country*. Bear in mind that this was a year in which nearly ten million Americans were still unemployed, when only forty-two thousand had incomes of over twenty-five thousand dollars a year, and when only three percent of the country's population earned enough to pay income taxes at all.

Here are some of the picture captions from that story:

Adolph Myerson, the "Cosmetics King," and his beautiful wife Fleuret [sic], née Guggenheim, of the copper-smelting fortune, take tea in the grand salon of their Manhattan mansion. Mr. Myerson, a descendant of an old French family, explains that the original family name, which is still the family motto, "Ma Raison" ("My Right"), became transliterated as Myerson in nineteenth-century America. The single goal that has fueled Adolph Myerson's success in the cosmetics industry: "To make American women the most beautiful in the world."

Sons Henry G. Myerson, left, 24, and Edwin R. Myerson, 7, stroll with their parents on Fifth Avenue. Henry Myerson is already a force in his father's business, while Edwin, a bright second-grader, says he wants to be "a Policeman" when he grows up!

Auburn-haired debutante daughter, Miss Naomi Myerson, center, hosts a party for young friends at The Stork Club. Miss Myerson, known to her friends as "Nonie," is a popular member of New York's younger social set.

"Merry Song," the Myersons' spacious summer retreat at Bar Harbor, on
Mt. Desert Island, Maine. A quarter-mile of manicured lawns and gardens sweeps down from the portico of the Georgian house to the sparkling blue waters of Frenchman Bay.

Mer et Son, the Myerson yacht, lies at anchor off Bar Harbor. The 70-
foot yacht, with a beam of 14 feet, a draft of 9 feet, and a gross tonnage
of 24.6, was commissioned by Adolph Myerson in 1932 and built by
Harvey Gamage. Like the names of the Myerson country homes, *Mer et
Son* ("Sea and Sound") is a playful sound-alike of the name "Myerson."

"Ma Raison," the newly completed Myerson estate in Palm Beach, Florida, which will provide the "Magnificent Myersons" with a winter retreat. Built of rose-colored stucco, in the Spanish-Moorish style, the main
house consists of 80 principal rooms under 2½ acres of red-tiled roof.
The property, which extends from the shore of Lake Worth to the Atlantic Ocean, includes an underground passageway, called "The Shell
Grotto," beneath South Ocean Boulevard, so that the family can stroll
from poolside to private beach and beach cabana without crossing the
street. The Bell Tower which rises dramatically above the rooftop of the
main house is an exact copy of the Giralda Tower in Seville, Spain. The
Myersons will inaugurate their new vacation home with a Christmas
party for 500 of the Palm Beach social set.

The latest "bud" to blossom on the Myerson family tree is baby Mireille
Myerson, 6 months old, the daughter of Mr. and Mrs. Henry G. Myerson, shown here with her mother, the former Alice Bloch of New York,
in the gardens of the family's summer home in Bar Harbor. Once again,
the family's fondness for playful, sound-alike names is apparent, for the
name "Mireille," pronounced the proper French way, to the ear becomes
"Miray," or the name of the Miray Corporation, which Baby Mireille's
grandfather founded in 1912. And without the Miray Corporation,
where would all this magnificence come from? *Mirabile ductu!* is all one
can say.

"Of course it was all my money," Granny Flo says to her interviewer. "I
didn't know it then, but it was. They've always been after my money, all of
them. They still are."

8

MIMI AND MARK SEGAL are sitting on the sofa in her office with the retouched photos of the Mireille Couple spread out on the coffee table in front of them. Mimi looks at one after another, and for several minutes neither says anything.

Finally, Mark says, "Do you notice something that's happened, Mimi, when we give the guy the scar? Something very interesting?"

"You tell me, Mark."

"It not only gives the guy a kind of mysterious personal *history*, the thing you said you wanted. It does something else. It makes him incredibly—there's no other word for it—it makes him incredibly *sexy*. I mean, don't get me wrong, guys don't turn me on. But this guy is now *sexy!* It's raw, naked, basic, animal *sex*, Mimi. I've never seen anything like it!"

"You're right. It makes him look hard and tough—the kind of hard edge he didn't have before."

"Hard, and tough, and mean—there's even a hint of *mean* sex there. I think this is going to turn women on, Mimi, turn 'em on in a way no ad campaign has ever turned women on before, I really do! Just to be sure, I brought a set of these prints home and showed 'em to my wife. She took one look and *shivered*, Mimi—shivered! She said, 'My God, what a hunk!' but it was the shiver that I noticed. Which has given me an idea."

"What's that?

"Since we're going to have to reshoot the first commercials anyway, if we decide to go with this, I thought, why not undress 'em both a little more?

Put him in a pair of bikini briefs. Put her in a teeny little maillot—she's got a great body. What do you think?"

"You mean the Calvin Klein bit? The Obsession bit, the nude bodies all twisted around each other? The naked men and women posed around Greek columns?"

"Not exactly that, of course. Different, but the same idea. Something that would capitalize on the sexiness that we've found is already there. Then, when he kisses her, it could be, like—wow! It would be like watching sexual intercourse on your twenty-three-inch screen! Mothers would scream at their children, 'Don't look!' "

Mimi thinks about this for a moment or two. Then she says, "No, I don't think so, Mark. And do you know why? First, because Calvin's already done it, and it would look as though we were copying him, no matter how different we managed to make it look. And second, because of taste. We've always been known for producing tasteful ads, and our customers are used to it, they like it, and I think they respect us for it. And don't forget, we'll be airing this commercial not just in New York and L.A. We'll be airing it in Salt Lake City, and Boise, and God knows the Bible Belt. But finally, I think it's because the scar makes him look sexy, yes, but just sexy *enough*. It's a case of less is more. I think we'd be overdoing it if we stripped them to their skivvies. The scar's enough. This is sexy, but it's also subtle."

"Sex can be subtle?"

She laughs. "Oh, yes. I'm older than you, Mark, and I know that sex can be subtle—very subtle, and it's nice that way. You sleep better afterward."

He scratches his red beard thoughtfully. "Well," he says. "Maybe you're right."

"I think I am in this case, Mark. I really think I am. I think we can achieve the same effect we want without the bulging crotch, if you see what I mean." She glances at her watch. "But look—I've got to run. I've got a kind of important lunch date. Tell the art department they've done a terrific job. Tell them, 'By George, I think we've got it! The man with the scar!' Get things in motion to reshoot the commercials. Get the best makeup man in town to do the scar. There used to be a man named Scott Cunningham, who specialized; I think he did the work for *Planet of the Apes*."

"What about the print ads?"

"The TV spots are more important. Once we've got the scar finalized for TV, we can see what the art department can do with airbrushing to match it. If that won't work, we reshoot the print ads, too!"

"Well . . . okay."

"You seem hesitant, Mark. What's wrong?"

"There's just one thing about this campaign that I hope you've thought of, Mimi."

"What's that?"

"This is turning out to be a ground-breaking campaign," he says, "now that we've got a man with a scar, and there's a certain amount of risk involved. We're going to be breaking a taboo."

"Taboo? What sort of taboo?"

"For years, advertising has observed a number of unwritten taboos. Self-imposed restrictions on the industry. For a long time, for instance, it was an unwritten rule that you didn't show a woman in a cigarette ad. Then, back in the thirties, Chesterfield broke the rule with a famous ad that showed a woman saying 'Blow some my way.' Until pretty recently, the same thing was true of liquor and beer advertising—you didn't show a woman with a glass in her hand, much less at her lips. For a long time you didn't use black people in ads—except in the black-oriented media. Now all that's changed, of course, but in this campaign we're taking on a new minority group: the physically disfigured, even the handicapped. It's pretty daring. I mean, even the Hathaway Shirt ads didn't show a man with an empty eye socket. This could backfire, Mimi. The scar could turn people off. That's the risk you're taking. I just hope you're aware of that."

"You think it's a big risk, Mark?"

"It could be—a very big risk, Mimi. A very, very big risk."

"But look: the whole idea of launching a perfume was a risk to begin with, wasn't it? Now we've taken the risk, we've got to take it all the way, don't we? So let's take it!" She jumps to her feet. "Oh, Mark," she says, "now I really am excited! Scared, but excited! Will you do me one more favor?"

"What's that?"

"Kiss me on the shoulder. Right here," she points.

"Kiss your shoulder?"

"It's for luck. I'm superstitious. This is going to be an important campaign, and I'm on my way to an important lunch. Whenever I'm about to start out on something important, I ask someone to kiss me on the left shoulder, for good luck. Would you mind?"

"Well," he hesitates. Then carefully, almost gingerly, he places a kiss on the left shoulder of the President and Chief Executive Officer of the Miray Corporation.

"Thank you! That should do it!" she says. "That's usually all it takes." Then she is off.

She has no sooner been seated at his table at the restaurant—sensing immediately that it has somehow all at once become *his* table, not hers, though her secretary made the reservation—than the captain appears carrying a telephone. "A Mr. Polakoff, sir, calling from Chicago," he says.

Michael Horowitz picks up the receiver. "Polakoff?" he says. "How are you, buddy? Now, listen, kiddo, I've made you my last offer. No, I don't want to hear what your price is, and I don't want to hear what your lawyer has to say. I want you to listen to me very carefully, kiddo. Are you ready to listen to me? . . . Then stop talking. Do you know what I want that twenty-five-by-ninety piece *for?* I want it for a *fountain,* kiddo—a fountain and a waterfall. That's right—it's called *landscaping,* and it's a mere *detail* of landscaping. Icing on the cake. And I think my offer is very generous, kiddo, because stop and think about it. When my hotel goes up on three sides of your twenty-five-by-ninety-foot lot, what're you gonna have? A vacant lot that's not gonna be worth shit, that's what—a vacant lot surrounded by a high rise. Why, you won't even have a parking lot! No, I'm not going to let you think about it. My offer is final, got that? Tell you what. It's now"—he glances at his watch—"it's now twelve thirty-six. You've got till five o'clock to fax me your agreement to the deal. If I don't hear from you by five o'clock, the deal's off—over, kaput, finished, no more hondeling. Got that, kiddo? And I'm talking five o'clock *my* time, not five o'clock *your* time, and five o'clock my time is four o'clock your time. Clear? Okay, kiddo. Take it easy. Talk to you later." He puts down the phone and smiles at Mimi. "I'll get my fountain," he says. "I'll get my waterfall." Then, "Well, where were we?"

"We really weren't anywhere," she says sweetly. "You haven't even said hello."

"Hi, kiddo," he says, brushing his lips against her cheek. "You're looking great."

"Thank you, Michael." She had forgotten about his habit of calling everybody kiddo. She studies his face for a moment or two, remembering.

Whatever it was, years ago, she had given it a name. My Michael feeling, she had called it. It came when he looked at her a certain way, when shadows seemed to cross his eyes, and they became wide and intense and luminous. That look left her feeling suddenly helpless, trembling, unable to control her thoughts and words. It was almost like an adrenaline rush, but instead of a surge of power and energy she felt a surge of powerlessness and inevitability. Once upon a time, the effect of the Michael feeling had been riveting, overpowering, but now, all these years later, she is certain that she has outgrown it, is immune to it. It is part of the dead past.

"Something to drink?" he says.

"A glass of white wine."

"Sounds good." He snaps his fingers for a waiter. "Two glasses of Chablis," he says.

A great deal of ink, as they say, has been used up in the press to describe Michael Horowitz. He has been called debonair. He has been called devious. He has been called rosy-cheeked, ruthless, rapacious, the Romeo of real estate, the Lothario of land deals. He has been called a wolf in preppy's clothing, the baby-faced bandit of Manhattan. He has been called the last honest man in the development business. He has been called totally untrustworthy. He is famous for saying, when looking over the plans for a competitor's project, "I could build it twice as tall in half the time for half the money." He has been called sly, feisty, scrappy, a tough fighter with street smarts. Diana Vreeland called him "*terribly* cute," and no one was quite sure what she meant by that. Did she mean she found him terrible or adorable? Asked to amplify on that appraisal, Mrs. Vreeland, who is the modern equivalent of the Oracle at Delphi, said, "He's *dreadfully* attractive." Then she added, "He's never *tired.*" Hmm.

Michael Horowitz has been called brash, bratty, brutal, and boyishly self-effacing. Within his organization, he is called "Mr. Wonderful." Is there a hint of sarcasm there? Among his enemies, he is often referred to as Michael Horrorwitz. He has also been called New York's Most Eligible Bachelor, and it has been said that when his lips affix themselves to a woman's mouth she becomes powerless to resist offering him more of herself. It is said that he receives mash notes from movie stars he has never met, among them Farrah Fawcett. One thing is certain: he is the premier deal-maker in New York City, if not in the entire country, if not the world.

One thing that Mimi notices is that, if he has made a pact with the devil to get where he is, part of the arrangement was to endow him with perpetual youth. He looks hardly different from the eager young man she met when he was a student at the Columbia School of Business thirty years ago. He has the same slightly crooked smile, revealing perfect teeth, and when he smiles, as he is smiling at her now, there are three dimples, one at each corner of his mouth, and one in his chin. Pink spots of color still highlight his cheekbones. Though never particularly tall—five nine in his stockinged feet—his physique is still trim and wiry, his stomach enviably flat. He is often seen running in Central Park, and Mimi is sure that he still works out religiously with his weights and exercise machines. In fact, as rich as he's become, he probably has his own private gym. He looks like a man with a private gym. If one did not know that he was a famous real-estate developer, one might take him for a ski instructor.

He still has the odd little habit of thrusting out his lower jaw just before he speaks and, simultaneously, tossing back a stray forelock of sandy hair that always seems about to fall across his eyes. It is a kind of personal tic. He does this now. "So," he says, "to what do I owe this singular pleasure? It's been a long time between drinks, kiddo."

"I'll get right to the point," she says. "I want to know why you're buying so much Miray stock."

He smiles again. "So you've noticed that? Well, for one thing, I happen to think you run a damn good company. For another, I hear that you're about to come out with a hot new product."

"Where did you hear that, Michael? Nothing's been announced."

"Listen," he says, "this is a small town. Word gets around. New York is a village. Only about two hundred people live here, and we both know them all. Remember how they used to talk about New York's Four Hundred? That was a hundred years ago, when New York was a lot smaller than it is today. Today, New York may be bigger, but it's also gotten smaller. Today, there are only about two hundred people who count in this town."

"Who are these two hundred people, Michael?"

"Well, kiddo, you're one, and I'm another, and that leaves about a hundred and ninety-eight others." He shrugs. "You want, I could make up a list."

"It would be helpful if I knew who's been leaking information about my company."

"You're denying you've got a hot new product in the works?"

"Not denying—nor confirming."

"Well, let's just say I heard it from one person or another—one of those two hundred people we both know. Hell, I don't even remember who it was that told me. A new perfume, I think they said it was."

"You own over four percent of us already. That's a lot of shares."

He whistles, as though genuinely surprised. "No kidding! Have I got that much? Well, kiddo, I'm a rich guy now, and when I buy I tend to buy big. Anything wrong with that?"

"No, but when you acquire as much as five percent of a company, SEC regulations require that you file a public notice of intent."

"Yeah, I guess I did know that."

"You're sure you're not planning some sort of takeover bid? Because if you are—"

"Takeover? Why would I want to take you over? What do I know about the beauty business? The beauty business is something I know zilch about. But I do know that whatever it is you're wearing, you smell awfully nice. Is that the new stuff?"

He is trying, she knows, to draw more information out of her, and to change the subject, all at the same time. "Shall we look at the menu," she says coolly, picking it up.

"I know what I'm going to have," he says. "A bowl of Kellogg's Raisin Bran flakes and a glass of cranberry juice."

"*Bran flakes*—at Le Cirque?"

"Don't you remember?" he says. "When you used to come over to my apartment at the grungy end of Riverside Drive? You were always bringing me things like bran flakes and bottles of cranberry juice. The bran flakes, you said, were because I needed roughage. The cranberry juice was supposed to be good for my liver."

"That must have been during my health-food phase," she says. "I've grown much fonder of caviar since then. Shall we start with some of their Beluga?"

"And my socks. Remember how you were always rearranging my goddam socks? You said my socks should be lined up in the drawer according to color. I guess that was your organizational ability showing through, even then."

"Probably." If he is hoping to evoke a girlish blush from her over these intimate memories of a long-ago relationship, he has taken the wrong tack. That eighteen-year-old girl of thirty years ago was an altogether different person, a girl she barely remembers.

"You still wore braces on your teeth. Remember how you hated those braces? I thought they were kind of cute."

"Really? Was I still wearing braces then? Well, perhaps."

"We've both come a long way from those days, haven't we, kiddo? In those days, you were just a shy little thing, half afraid of your own shadow. And I was so—"

The maitre d' appears again, carrying the telephone in his hand, but Michael motions him away with a wave. "No more calls, Charlie," he says.

"—And I was so much in love with you."

"I'm going to have the veal," she says.

Further downtown, at a less fashionable eating place, Granny Flo Myerson is having lunch with her friend Rose Perlman. They are lunching at the coffee shop at Altman's. "You can trust Altman's," Granny Flo said when making the date. "I don't think their menu has changed one bit since I was a girl. Now that Schrafft's has gone, all that's left is Altman's." They have both ordered the tomato surprise. The surprise is that the tomato is stuffed with cottage cheese.

"I didn't intend to lunch out today," Granny Flo is saying. "What I'm trying to do is avoid Edwee. He keeps calling me and *calling* me, wanting to come by and *see* me. He called this morning, *insisting* he had to see me today. I told him no, I can't, I'm busy. I told him I'm going out to lunch and don't know when I'll be back. That's when I called you, in case he came by anyway, got the hotel to let him upstairs, and caught me in a lie. We can spend the whole afternoon here, if you'd like, and do some shopping. You can tell me what we're looking at. Is this my salad fork? Yes. Edwee wants to put me in a nursing home."

"*What?* He can't do that, can he, Flo?"

"That's what he says he's going to do. He says he's going to have me put on probation, or something like that. He's got these forty lawyers working on it."

"But that's *awful*, Flo! You need to see a lawyer—fast. Isn't your grand-daughter's husband some sort of big-shot lawyer?"

"Yes, but everybody says that Mimi's mad as hell at me. I said something that wasn't particularly nice to Alice the other night."

"Who's Alice?"

"Mimi's mother, Alice."

"Oh, yes. The one that drinks."

"That's right. Honestly, Rose, I think you were smart or lucky, or maybe both, never to have had children. Sometimes I wish I'd never had any. But tell me something, Rose. With no children, what do you do for aggrava-tion?"

"How is your grandmother?" Michael says. "As ditsy as ever?"

"Oh, yes. Granny never changes."

"But let me tell you something about that old belle," he says. "The old belle is crazy like a fox. When I was helping her break up that place in Maine, she had her head over my shoulder every minute, counting every penny. And when I was selling the Madison Avenue house for her, she suddenly said to me, 'What about the air rights?' I mean, is that crazy, or is that smart? *Air rights!* She knows about air rights, for Chrissake!"

"And now you've bought Grandpa's Palm Beach place."

"That's right. So you heard about that."

"Well, it was in the *New York Times*. I also heard that Grandpa's founda-tion wanted ten million for it, and that you got it for four-point-two."

He wrinkles his nose. "It was more than that," he says. "Look, that place had been on the market for years. Nobody wanted it. It wasn't that I was trying to jew them down, kiddo. I made an offer. The foundation dropped their price. I upped my offer. We met in the middle. I bought it the way anybody else would buy a house. In fact, I felt I was doing the old man's foundation a favor, by taking it off their hands."

"You probably were."

"But it's funny. I was thinking of you the other day—the day you called me, in fact. It was like thought transference. About the house."

"What about it?"

"The place is pretty run-down, standing empty all those years. It needs a lot of work. I was thinking, maybe I'll see if Mimi can help me put it back together the way it was in the good old days."

"You wouldn't like it the way it was. It was hideously ugly. It was filled with palm trees, and there was a dining room table made out of mosaic from St. Peter's in Rome. It was the ugliest table I've ever seen, and Grandpa liked to boast that it cost fifty thousand dollars. That's all the furniture was —ugly and expensive."

"Then maybe you could help me fix it up the way it *should* look. Think about it, kiddo. You've always had great taste. You always had taste, and you always had class. Could you, Mimi? Come down to Palm Beach for a few days, be my guest, and help me pick out some things? Me, I've got no taste, and no class. I never will. But you do. Would you give me a hand with the place?"

"I hardly think that would be appropriate, Michael."

"Why not?" He shrugs. "Well, think about it, anyway."

"Why would you want such a big place? Just one person. Why would you need twenty bedrooms?"

"Sentiment, maybe. Maybe I thought it would be nice to own a little piece of something that was yours."

"But it wasn't my place. It was Grandpa's place. I was never in it more than once or twice. And Grandpa wasn't very nice to you, if you remember."

His gaze at her is open and steady. "So you do remember some things," he says. "That's right. He wasn't nice to me at all. Or even to you."

"Is it to own a little piece of me that you're buying up Miray shares?"

"Could be," he says. "It's possible."

"Or is it to get revenge on Grandpa?"

Jutting his chin and tossing back the wayward lock of hair, he says, "Also possible. You won't know which, will you, unless you take me up on my invitation to Palm Beach."

"That's out of the question, Michael."

"Because of that shegetz you married? I still find you very attractive, you know. You're still the most beautiful, desirable woman in the world to me. Nobody else ever came close. Nobody else made me eat bran flakes. Nobody else made me see white stars."

"Good afternoon, Mr. Myerson," Patrick, the Carlyle's doorman, says, holding open the cab door. "But I'm afraid your mother has gone out for the afternoon."

"I know that, Patrick," Edwee says. "But there are a couple of things she wants me to see to in the apartment." He presses a folded bill into Patrick's gloved hand.

"Thank *you*, Mr. Myerson!"

George is on the front desk. "Good afternoon, George," Edwee says. "Mother had to go out to lunch, and she asked me to check on a couple of things in the apartment. Can I borrow a key?"

"Certainly, sir." Another folded bill is pressed into George's hand and acknowledged with a smile.

Upstairs, Edwee lets himself into the apartment, and immediately Itty-Bitty appears at his mother's bedroom door and begins to bark, a series of sharp, high-pitched yips.

"Oh, shut up, you stupid animal," Edwee says.

This visit amounts to something of a feat of daring on Edwee's part. Or perhaps one should say a series of feats, for this is not the first visit he has made to the apartment, alone, when he was certain she was elsewhere. He has attempted, in fact, to establish something of a pattern of visits, and it is part of a plan so that, if Patrick and George are ever questioned about it, they will say, truthfully, "Oh, Mr. Myerson visited his mother's apartment often." That way, responsibility for the breach of security will fall on their shoulders, not Edwee's.

He opens the door to his mother's kitchen, and a roach scuttles across the floor and buries itself in a crevice beneath the sink. Even at the Carlyle—roaches. Since roaches are not known for celibacy, Edwee is certain that this one has numerous relatives housed elsewhere in the building's innards. The whole city is roach-infested, he thinks, even the best addresses. And this gives him an idea for an article, perhaps for *Art & Antiques*, on how New York has fallen off in recent years, to the point where even the finest buildings have become afflicted by these crawly creatures.

"Far from eremitic," he writes in his mind, "the universal roach thrives today against a backdrop of brocades and bibelots, mousseline and marquetry, undaunted by the grandeur of *le gratin.*" He likes it. It scans. He likes those alliterations—"brocades and bibelots," "mousseline and marquetry." He must write that down when he gets back to his desk.

Itty-Bitty still yaps at him shrilly from the kitchen door.

He is still toying with the idea of somehow putting his mother out of her misery. Some sort of poison would seem to be the best way. He opens the door to her small refrigerator. All that it contains is a bag of Goldfish crackers. It would seem difficult to inject poison into a cracker. Perhaps he could prepare some delicacy for her in his kitchen and present it to her. But would she eat it? No, she would probably be suspicious, since he has never cooked anything for her before. Then there is her drinks cart in the living room with its various decanters, but the trouble is that his mother does not drink. The liquor is there for friends who visit her, and of course for the hotel staff who obviously help themselves to it. A poisoned decanter of whiskey would only end up polishing off one of his mother's friends, or one of the night maids.

He returns to the living room, with Itty-Bitty yapping at his heels.

There is the Goya, his Goya.

He thinks: Francisco de Goya y Lucientes (1746–1828); street fighter, possible murderer, heavy drinker, vagabond part-time bullfighter, cartoonist, influenced by Tiepolo, discovered by Mengs, official court portraitist to four successive monarchs of Spain, who never seemed to notice how he mocked them in his work, how degenerate and ineffectual he made them look, how mercilessly he satirized them on his canvases, turning them into parodies of grandeur—genius.

This particular portrait is of the Duchess of Osuna, one of several she commissioned him to do, indicating that she must have admired the way he portrayed her—looking arrogant and stupid, and far from beautiful, with small, dull eyes, a large nose, a small, cruel mouth and bony outsize hands covered with rings. How had Goya been able to keep from laughing out loud at Her Grace when he had her in that pose? Genius again. *"Usted es divina . . . divina,"* Edwee can hear the Master murmuring to his subject.

That masterpiece belongs to him—and now Philippe de Montebello has seen it and must be itching to get his hands on it. It seems almost an obscenity that the eyes of the Metropolitan's director should ever have come into contact with that painting—those grasping, greedy eyes.

Now Edwee does something he has never done before. Moving a set of library steps to the wall, he climbs to the top step and lifts the painting from the wall. It is not easy. The portrait of the duchess is about a meter in width and two meters high, and, in its frame, it is heavy. But Edwee manages to get it down, sets it on the floor, and places it with its face against the wall. He has never seen the back of the painting before, and now he studies it.

The back of the canvas is dusty and threaded with tiny cobwebs. It has not been off the wall in fifteen years, and, indeed, the space on the wall where it hung is marked by a pale rectangle against the yellower paint. The back of the canvas, as well as the frame, is covered with squiggles of almost indecipherable handwriting, some of it in Spanish, some in English: verifications, notations of provenance and ownership, as well as official customs and export duty stamps in French and English. This painting, Edwee knows, is one of three his mother purchased from the art dealer Joseph Duveen and his aesthetic sidekick, Bernard Berenson. His mother had disliked Duveen, distrusted him, suspected him of charging inflated prices—which was certainly true—but had been forced to use him to acquire certain pieces that she wanted. Some of this writing may be in Duveen's or Berenson's hand, Edwee supposes, and he removes the small magnifying glass he always carries in his vest pocket and examines the various notations more closely. Much of the ink is very faded, but he suddenly spots, sure enough, the handwritten words, "vrai—B. Berenson." The authentication.

For a brief, quite ridiculous moment, Edwee considers simply carrying the painting out of the apartment with him on its cord—it is rightfully his—

down the elevator, out into the street, into a taxi, and home. But this he knows would be impossible. Lackeys such as Patrick and George might be bribable in terms of letting him into the apartment, but they would certainly draw the line at permitting him to remove anything, particularly a large oil painting. Even if Edwee could double-talk his, and the Goya's, way past George and Patrick, its loss would be noticed immediately—that pale rectangle on the wall. The police would be summoned, the insurance company would be notified, the entire staff of the building would be questioned, and either Patrick or George would be forced to reveal that Mr. Edwin Myerson had been in the apartment on the day of the crime and had been seen carrying off a large, heavy, rectangular object. The jig would be up. Then would come the ghastly publicity, then the lie-detector test, then the search warrant for Edwee's house. Next would come the trial, and the conviction—for grand theft, not even a white-collar crime—and the sentencing to the New York State Penitentiary at Ossining, and the years spent over a workbench making license plates. It would never work.

But, all at once, as he stares at those faint little squiggles of handwriting on the back of the canvas, the idea comes to him. *Of course!* Why had he never thought of it before? Simply because he had never thought of taking the picture off the wall and examining the back of it! Like all great notions, it was splendidly simple. Now, almost breathless with excitement over his plan, Edwee lifts the painting, mounts the steps again, and rehangs the Duchess of Osuna on her hook. Appropriate telephone calls must be made, just one or two. All the little details can be worked out later, though there isn't much time. He strides toward the front door of the apartment.

The little dog tries to block his way, still barking noisily. Crouching on its forepaws, its rear end in the air, it snarls angrily at him. Suddenly it leaps forward, seizes his trouser leg between its teeth, and, with one sharp pull, succeeds in breaking the threads that secure the cuff to the trouser leg. Edwee gives the dog a sharp kick in the ribs, and the animal runs howling into its mistress's bedroom.

Now Edwee knows what people mean when they say they feel as if they were walking on air. It is sheer euphoria, and Edwee marches—skips, floats, soars—out of the apartment, down the corridor to the elevators, where he jabs the button several times.

"Did you find everything in order, Mr. Myerson?" George asks him when he reaches the lobby.

"In quite perfect order, George," he says warmly. "Yes, everything is quite perfect, thank you."

"Taxi, Mr. Myerson?" Patrick asks him at the door.

"No, thank you, Patrick. It's such a fine afternoon, I think I'll walk."

But this is a lie. Edwee is simply too impatient to wait for Patrick to

whistle for a cab. He will find an east-bound taxi on 70th Street. Loping
down Madison Avenue, one trouser cuff flapping in the breeze, Edwee Myerson sings—sings to himself on a perfect New York summer afternoon.

"I just want you to know that I'll fight any attempt to take over my
company," Mimi says. She is trying to return this conversation to the level
of the sort of business discussion she had originally intended it to be. "I've
already taken the matter up with legal counsel. I'm quite serious, Michael.
You see, I don't want this company just for myself. I plan to retire in a few
more years. I want it for my son. I want it for Badger."

"Don't give me that crap. You love the business you're in; that's why
you've been so successful. You love the glamour, the power, the money—all
of it. It's like Christmas. What's Christmas for, kiddo? It's not just for
giving presents, it's for getting them. It's for reaping the rewards of being
good all year. That's what people like you and me are in business for—seeing
the results pile up. People like you and me, we like it to be Christmas every
day. Do you remember saying that? Because that's what you said to me
once, a long time ago."

"Really, Michael, I—"

"And how is your son?" he says, and she watches as his eyes seem to grow
wider, darker, and all at once there it is again, unbidden, the Michael feeling, the feeling she thought she had outgrown, become immune and insensitive to. She quickly averts her eyes, and to hide a certain trembling that she
feels in her fingertips, she reaches for her bag and gloves to go.

"Badger's fine," she says. "But now I've really got to get back to my
office."

As they are leaving the restaurant, she sees her husband at a corner table.
He looks worried, staring darkly at the tablecloth, his napkin clutched in one
hand. The young woman with him looks troubled, too, even angry, and her
hands are balled into fists on the table. Yes, she is pretty, blond hair, cut
straight, with bangs. Well, he has good taste in women, at least. She thinks
wildly: Why did I choose Le Cirque? Was it because that was where I
overheard Edwee say he'd seen them? Or was this restaurant Michael's
suggestion? She can no longer remember. Why would they choose this place
for their rendezvous, if that's what it is? Le Cirque is certainly not the place
one would choose if one wanted to be inconspicuous. She turns away
quickly, not wanting to catch his eye. At least this nameless woman now has
a face.

"Someone you know?" Michael asks.

"No. I thought I did, but no."

What have they been discussing? she asks herself. Has she just told him that she thinks she's pregnant? Is she the type who would try to trap a man with a time-worn ploy like that?

"Come to Palm Beach with me," Michael says. "Do you know why I've been buying your stock? Because I suddenly knew I had to see you again, and this was a quick way to do it. Remember the little white stars? I love you, Mimi. You never loved that shegetz you married, did you?"

Mark Segal is waiting for her at the elevator and follows her down the corridor to her office. "We've got a little problem," he says.

"Oh? What's that?"

"I've been on the phone with Dirk Gordon's agent."

"Who's Dirk Gordon?"

"Our male model." He follows her into her office. "His agent wants a hundred-thousand-dollar bonus for the scar. He says it could adversely affect his career."

"No!" She slams her fist on her desk. She is still under the stimulus of her meeting with Michael. "No," she repeats. "What career? He didn't have any career until we found him! There are a hundred other models in New York we could use just as well. Tell his agent that, and tell him—tell him he's got till five o'clock to drop this demand, or else the whole deal's off."

"I like a boss who makes quick decisions," Mark says.

Mimi's secretary is standing at the door. "You have a call from Charles, the captain at the Le Cirque restaurant."

Mimi thinks: Did I leave something behind? She picks up the telephone.

"I have a very grave apology to make to you, Miss Myerson," he says. "I feel we may have caused you great embarrassment. You see, I just had a call from Mr. Horowitz, and he was quite upset, and quite rightly so. I had no idea, you see, that Mr. Bradford Moore was your husband. Had I known, I would have alerted you that Mr. Moore would also be lunching here today. But I have spoken with my waiters, and they are very confident that Mr. Moore did not see you lunching with Mr. Horowitz. Still, I do apologize, Miss Myerson."

"My husband," she says quickly, "was lunching with a client, a Mrs. Sturtevant, whose divorce he is handling. Mr. Horowitz and I were lunching on another business matter. My husband and I were both aware that we were lunching in the same place but chose not to interrupt each other's business meetings. No apology is necessary, I assure you."

"I see. Thank you, Miss Myerson. Le Cirque appreciates your patronage."

Returning to her apartment, Fleurette Myerson makes her way across her living room, touching the familiar objects with outstretched hands, with Itty-Bitty leaping happily at her heels. Suddenly she encounters an unfamiliar object. The library steps are out of place. Someone has moved them against the wall.

It cannot have been one of the maids. The maids come in the morning to do up the rooms, and the night maid appears promptly at seven to turn down her bed. It was either Nonie or Edwee. She sits down in her favorite chair, thinking what to do next. Then she picks up the hotel phone.

"Yes, Mrs. Myerson?"

"Were either of my children in my apartment this afternoon?"

"Mr. Edwin Myerson came by for a few minutes, ma'am," the clerk says.

She replaces the receiver on its hook. Now what to do? Is there no one left in this family whom she can trust or turn to?

Then she remembers Mr. Greenway, who seemed so kind. Perhaps he will have a suggestion as to what she ought to do. She could tempt him by remembering more of the things that were in her husband's diary. She could tell him *exactly* how Adolph forced his brother Leo out of the business, which is one of the things Mr. Greenway seems to want to know. Mimi seems fond of this young man. Perhaps he can provide her with a bridge to peace with Mimi.

9

IN HER APARTMENT at 200 East 66th Street, Nonie Myerson and Roger Williams are in her bedroom, with the curtains drawn, where they have just made love. Roger has shifted his weight to one side and has lighted a cigarette. Normally, Nonie does not allow anyone to smoke in her apartment, but of course Roger is an exception.

Making love is perhaps the wrong term, because love had very little to do with it. Nonie considers herself a sensible woman, a realistic woman, and is cynical enough to know the difference between a sexual act and love. The sexual act is a glandular function, and love is—well, love is something Nonie has learned to distrust over the years; it has betrayed her too often. Many men have made love to Nonie Myerson and some of them have said they were in love with her, and a few of these she has thought she loved. But this is quite different. She does not love Roger, and Roger does not love her. What they have performed together is more like a business handshake, a quid pro quo. He makes love to her (What else to call it? Every other term that comes to mind is vulgar.) because he assumes she expects him to, and she lets him because she knows that is what he assumes. That is all. Oh, she admits that she finds him attractive. He is good-looking in a hard-boiled sort of way, lean and well-built, with chiseled pectorals, tight buttocks, and long, splendidly muscled legs. What older woman wouldn't be delighted to be taken to bed by a virile, youthful specimen like that? And, to be sure, when they are making love, he whispers husky comments to her such as "You're terrific. . . . You're so beautiful. . . ." But Nonie is not fool enough to be taken in by any of that. That does not add up to love. No, each wants the other for different reasons. She wants him for his demonstrable ability—by making a call to Zurich, then to Chicago, in quick succession—to make eight thousand dollars a minute. He is her golden opportunity to get back into the business world, where she belongs, because business is in her blood, inherited, no doubt, from her father. And Roger wants her because, let's face it—Nonie most certainly does—she is a Myerson, and a likely avenue to the kind of money he needs to put his talents to work. The sex is incidental, just a way of demonstrating that they trust each other, want to work together, that each wants something that the other has; a pleasant prelude to exploring more serious possibilities, a handshake.

This afternoon, of course, she could tell that his heart wasn't really in it. His performance was halfhearted, even listless, and she is sure he didn't come, only pretended to. And this, no doubt, is because she had been unable to bring him any good news. He lies beside her on the bed, naked under the single sheet, his erection gone, the cigarette drooping from between his lips. She touches his shoulder with a fingertip to reassure him and says, "That was lovely, darling."

He swings his bare legs over the side of the bed and sits there for a moment, shaping his ash on the edge of an ashtray. Then he says, "Let's face it, Nonie. This isn't working out."

She sits up as well. "What do you *mean?*" she says. "What isn't working out?"

"It doesn't look as though we're going to get any money out of your mother."

"Just be *patient*, darling! These things take time. I've got a few more aces up my sleeve. I know how to work on her."

"I don't like the way things are going."

"She's always come through before! It just takes time."

"What if she's telling the truth? What if she just doesn't have the money?"

"How could she *not* have the money? She got trust funds from each one of her Guggenheim uncles, as well as from her father, and she had seven uncles! Daddy . . . dipped into them a bit before he died, but Mimi reestablished them for her. She got nearly a third of Daddy's Miray shares, and think what they must be worth now! She's loaded, Roger; she's the richest Myerson of us all, except perhaps for Mimi."

"And Mimi is—I mean, I suppose there's no point in trying to approach Mimi?"

She hesitates. "The truth," she says, "is that Mimi's never liked me."

"Why not?"

"It's because of her mother, because of Alice. Alice has always been such a . . . *difficult* woman. None of the family could ever get along with her.

Alice is an alcoholic, and she was always coming around, hat in hand, begging for money from everyone—from Mother, from Edwee, from me. Don't ask me why. Daddy paid Henry a good salary, but he and Alice never seemed to have any money. Because of her drinking, I suppose. She'd trot little Mimi around—literally, from door to door—talking about how poor they all were, asking for money. It got so we'd all practically run and hide when we saw Alice coming, with her little girl in tow! Mimi grew up resenting us. It's not that Mother and Daddy weren't generous with them. Why, they bought presents for Mimi that were nicer—nicer than anything they ever gave to me! Alice just couldn't seem to handle money. But Mimi's very protective of her mother, and she's well taken care of now."

He is shaking his head back and forth.

She leans back against the pillows. "Isn't it ironic?" she says.

"Isn't what ironic?"

"If *I'd* taken over the company after Henry died, I could have been where Mimi is now—in the driver's seat!"

"Yeah. Well, you didn't, and this whole thing isn't working out, Nonie."

"*It will!* Just give me a few more days, Roger, to work on Mother. Let me work on this nursing home thing. She's terrified of going into a nursing home, and if I can make her think—"

He is still shaking his head. "This is no way to get a business started, with a lot of goddam threats, with a blackmail—"

"Who's *threat*ening? I'm just saying—"

"You told me that getting the backing from your mother would be a piece of cake, Nonie. It's turning out to be a goddam can of worms. I'm going to start looking for a new financial partner."

"You can't!" she cries in a panic. "You can't do that! I'm your financial partner!"

"Yeah, well, where's the financing? Look, I need to get this thing off the ground. I can't sit around, day after day, twiddling my thumbs, waiting for you to—"

"Just a few more days. Give me through the weekend. Give me till Monday. I'll have it by then, I *promise.*"

He sits there, with his back to her, still shaking his head.

He can't, she thinks. He can't back out now; they've only just begun. She still knows too little about him. He is terribly difficult to reach. All she has for him is an unpublished telephone number, which he has cautioned her to give out to no one, and when she calls this number it is invariably answered by a disembodied male voice, not even his own, on a machine that says, "You have reached five-five-five-one-eight-eight-oh. If you wish to leave a message . . ." She has not been to his house, doesn't even know where he lives, though the telephone prefix indicates it is somewhere in lower Manhattan. Why this secrecy? He has hinted that it has something to do with an old girlfriend who has been bothering him. She does not know whether he is married or not, though he wears no wedding band. He has been very unforthcoming with details about his past, his childhood, his education, his family, though she has told him everything about hers. All she knows about him is that she met him three weeks ago at a cocktail party, that they happened to leave at the same time, that it was raining, that he suggested they share a cab and he would drop her off, that she asked him up for a nightcap, that he told her he was a foreign currency trader, temporarily between jobs, looking for backing for a new venture, and then one thing led to another, and here they are.

He stands up, stubbing out his cigarette in the ashtray. "Sorry," he says, "but it's no go. I'm going to find another partner."

"You can't!" she screams. And then, "You mean you're going out to look for another rich woman, who'll let you fuck her, who'll try to help you the way I've been trying. And then if she doesn't help you just like *that*, you'll walk out on her? Well, you can't do that to me, you gigolo bastard! I'm not going to let you do that to me, you gigolo bastard, because you and I have an agreement. We agreed to be partners in this, full partners, fifty-fifty. We have a contract!"

With his back to her, he bends forward slightly, spreads his cheeks with his fingertips, and farts. "So much for your contract," he says. Then he walks into the bathroom, and a moment later, she hears the shower running.

"He was very—evasive," Mimi says to Badger. "That's the only word I can think of to describe it. Evasive. He kept trying to change the subject. He kept trying to play dumb. 'Is *that* how much of your stock I own? Golly!' He's very clever. I don't trust him, Badger. I genuinely think he's after us. In fact, I'm positive he is."

He nudges his chair closer to her desk and rests his shirt-sleeved elbows on her desktop. "I've been thinking about this," he says, "and I think I've come up with a plan that could stop him in his tracks."

"What is it, Badger?"

"Privatization."

"You mean—?"

"Exactly. We go private. We become a private company again."

"But we have thousands of stockholders, Badger."

"There are two ways of doing it," he says. "The first would be for the family to offer to buy back the stock from individual stockholders—at an attractive price, of course, that would have to be somewhat higher than the market. I don't need to say that this would cost us a lot of money. But there's another way, besides a buyback, that would be much simpler . . . and cheaper."

"Oh? What's that?"

"Telescope the stock. I'm talking about a reverse split. It's not unheard-of. Instead of buying back publicly owned shares, we'd convert them. Every one thousand shares of old stock, for instance, would be converted into one new share. Holders of less than a thousand shares would be paid in cash for their holdings—again, at an attractive price. Right now, individual members of the family own, collectively, about thirty percent of our stock. Various family trusts vote another ten percent. That leaves sixty percent, more or less, in public hands. But remember that a lot of our stock is owned by people who own just one or two hundred shares, or odd lots. With these small shareholders bought out, the family would be majority owners of the company, and nobody could touch us. Also, a reverse split would bring the number of stockholders to under three hundred people, and you know what that means."

"The SEC . . ."

"Exactly. A company with less than three hundred stockholders is not subject to SEC regulations. The company would be deregistered. Do you realize how much money that would save us annually? Hundreds of thousands saved each year, by not having to report to the SEC, and not having to comply with the regulatory requirements of being a public company."

"I see what you mean," his mother says carefully.

"So several things would be accomplished all at once. The family would control the company, with no regulatory agency hanging over its shoulder telling us what to do. The company's management decisions would be simplified by not having to defer to a lot of different outside stockholder interests. With a larger share of the company in our hands, we could find ourselves a good deal richer. Also, if at some future time we decided to sell this company, we could name our price. And, finally, Mr. Michael Horowitz, with his lousy four-plus percent of the stock, would find himself out in the cold, wondering what hit him."

"Byzantine," she says. "Byzantine, the way your mind works, Badger."

Badger sits back in his chair, looking pleased with himself. "Thanks, Mom," he says.

"Of course a reverse split would have to be approved by a majority of stockholders. Which may not be easy."

"But which may not be that hard, either. How many small stockholders even read that proxy material they get in the mail? Most of those proxies go straight in the wastebasket."

"But a failure to vote is counted as a vote *against* the proposal."

"I've thought of that, too. It's all a question of how the proxy is worded.

If it's worded as a vote against privatization, those who don't vote could push our plan through. Meanwhile, the holders who have large blocks of shares have nothing to lose, either way. Whichever way the company goes, the dollar amounts of their investment stay the same. In fact, we may be able to persuade some of these large shareholders that they have a lot to gain from a negative vote."

"And Mr. Michael Horowitz? I have a feeling he reads his proxies very carefully."

He smiles. "That," he says, "is when the fun will start. That's when things may begin to heat up a bit. That's when we'll see what his true colors are—if he starts trying to line up other stockholders against our plan. That's when we'll see if this is going to be a little scuffle, or an all-out war."

"It's going to cost us money, isn't it."

He spreads his hands. "Sure. Some. But worth it, maybe?"

"How much? How much exactly?"

"Look," he says, "I haven't done a feasibility study on this, you know. I'm just suggesting this as an idea—an idea that would make it impossible for *anybody* to take us over. Horowitz, or anybody else. An idea whose time has maybe come. You see, this is what I think. I think that when you took this company public back in nineteen sixty-two, it was a brilliant move—at the time. You saved us from what looked like certain bankruptcy. But this isn't 'sixty-two, it's 'eighty-seven—the age of the takeover. Privatization could be a second brilliant move, in light of what's happening to companies like ours today. Look at Revlon, Germaine Monteil, and Charles of the Ritz—all bought by Ron Perelman in the last two years. Look at Giorgio, bought by Avon. As far as financing goes, we could get it. We'd have no trouble finding somebody on Wall Street who'd underwrite us. Who were the underwriters in 'sixty-two?"

"Goldman, Sachs."

"Hit some of those boys again!"

"All right," she says. "Let's go ahead. Let's do a feasibility study. Find out how many major stockholders are involved. Find out how many small shareholders we'd need to buy out. Find out how much it will cost. Sound out an underwriter. Find out—"

"Okay, but there are two things we've got to agree on before I even leave this room."

"What's that?"

"First, this has got to be kept absolutely confidential—between you and me, period. If word hit the street that we're even *thinking* of such a move, our stock would go crazy. No one should even know that you and I have had this conversation. I mean, for the time being I wouldn't even tell Dad."

"I agree."

"And, second, every family shareholder, at some point down the line, must be in unanimous agreement with the plan, if we're going to pull it off at all. *Every* family shareholder."

"Including the Leo cousins, you mean."

"*Exactly.* Those mysterious Leo cousins none of us has ever met. We're going to need to get them on our team."

She sighs. "The damned Leo cousins, who've been taught from the time they were in diapers that I run a kind of evil empire. That anything the Adolph Myerson branch of the family wants to do has got to be to their disadvantage. That if we're for it, they're against it. That's going to be a tough one, Badger."

"The Leo cousins are going to have to be reintroduced to their Adolph cousins. Someone's going to have to raise a white flag. They're going to have to be persuaded, one at a time, that coming back into the family fold will not only be to their *distinct* advantage, but that it may also save their skins —vis à vis what our friend Horowitz seems to be up to."

"And how, pray, do we accomplish that?"

"The Leo cousins all have names. They have addresses and telephone numbers. Quite a few of them live right here in Manhattan. Some of them we may have been passing on the street, every day."

"But how do we approach them?"

Slowly, he points his finger at his mother. "Who's the salesperson *extraordinaire?*" he says. "Who's the famous charmer, the famous diplomat? Who's the Great Persuader in this company?"

She laughs, a little uncertainly.

"And what better way to persuade the mysterious cousins than by explaining to them that you're about to launch the most exciting new fragrance in the world?"

"Oh, Badger, do you really think it will be?"

"I said you've got to persuade them that it will be."

"But what if it flops? Mark's very nervous about this ad campaign. It could backfire on us—the disfigured face. If that happens, we could be left with fifty million dollars' worth of—"

"Shit on our face. But we're not going to let that happen, are we?"

Mimi hesitates. "But what if—" she begins, "—what if Michael is telling the truth? What if he isn't after us at all? We'd be going to all this effort and expense for nothing."

His look at her is incredulous. "What are you talking about?" he says.

"I mean he told me he has no interest in the beauty business. Doesn't understand it, has no interest in it."

He continues to look at her wide-eyed. "And you *believed* that?"

"Well, there's a possibility he's sincere, isn't there?"

"Michael Horowitz, *sincere?* The guy's famous for dirty deals!"

"But what if he's just playing games with us, a kind of cat-and-mouse game, Badger?"

"But what the hell *for?* From what I know of this guy's reputation, he doesn't go into a deal for fun and games. When he buys something, it's because he *wants* it."

"But he denied this. He said—"

"I can't believe I'm listening to this!" he says. "A minute ago, you were all fired up about this. All at once you're waffling!"

"I'm not waffling! I'm just saying—"

"A minute ago, I heard you say you didn't trust this character! I heard you say you were *positive* he was after us! Now you're saying he's maybe a good little Boy Scout, after all!"

"I did *not* say he was a Boy Scout! I said, can we give him the benefit of the doubt?"

"Playing devil's advocate? For that little kike bastard?"

"Don't ever use that term in front of me!" Suddenly she is very angry. This is something she is famous for never doing, losing her temper.

"Well, that's what he is, isn't he? His father was a caterer in Queens!"

"And *my* grandfather was a housepainter in the Bronx," she says, just as furiously. "Is that better than a caterer in Queens?"

"Yes, god damn it!" he shouts. From the anteroom outside Mimi's office, there is the sound of Mrs. Hanna, Mimi's secretary, rather conspicuously clearing her throat. Mimi hears this, rises quickly from her desk, goes to the door, and closes it, leaning her back against it.

"Is this something they taught you at Yale?" she says through clenched teeth. "To talk like a bigot and a snob?"

"They taught me to recognize a lowlife when I see one!"

"Michael Horowitz is more of a gentleman than you are. And a better Jew."

"Me? A Jew? Don't give me that crap!"

"Why do you think you weren't taken into Skull and Bones? Because you're a Jew. The captain of the golf team, but you weren't taken into Skull and Bones!"

"You're full of *crap!* You know why I wasn't tapped for Bones? Because Tony Beard blackballed me—after I saw him move his ball from a bad lie in the semifinals, that's why! If the Myerson half of me is Jewish, the other half is Protestant. And I've never been inside a synagogue in my life."

"You might try. You might learn something, because you're a Jew. Jewishness comes from the mother. It comes from the mother's milk."

"I can't *believe* I'm listening to this crap," he says. "Next thing you're going to tell me is that you breast-fed me, for Chrissake."

"As a matter of fact, I did. Though I don't expect you to remember it."

He averts his eyes. He rises, crosses to the window, and stands, his hands thrust deep in his trousers pockets, his back to her, looking out at the afternoon. "Anyway," he says, "we weren't talking about breast-feeding. We were talking about why you can't seem to make a business decision, which is supposed to be your goddam job."

"My job," she says, and for the first time her voice has the beginnings of tears in it, "has involved a bit more than that, you might want to remember. It's also been trying to hold this family together. It's been trying to help my mother all these years. It's been listening to Nonie's complaints. It's been trying to keep Edwee out of trouble. It's been coping with Granny. It's been dealing with the tragedy that was my father. It's been trying to pick up the pieces of the shambles and mess that were left after Grandpa died, and it's been doing all these things for years, since you were too young to know about any of these things, or even remember. That's also been part of my goddam *job.*" Surprisingly, though tears were threatened, Mimi's eyes are dry when she finishes saying this, and she is pleased with herself for this.

"We weren't talking about that, either. We were talking about a New York wheeler-dealer who's showing every sign of wanting to take over this company in a very unfriendly way—a guy you said you positively did not trust."

"And you're watching me have second thoughts about him. You see, I think . . . I think Michael admires us in a certain way. I think he'd like to feel he's a part of us—not a big part, but a little part. Maybe that's all it is. Michael has his sweet, kind of boyish and innocent side. He's not *all* bad."

He turns and faces her, and whistles softly. "Hey," he says, "what's going on here? Did this guy *seduce* you, or what?"

"Of course not!" she cries. "What a ridiculous thing to say."

"By golly, I think he must have! This guy who's managed to lay every good-looking broad in town."

"Are you implying that I am one of Michael Horowitz's *broads?*" They are shouting at each other again.

"That's gotta be it: that baby-face got to you. You were taken in by those baby-blue eyes and cute little dimples! You've goddam fallen for the little prick!"

"Shut up, Badger! I will not listen to this garbage!"

He slams the palm of his hand on the windowsill. "Then stop waffling, Mom! Because that's what you're doing, waffling. Make up your effing mind. Is this guy a snake, or isn't he? *You're* the one who had lunch with him. Me, I've never met the creep!"

"The lunch was *your* idea, not mine! You're the one who got me into this mess, you know!"

He stares at her. "All I know," he says, "is that I'm talking to someone I used to think was a pretty smart lady, but who suddenly isn't making a hell of a lot of sense."

"Are you questioning my judgment?"

"If you want an honest answer—*yes.*"

She is pacing now, shoulders hunched, back and forth across her office carpet, like a sleek leopardess circling her prey, but her voice is wondering. "I wanted this company," she says, "not for myself, but for you. I always wanted it for you, to take over someday from me."

"That's a lot of self-righteous, self-pitying crap."

"But maybe I was wrong. Maybe this company isn't for you. Maybe you find it . . . humiliating, to be working for a woman, and a woman who happens to be your mother in the bargain. Maybe that's it. Maybe it's time for someone new, someone like Michael, to come in and take this company over. Maybe that's why I can sympathize, a little, with what Michael says he wants."

"More self-righteous, self-pitying crap."

"I'm losing you, aren't I, Badger. I can feel it, that I'm losing you. I feel it in the terrible things you've said to me today. I'm losing you. I feel you slipping away from me."

He moves toward her and takes her by the shoulders, turning her so that she faces him. "Listen to me," he says quietly. "All I know is that Horowitz is a fighter, and a fighter who, if he has to, doesn't mind fighting dirty. All I'm saying is that *if* you're going to have to fight him, you're going to have to be prepared for a dirty fight. You're going to have to go after him with a killer's instinct. Where's your killer instinct, Mom? It was old Adolph's killer instinct that built this company, wasn't it? The way he went after the Revsons, after Arden, after Rubinstein. If you're going to find yourself in the ring with Horowitz, you're going to have to decide what you think of him. Because if there's going to be a fight, and if you're going to win it, you're going to have to go for the jugular." Suddenly, he thrusts out his lower jaw sharply and, in the same motion, tosses a lock of sandy brown hair from across his forehead. "You're going to have to *hate* him! You've got to be *prepared* to hate him. So don't let yourself fall under his famous spell!"

"What?" she gasps. "*What?*"

"I said we've got to be prepared. We've got to line up our ammunition. He's got his toe in the door already. And once the camel gets into the tent—"

"No," she says, her eyes blazing. "I meant what you did just then, with your chin. Your hair. Have you always done that?"

"I don't know what you're talking about."

She moves away from him toward her desk and slumps limply in her chair, feeling faint. "You're right," she says. "Michael has no right owning any part of this company. Do your feasibility study. Do it as quickly as you can. Get the cousins' names, addresses. I'll contact them. We've got to get rid of Michael Horowitz as fast as we can. I think you're right. He's a dangerous man."

"You're the boss," he says.

"And you're the next boss. Remember that."

The slim, stylishly dressed woman swings out through the 50th Street door of Saks Fifth Avenue and immediately an alarm goes off.

A uniformed guard steps toward her. "Excuse me, madam," he says politely, "but may I just glance at the contents of your shopping bag?"

"What?" she says in a cultured voice. "What did you say?"

"I think," he says, "that one of our salespeople may have neglected to remove the magnetic tag from one of your purchases. It caused the alarm to sound. If you'll just let me look at the contents of your shopping bag, I think we can locate the problem."

"Why, I've never heard of such a thing!" the woman cries indignantly. Other shoppers, heading out into the late-afternoon rush hour, pause to observe the scene.

"They've caught a shoplifter!" one woman says loudly to her companion.

"I must ask that you open your shopping bag," the guard says. "Otherwise, I must—"

"Well, certainly!" the woman says. "But honestly, I've never been subjected to such a—"

"Ah," the guard says, lifting a man's alligator belt from the shopping bag. "Here is the problem. You see! The magnetic tag has not been removed from this article. You have your sales slip for this, of course."

"Certainly! It's in there somewhere, I suppose!"

The guard extracts a pink slip of paper from the bag and examines it. "I'm sorry," he says, "but this is from the women's shoe department, for the pair of shoes that I assume are in that box. I see no sales slip for a man's belt."

"This is ridiculous!" the woman cries. "I've been a Saks charge customer for years! Never have I been subjected to this sort of thing before!"

"Perhaps if we can go back to the small leather goods department, we can straighten this out," he says, taking her arm.

"*What?*" she says, pulling away from him. "I'm in a terrible rush! This is most inconvenient. Don't you know who I *am?* I am Naomi Myerson!"

"I'm sorry, ma'am, but I must—"

Suddenly she snatches the alligator belt from his hand and flings it in his face. "Take your damn belt!" she cries. "And if that belt turns up on my next Saks bill, I'll sue! Do you hear me? I'll sue!" She hurls herself through the second set of swinging doors and out into the rush-hour street.

It is evening now, and Mimi and her husband are sitting in their living room, sipping a martini before dinner.

"How was your day?" she asks him.

"Oh, routine," he says. "Today was our monthly partners' lunch. No big issues to discuss."

"Ah, your partners' lunch," she says. She sips her drink. "Where did you do it this time?"

"At the Downtown Club. And you?"

He has obviously forgotten that today she was lunching with Michael. "Oh, I was fairly busy. I just had a sandwich at my desk."

She gazes into her cocktail glass. And so here we sit, she thinks, two famously successful people in a two-career household, so smiled upon by fortune. And this is the point to which twenty-nine years of marriage have brought us. We sit here, domestic as that silver cocktail shaker—that cocktail shaker that was a wedding gift, that has all the names of Brad's ushers at the wedding engraved on it—and tell lies to one another.

Palm Beach, Michael had said, come with me to Palm Beach. Palm Beach, that latest triumph of the Jewish Renaissance. She has always hated Palm Beach, and all those other places that were always her grandfather's places, never her own. If he had suggested Srinagar or Ootacamund or Katmandu, or some other more exotic place—the Blue Mountains of New South Wales, he had once suggested in a moment of fantasy, where they would start a sheep ranch—would she have flown there with him?

"You never loved the shegetz you married, did you?"

Right now, she does not have the answer to either of these questions.

10

Granny Flo Myerson (interview taped 8/27/87):

Leo was a crook. I think I already told you that, but what I didn't tell you was that his son, Nathan, also was a crook. In fact, Nate Myerson was worse than a crook, he was a rat. Nate had it in for my son Henry, but I'm getting ahead of my story. My Adolph may have had a lot of enemies, but he wasn't a crook. Leo and Nate were both crooks. They're all dead now, so I can say this.

Leo was five years younger than Adolph, and my goodness, I don't think those two ever got along. Even when they were in the painting business in the Bronx, they were always scrapping. Adolph would want to do things one way, and Leo would want to do it another. It was always like that. I think I told you that Leo was much the better-looking of the two brothers. Oh, my, Leo was a looker, for all his crookedness. Leo looked a little bit like What's-his-name, the movie star, Douglas Fairbanks, and Adolph was short and fat. Leo had all the girls—even after he was married he had girls—and Adolph could never get a girl, until I came along and proposed to him. Those two used to sit right behind my family at temple, and my eye was always on Leo, even though I knew it was Adolph's eye that was always on me. I think I told you that I'd have rather married Leo than Adolph, but how could I do that? Leo already had a wife, named Blanche. These people are all dead now. Blanche was all right, though I didn't have too much to do with her. At least Blanche was nicer than Leo turned out to be.

You see, even though Leo was five years younger, he'd married earlier—around nineteen hundred, it seems to me. I married Adolph in nineteen fifteen, and Adolph was already forty-five! By then, Leo and Blanche already had a family. There was the son, Nate, that I told you about, and two little girls, Minna and Esther. Nate, I told you, is dead, and under mysterious circumstances that I'll get to later. I don't know what's become of Minna and Esther, because the family's been out of touch with those cousins since before the war. They may be dead too, for all I know, but if they're alive they'd be pretty old ladies now—nearly as old as me!

But the point of it is that Adolph never got along with his brother. Part of it was because of Leo's way with the ladies, but that was only part of it. Adolph used to say that Leo was stupid, and Leo used to say that Adolph was cheating him out of his share of the money, but it wasn't true. One thing I can say about my husband is that he never cheated. He did other things, but he didn't cheat his brother. If anything, he was too fair with him —fairer than Leo deserved. Anyway, after my husband invented nail polish, things got quite worse. Of course I can't say that my husband invented nail polish, can I? It'd been around for some years. It was the *quick-drying* nail polish that was new. That was the thing. That, and the catchy names, like Three Alarm.

Anyway, Leo thought he should get all the credit for it. He'd say, "Where would you be if I hadn't put the whatchamacallit in it, the chemical that makes it quick-drying? Where would you be without me, Mr. Big Shot?" And Adolph would say, "And where would *you* be if I'd let you throw the whole batch out, like you wanted to do? Where would you be if I hadn't seen the possibilities?" They'd argue like that all day long, and it would make my husband crazy. He'd come home at night and read to me from his diary about how Leo was making him crazy. I remember a lot of days where the diary began with "How many times did Leo make me crazy today?"

Anyway, in those days there was a lot of dirty work in our business—a lot of dirty work at the crossroads. In the nineteen twenties, particularly. There were payoffs. Under-the-counter payoffs. You'd pay a store owner, or one of his clerks, to display your products in the front of the store, or on top of the counter, or along the center aisle, and to push your competitors' product into the back, where it wouldn't be seen. Of course the competition did the same thing, and so the payoffs got bigger and bigger if you wanted your brands to get a good display in a store. Some people say it still goes on today. I wouldn't know. You'll have to ask Mimi about that, but I'll bet she won't tell you. I don't know if it's exactly against the law, but it's dirty business.

I'll tell you how some store owners worked. The Miray salesman would come into a store, complain about his display, make the payoff, and bingo! Up would go a big, fancy display of Miray right inside the front door. Half an hour later, a salesman from Revlon or one of the others would come into the same store, complain about his display, make the payoff, and bingo again! Down would come the Miray display, and up would go Revlon's in the same spot! This could happen a dozen times a day! People complain about the cost of cosmetics. They say a night cream that retails fifty dollars has only a few cents' worth of ingredients in it. They say the rest of the cost is for packaging and advertising, but that's not true! It's not packaging and advertising that push up the cost, it's the payoffs! My husband explained it all to me, how it worked. It was all in his diary, how much he paid off, and who to, to get his products displayed at *all*.

That was one reason why, in the late nineteen twenties I think it was, my husband decided to pull Miray out of the dime stores and drugstores, where the payoffs were worst, and sell only in the big department stores, which were supposed to be respectable. Well, let me tell you something: The big stores may have been a *little* more respectable, but there were still payoffs, and I'm talking Wanamaker's and Saks and Best's and Lord & Taylor, I'm not talking dreck. In those days, anyway. The only difference between the fancy stores and the dime stores was that the big stores were too busy to change their displays every half hour! Except for Altman's. I've always trusted Altman's. My family were friends with the Altman family, and they were always respectable people. But Saks! Saks used to be owned by the Gimbel family, who were from out West somewhere, and my husband used to say, "Beware of the Gimbels!" He'd say, "I helped make Frank Woolworth rich, now I'm making the Gimbels rich!" Think of that: if it hadn't been for men like my husband, who would she be, this Barbara Hutton?

Anyway, where was I? Oh, yes, the payoffs. It was worst in the nineteen twenties, and even in the nineteen thirties, right up to just before the war. Today, I don't know about. Ask Mimi. In the nineteen twenties and 'thirties there were even worse things than that. This is a very competitive business, as I guess you know. The competition in this business is fierce, it's cutthroat. There were real strong-arm tactics used to keep a competitor's product off the shelves. They'd use the Teamsters to misdirect a competitor's shipment, or to get it "lost" or hijacked. There'd be kidnap threats, even murder threats. It was no holds barred! This was during Prohibition that all this started, but it went on even afterward. In the nineteen twenties was when cosmetics began to be big business. That was when even Wall Street began to take a serious look at companies like ours. Before that, we were thought of as kind of like the movie business, strictly small-time stuff. But now that even Wall Street was looking us over, it meant the competition was even stiffer. It became like a war between the cosmetics companies.

Then, in 'twenty-nine I think it was, there was a kind of scandal, at least it could have been if it hadn't been covered up. A Revlon—I think it was Revlon, yes, I'm sure it was Revlon—a Revlon shipping van was found in New Jersey with its tires slashed and a bullet hole through the windshield.

The driver was gone, they never did find him. But there were bloodstains inside the cab, and in the back, all the shipping crates and cartons had been ripped open and their contents smashed to smithereens. A witness said she'd seen what sounded like one of our Miray cars in the vicinity the night it happened.

Well! As you can imagine, Adolph was fit to be tied when he heard about this! He called Leo on the carpet and wanted to know what he knew about this. Leo just laughed in Adolph's face. Leo admitted he knew that something like that was going to happen. Leo admitted that, behind Adolph's back, he'd been hiring gangsters—The Mob!—to frighten the competition. That made Adolph just about hit the roof, but Leo said, "It's just a part of the price of doing business." Can you imagine that? Anyway, the witness changed her story, said she could have been mistaken (someone must have threatened her or bought her off), and that scandal went away on us. But you can imagine how knowing that Leo was doing things like that made Adolph even crazier. That was when Adolph began filling the pages of his diaries with lots of entries under the heading "Plan to Get Rid of Leo." It took him almost ten years to do it, but he did it.

I mean, the under-the-counter payoffs were one thing—everybody did that—but using The Mob, that was too much for Adolph.

Then, I think I mentioned that Leo had this son, this Nate. In nineteen thirty-one, this Nate was about thirty, and Leo began pushing Adolph to give Nate some big job in the company. Well, by then, Adolph didn't want Leo in the company, and he certainly didn't want Nate! Nate was a bum! Meanwhile, Adolph had always planned that our son Henry would take over the company someday—that was Adolph's dream. Our son Henry was born in nineteen sixteen, and so in nineteen thirty-one, Henry was just fifteen, just a little boy, but that was another reason why Adolph didn't want to let Nate into the company, to be there standing in our Henry's way when the time came.

Henry was just fifteen years old when Nate—his own cousin, a grown man—approached him.

Henry was . . . so young. Young, even, for fifteen. How can I describe my Henry to you? He was innocent, a beautiful child—not like Edwee, not at all. Henry believed in the goodness of things, even then. Sometimes, I think that Henry was too good a person to live out a full life. Of course, that Alice he married was no help to him, no help at all. Any brains, any goodness that are in Mimi came from her father's side, not from that Alice. Even Mimi's looks come from Henry.

Henry was—how to describe him? Henry was my angel on earth. He was my Henny-Penny—that's what I called him. Do you know that story about Henny-Penny? "Run, run, the sky is falling!" I didn't know it, but the sky was beginning to fall on Henry even then. Later, if Alice knew it, she was too stupid to know what to do about it! Henry could have had . . . such a future! Do you know that story in the Bible about old King David when he hears that his son Absalom has been killed? He goes to the tower over the gate and cries, "O Absalom, my son, my son Absalom. Would God I had died for thee, O Absalom, my son, my son." That's how I felt when I heard that my Henny-Penny was dead . . . like going to a tower . . . and crying out to God. . . . Oh, you don't know it, but it's a terrible thing for a mother to outlive her firstborn son . . . terrible. . . . Excuse me, I'm sorry. . . . Do you mind turning off that machine until I . . . [unintelligible] . . .

All right. Yes, I'm fine, now. Let's go on. Where was I? Oh, how Nate corrupted Henry, and turned him against his father. Nate approached Henry—Nate, a grown man, his first cousin, and Henry, a child of fifteen—and said to him, "Do you know how your father and my father run that company of theirs? That swell little company that you're supposed to inherit? They hire gangsters to run it, that's how! Gangsters who kill people who get in their way! What do you think of that? They actually kill people!" It seems that Leo had actually boasted to Nate about his gangster connections, and how he used them! Can you imagine that?

Henry—so young, so innocent, so trusting—ran to his father and said, "Is it true, Daddy? Is it true what Cousin Nate says—that you pay to have people killed?" Of course Adolph denied it. How could you not deny a question like that, coming from your own young son? But I know that Henry knew from his father's reaction that his father was lying to him. Children know these things. You can't lie to a child. And I don't think Henry ever trusted his father again. I don't think he ever believed in his father's business again. I don't think Henry ever even trusted *me* again, because I was there when his father tried to deny all these things, and of course I had to deny them too, even though I knew the truth. I had to stand behind my husband.

I honestly think Adolph could have killed Leo then, killed Leo *and* Nate, killed them both, if he could have figured out a way. Sometimes I think he should have—for killing his son's love for him, for robbing him of his innocence, for poisoning a son's mind against his father, and even me who loved him more than the world itself! Because that was what it was like—a poison in the mind of an impressionable young boy. Because Henry never forgot it. Years later, Henry came back at his father and accused him—but I don't need to tell you that all this made my husband more determined than ever to get his brother out of the company—*forever.*

There's a picture of my Henry over there on that little table in the corner.

It was taken when he was about thirty. Go take a look at it. See that sad, mistrustful look in his eyes? It was there from that day in nineteen thirty-one onward. But see how handsome he was? Can you see Mimi's face in his? I can, or could. I used to pick up that photograph often, and study that face, and that look, and curse Leo and Nate for doing what they did to him. Of course, I can't see that photograph anymore, but I can still see the face, and the look, in my mind's eye. Now, turn off your machine again because this next I am going to tell you is for off the record. . . .

"Payoffs?" Mimi smiles. "We're a bit more sophisticated nowadays than we were in my grandfather's day. Today, it's called public relations. I have a whole department devoted to it. A retailer or salesperson would be insulted today if you went up to him and handed him an envelope full of money, the way my grandfather used to do. But we're still very nice to our friends the retailers, as we say. We take them out to lunch and dinner, we have parties for them. We remember them at Christmastime with a little note and a little gift. I make it a point to make regular personal visits to the stores where our products are sold. I visit with the buyers, chat with the salesgirls, tell them what a terrific job they're doing, how great they look, offer them little hints on how to make their jobs easier for them. There are certain special salespeople to whom we pay special attention. See that Rolodex file on my desk? It's full of the names of special salespeople who've done well for us over the years. It's got their names, their home addresses, their spouses' names, their children's names and ages, their birthdays, their glove sizes, everything we can find out about them. On Christmas, these special people get very special gifts from us and a personal note from me. There's Miss Libby from Neiman's in Fort Worth, for instance. Every year for the past fifteen years, Miss Libby personally sells over fifty thousand dollars' worth of our products. Naturally, we're extra nice to the little jewels like Miss Libby. On her fifteenth anniversary with the store, I sent Miss Libby a Cartier pearl choker—pearls, because I'd heard her say that the only jewels she ever wore were pearls. I like to think we're especially good at remembering to add these personal touches.

"And of course we're always giving away free samples of our products. Sampling, as it's called, has always been a big part of this business. Every day, we give away cartons and cartons of free samples to our friends and would-be friends. Everybody loves to get something that's free—I don't care how rich the person is. Even if it's a free bunch of parsley in the supermarket, the shopper will take it whether she needs parsley or not! My grandfather used to say, 'If it's free, take two.' In fact, it was the whole practice of sampling that made me come up with the free-gift-for-purchase idea. Yes, I was the first manufacturer to do that. For every purchase of a Miray product, the customer gets one—or two or three or four—free samples of some of our other products. It's an incentive for the purchaser, and also for the salesperson because it gives her an extra selling tool. We'll be doing that with the new fragrance: every woman who buys a bottle of the perfume will get a free sample of the men's cologne for her husband, lover, or whatever. Vice versa for the men who buy the cologne.

"Of course when I first took over the company in 'sixty-two, after my father's . . . accident . . . there was no money anywhere. The creditors were hounding us, and there was even talk of Chapter Eleven. During his few years as head of the company, my father had made what, in retrospect, turned out to be some unwise business decisions. It was up to me to try to reposition our products in the marketplace, to reposition the whole Miray name. There was no money for special gifts or dinners for buyers or pearl chokers for salesladies. There was not even enough money to pay the salaries for a sales force. I had to go out to the stores myself, trying to sweet-talk the buyers into stocking us. I walked up and down the aisles myself, with my little tray of free samples, passing them out. I even became an unpaid saleslady, standing at a counter, helping customers apply their makeup, suggesting lipstick and eye shadow shades, giving little beauty tips on this and that, hoping they'd end up buying something.

"Of course, being a woman presented special problems. Most retail-store cosmetics buyers are men, and naturally, I encountered situations where a buyer would offer to stock my goodies in return for something else, if you know what I mean. This required a certain diplomacy and tact. I had to be nice to these guys, but I couldn't—even if I'd been willing to take them up on their suggestions—run the risk of getting the reputation that the Miray girl was an easy lay. I had to be gentle, but firm. I developed little techniques. Instead of crying, 'Unhand me, sir!' I'd smile and say, 'Oh, guess what! I've got a beautiful new eye shadow that I know your wife or girlfriend would just love to try!' And I'd unhand him by dropping a free sample in his hand. It worked, for the most part, though there were a few stores that I listed in my date book as 'Problem Areas.' I think, in the long run, that most retailers learned to like and respect me for my attitude. Of course, the biggest compliment from these guys was, 'You're all business, aren't you? You think like a man!'

"We also do a lot of cooperative advertising. It's another way we're nice to our friends the retailers. There's nothing really new about this, except that we were the first *cosmetics* company to do it. If a store is running a full-page ad for evening wear, for instance, we'll suggest that they feature one of our lipstick shades as an accompaniment to the dress—and we pay for part of their ad. I think it helps our customers to think of Miray products in terms of fashion, and of course the stores are delighted to have us share their ad costs. . . ."

Mrs. Hanna appears at the office door carrying a large arrangement of snowdrop anemones. "These just arrived from Max Schling," she says. "Shall I put them on your coffee table?"

"What beautiful flowers!" Mimi exclaims. "Who sent them, Mrs. Hanna?"

"There's no name on the card. All it says is 'Remembering little white stars.' Do you want me to call the shop and ask them?"

Mimi frowns. "No, never mind. Just set them over there."

She sits for several minutes, her face expressionless, staring at the pale clusters of flowers rising from their green cleft leaves, saying nothing.

"They might be from your grandmother," I suggested after a while, to break the silence.

"No. I know who they're from. Why would my grandmother send me flowers?"

"She's genuinely sorry about the way she treated your mother the other night. I spent some time with her this morning. She asked me to tell you how bad she feels."

"Then why hasn't she called me to say so?"

"I think she's a little afraid to."

"Ha! Her? *Afraid?* Oh, this has gone on for so long between her and my mother—for years and years, since before I was born. Old resentments, ancient grudges, hard feelings that have never changed, bitterness—wounds that will never heal. I've grown so used to it I hardly pay any attention to it anymore. Tell Granny to call me if she's got anything to say to me. I'm certainly not going to call *her*. But if she calls, I'll talk to her—though I can assure you that talking to her won't change anything. It won't change anything at all."

"What's at the root of it, do you think?"

"It's all so complicated. I don't even understand all of it myself. Now, where were we? Oh, yes, how we help our friends the retailers. Well, we always mention their stores in *our* advertising, for one thing. We help them with special in-store promotions. We provide them with special display materials, which they're free to use or not, but which many of the stores do use. We provide our own specially trained salespeople for demonstrations, makeup lessons. We make it clear to them that we're always available whenever they might need a helping hand. . . ."

"I know it's none of my business," I said, because it really wasn't, even though I had somehow been drawn into it by the old lady at the Carlyle, whose sense of dread had been either real or feigned or imagined, and who had pulled me into some sort of family web of disagreement about which, at the time, I had no knowledge, asking me to be a messenger and an intermediary between herself and her granddaughter. "But I really think your grandmother is frightened of something she thinks is about to happen to her. All I know for sure is that it involves Edwee and Nonie. I think she's asking you for a helping hand right now."

"Sometimes I think that my grandmother has ice water running in her veins. If she does, she got it as the result of a transfusion from my grandfather, who was the coldest fish you ever saw. I mean, it wasn't just what she said that was so completely off the wall—about my mother having killed a man, referring to my father's tragic . . . accident. He was—"

"He was a suicide," I said, as gently as I could.

She hesitated then. "My mother and I disagree on that," she said. "My mother has always felt that it was suicide, and that was what the coroner concluded in his report. That was the way it was reported in the press. But no note was found. And I've always preferred to think—to hope, I guess—that it was an accident, that he was cleaning his gun, perhaps, and it accidentally went off. Then again, it could have been—"

"Foul play?"

"Yes! My grandfather had many enemies. I suppose we'll never know for sure what happened. But, in my opinion, my father was systematically destroyed by his parents, from the time he was a little boy. In the company, they gave him titles, but no responsibilities. They gave him jobs, but nothing to do. They refused to listen to any of his ideas. They killed his spirit."

"Your grandmother feels that your uncle Leo had a lot to do with this."

"I never knew Leo, who was my great-uncle, by the way, and not my uncle. That may be true—a case of Grandpa battling with Leo, and my poor father caught in the crossfire in the middle? It may have been something like that."

"Your grandmother says it was all detailed in your grandfather's diaries."

"You see? You see how she likes to stir things up, talking about diaries? I never heard of any diaries. Wouldn't my father have mentioned it if there were diaries? Edwee and Nonie never heard of any diaries. But that's how Granny likes to keep things stirred up. Her remark at my dinner table was not only deliberately cruel, and horribly insensitive, it was mischievous! My God, my mother is just back from the Betty Ford Center, trying to start a whole new life. I talk to my mother every single day, trying to keep her spirits up, her determination up. What Mother needs now is not another kick in the teeth from her mother-in-law, but the support of every member of this family! Now that Granny wants something from me, she regrets her mischief! See how she uses people? She uses you to get to me by talking about these damned fictitious diaries! More mischief!"

"I got the impression that the diaries were a form of private communication between your grandfather and grandmother, in which he told her everything that was important in his life, things he didn't like to talk about, so he wrote them down."

"Maybe so! He was that devious. All men are devious, aren't they? Why are men so much more devious than women? Women can be mischievous, yes, but men are devious. Oh, damn, damn, *damn!*" Suddenly, with the pointed toe of her shoe, she kicked sharply at her office wastebasket, tipping it over and half-spilling its contents across her carpet, and I realized that she was weeping. I could not believe that I was seeing this normally poised and self-collected woman crying, and I groped in my pocket to see whether I had remembered to insert a handkerchief, but I had not. "Oh, damn!" she sobbed, and then, "Want some flowers? Take those damn flowers out of here!"

In his cluttered office on Sutton Square, Edwee Myerson is on the telephone. "This is Mr. Edwin Myerson calling from the Miray Corporation," he says to the woman he has finally tracked down.

"Oh, yes, Mr. Myerson," the woman says. "I suppose you've heard by now that he's agreed to go with the scar bit. He's not happy about it, but he's agreed to go along."

"The scar bit," Edwee says, having no idea what this woman is talking about, but willing to play along. "Of course," he says. "I understand."

"I'll spare you the few choice words he had to say about *Miss* Myerson," she says. "But don't worry. He's still in the ball game with Miray."

"Good," Edwee says. "And I have some news for him that may make your client a little happier."

"About how you're going to handle the scar bit? Good. He could use some cheering up."

"But I seem to have misplaced the chap's telephone number."

"Hang on. I'll get it for you," the woman says.

11

*T*HE *YEAR WAS* 1957, and Mimi was eighteen, and she was sitting on a bench by the frozen pond in Central Park, lacing her skates. "Damn!" she muttered as one of her laces broke.

"Here," the pink-cheeked young man sitting next to her said, reaching into the pocket of his red parka. "I always carry an extra pair. Be my guest." And he handed her a new pair of laces.

She had hesitated. "Thank you," she said. "But I can just tie a knot."

"Knots look dumb," he said. "You don't want to look dumb, do you?"

"No, but—"

"Then gimme your right skate," he said briskly. "I'll start working on that one, and you can start with the other one."

"Really, I—"

He snapped his fingers. "Stop talking and gimme your skate. It's not like taking candy from a stranger, you know. I bet you're the kind of girl who was told never to take candy from a stranger. A pair of shoelaces isn't candy, for Chrissake." Accepting her skate, he said, "You know, a guy could make a fortune selling shoelaces singly, instead of in pairs. Ever think of that? Nobody ever breaks more than one lace at a time. What are the odds against breaking both laces at once? That's all business is, knowing the odds. Guy could make a fortune from an idea like that." He had gone busily to work removing the broken lace and inserting the new one.

When he had finished, and both her relaced skates were on, he stood up. "Buy you an ice cream cone?" he said. "Hell, maybe that is like taking candy from a stranger, but I'm not the Black Dahlia Killer, as maybe you can tell."

"Who are you?" she asked.

He winked at her. "It's not who I am that matters," he said. "It's who I'm going to be. And you know who I'm going to be? The richest guy in New York, is all. Think I'm kidding? I'm not even out of Columbia Biz School, and I've got a project going: low-income housing in Newark. Government subsidized—not a penny of my own money in it. I'm a genius, is what I am. You'll find that out when you get to know me better. C'mon, let's get ice cream."

They skated together across the pond, and Mimi thought that this was the most extraordinary young man she had ever met.

As they stood in line in front of the refreshment stand, he cupped his mittened hands in front of his mouth and blew out misty puffs of breath. He said, "You know? Guy could make a fortune from a place like this. How come they only sell ice cream and soda pop? Who wants cold food on a winter day? Why not hot things? Hot chocolate, hot dogs, hot apple cider, hot bagels, hot pastrami sandwiches. Hot potato salad. Hot cross buns. Hot cole slaw. Hot sauerkraut. Hot tamales. Hot apple pie. Hot chicken soup. Hot buttered popcorn. Hot buttered rum. I've seen you around here before."

"I come fairly often, yes."

"Always alone?"

"Usually, yes."

"No friends?"

"I go to school in Connecticut," she said. "This is our midwinter break, and most of my friends live in other cities."

"Other cities like where?"

"I have a good friend who lives in Akron," she said.

"That's a hellhole," he said. "I've never been there, but I've heard that Akron's a hellhole. I've heard that if they were going to give the world an enema, Akron's where they'd put the tube." He was paying for their ice cream cones now, rather showily, with a hundred-dollar bill, and the cashier, looking pained, was counting out his change, most of it in singles. "No," he said, "New York's the only city in the world for me. Remember that you heard it here, Mimi."

She gasped. "How did you know my name?" she said.

He grinned at her. "I'm psychic," he said. "But there's a name-tag sewn inside your skate. Your eyes are a wonderful color."

She laughed. "My beige eyes," she said.

"Silver," he said. "I'm also into self-improvement. I want to know more about culture, and the finer things in life. If a man's going to be successful, he needs to be well-rounded. Every week, I try to learn about something new, and before I'm done I want to know at least something about everything there is to know. This week I've been learning about silver. The finest English silver is from the George the First period. Did you know that? A lot of people think it's George the Third, but George the First is finer. You know that James Robinson shop on Fifty-seventh Street? That's where I learned about George the First silver. And do you know what the finest silver needs? It needs to be polished every single day. That's what gives it that special creamy luster. That's what they told me at the James Robinson store. That's the color of your eyes—the color of old silver that's been polished every single day. You Jewish?"

"Yes, as a matter of fact."

"I thought so. Not that you look Jewish. You don't. You're a sort of blonde, but they're always blonder, the *goyim.* I can usually tell. Not always, but usually."

"Does it matter if I am?"

"Not to me, it doesn't. But it would to my mother."

"What does your mother have to do with it?"

"When I take you home to meet her, it will matter."

"Why would you take me home to meet your mother?"

"Because you're the girl I'm going to marry."

"*What?*"

He was skating away from her now, skating effortlessly backward in an easy, splay-legged motion, still grinning at her, licking his ice cream cone, and there was a drop of chocolate ice cream glistening on the tip of his nose. "Gotta run now," he said. "Gotta run over to Jersey and check on my job. See you here tomorrow—same place."

"Wait!" she cried. "I don't even know your name!"

"Michael Horowitz," he called back. "See you tomorrow, kiddo," and then he was gone, a blur of red parka that disappeared among the other skaters.

But the next afternoon he had not come, and she waited for him at the same bench by the pond, her arms crossed about her middle for warmth. She had been on time, even a little early, for him, and after half an hour she decided he was not going to come. She knew, she thought, everything she ever needed to know about men, and she knew, or thought she knew, everything she needed to know about sex. At school, there was Old Pete, who was a janitor in the gym. Old Pete's office, if you could call it that, was a mop and broom closet in the gym basement, where he sat much of the day smoking endless cigarettes and reading comic books, and whenever a group of Miss Hall's girls gathered outside the cellar light that was his headquarters' only window, Old Pete would usually put on a little show for them, carefully opening his pants, taking out his swollen thing, and swinging it back and forth, pointing it at them, and stroking it as his audience watched wide-eyed. Word that Old Pete was in the middle of one of his performances would spread like wildfire across that lovely, elm-dotted campus, from one ivy-clad dorm to the next: "Old Pete's putting on his act!" And the girls, in the green plaid skirts and middy blouses that were their uniforms, would hurry down the well-raked gravel walks to the basement window of the gym, always careful to be sure that no faculty member was aware of this surreptitious congregation of well-bred, well-brought-up young ladies. What would the parents of these well-bred, well-brought-up young ladies have thought if they knew that such a thing went on at the fashionable Miss Hall's School for Girls in Connecticut? Who knew? But that was sex, Mimi knew. "The man sticks his thing in you," the older girls knowingly explained. "It doesn't really hurt."

As for men, she knew what the other girls said. Because all men liked sports, the rougher the sports the better, men liked to play games with you. They played cat and mouse. They teased you, taunted you, and led you on until, if you weren't careful, you found yourself in a dangerous place from which there was no escape: pregnant. Then they tossed you aside, never to be heard from again. If you accused them, they would simply deny it, and there was no way of proving—unless he admitted it, which he hardly ever did—that this one or that one was the one who made you pregnant. And so you were left all alone, with no one to befriend you. This had happened to at least one girl at Miss Hall's School. She had been whisked away, in tears, in a chauffeur-driven car—not even her parents would come to collect her— and she had never been seen or heard from again. She had vanished without a trace, dropped off the face of the earth.

In their cat-and-mouse games, men liked to "string a girl along." Often, they strung several girls along at the same time, just for the hell of it, leading a girl deeper and deeper into the web of deceit until, bored with a girl who seemed too willing to be trapped, they simply cast her aside and went on to another one. For each new girl, each man had "a line." The fishing imagery was no accident, for that was all it was, a casual fishing outing in which each fisherman tried to get a bigger, juicier specimen to nibble on his bait. Once he caught her, he either tossed her back into the pond or brought her home and fried her for dinner. This may seem a naive view, but remember that this was Miss Hall's School for Young Ladies of Sheltered Sensibilities, and the more hard-bitten knockabout era of the 1960s had not yet dawned. After she had waited nearly an hour, Mimi decided that Michael Horowitz was no different from any of the others. She had stupidly fallen for his line too quickly. He had moved on to more exciting fishing grounds. He had

stood her up. He probably did this sort of thing every day. To mix metaphors, she was just another notch on his belt. She decided that she did not
even like him. He was too cocky, too boastful and braggarty, too full of
himself, too show-offy—that hundred-dollar bill! She decided that if she
ever saw him again she would simply hand his skate laces back to him
without a word. She gathered up her skates to go.

But, just then, she saw a figure in a red parka running toward her through
the park.

"Sorry!" he said breathlessly when he reached her. "Got tied up at the job
in Jersey. No way to call you. Look—I've got to run again, but can you have
dinner with me tonight? Can I make it up to you with dinner?"

"Well, I suppose so," she said.

"Good! Thank God you waited!"

"If I waited any longer, I'd be frozen stiff."

"How's the Rainbow Room? Do you like the Rainbow Room?"

"That would be very nice," she said. She had never been to the Rainbow
Room.

"Good. Meet me there at seven-thirty. I'll have the reservation." He blew
her a kiss and was off again, in another blur of moving red parka.

"The Rainbow Room!" her mother cried excitedly. "Your father and I
were there years ago. They have dancing there, you know, so what do you
think? Your ballerina? Or your blue sheath? Yes, I think the blue sheath,
don't you? And your blue coat, but first I think we should snip the padding
out, don't you? I just don't know what people are wearing this winter.
Everything in the stores looks so awful—I mean sequins, and all that. Or do
you think your ballerina—or is that too long? The New Look is long gone, I
know that much, but there isn't time to raise the hem. No, I think the blue
sheath, *definitely*. What time is he picking you up?"

"I'm to meet him there."

"*Really?* In my day—"

"He's coming in from New Jersey. It's easier."

"Then you'll need taxi money. You can't take the bus to the Rainbow
Room! Don't worry, I have taxi money. Where did you meet this young
man, anyway? At one of your school dances? Who is he, anyway?"

"He says he intends to become the richest man in New York."

"How exciting! Now quick, run fetch me your blue coat so I can snip out
the shoulder pads. I know that shoulder pads are definitely *out* this year. Is it
a boy you met at the Choate dance? Of course it must be. Choate means
he's from a fine family."

Over the years, Mimi had learned that her mother had, once upon a time,
been a woman with great expectations for her future. After all, hadn't she

married Henry Myerson, the son of Adolph Myerson, the Cosmetics King, and of Fleurette Myerson, *geboren* Guggenheim, the copper-smelting heiress? She had done this, and yet, mysteriously, the expectations had never come to pass. That glorious future she had assigned herself had managed to betray her, the great promises had not been kept, and, little by little, and bitterly, the dream had begun to die a long and lingering death. Sinister forces that no one seemed able to explain had cheated Alice Myerson of all her hopes. Who was the author of this villainy? At that point in her life, Mimi herself had no clear idea, but suddenly that night she saw all her mother's aborted dreams become refocused on her daughter's new beau.

Her mother, the former Alice Bloch, had been the pretty daughter of Sigismund and Nettie Bloch, members of a fine old German-Jewish family. In the teens and twenties, Sigismund Bloch had prospered, wore the title "Private Banker," and "kept an office," as they said in those days, in Wall Street—an office he rarely found it necessary to visit. But in the Great Crash of 1929, Bloch's bank had been one of the first to go under, and Sigismund Bloch had lost everything. He never recovered from the shock and died several years later of a disease the family diagnosed as "melancholia." Not long after that, his widow followed him to the Bloch family mausoleum in Salem Fields, the only piece of property the family had been able to retain, a marble edifice of extravagant design with a splendid view of the Manhattan skyline.

With Alice's marriage to Henry Myerson, it was assumed that the Bloch family's misfortunes were about to reverse themselves. It was assumed that the new Mrs. Myerson would become the chatelaine of grand houses such as those her in-laws occupied. It was assumed that Alice would embark upon the pampered, servant-attended sort of life that the other women of the uptown German-Jewish crowd enjoyed, lives of bridge clubs, luncheons at the Plaza, formal teas with daily-polished-silver tea services, calling cards, croquet on summer lawns overlooking the Atlantic, and a once-yearly (at least) "important entertainment," where as many as two hundred and fifty white-tied gentlemen—and their spouses, wearing the required looping strands of Oriental pearls—sat down for dinner in a house on Fifth or Madison. You could look at Henry and Alice's wedding photographs—the radiant young couple surrounded by their friends and relatives: little Granny Flo; Grandpa Myerson looking magisterial in his goatee and pince-nez; the massive Guggenheim uncles and their Junoesque wives—and see the bright promise of that privileged future shining in Alice's eyes.

But it had never come to pass, none of it. At first, Alice and Henry had been lavishly entertained by their contemporaries and their contemporaries' parents. They had been on everyone's invitation list. But gradually it was noticed that Henry and Alice were not reciprocating in kind. At first, the

Henry Myersons were accused of laziness, then of penuriousness, then of both. "You can't accept Scotch salmon and pay back with tunafish," Mimi had overheard someone say of her parents. She had also heard her parents described as "peculiar." It seemed inconceivable that Adolph Myerson's son and daughter-in-law could not afford to live on the scale that had been designated for them. They were supposed to have all this money. Where was it?

Mimi knew that money was part of the key to the conundrum. But another part was more mysterious and involved certain family secrets that had to be kept. One of the secrets was the unanswered question in her mother's repeated cry: *Where is the money?* As a little girl, she had sometimes asked her father, "Daddy, are we poor?" He would answer her with another question: "You're not starving, are you? Think of the starving Armenians!" Or he would respond with a challenge: "If you'll lose ten pounds, I'll give you ten dollars." Because as a child, she had been chubby, and it was not until she was twelve or thirteen that the hated fat began suddenly to melt away. Or he would answer with a riddle, one of his little jokes that her mother called "Daddy's groaners." "Why didn't the children of Israel starve in the desert?" he would ask her.

"Why didn't they?"

"Because of all the *sand which is* there."

"Are we an unlucky family, Daddy?" she had asked him once.

"Unlucky? Why do you ask that?"

"Mama says we were all born under some unlucky star."

"Nonsense. Want to know the formula for good luck? Give me your left shoulder. It has to be the left one."

She offered it to him, and he kissed her shoulder lightly. "There," he said. "That's the good-luck kiss. Then remember the secret, magic words: 'With a kiss on my left shoulder, my heart will beat a little bolder.' "

When Mimi had gone off to Miss Hall's School, she had gone on a full academic scholarship, but she had been told that she must never, on pain of the most horrible punishment imaginable, mention this fact to her grandparents. In the beginning, Mimi had thought of her scholarship as an honor. She soon realized that her mother considered it a disgrace. And still another key lay in her mother's repeated assertion that the most important mission in a young woman's life was "to make the right sort of marriage." It was perfectly clear that Alice Myerson, who had thought she was making the right sort of marriage, had not, in fact, done so.

And so, at a quarter to seven on the night she was to meet Michael at the Rainbow Room, Mimi waited as her mother, working with nail scissors, cut out the shoulder pads of her two-year-old blue coat, her mother taking a sip of her drink with whichever hand happened to be free. "Oh, this is so exciting, isn't it?" her mother said. "This could be a big change for you, couldn't it—this Choate boy? Of course, in my day, if a Choate boy was taking a girl out to dinner, he'd call for her in a taxi and come in to be introduced to her mother, or at least have his family send around a car and driver to pick her up. But times change, I suppose. And—oh, God! I nearly forgot! In addition to taxi money, you'll need money for the matron! When you go to the ladies' room to freshen yourself— you'll have to go there after dinner to freshen your makeup; after all, you're a Myerson!— there'll be a matron there. Right by the washstand, you'll see a little saucer with coins in it. That's where you leave the tip for the matron, after you've washed and dried your hands. Some people leave only fifty cents, but I think you should leave a dollar; after all, you *are* a Myerson! Don't you dare tell your father I gave you a whole dollar to do this, but I think it will look better, and after all, it *is* the Rainbow Room! Tommy Dorsey's band—that's what was playing at the Rainbow Room when your father took me there. Goodness, that was years ago. Oh, my God . . . oh, *no!*"

"What happened, Mother?"

"I've cut a little hole in the lining! I didn't mean to! Oh, my God, you can't wear this coat, Mimi!"

"It's just a tiny little tear, Mother. It's only the lining; no one will ever see it."

"But what about when your nice boy from Choate helps you into your coat after dinner? If he sees this hole, what will he think of us? He'll think we're as poor as Job's turkey!"

"I'm sure he won't notice. Here, let me take out the rest of the stitches." She saw that her mother's hands were trembling.

"No, no. I've just got a few more to go. Oh, Mimi, are you sure he won't notice? This is such an important night for you!"

"I'm positive he won't notice. He's not the noticing sort."

"Thank goodness it's a little way down inside the sleeve." Working with her nail scissors at the stitches, she went on, "It was years ago, when he took me to the Rainbow Room. It was before you were born, Mimi—before you were even born—when you were no more than a twinkle in your father's eye!" And Mimi watched as, with one hand, her mother brushed a tear from her own eye. "Your father has always been kind to me, I have to give him credit for that. He's never been guilty of an act of"— she worried at the stitches with her scissors tip—"deliberate . . . unkindness. . . . I have many happy . . . memories. They photographed us there that night, and on Sunday our picture was in the Rotogravure. . . . The Magnificent Myersons, they called us. . . ."

*   *   *

"I'll have my usual, Scotch and soda," Michael said, and the captain, who really did seem to know him, nodded. Michael was always good with head-waiters, was always authoritative, and always tipped them well.

The captain looked at Mimi, who took a deep breath and said, "I'll have a dry martini."

"Excuse me," the captain said, "but may I see the young lady's ID?"

"*What?*" Michael cried in outrage. "Don't you know who this young lady is? This is my twin sister, my fraternal twin sister, who is actually three minutes older than I am! This is an insult, asking my twin sister for her ID!"

"Certainly, Mr. Horowitz," the captain said. "I do apologize, Mr. Horowitz."

"My twin sister has ordered a dry martini. Now get us our drinks."

"Certainly, sir."

"You have to show them who's boss," Michael said, after the headwaiter had left them. "By the way, how old are you?"

"Nineteen," she said, adding a few months for good measure.

"That's old enough. But I guess you do look younger. I'm a few years older than you. I'm twenty-five. You're shy, aren't you."

"Yes, I guess, a little."

"Some people say shyness is a form of selfishness. Do you agree with that?"

"I don't know. I've never thought about it."

"I don't agree. Because I think shyness can be cured by practicing the art of self-esteem—so shyness is the opposite of selfishness, don't you think? I used to be shy. Or at least I was considered a shy little kid. Then I read a book called *How to Win Friends and Influence People* by Mr. Dale Carnegie. It changed my life. I'll give you that book to read, if you'd like. It could change your life, the way it changed mine."

"Thank you," she said. "I've heard of the book."

"And so," he said, grinning at her, "aside from those little differences—our ages, and the shyness thing—what do you think of my plan?"

"What plan?"

"For us to get married, of course!"

"But Michael, I hardly know you!"

"Plenty of time for that. I didn't mean get married *tomorrow*, for Chris-sakes. How about June? There's a song—'It was just a wedding in June . . .' "

"But Michael," she said a little wildly, "don't I have to love you? Isn't love supposed to be a part of it? I mean, I'm not even sure I even *like* you!"

Their drinks arrived just then, and when the waiter had left, Michael touched his glass to hers. "You may never like me," he said, looking straight into her eyes. "But I'll tell you this much, kiddo. You may never like me, but at least you'll never forget me."

He had been right about that.

12

$M_{RS.}$ *RICHARD BERNHARDT* is a thirtyish housewife in Scarsdale, and she comes to the door of her pleasant, Tudor-style house on Rockinghorse Lane to greet her visitor. "What a great pleasure," she says as she offers him her hand. "Your reputation, as they say, precedes you, sir!"

"That could be taken two ways, of course," he says.

She laughs easily and leads him across the wide entrance hall and into her sunny living room, which is decorated with floral Clarence House chintz and overlooks the sparkling backyard pool. "Can I get you something?" Louise Bernhardt asks. "Iced tea? Lemonade? A drink?"

"Nothing, thanks."

They seat themselves on the sofa in front of the fireplace, the opening of which is filled with a hand-painted paper fan, for summer. Arrayed on the mantel is a handsome collection of polished pewter tankards. Louise Bernhardt has a certain reputation as a housekeeper and, in her living room, it shows.

"Needless to say, I'm consumed with curiosity as to why you called and wanted to see me," she says.

"I'll come right to the point," he says. "If you know my reputation, you know I'm not the kind of guy who likes to beat around the bush."

"Good," she says. "Neither am I."

"I'm interested in you because you're a member of the Myerson family."

She hesitates. "My grandfather was Leopold Myerson, that's true," she says. "He was an early partner of Adolph Myerson's. But other than that—"

"And you are a stockholder in the Miray Corporation."

"Yes. All of us are. There are six—no, seven—grandchildren."

"Eight, actually."

"Eight?"

"Esther's three children."

"Did Aunt Esther have three? Oh, you're counting Norman. Poor Norman is . . . retarded, you know. We don't usually count poor Norman."

"Norman Stein is still a shareholder."

"Well, yes, I suppose he is. His brother Gil handles his affairs for him. Gil is a darling. Norman is in Shady Hill."

"I know all that."

"Well," she says brightly, "you've certainly done your homework on the family. Why this interest in us?"

"I'm interested in buying your Miray stock, Mrs. Bernhardt," he says.

"All of it?"

"All."

She rises and fishes a cigarette out of a gleaming silver box on the coffee table. "I hope you don't mind if I smoke," she says. "Really, we're the last persecuted minority in America, we smokers!" She lights her cigarette with a heavy silver table lighter, of the variety that usually does not work. In Louise Bernhardt's house, however, everything works, including the lighter.

"When I left Manhattan this morning, Miray shares were trading at sixty-nine and a half. I'm willing to offer you seventy-five and a quarter, Mrs. Bernhardt. That's nearly ten percent above the current market."

"Mmm," she says into the cigarette smoke. "Well, I should tell you that my grandfather used to say that we should never sell our Miray stock, no matter what. He was really quite adamant—even rabid—on the subject. He made my father, Nathan Myerson, promise never to sell. He was simply rabid on the subject."

"I understand that, Mrs. Bernhardt."

"My grandfather made all of his children and grandchildren promise—"

"I understand that, too."

"It's a very hard thing you're asking me to do, to break a solemn promise I made to my grandfather."

"Let me say that I'd consider offering you seventy-seven and a half. That's slightly more than ten percent over the market."

"Yes," she says, picking an invisible piece of lint from the front of her white silk slacks. "Well, I'm sure you don't expect a decision from me this afternoon. I'd like to consult my brothers, Sam and Joe."

"I'll be speaking to them as well."

"And my husband, Dick. And I think I'd also like to consult my children. They should be a part of this, too, since this represents part of their inheritance. I must say, Miray has always been very good to us—at least since

Adolph's granddaughter took the company over. They've never skipped a dividend, and, as you know, there've been two splits."

"I know that."

"Will you be speaking with Mimi Myerson, too?"

"On a somewhat different basis, yes."

"I don't know her. We've never met, though she must be a very clever lady. There was some sort of family falling out years ago between my grandfather and his brother. I've never known what it was about, but it does seem silly, doesn't it, after all these years? Two branches of the family which refuse to have anything to do with one another?"

"These things happen, in families."

"Alas, yes. Is Mimi's son in the business now? I think I read—"

"He's the one I'm after."

"*After?*" She laughs. "Goodness, you make it all sound rather sinister!"

"I meant that . . . in the abstract," he says.

"I see. Business talk."

"So," he says, rising from the sofa, "here's my card where I can always be reached. You talk it over with your husband, your brothers, your kids. And let me know."

"I'll do that."

"All I can say is that, in today's market, I don't think you'll find a better offer, kiddo."

She starts toward the front door with him, then hesitates. "If you're interested in the family, and the company, Mr. Horowitz, there's something that you might like to see. . . ."

To say that Nonie Myerson was astonished by her brother's invitation to his house for dinner tonight would be an understatement. At their last meeting, she had thought he was going to hit her, and that only an extraordinary exercise in self-will had prevented him from doing just that. Knowing Edwee's pattern of lengthy sulks after any sort of family disagreement, she had expected that it would be weeks, even months, before she heard from him again. And yet, this very morning, there he had been on the telephone, all jolly-voiced and cajoling, murmuring something about burying the hatchet, and calling her "dear girl," and begging her to come to dinner.

"I'm going to be cooking," he said, "and there may be one or two others. Also, there's a small bit of family business we need to discuss. Come at seven, dear girl."

And so, with that hint about family business, she had accepted. It was likely that Edwee's plan to place their mother in a nursing home had struck some sort of legal snag that even forty lawyers from Dewey, Ballantine had been unable to sort out without Nonie's cooperation. And, since she was revising her thinking about the nursing home notion as it might affect her dealings with her mother, Nonie had decided that it would be useful to her cause to find out what, exactly, was on Edwee's mind.

Now she has been ushered into Edwee's office on Sutton Square by Edwee's Filipino butler, and Edwee has closed the door conspiratorially behind them. He is still wearing his full white apron and tall chef's bonnet, which, with his long silver hair flowing out beneath it, makes him look more than a little ridiculous, she thinks.

"We're having a salmon and sea-scallop tart, vermicelli with caviar and *sauce aux truffes,* veal paillard with sorrel sauce, cold chestnut soufflé, and a mango mousse," he announces. "I'm particularly pleased with the mousse. Will you have a glass of Perrier?"

Nonie nods. Perrier is the only liquid that Edwee permits his guests to drink before one of his little dinners. Anything stronger, he insists, would dull the palate to the flavors of his dishes and their accompanying wines.

"Sit down, dear girl," he says, uncapping the little green bottles and emptying them into champagne flutes. "I asked you to come a little early, because there is a matter of some delicacy that I need to discuss with you. And Gloria is—"

"How is darling little Gloria?"

"Gloria is . . . indisposed. Poor Gloria won't be joining us tonight. She's having something light sent up to her on a tray." He hands Nonie a glass and suddenly winks at her. "The fact is, we think we're pregnant."

"Pregnant! For the first time in her life, do you think?"

"Yes. We've been experiencing a little morning sickness for the last few days, and we're twelve days late getting our period."

"You *both* are? This will make medical history, Edwee!"

"Yes! Isn't that extraordinary? Oh, not the late period, of course, but I've been experiencing the morning sickness *too.* Doctor Katz tells me that this often happens with the husband. It's called a sympathetic pregnancy. Do you suppose I'm going to start swelling up like a balloon? Doctor Katz says I just *might.* Anyway, we won't know for sure until tomorrow, when we have our appointment with the OB-GYN."

"Really, Edwee. It's too . . . mind-boggling." She does not voice the question that immediately flew into her mind: how the sort of sexual gymnastics Edwee described to her earlier could possibly have led to a pregnancy.

"Exciting, isn't it? And you're the first to know, because we're really quite, quite sure. Aren't you pleased? Won't it be nice to have a new little nephew, or a new little niece who'll be a bit more *simpatico* than our crass and calculating Mimi?"

"I didn't know that you found Mimi crass and calculating, Edwee."

"Mimi's only interested in money; that's all she's ever cared about. The finer things in life have always escaped her. All she sees are dollar signs. It's tragic, really, but that's the way she's always been—a life single-mindedly dedicated to the almighty dollar. I pity people like Mimi, who've never let their souls be lifted by art, music, poetry, the dance, the higher forms of love or beauty, even *haute cuisine,* and who care about nothing but money."

That, Nonie thinks, is easy for him to say, since he has always had more money than he ever needed. But she doesn't say this. Instead she says, "But that isn't what you wanted to talk about, it it? You mentioned some family business. I assume it's about putting Mother in the nursing home."

"Hmm? Oh, no. No, I've given up on that idea. No, that won't be necessary."

"What?" she cries in some dismay. "What do you mean? I thought you had the home all picked out. I thought we—"

"No, no, no," Edwee says. "No, you were right. It would be too cruel. We could never do a thing like that to our dear mother—to make her give up her lovely apartment, her darling little dog, her friends, room service. You and I could never live with ourselves, Nonie, if we were to be a party to a thing like that. You were absolutely right."

"But I've changed my—"

"No, what I wanted to talk to you about was something quite different. It's that I suddenly remembered the other day that you have been to 'I Tatti,' and that you're the only one in the family who has."

"That I've been *where?*" She is now more mystified than ever.

"To 'I Tatti.' Bernard Berenson's villa outside Florence."

"Well, yes. Years ago. It was when I was married to Horace. No, it was when I was married to Erik. It was before the war, and Berenson invited Erik and me to lunch."

"Ah," he says. "Do you remember what you talked about?"

"Not really. I remember there were some other people there, and I remember I thought he was charming. B.B., everybody called him. And his wife, Mary. I thought he was a darling little man, with that white, pointy beard and those big, sad eyes. Why do you ask about him?"

"It's important. Mother would never go to 'I Tatti.' She didn't trust Berenson. She never met him. But you were there. You met him and talked with him."

"Well, yes."

"You also remember when mother bought the Goya. I was too young."

"Oh, I remember vividly. It was in the early thirties. And I remember the price: fifty thousand dollars. I remember how Mother agonized over that. It seemed sinful, she said, almost sinful, to spend that kind of money on a piece of art when the world was sinking into a Great Depression, when vice-presidents of banks were selling apples on street corners. Well, how much is that Goya worth today, Edwee, do you suppose? Fifty million? Astonishing, what's happened to art prices."

"And when you were at 'I Tatti,' did Berenson mention the Goya? Think hard. It's important."

"He may have. I really don't remember, Edwee. Goodness, it was more than forty years ago when Erik and I were there."

"But he *may have.*"

"Yes, I suppose so."

"What *exactly* did he say about it?"

"I don't remember if he said anything about it at *all*, Edwee."

"You see, Mother bought the painting from Joseph Duveen, presumably with Berenson's endorsement. But Duveen is dead, Berenson is dead, Mother is senile, and of course Goya is dead. You are the *last living link* between Berenson and that painting, Nonie."

Nonie frowns slightly. She does not particularly like being called the last living link between something and something else.

"So it's important for you to try to remember whether Berenson said anything at all to you about Mother's Goya."

"Well, I guess he may have mentioned it—said he was pleased that it had joined Mother's collection, or something like that. It was considered an important piece. But I don't understand. What's all this business about the Goya? The Goya's going to the Met, as you well know—thanks to Mother's sudden outburst of generosity!"

"Not necessarily," he says. "It may not necessarily be going to the Met."

"Of course it is. You heard what Mother said. She had Philippe de Montebello in and told him he could have whatever he wanted. He'll certainly want the Goya."

"Ah, but will he, dear girl?" he says. "You see, there's a strong possibility that the Goya is a fake. A very strong possibility."

"Oh, no! How awful!"

"Yes," he says. "You see, Berenson's specialty was Italian Renaissance painting. That was his forte, Italian painting from the fourteenth to the seventeenth century. Goya was not Italian, and he was late-eighteenth–early-nineteenth century, as you know. Berenson was weak—by his own admission, Nonie—when it came to the Spaniards. He was on very shaky ground—he admitted this, too—when it came to the later period of Goya. He may have had grave doubts about the authenticity of our Goya, and he may have expressed these doubts to you."

"Well, he didn't. I'd have certainly remembered it if he had."

"You know that Berenson, on more than one occasion, authenticated paintings that he was unsure about because Duveen made him do it. Berenson worked for Duveen, of course, and it was Joseph Duveen who made Berenson a rich man. Without Duveen, your friend B.B. would not have been able to afford luxuries like 'I Tatti.' "

"Please don't call him my friend, Edwee. I only met him that once, at lunch, and there were quite a few other people there. I remember Garbo was there, and the Duke and Duchess of Windsor. No, wait: the Duchess was there, but the Duke wasn't."

"Berenson was essentially Duveen's employee. If Duveen had a rich client who wanted, say, a Caravaggio, Duveen would force Berenson to certify a particular work as being by Caravaggio when, in fact, Berenson suspected that the quote-unquote Caravaggio was actually a Guido Reni, or some lesser master, or an outright forgery. A number of instances of that sort of hanky-panky have come to light since the great B.B.'s death."

"But what makes you think Mother's Goya is a forgery, Edwee?"

Edwee makes a steeple of his fingers. "As you know," he says, "and I hope this doesn't sound immodest, but I have a certain reputation as an art historian, I have examined the painting very carefully, and there are certain details, certain brushstrokes, that strike me as incompatible with Goya's work. On the other hand—and I am modest enough to admit this—my reputation is as an amateur, not a professional. I have been called—and I admit this, Nonie—a dilettante, rather than a true connoisseur, in the art world. But you were a witness. You were there."

"A witness to what? What are you driving at?"

Edwee leans back in his chair, his fingers still steepled, and closes his eyes. "Let us try to picture a scenario," he says. "You and Horace were invited to 'I Tatti' by B.B. for lunch—"

"It wasn't Horace. It was Erik."

"It was a lovely summer's day. The war was over."

"As I recall, it was raining, and it was *before* the war."

"Let me continue, please," he says. "The time doesn't matter. It was a lovely summer's day. The war was over. B.B. took you by the hand and led you outside into his garden. Erik stayed behind in the villa with the other guests—this is important, because Erik is still around. B.B. led you out into his garden—he was very proud of his garden at 'I Tatti,' you know—"

"He didn't show me any garden. He showed us his library, I remember. I don't recall seeing any garden."

"Please let me finish, dear girl. As you and B.B. strolled through his beautiful garden, and he pointed out the specimen trees and plantings, you admired the blossoms of the tall lupines and delphiniums, the strong violet hues of the lobelia blooms, the dark greens of the Lombardy poplars, the shadows of the cyprus trees, and you remarked that these colors, this palette of garden hues and shades, reminded you exactly of the colors of the Duchess of Osuna's gown in your mother's Goya. With that, a look of deep distress came over B.B.'s normally serene face! He seized your elbow. 'The Myerson Goya,' he whispered. 'I should never have let your mother buy that picture. It is most assuredly a forgery, though a clever one. I have lived too long with this guilty secret! It was a robbery to sell your mother that painting for that price! I begged Duveen not to force me to authenticate that painting. But the rascal reminded me of what my share of the commission would be, reminded me that there was a world depression, reminded me of the unpaid doctors' bills that were mounting on my desk to care for my beloved Mary, reminded me of the money it was taking to support Mary's sister's cocaine habit. He threatened to withhold from me certain other commissions that were due me if I did not authenticate this one painting. And so I succumbed to the devil Duveen, may he twist eternally in his grave.' Then he added 'Do just one thing for me, Mrs.'—what was Erik's last name?"

"Tarcher. Erik Tarcher."

" 'Do just one thing for me, Mrs. Tarcher. Never tell your mother what I have just told you. It would hurt her too much to know how thoroughly she had been fooled.' As the years went by, you kept your promise. Indeed, you had almost forgotten this singular episode in B.B.'s garden because, after all, at the time you and Erik were in Italy on your honeymoon."

"We'd been married at least four years."

"Indeed, you'd forgotten this singular episode until, the other day, you heard that your mother was planning to give this painting to the Metropolitan Museum. This triggered your memory, and you became concerned lest the museum be drawn into this deception."

"Well, it makes an interesting story," she says. "Except that none of it is true." Then, all at once, she begins to have a glimmer of what Edwee is up to. She has found herself unwittingly involved in some of Edwee's schemes before, and she knows that she must watch her step. Edwee's schemes often lead to traps, and she knows that she must proceed very cautiously from this point forward. "I think," she says, "that this is a story, or something like it, that you want me to tell someone. Who?"

His eyes are open now. "The Met wouldn't touch that painting with a ten-foot pole if there was even the slightest *question* of its authenticity. Neither would John Marion at Sotheby's, or any other auctioneer or dealer, in spite of some of the funny games they play at those places."

"And?"

"The Goya would be ours."

"Ours?" She has a brief mental picture of her brother and herself lugging the heavy painting back and forth between each other's houses, between 66th Street and Sutton Square, once a month, on a kind of time-share basis.

Shades of Fortune

"Why would we want it?" she says. "A fake Goya? Or maybe it isn't a fake, is that it? I think it isn't a fake, correct?"

"It's still a very handsome painting, either way," he says evasively. "The field of art authentication is a very inexact science. You can get one so-called expert to stand up before a judge and jury and swear that a painting is authentic. And you can get another so-called expert to swear before the same judge and the same jury that it isn't. It's when the authenticity is *questioned* that the museums and the dealers want hands off. That's when it becomes a hot potato. My own expertise in questioning the authenticity of this one will certainly help. But your firsthand account of your conversation with B.B. should cinch it, don't you think? The Goya will become the hot potato that nobody will want to touch . . . but us."

"Us," she says. And then, "Edwee, I think you're crazy. You expect me to make up some cock-and-bull story—to tell an outright lie about a conversation with Berenson that never happened—just so you can get that Goya? Yes, I think you are quite crazy."

"Just a little white lie," he says in a wheedling tone. "After all, it *could* have happened."

"I am a woman with a certain reputation for integrity, Edwee. I am something of a public figure, whether you realize it or not. I don't intend to sacrifice my integrity, my credibility, for something like this."

"Your credibility could be a plus factor," he says. "Your credibility could mean that people will be inclined to believe what you say."

"As a magazine publisher, my dedication was to editorial integrity. In any future venture I may undertake, I will need that reputation for total integrity. I cannot afford to sacrifice, or to risk sacrificing, that reputation."

"Your integrity didn't prevent your magazine from folding," he says.

"How was I to know that Johnny Fairchild would attack me in *Women's Wear?*"

"Wasn't there a little more to it than that, dear girl? Wasn't there a little flurry of complaints within the advertising community when it turned out that you were charging different advertisers different rates for the same space?"

"That was—"

"And I seem to remember hearing something about padding circulation figures?"

"That was never proven!"

"And what about your little predilection for pinching things from here and there—from department stores, and other people's houses? Every time you leave my house I feel I should count the silver!"

"And what about *you?* What about that Collier business? What about that business with the Florida police? Talk about *morals!*"

But wait, she thinks. Wait. There is nothing to be gained by either of them from this sort of quarreling. Slowly, unexpectedly, it dawns on her that her baby brother may be playing right into her hand. He wants something. What he wants is not necessarily to put their mother in a nursing home. It is clear what he wants now. He wants the Goya. What she had not guessed was how desperately he wants it. He will risk his own reputation as well as hers to get it, and he needs her to help him get it. Well, anyone who wants a thing as badly as that should be willing to pay for it, shouldn't he? Of course he should. It is known as the law of supply and demand. In life, as in the marketplace, one gets what one pays for.

She stands up and moves across the cluttered room toward the east-facing windows, which overlook Edwee's perfect garden and the river. The summer is ending, and the days are growing shorter, and from the borough of Queens lights are beginning to flicker on. The days are growing shorter for me, too, she thinks. All around me, time is running short. The safety catch on her gold bracelet has come loose, and she fiddles with this with her free hand, playing for time, while in her mind she composes what she will say to him next.

"You know, I think Goya would rather like my idea," Edwee says quietly. "There's something very Goyaesque about it, isn't there? He was the most cynical of painters. He painted the Duchess of Osuna in a way that revealed all her ugliness and ignorance, her venality and greed and decadence and self-indulgence. Yet he managed to make her think that the result was a portrait of a great beauty. He must have, because she commissioned him over and over again. He managed to paint a screen over her own eyes, so that what she saw on the canvas was something entirely different from what was so clearly there. Remarkable, isn't it? It is as though he was able to hypnotize his subjects while he painted them. Beauty is in the eye of the beholder, but what is in the eye that the beholder beholds? A totally different vision. Four successive Spanish monarchs and their families and courtiers were fooled that way by him."

"What a pretty little speech, Edwee," she says, still fiddling with the safety catch, while all around her the room looms large and electric with possibilities.

"Someday I may write an essay on the subject."

"Do," Nonie says, studying the walls of Edwee's room, his collections arrayed along the bookshelves and in vitrines. Suddenly the room itself seems to her Goyaesque, rich and ripe and ready for intrigue and high deception.

"Edwee," she begins carefully, "you are a very rich man. I, of course, am something of the poor relation. This is a very valuable painting we're talking about, correct? Fifty million dollars? Just to take a wild guess at what it might be worth. How much would it be worth to you, Edwee, if I were to do this?"

He looks very unhappy now. "We'd have joint ownership, the two of us, of a great art treasure," he says. "After all, we're Mother's only direct heirs. The old battle-ax can't live forever!"

"Would it be worth five million dollars to you, Edwee?" She smiles brightly, straightening her bracelet. "Would it?"

But at that moment their conversation is interrupted by Edwee's Filipino houseman, who opens the door a crack and says, "Your other guest is here, Señor Myerson."

"Thank you, Tonio."

"Would it, Edwee?" she says again. "Edwee, you're looking a little ill. Are you all right? Is it your morning sickness again, do you think?" She taps his shoulder. "Now for goodness' sakes, get out of that silly chef's apron and hat. You look exactly like the little man on the Chef Boyardee spaghetti can."

Nonie follows her brother out of the office and down the long walnut-paneled gallery, past the collection of Greek amphorae, which, tonight, are individually lighted from concealed spots. The pricelessness of things, she thinks, the pricelessness of dreams, of all the dreams that money can buy. She hooks a hand in his elbow. "Five million," she says. "That's my price, sweetie."

"You drive a hard bargain, Sis."

They start down the short flight of carpeted steps into Edwee's sunken living room where, at the far end, a blond young man in a dinner jacket who looks vaguely familiar awaits them.

"Dirk, you remember my sister, Nonie, don't you?" Edwee says.

"Did I wake you, Mother?" It is Badger on the phone.

"No darling. I'm in bed, reading. What's up?"

"I wouldn't bother you this late, but I've learned something that you ought to know."

"What's that?"

"Our friend Horowitz has been talking to some of the Leo cousins."

She sits up straight in bed and cradles the receiver between her chin and shoulder. "How do you know this?"

"My squash-playing buddy who works for him. He's turning out to be quite a nice little source of information. We were having drinks tonight, and Horowitz's name came up. My friend said, 'Guess what my crazy boss did today. He flew up to Scarsdale in his helicopter . . . took his helicopter to fly twenty miles to Scarsdale.' I said I had some cousins in Scarsdale, people named Bernhardt. He said, 'That's funny, he went up there to see a Mrs. Richard Bernhardt.' I said 'Funny coincidence,' or something like that, but Mrs. Richard Bernhardt is one of Leo Myerson's granddaughters, Mother."

"I see."

"So it looks as though our friend may already be a jump ahead of us."

"Obviously. Damn!"

"I think if we're going to act, we'd better act fast."

"Yes. I agree. Absolutely."

"I have all the cousins' names, addresses, and telephone numbers. Do you want me to give these to you now, or shall we wait until the morning?"

"No, give them to me now." She fishes a pad and ballpoint pen from the drawer of her bedside table.

"Okay. Leopold Myerson's son and two daughters are all dead, but their children are all very much alive, and they all own shares in varying amounts. There are eight of these—or seven, if you don't count one who's in a loony bin. His brother's his custodian and votes his shares. One of the larger shareholders is this Mrs. Richard Bernhardt, Eight Rockinghorse Lane, Scarsdale, area code nine-one-four . . ."

"You're a genius, Badger," she whispers. "Have I told you that lately?"

Long after he has hung up, Mimi sits up in her bed, studying the list of names, memorizing them. The trouble is, she thinks, that she still has not decided on what might be the best way to approach these people. With a letter? Or a telephone call? Or a telephone call followed by a letter? Finally, she decides to discuss this with Badger first thing in the morning. She closes her book, using the list of names to mark her place, and turns out her lamp.

Sleep comes with difficulty tonight. Memories and questions crowd her mind. "Little white stars," he said. "Did you see them, too, Mimi?"

"Yes."

And then, much later, she has the dream again. It is always the same: the dark shape flying across the windshield, the shouts, the horns honking, her mother's screams. But suddenly the dream changes, and it is no longer her mother sitting beside her in the car. It is Michael, and he is laughing, but then she sees that he is weeping, too. "Don't cry," she tells him. "Don't cry, dear Michael. It wasn't my fault, my darling. It wasn't my fault."

Nonie Myerson lets herself into her apartment and rushes to the telephone and dials his number. After three rings, the oddly disembodied male voice answers. "You have reached five-five-five-one-eight-eight-oh. If you wish to leave a message, please wait for the sound of the tone."

The tone comes, and Nonie says, "This is a message for Mr. Roger Williams. This is Naomi Myerson calling. The message is this: Have secured necessary funding. Repeat. Have secured all necessary funding. Please call me at home as soon as you possibly can. Urgent." Agonizingly, she hopes it is not too late.

Alone in his living room now, Edwee Myerson turns to the blond young man and said, "Come upstairs with me for a minute. I have an interesting idea."

The young man follows him up the curved staircase, a bemused expression on his face.

At the top of the stairs, Edwee taps on a closed door. From behind it come the sounds of a television set.

"Is that you, Daddy?" she says.

He opens the door a crack.

"Johnny has Eddie Murphy on," she says. "He's really *funny.*"

"Feeling better, Pussyface? Good. I have a little surprise for you."

She turns her head from the huge television screen that occupies the entire wall opposite her bed. A look of alarm crosses her face when she sees he is not alone, and she pulls the satin sheet up across her bare shoulders.

"Isn't he pretty?" Edwee says. "I thought we'd try something a little different tonight: a threesome. What do you think, Pussyface?"

Still looking frightened, she studies the young man's smiling face, and gradually her look of alarm grows softer. She settles her blond head back against the many multishaped, lace-edged pillows on her bed and, with one arm, reaches out and turns off the television from the remote-control unit. She giggles. "Hell, I'll try anything once," she says.

The younger man begins loosening his tie.

"Mind if we videotape this?" Edwee says.

13

SOMETIMES MIMI'S FAMOUS—at least within the industry—
"Mimi Memos" were not about proposing new projects or developing new
products, but were simply sent out to impart cosmetological lore to the
people who worked for her. Since she learned that many of her employees
saved the memos, she decided that they were good for employee morale.
These "general" memos had the effect of reminding her staff that they were
part of an ancient and respected industry, not just a glitzy and show-bizzy
trade. They were designed to inform, educate, and amuse, and they always
revealed how thoroughly Mimi had immersed herself in her subject.

For instance, there was this one from 1973, after Mimi had headed Miray
for about ten years and was well on her way to making Miray the second-
largest (second only to door-to-door Avon) cosmetics manufacturer in the
country:

MIRAY CORPORATION
Interoffice Memorandum

TO: All employees
FROM: MM
SUBJECT: This & That

Humans have been using cosmetics for at least 8,000 years. Archeolo-
gists have uncovered palettes for grinding and mixing face powders dating from 6000 B.C. In ancient Egypt, by 4000 B.C., beauty shops flour-

ished. Women tipped their fingers and toes in reddish henna, accented the veins on their breasts in blue, and painted their nipples gold!

Egyptian men were just as vain, and Egyptian tombs are frequently found with makeup kits for the afterlife. In the 1920s, when King Tut's tomb was opened after more than 3,000 years, jars of skin cream, lip color, and rouge were found there—still usable, and still fragrant of oleoresins.

By 850 B.C., Phoenicia was the fashion and cultural capital of the civilized world, and cosmetics were introduced to Israel by Queen Jezebel, the wife of King Ahab, and the Bible refers to her use of makeup (2 Kings 9:30): "And when Jehu was come to Jezreel, Jezebel heard of it; and she painted her face . . ." From her window in the palace, in her makeup, she taunted Jehu, who was her son's rival for the throne, until Jehu, tired of this treatment, ordered her eunuchs to throw her out the window. When she landed, Jehu trampled her to death. Since then, Jezebel became the symbol of the scheming, evil woman, and for many years she gave cosmetics a bad name.

Cosmetics became fashionable in England under Queen Elizabeth I, who had her own beauty formula. After bathing in a very hot bath to open the pores, she splashed her face liberally with red wine, which stained her a pretty pink color. Soon fashionable women were bathing their entire bodies with wine, including Mary Queen of Scots, who had the temerity to ask for an increased living allowance in order to afford this luxury!

By the 18th century, English women of all classes were using such a variety of paints, creams, stains, and rouges to such an extent that it was suspected that the sinister purpose behind women's makeup was to lure unsuspecting males into marriage. In 1770, a drastic law was enacted by Parliament, stating "that all women of whatever age, rank, profession, or degree, whether virgins, maids, or widows, that shall, from and after such Act, impose upon, seduce, and betray into matrimony, any of His Majesty's subjects, by the scents, paints, cosmetic washes, artificial teeth, false hair, Spanish wool, iron stays, hoops, high heeled shoes, bolstered hips, shall incur the penalty of the law in force against witchcraft, and like misdemeanors and that the marriage, upon conviction, shall stand null and void."

Needless to say, we women prevailed, and this law did not stay on the books very long.

From England, the idea that cosmetics were an important adjunct to fashion quickly spread to the royal courts of France, Italy, and Spain. Cosmetics were much favored by the court of Louis XIII, and one of the most legendary royal advertisements of their efficacy was the beautiful

Anne of Austria. But it was the Empress Josephine, the wife of Napoleon I, who can really be said to be the mother of the modern cosmetics industry. From her native island of Martinique, she brought to Paris trunkloads of exotic creams, rouges, powders, and dyes that the French public immediately wanted for themselves. This demand inspired French scientists to try to duplicate these artistic beauty aids on a scientific basis.

It is thanks to Josephine that, for many years, the French dominated the cosmetics industry.

Until *we* came along, that is!

Which brings me to the real point of this memo. There's been a lot of talk in our industry lately about collagens and various cellular anti-aging emulsions being developed in Switzerland and other parts of Europe, and I've been asked whether we shouldn't jump on this bandwagon and intro- duce an anti-wrinkle cream of our own. The fact is that collagens and elastins are simply fibrous animal proteins that are used in the tanning of leather. Our chemists have analyzed these products and found that they are quite useless when it comes to the actual elimination of wrinkles. All these products are *moisturizers,* and the regular use of moisturizers (on most skin) will delay the appearance of wrinkles, but—as yet—there is no known substance that will actually *remove* or *prevent* wrinkling. I feel we would be doing our customers a disservice if we offered a product that made such claims. Meanwhile, of course, research continues. . . .

Despite her sophistication, Mimi often thinks that in some ways she had what amounted to a sheltered childhood. As an only child, with only her dolls for playmates, and with parents who spent much of their time express- ing their displeasure with one another, she had become—quite contentedly, it seemed to her—something of a loner. Her grandparents remained myste- rious beings to her, even though she saw them nearly every Sunday after- noon at their house for tea. They gave her elaborate presents, like the ermine jacket and the dollhouse, and yet they remained always distant and aloof, and she knew that her mother was frightened of them. They held some indefinable power over her parents' lives. But there was always an insurmountable barrier, a wall implacable and stern, that stood between their house and hers.

Once, when leaving her grandparents' house after one of those teas, she had made the mistake of saying to them, "I'll see you next Sunday, Grand- mama, ma'am, and Grandpapa, sir," before performing her farewell curtsy. She knew from the expression on her mother's face that she had said some- thing terribly wrong, and afterward her mother was very angry about it.

"Never tell them you'll see them next Sunday!" her mother said. "That was *very* rude. That's like asking to be invited to someone's party."

"But we go there every Sunday."

"We go there because *they* ask *us*, not the other way around. It's up to them to issue the invitation. Did you notice that neither of them said anything when you said that? That's how shocked they were! Now I don't know whether we're to be invited there next Sunday or not. What will your father say if we're not?"

But of course they were.

She knew that these Sunday visits were terribly important to her mother. And yet, at the same time, she knew that her mother dreaded them and always required several swallows of her medicine before setting forth downtown—"liquid courage," her mother sometimes called it. It was all very confusing, and in the end, it was easier to let the confusions of her young girlhood flow around her and past her and wash over her, and to keep her questions to herself.

At Miss Hall's school, being on an academic scholarship meant that, socially, Mimi was a member of a caste very different, and apart, from that of the majority of the girls. Her scholarship meant that there were certain "scholarship duties" that she and the few other scholarship girls were required to perform. These duties were posted weekly on the school's bulletin board. Scholarship girls had to wait on tables in the school's dining room a certain number of weeks in every year, and this meant getting to the dining room early and eating meals separately, in the kitchen, before the dinner bell rang and the rest of the school trooped in. A certain number of hours also had to be spent pushing brooms and dustmops in the school's corridors, while the rest of the school, gossiping and laughing, passed to and fro, on their way to this or that. A scholarship girl, busy with her duties, became invisible, and Mimi had learned to make the best of her invisibility, and even to enjoy it. What else was there to do? They can't see me, she told herself, and I can't see them. For me, they don't exist.

Scholarship duties also prevented her from joining certain extracurricular activities and clubs that the other girls joined, and even from taking part in certain sports. She told herself that she was lucky, that these were things in which she had no interest anyway. If anyone had told her she was lonely, she would have laughed at them. She had learned to enjoy the company of herself the best.

There was a word in the school in those days that everyone used. It was *hypocrisy.* Everyone complained of the hypocrisy of teachers, the hypocrisy of the school administration, even Headmistress, the hypocrisy of parents, the hypocrisy of boys, and the hypocrisy of anyone whom you didn't particularly care for. Mimi herself had noticed glaring examples of what she considered hypocrisy at Miss Hall's and was therefore a little taken aback to discover that she herself had been branded a hypocrite.

A girl named Barbara Badminton from Locust Valley had confronted her with this accusation one afternoon in the corridor. Planting herself squarely in front of Mimi, Barbara Badminton had said, "You know, you're a real hypocrite, Myerson. You're the biggest hypocrite in this entire school."

"Really? Why?"

"Your grandfather's Adolph Myerson, isn't he? He's supposed to be one of the richest men in the entire country, isn't he? Then why are you on scholarship? The rest of us have to pay the full tuition, but you don't pay anything. It's not fair!"

Later, she had overheard Barbara Badminton and some of her friends whispering about her in the common room, while Mimi ran her dustcloth along the chair rail in the room next door.

"You know why that hypocrite Myerson is on a scholarship, don't you?" Barbara Badminton said. "It's because she's a J-e-w, and all the J-e-w's ever want is to get everything they can for free. That's why they're all so rich. My father said so."

Mimi decided that it was beneath her dignity to let remarks like that upset her. But she could not resist a condescending, and totally patronizing, smile in Barbara Badminton's direction when that semester's grades were posted and Mimi received four A's and one A-plus, while Barbara Badminton got two C's, two D's, and one D-minus.

Winning good grades, of course, is not always the passkey to instant popularity.

In chemistry class, Barbara Badminton sat at the desk behind her, and a few weeks later, during a quiz, Mimi felt a fingertip touch her shoulder. She half-turned, and Barbara Badminton hissed, "What's the atomic weight of nitrogen? Give me the answer and I'll be your friend!" Mimi simply turned back to the test, making sure that her left arm covered the answers as thoroughly as possible as she filled them in.

"Bitch!" Barbara Badminton whispered.

After that, Barbara Badminton's enmity was even more open and outspoken.

In 1957, the year she met Michael, most of the other girls at Miss Hall's School were talking about debutante parties—the balls and tea dances they had been invited to in Lake Forest or Shaker Heights or Sewickley or Greenwich or Tuxedo Park, or the ones that their parents were giving for them. Every day, the girls who were members of the Badminton Set compared the invitations that appeared in their mailboxes, and in their dormitory rooms their dresser mirrors sprouted with little black-and-white engraved cards marked "Accept" or "Regret."

"Are you having a coming-out party, Myerson?" Barbara Badminton asked her haughtily.

"No, as a matter of fact, I'm not," she said.

"I know why," Barbara Badminton said. "They don't let Jews have coming-out parties, that's why. They don't even let them in the *Social Register*, and that's a fact."

"No, that's not the reason," Mimi said sweetly. "I can't very well have a coming-out party when I'm engaged to be married, can I?"

"Oh, yeah? Where's your ring?"

"We're picking it out this summer," Mimi said.

"I don't believe you!"

"Excuse me, I'm on my way to the library," Mimi said.

"You think you're hell on wheels, don'tcha?"

The story, true or not (and not even Mimi was sure whether it was true), quickly made its way to the others in the Badminton Set who were, if nothing else, impressed. But being the first girl in one's class to become engaged is not a ticket to popularity, either.

One of the hit television shows of those days was called *Catch Me If You Can*, and it was easily the biggest of the big-money quiz shows that dominated the airwaves. With its sinister-looking, hermetically sealed "isolation booth," the show posed a series of increasingly difficult questions to a series of contestants. But the contestant who, almost single-handedly, had made *Catch Me* a hit was a tall, dark curly-haired young man of vaguely Central European origins called Prince Fritzi von Maulsen. Prince Fritzi claimed to be one of the many great-nephews of Queen Victoria, and when he first appeared on *Catch Me* as a contestant, he quickly demonstrated an astonishing ability to answer questions ranging from American baseball to nuclear physics, from Shakespeare to science fiction.

The youthful prince was also an enormously appealing television presence, furrowing his brow boyishly as he struggled to come up with the answer to some particularly abstruse question. Soon this charmingly foreign-accented young nobleman was receiving over ten thousand pieces of fan mail a week, many of them containing marriage proposals. When he correctly answered the question that asked where in *Coriolanus* Volumnia says, "For the love of Juno, let's go" (Act II, Scene 1), he became the biggest money winner in the history of television, walking off with total winnings of $175,000. Now he was not only handsome and titled and brainy, but also rich. Following Mimi's announcement of her engagement, Barbara Badminton began telling all her friends that none other than Prince Fritzi von Maulsen had been invited to her coming-out party, and had accepted

Her family, Barbara Badminton explained airily, had known the von Maulsens "forever—we've stayed at their *Schloss*," and she added that

Prince Fritzi was just as sweet in person as he was on the tiny screen, "or even sweeter, and ever so much sexier." To this news she was soon adding the fact that Prince Fritzi had "practically" proposed marriage to her, and that she was considering becoming his princess.

"But wouldn't it be kind of scary to be married to a man who's as smart as that?" Mimi had heard one of Barbara's friends ask her.

She had heard Barbara giggle. "He told me they give him the answers to lots of those questions ahead of time," she said. "Because he's so good for the ratings. It's not really cheating."

Meanwhile, Mimi had had no idea, no preparation, for what it meant to be in love. It was something her mother had never discussed with her, and it was something that was not taught in school. In the books she had read, people "fell in love," but hardly anywhere had she found a description that matched her own terrifying sensation of it. To her, it was like falling off the edge of the earth, it was like a loss of gravity. When she thought of him, her lungs seemed to collapse within her, she was unable to breathe, there was a yawning ache at the pit of her stomach that was almost nausea, her eyes glazed and familiar objects refused to come into focus, and the words of the book she was reading would dissolve into meaningless squiggles on the page. It was not a venereal longing, really, and it seemed to have nothing at all to do with what sex was. Indeed, it made those demonstrations of Old Pete's from his basement window seem almost comical. It seemed to have no body, no form, no specificity. But just the thought of the fine, soft hairs on the back of one of Michael's hands could bring on one of these violent surges, and she would lose her balance on the stairs and have to seize the banister for support. Or it could happen just as easily in the history classroom, in the middle of a lecture, the dizziness, and she would have to excuse herself and go to the washroom and, with trembling hands, splash cold water on her face.

There were other symptoms. She seemed to have lost all appetite for food and had to force herself to eat, to force the straw-tasting Salisbury steak down her throat. She seemed to have lost all awareness of other people, to have been sucked into a kind of void or airless vacuum, and when this happened all the members of the Badminton Set could have stood in a circle all around her, taunting her and calling her names, and she would have been unaware of them. She had trouble concentrating, had difficulty remembering not only names of presidents and dates of wars and atomic weights, but also which dresser drawer contained her stockings and which held her sweaters. Her English teacher, Miss McCauley, was the first to mention it to her.

"Your work's been slipping this semester, Mimi," Miss McCauley said. "Is anything the matter?"

"No, no."

"You forgot that the essay on Coleridge was due today? That's not like you, Mimi."

"I know, I—"

"You're not ill, are you?"

"No, no." And that, apparently, was when she fainted, felt her legs go weak and fell in a heap on the classroom floor.

When she woke, she was in a bed in the school infirmary, and the doctor was standing over her. "Can't find anything wrong with you," he said. "Your pulse is fine, your blood pressure's fine. Are you about due to have your period?"

She nodded yes.

"I suspect that's it," he said.

At times, she wondered whether in fact she was sick. Early one morning she woke, shivering with icy cold, and discovered that her sheets and bedclothes were soaking wet. It was either from a feverish dream, or she had wet the bed. But she knew what it was. She was in love.

And it all happened so suddenly, almost without warning. They had met several other times during that midwinter break. They met for skating in the park, and he took her to see the movie *Funny Face*, with Fred Astaire and Audrey Hepburn, and afterward he did a fair imitation of Astaire, touching the tip of her nose with the tip of his finger and saying, "I loff your fah-nee face, your fah-nee face." And they went to see *The Bridge on the River Kwai*, and as they were leaving the theatre she said she loved the picture but didn't understand the ending, and so he insisted on going back into the theatre to see the movie over again until she got the point that the English officer, Alec Guinness, had become so obsessed by the bridge he was building for his Japanese captors that, in the end, he was firing on his own countrymen to defend the bridge from destruction. All through that second showing he held her hand.

One of the thrilling things about him, she realized, was his supreme self-confidence. In any situation, he moved in immediately and almost casually took command of whatever it was. This made even the most banal occasions seem somehow glamorous. He seemed to be an authority on everything. For instance, when they had gone back to see *The Bridge* a second time, the attendant at the door had said that it would be necessary to buy two new tickets. "I have my stubs from the earlier showing," Michael said airily, producing them. "I happen to know that tickets for a movie are good for as many showings of the film as the purchaser wishes to view on any particular day. If there's any question, send out the manager." They had gone sweeping back into the theatre like royalty. "You have to know how to talk to these people," Michael said.

There had been no more dinners at the Rainbow Room, but there had been pizzas and hamburgers and hot dogs in more pedestrian establishments, and, during this two-week period, there were many days when he was too busy with his studies, and with his project in New Jersey—"the job," as he called it—to see her at all. He had kept repeating that he was going to marry her, but she had decided that this was some sort of little joke with him.

Then, on their last night together, he had very gently taken her in his arms, said, "May I?" and kissed her.

It was certainly a pleasant kiss, bringing with it a bright little tingle of excitement, a little thrill of grownupness that gave her happy dreams that night. But that was all.

Then, a few days after she had returned to school in Connecticut, there was a letter from him in her mailbox. "Dear Mimi," it began.

I have just realized that I have been guilty of a very serious oversight during our recent times together. I realize that I have neglected to tell you that I love you. Let me try to correct that oversight now. I love you, Mimi. I love you. I love you. I love you. I love you. I love you. I love you. I love you. I love you. . . .

And he had gone on like that for at least twenty handwritten pages.

She had immediately picked up a pen and a sheet of embossed school stationery, with its motto, *Deum Servire*, which the girls in the Badminton Set claimed to find "fantastically hypocritical," and wrote:

Dear Michael—I love you too!

That was when it happened, all at once. She could not catch her breath, her vision blurred, and that groaning ache rose from the pit of her stomach, not nausea but something much more eruptive and overpowering and debilitating, and she knew she was in love, and that it was nothing like anything she had ever read about in any book. She had blindly sealed and addressed the letter, unable to write another single word.

Today, thirty years later, Mimi Myerson Moore admits that she has never quite felt that way since.

That Michael feeling.

14

*O*F COURSE I want to meet him," her mother said. "I am dying to meet him, and your daddy is dying to meet him, and we *will* meet him, your lovely Choate boy. But—"

"I told you, Mother, he's not from Choate."

"Of course. I forgot. Where did you say he went to school?"

"He's just graduated from Columbia Business School."

"Oh, yes, that's right. You did tell me that. That means he's older than you, but that's all right. Oh, this is so exciting, isn't it, Mimi? Your first beau!"

"He wants to marry me, Mother."

"Yes, yes, you told me that. But the thing is, before we go into this any further, before your daddy and I even meet this young man and discuss all this, there is something you must do first."

"What's that?" she asked, even though she was fairly sure she knew what the first thing was.

"You must discuss this with your grandfather, Mimi. You know how hurt he gets when he thinks anything is being planned behind his back, when he even suspects that something has been planned behind his back."

Mimi said nothing.

"A letter, I think," her mother said. "Yes, I think a nice letter from you on your personal stationery, asking if you can come to see him. On a matter of a personal nature. Concerning your future. Yes, I think that would be the way to put it. That you would like to see him on a matter of a personal nature, concerning your future."

"Why does everything have to have his approval, Mother?"

"Why? Well, you know *why*, silly! Because he *controls* everything. Everything you, or I, or your father does, your grandfather controls. Surely you know that. And until he dies"—suddenly her mother's eyes went blank—"until he dies, that's the way it's going to be."

"What does he control, exactly?"

"Why, the money, of course! Where would you or I or your father be if it weren't for his money? Where would we be? Out on the street. Beggars. He knows that, and that's why he must be a part of any family decision."

"Then why couldn't we tell him that I went to Miss Hall's on a scholarship?"

"*What?*" her mother cried. "But that was something entirely different, Mimi. Entirely different! You must never tell your grandfather that. Never!"

"Why is that different, Mother?"

"Because it just . . . *is*. If your grandfather found out that we couldn't afford, well, he just wouldn't understand, that's all."

"Why wouldn't he understand?"

"Oh, Mimi, it's all so complicated. Can't you just take my word for it that he wouldn't understand? You see, he thinks he pays your father this big salary, enough for us to live in the lap of luxury, the way *he* does. But if he knew where the money goes—"

"Where does it go, Mother?"

"If he knew where the money goes, that would be the end of everything —for all of us."

"But where *does* the money go?"

Her mother hesitated, and her eyes withdrew. "It just . . . goes," she said. "Things are expensive. Bills . . . bills. Shall I show you the stack of bills on my desk? Dentists' bills, doctors' bills—"

"None of us have been to the dentist or a doctor lately."

"Other bills. Take my word for it, there are bills. I could show you the stack of bills on my desk, if you'd like."

"I'm afraid I still don't understand, Mother."

"Can't you just take my word for it? I'm the one who pays the bills, so I ought to know, shouldn't I? But you're not to mention a word of this to your grandfather. As I say, he wouldn't understand. Now run and fetch a pen and a sheet of your good stationery—the one with your initials on it—and we'll write a nice letter to your grandpa. That's the first thing we have to do."

Mimi had found a sheet of letter paper in her desk drawer and returned with it to the living room.

"While you're up, freshen my drink, will you, darling? I need a bit of my medicine before I dictate this letter."

Mimi carried her mother's glass to the drinks cart and fixed her mother's drink the way she knew she liked it: whiskey, with lots of ice, and a tiny splash of water on the top.

"Thank you, darling," her mother said, accepting the glass, and after a quick sip, her spirits seemed to improve, as they usually did. "You see, I nurse my drinks," her mother said. "That's the secret. I suppose you've heard your father tell me that he thinks I drink too much, but what he doesn't understand is that I always nurse my drinks. That's why I never become intoxicated. If you ever take a drink, Mimi, drink it very slowly. Nurse it, as I say. That's the ladylike way, and you'll never become intoxicated. Now, where were we? Oh, yes, your letter. Sit here beside me, darling." She patted the sofa. "Have you got a good writing surface? Yes, the telephone book will do nicely. Is the light over your left shoulder? Good. For reading or writing, the light should always be over your left shoulder, but you knew that. All right. Let's begin. 'Dear Old Moneybags.'" Her mother giggled. "No, don't write that; I was only teasing. 'Dearest Grandpa—'"

" 'Sir'?"

Her mother laughed again. "No, silly! You don't call him 'sir' in a letter! That's only to his face. Now let's begin. 'Dearest Grandpapa. Having graduated from Miss Hall's School with honors'—that's true, isn't it?"

"I was on the Honor Roll."

"Yes, I thought so. The school sent us your report card, but I've forgotten where I put it. Probably with all the bills! So let's change that. Let's say, 'Having graduated from Miss Hall's School with highest honors'—that's not too much of a fib, is it? Anyway, it sounds good and it will impress your grandfather, so leave it in. 'Having graduated from da-dee-da with highest honors, I now face the challenge of my future.' I like that, don't you? 'The challenge of my future'? Yes. 'But before charting the next phase of my life, dear Grandpapa, I need the kind of sound advice that only you can give me. A number of interesting possibilities present themselves, including a proposal of marriage from a splendid young man.' No, leave that part out. Don't say that, because it sounds too much as though you've already made up your mind, which you haven't. You'll wait to mention that when you see him. Just say, 'A number of interesting possibilities present themselves. May I, at your convenience, come to see you and discuss these with you, along with . . . along with'—oh, I had a good phrase a minute ago, but I've forgotten it!"

"Matters of a personal nature?"

"Yes, that's it! 'Along with certain matters of a personal nature which will affect the future course of my life. I look forward to your reply. Sincerely yours.' Oh, my God! I almost forgot the Wicked Old Witch of the West! Before 'Sincerely yours,' add, 'My dearest love to Grandmama.' There. Now read it back to me."

Mimi did, and when she was finished, her mother clapped her hands and then took another swallow of her drink. "Perfect!" her mother cried. "Sign it, seal it, and send it off! Oh, I'm so happy for you, Mimi—you and your wonderful Choate boy!"

"He isn't—" she began, but decided to let it pass.

"It's a perfect letter. It's sure to win him over. Quick. Drop it in the mail."

In Mimi's opinion, the letter seemed a little too starched and formal, but she did as she was told.

"Well, how'd it go?" he asked her when she met him. "What'd your folks say? When do I get to meet them?"

"It was just my mother. My father wasn't home. She wants me to see my grandfather first."

"Your *grand*father?"

"Old Moneybags, she calls him."

"Hell, we don't need his money!"

"I know, but it's sort of a family tradition, discussing everything with my grandparents first. It doesn't mean anything." But she did not really want to talk about it. She did not really want to talk about anything. It was enough to be with him, just walking down the street with him with their shoulders touching and their fingers linked.

At the edge of the park, he motioned her to a bench and said, "Sit down a minute. I want to show you something."

They sat, and he reached into the pocket of his jacket and withdrew a small blue box. "For you," he said. "Open it."

"From Tiffany . . ."

"Go ahead. Open it."

She opened the box and inside, nested in a white velvet cushion, was a diamond solitaire.

"A diamond is forever," he said. "I want you forever."

"Oh, Michael!" she cried, and suddenly she burst into tears.

"Hey," he said. "What's this? It's only a little old engagement ring. What are you crying for?"

"I can't . . . help it," she sobbed.

"Come on, cut it out. You look terrible when you cry, you really do."

"It's just the . . . the hypocrisy . . ."

"Hypocrisy? What are you talking about, kiddo?" His arm was about her shoulders now.

"Pretending . . . people pretending they care about people that they really wish would die. . . ."

"I don't understand. What's wrong?"

"I'm crying because . . . because it makes me sad because . . ." Her voice was muffled now because her face was buried in the thick folds of his jacket sleeve, and her sobs became more violent, and he sat there, helpless, letting her cry and cry.

But she could not tell him why she was crying, because it seemed she was crying for everything: for her mother and her unhappy father, for all the Sunday teas on Madison Avenue, for the scholarship girls, and even for Barbara Badminton and the Badminton Set and Old Pete, but mostly it was because she had never believed that something like this would ever really happen to her, never really believed that Michael had meant it when he said he loved her, never really believed that anyone would ever care for her enough to say "I want you forever" in just that way, and because, even with the ring box in her hand, she still could not believe it and was afraid she never would.

Finally, she sat up straight. "It's because I've never seen such a beautiful ring . . . it's so beautiful . . . too beautiful . . . it's the most beautiful ring I've ever seen . . . the most beautiful in the world, I think. I'm sad because I've never seen . . . such a beautiful ring. Oh, Michael, I love you so. . . ."

15

*H*E WANTS TO SEE YOU at his *office?*" her mother said to her. "My goodness, I've never *been* to his office! But that makes it much more formal, doesn't it. If it had been at the house, you could have been more casual. I think a suit, don't you? How about your beige Davidow with the piping? Or your light blue David Crystal? No, too springy, I think. I think the Davidow, with a very simple off-white blouse—high-neck, of course—and a gold circle pin, or a strand of pearls, but not both. You know how your grandpa hates women who wear too much jewelry! Small gold earrings if you wear the pin, or seed pearls with the pearls. You'll have your hair done, of course. And a hat? Yes, I think so, Mimi. I do think a little hat, a little sailor, perhaps, or—who knows?—even a little beret might be pretty. Fix me a quick drink, darling, and we'll run down to Saks and see what we can find. Thank you. Of course, you'll want to tell whoever does your hair that you're going to be wearing a hat, so he can leave your hair flatter on the top and fluffed up on the sides. Of course, not too much makeup—lipstick, and a little cream rouge. Not too much with the eyes. Needless to say, your grandpa has some pretty strong theories about makeup—after all, that's his business! But even though he makes the stuff, he hates it when a woman wears too much. And don't forget hose. He can't stand women with bare legs. And shoes with a medium heel. He hates me when I wear high heels because they make me as tall as he is! Don't you have some beigey alligator-type pumps with a medium heel? If you wear those, I have a beigey alligator Chanel-type bag with a long gold chain that would go nicely, I could let you borrow. And—oh, I almost forgot: *gloves!* Shortie white gloves, just to the wrist, and make sure they're white and clean-clean-clean. You'll remove the gloves, of course, as you enter his office. And, for God's sake, don't wear the ring! The ring will make it look as though it's official, which it isn't, and won't be until we're ready to announce it. Don't wear the ring, whatever you do. He notices *every*thing. . . ."

Her mother had planned her wardrobe for this meeting with her grandfather as though it were for her first day at school.

"What did you say the young man's name was?" her grandfather said.

"Horowitz," she said. "Michael Horowitz, Grandpa."

"Horowitz," he repeated. "There was a family named Horween in Chicago. I believe their name was originally Horowitz. They were decent people."

"Michael doesn't believe in name-changing, Grandpa."

"Well, there are two schools of thought about that, of course."

They were sitting in her grandfather's big office on Fifth Avenue—the same office that Mimi uses now, though one would never recognize it.

In those days, Adolph Myerson's New York office seemed a dark, cavernous, almost forbidding place, with its heavy oak-paneled walls and ceiling, the thick Persian carpet on the floor, and the deep red-velvet window hangings that all but blocked out any sunlight from the street outside. All around the room, on various tables and stands, were the signed presidential portraits, from Harding onward—though Roosevelt and Truman were missing —and, front and center, a photograph of the current White House occupant, Dwight D. Eisenhower, signed breezily, "For Adolph—cheers from Ike." All the photographs were in heavy silver frames, and in other frames were copies of the various medals, citations, awards, honors, and degrees that had been bestowed upon Adolph Myerson in the course of his long career.

Behind his big, leather-topped desk hung the portrait of Adolph Myerson himself, the man who had guided the Miray Corporation from its inauspicious beginnings on the Grand Concourse to its present world eminence. It was a portrait, naturally, of a more youthful man than the one she sat opposite now. The small moustache had been black when the portrait had been painted, and the pince-nez that he wore about his neck had not yet become a part of his habitual attire. But there was something odd about the portrait that struck her right away. He stood, full length, beside a fireplace, his right hand resting on the mantelpiece, but the painting seemed out of balance, off-center. Her grandfather's figure occupied the right-hand edge of the canvas, while the rest of the frame consisted of a depiction of the fireplace and empty wall. Later, she learned the reason for the painting's strange imbalance. Originally, it had been a portrait of the company's two cofounders, Adolph and Leopold, standing on either side of the fireplace. But when Leopold had left the company, or even somewhat before, Adolph had ordered his younger brother painted out of the picture and replaced with woodwork and an ornamental mantel clock.

Still, despite this oddity, her grandfather's office was a room designed to announce to the visitor that this was the office of a Very Important Person, who always dressed in dark, English-tailored suits. Behind his desk now, he removed his pince-nez and rubbed the bridge of his nose. It was a gesture, those in the family knew, that usually indicated displeasure. Though Adolph Myerson was then eighty-seven years old, he was still, Mimi had to admit, a commanding presence—even though he was not tall and had grown somewhat portly. His nose was long and thin, his steel-grey moustache and pointed beard were perfectly trimmed, and he sat ramrod-straight in his chair.

He replaced the pince-nez and, through their glittery lenses, fixed his deep-set, penetrating eyes on her. "Horowitz," he said once more.

"Yes, Grandpa."

"In real estate, you say."

"Yes, a builder. He's just graduated from Columbia Business School."

"Columbia. We've always been a Princeton and Harvard family, of course."

"Princeton doesn't have a business school, Grandpa."

He leaned forward in his chair. *"But Harvard does!"*

"Yes, Grandpa, that's true. Harvard does." Whenever she was with him, he had a way of making her feel just like a little girl. But that, she supposed, was part of the secret of his business success: he made everyone around him feel insignificant.

"Who are his people? I don't know any Horowitzes in New York."

"His family has a catering business in Kew Gardens," she said. "It's very successful. They have over a hundred employees. They do—"

"Kew Gardens," he said. "Where is that?"

"On Long Island, Grandpa."

"Oh, yes. It's in Queens, actually, isn't it? A Jewish section of Queens. But out there they say they live on *Lon Gisland.*" He laughed, but his laugh was not one of amusement. "Jackson Heights used to be a nice neighborhood. Haven't been there in years, of course."

"Michael's very nice, Grandpa," she said. "I know you'll like him."

"He hasn't got you pregnant, has he?"

She gasped. "Of course not!"

"A caterer's son," he said. "Your grandmother and I never use caterers. We've always had our own staff."

"I know that, Grandpa."

"And I certainly can't use any building contractors in this company. Chemists and druggists we use to test certain products, but we can't use any builders, I'm afraid, in case that's what he has in mind."

At first, she didn't understand. Then she said, "But he doesn't want to work for Miray, Grandpa! He's got his own business. He's building—"

"Tell me something," he interrupted. "Is he dark-complected? They often are, these Orientals."

"No," she said, suddenly alarmed at the way this conversation seemed to be heading. "He has brown eyes, light brown hair, and his skin is . . . well, no darker than yours or mine."

"Can't have you giving me any darky great-grandchildren!" Once more there was the short, unamused laugh.

"Right now, he has a nice tan . . . from working out of doors a lot on his job in New Jersey."

"New *Joisey*," he said. "Tell me, Mireille, where did you meet this Mr. Moskowitz? Or is it Lupowitz?"

"Horowitz," she said. "Actually, we met when we were skating in Central Park. I broke a skate lace. He replaced it for me, and we—and he asked to see me again. It was last winter," she added a little lamely.

Once more he removed his pince-nez and rubbed the bridge of his nose a little harder than before. "Quite frankly, Mireille," he said, "you disappoint me. This Jewish caterer's son from Kew Gardens named *Horowitz*. We've never associated with that element in New York. Horowitz."

"What's wrong with the name Horowitz? Vladimir Horowitz, the great pianist!"

"I'm not musical," he said. "I'm talking about the element these people represent. They're Russians. They've just come down out of the trees. You're a Myerson, Mireille."

"Were the Myersons all that great—before you, that is?"

"Myerson is a very old and distinguished name," he said. "Before immigrating to Germany, where my parents came from, and where the name became somewhat corrupted, we were prominent in the seventeenth and eighteenth century in France, where the name was Maraison, from the family motto, 'Ma Raison,' which translates as 'My Right.' It is a motto closely connected to the royal 'Dieu et Mon Droit.' There was a castle called Ma Raison near Epernay, in the Champagne country, and there were Maraisons who were counts and countesses, members of the Court at Versailles. On my mother's side, the Rosenthal family—"

"But your family were from the Lower East Side, weren't they?"

There was a stony silence, and then he said, "I have had the family pedigree prepared. I will gladly show it to you if you're interested." There was another silence and then, in a different voice, he said, "You're very pretty, Mireille."

Startled, she blinked. He had never said anything like that to her before. "You really are. A very pretty girl. You have a pretty little nose, and unusual grey eyes. You don't look Jewish at all. I see you're wearing Pink Poppy."

"Pink Poppy?"

"On your nails. That's our Pink Poppy. It's very becoming. Now here's a new shade I want you to try." He pulled open one of his desk drawers. "We're going to be introducing it for fall. We're going to call it Fire and Brandy. It's a bit more sophisticated, more for evening. And here's another shade you might like: Hot Geranium. Another winter shade." He began removing the little bottles from his drawer and placing them on his desk. "But for a summer shade, try this: Saffron 'n' Spice. And the coordinated lipsticks, of course—a Miray innovation, as I'm sure you know. And here's a new eye shadow that would go well with your coloring. And this: brand-new, a night cream we're testing in selected markets."

As the collection of little tubes and jars and bottles grew on his desktop, she realized that he was sampling her, the way he sampled the buyers from Bonwit's and Bloomingdale's. "Don't worry about how you're going to carry all these things home," he said. "I have a shopping bag," and from another drawer he produced one of the small and elegant signature shopping bags that the stores gave out: bright, shiny red with the name "Miray" in white, the long, ribbonlike serif of the letter *M* curling backward and trailing through the loop of the *y*.

"Try this," he continued, producing more samples from the endless collection in his drawer and dropping them into the red bag, "and this: a bee-pollen eye gel . . ." Then, in the same cajoling tone, he said, "Mireille, you're my only granddaughter. Naturally, I have a special place in my heart for you. Please consider carefully what you are proposing to do. Do you want to become a Mrs. Horowitz, a name that will associate you with that Jewish element? I suppose you've often wondered why your grandmother and I no longer go to services at Temple Emanu-El."

She hadn't wondered, but she nodded.

"It's because that element has completely taken over there. If you let one in, others follow. They bring in their friends and all their relatives, the cousins, their aunts and uncles, their sons-in-law, and before you know it the place is overrun with them. The same thing has happened at the Harmonie Club, which is why I no longer am a member there—which I miss, because I used to enjoy the pool. The place is overrun. The only place that's left is Century, the only place that's been able to uphold the standard. But the Orientals are already pounding on our doors out there, trying to get in.

There's some publisher named Kopf or Kupf or something, who's been put up. Your Mr. Horowitz could never become a member of Century, Mireille."

"I'm sure Michael has no interest in joining Century, Grandpa."

"Don't be too sure," he said. "They all want to get into Century, these people. They regard it as a status symbol. They fail to realize that a club is a place where people of similar tastes and interests like to gather, nothing more than that."

"Michael isn't a golfer, Grandpa."

"Then look at it another way. Won't it look a little peculiar that Adolph Myerson's granddaughter's husband is *not* a member of Century? What will people say to that?"

She looked around the room helplessly, looking for some way to counter the illogic of her grandfather's logic.

"Is he interested in any sports, this Horowitz? Football or baseball?"

"Well, he's a Yankees fan."

"Yes. These Orientals often are, though they don't play sports well."

"A very *moderate* Yankees fan."

"But the point is to find someone whose name will do your family proud, someone whose family and position are in keeping with our own position in New York society. As I say, you don't look Jewish. Why marry someone whose name and background will stigmatize you unnecessarily and associate you in people's minds with everything that is deplored about the Jewish race? Of course, if the man you marry has to be Jewish, there are plenty of nice—"

"You sound like an anti-Semite, Grandpa!"

"I? On the boards of the United Jewish Appeal and the World Jewish Congress, not to mention a dozen other Jewish philanthropic organizations across the United States? Surely you cannot be serious, Mireille. And I have no time for jokes." Then he had spread his hands out flat on the leather desktop in front of him, in his best professional manner, and the expression on his face now was similar to the one he wore when he posed for the portrait that hung on the wall behind him: that of a weary but patient teacher who is forced to explain, all over again, a very simple problem to a particularly dull-witted pupil. "Let me tell you something about the Jews, Mireille," he said, "something that you seem not to understand. Not all Jews are alike, just as not all Christians are alike. There are essentially two types. There are people like us who, through hard work and a reputation for integrity, have earned themselves prominent positions in the business community, and who have many Christian friends from the highest social and government echelons in the country—like my dear friends Ike and Mamie Eisenhower. We are welcomed in the finest Christian homes and are guests in the finest Christian clubs. We are assimilated Jews, in other words. We recognize that we are a small minority, living in an essentially Christian country, and we realize that we must abide by the majority rule. That is the American way. Then there is another type, which refuses to adapt. I call them Old World Jews. They haven't changed their ways since the Middle Ages. They abide by archaic dietary laws. They practice their religion in a language no one can understand. They live in ghettos—middle-class ghettos, to be sure, in places like Kew Gardens and Woodmere and Fort Lee and the Green Haven section of Mamaroneck. They're tight-knit, distrustful of outsiders, still actually afraid of Christians. They tend to be entrepreneurial types. You'll find many in the entertainment business—catering, for instance. In my business, I've had to deal with many of these types—Revson, for example. Because they don't trust me, I've learned that you can't trust them. They're the type who, as they say, will try to 'jew you down' in a business deal. I don't personally find them attractive, but I've had to do business with this type so often that I know it well."

"You're talking about stereotypes, Grandpa."

"I am indeed! Because the stereotype exists. We used to call them kikeys. I realize that that is not a flattering expression to use, but I still think of them that way. I do not wish to see the only granddaughter of Adolph Myerson marry into a kikey family. Surely the only granddaughter of Adolph Myerson deserves something better than that. Surely Adolph Myerson himself deserves better treatment that that."

It was, Mimi knew, another danger signal when her grandfather began speaking of himself in the third person.

"Let me tell you something else about these people," he said. "Typically, they will have three sons. One they make become a doctor, another they make a lawyer, and the third they will make an accountant. Do you know why this is? So that one son can give them free health care, the next will give them free legal advice, and the accountant will prepare their taxes for them—free. If I've seen this happen once, I've seen it a thousand times."

"But Michael is a *builder!*"

"And let me tell you one more thing. Builder starts with the same letter as *borrower*. These people never put up anything with their own money. They borrow from the government, they borrow from banks, they borrow from their relatives. They are always in debt. They actually measure wealth by how much they owe. I assume that the Kew Gardens caterers are aware that we are a family of means?"

"I don't know that!"

"I'm sure they are. I'm sure that the Kew Gardens caterers hope that if their son marries a rich woman she will help him extend his line of credit. Why else would they support such a . . . such an obvious mismatch."

"But I love him, Grandpa!" she had cried. "You're making him sound just terrible."

"I'm saying he's marrying you for your money, Mireille. And the caterers are aiding him and abetting him in this pursuit."

"It's not true," she said desperately. "He didn't even know who you were until after he'd asked me to marry him. And besides, I'm not rich."

"That's true," he said quietly. "You're not rich yet. But you could be one day. Very rich. You are an heiress, Mireille."

"Michael doesn't care about any of that! He loves me!"

His gaze at her through the pince-nez was even. "Have you met this young man's family?" he asked her.

"Not yet." She felt herself close to tears. She felt her mouth going suddenly dry and could also feel perspiration streaming down her sides, under her blouse.

"Well, let me tell you what you will find when you do," he said, and he withdrew his large gold watch from a vest pocket and consulted it. "Let me just tell you this, young lady, and then I must send you on your way. You will find a short, swarthy, bald Jewish man with a Bronx accent who chews on a cigar. You'll find his peroxide-blond wife who has a floor-length mink coat, wears diamonds from head to toe, who goes to the Fontainebleau for Christmas and plays mah-jongg. You'll find a couple who want a wedding at the Plaza with two rabbis, and the kind of barbaric ceremony where the bridegroom smashes a wineglass with his heel. Naturally, they'll want to cater the reception, and I'll be expected to pay for everything. I'm not saying you'll find this in every exact detail, but this is the element you will be dragging yourself into, and dragging your family, and your family's good name into, if you persist in pursuing this unfortunate, this totally inappropriate, relationship to the point of marrying this David Horowitz."

"His name is Michael," she sobbed. "How can you sit there and say such things about people you've never met?"

"Mark my words, young lady—"

"Oh, stop! Just stop this!" she cried, and she reached blindly beside her chair for her gloves and her mother's Chanel bag to go. Then she said, "I don't care. I don't care what you say. I love him, and I'm going to marry him, and there's nothing you can do to stop me—nothing! You can go to hell!"

He looked momentarily so startled—the pince-nez seeming to teeter on his nose—that she realized that it had probably been years since anyone, within the family or out of it, had challenged him or defied him or even questioned him, and she saw that the experience was so new and so strange to him that he was, at least briefly, caught quite off his guard and was, quite literally, speechless. He removed the pince-nez completely and placed them on his desktop, lenses down, in a gesture of fatigue. Then he said evenly, "That may be true. There may be nothing I can do to stop you, but there are other things that I can do. If you were expecting to receive any inheritance under my will, that instrument can be redrawn so that you receive nothing. I will, in the process, find it quite within my power to forget that I ever had a granddaughter."

"I don't care! I don't need your money! I don't even want it!"

"And that's not all that I can do to prevent you from doing what you say you mean to do. If you persist in this, you will see that there are other things that I can do. Now, I have nothing more to say to you. I will, I assume, be apprised of your decision when you have had a chance to think this over." He looked down at his desk and began quickly moving pieces of paper about with his hands. "Right now I have people—important people—waiting to see me. I have a company to run. Good day." With one hand, he gave her a quick gesture of dismissal. "Don't forget your shopping bag."

"Good!" he said when she was able to reach him on the phone to tell him of her meeting with her grandfather. "Good for you! You told the old bastard off. To hell with him. We don't need his money, and now we won't have to go around kissing his ass the way your parents have always had to do."

"But what about what he said, that there were other things that he could do?"

"Bluffing. Just bluffing. After all, what else could he do?"

But, for the first time, she thought she heard a note of uncertainty in his voice.

Henry Myerson stood in front of his father's desk while his father affixed his signature to a thick sheaf of documents. Finally, after several minutes, without looking up from his paperwork, Adolf Myerson said, "What time is it?"

"Ten after four, Father."

"Good. This won't take long." Then, still signing papers, his father said, "I understand that you borrowed a certain sum of money from your mother the other day."

"A small sum, yes."

"I am aware of the amount. Please let me be the judge of whether the amount is small or not."

"Yes, Father."

"Your mother has funds of her own, which she is free to dispense as she pleases," he said. "But the trouble with your mother is that, though she is not soft-headed, she is soft-hearted. She is generous to a fault, and she has no money sense. I have to go over her accounts periodically and sort things out for her. She is particularly soft-hearted where you are concerned. I am sure that it will not come as news to you that she favors you among the three children. This is natural, and understandable. You are her firstborn, her oldest son, her pet. That you are your mother's favorite is human nature. In fact, as you were growing up, there were times when I felt that, if I had not applied strict discipline in the household, you might have turned into a mama's boy, or like your brother."

For the past several years, due to certain occurrences that had come to light, it had been noticed that Adolph Myerson no longer referred to his younger son by name. He was no longer "Edwee" or "Edwin" but was "your brother" or "my other son" or sometimes just "the other one."

"These borrowings of yours," he continued, "these small loans, as you call them, have gone on for some years. I am afraid that you are taking advantage of your mother's generous nature, that you regard her as a soft touch, an easy mark, that you are using her, bleeding her, because her resources, though considerable, are not limitless. I am not pleased with this situation, Henry."

"Yes, Father."

His father put his signature on the last of the stack of documents, and a small smile crossed his lips. "There," he said. "A four-million exclusivity agreement for our boutique at Magnin's. All the California stores. We've beat that shit Revson." He looked up at his son for the first time. "I'm not pleased, Henry," he said, "and I'm also puzzled. You are paid an excellent salary. Next to my own, it is the highest salary in the company. You are paid enough to live well, even luxuriously. Why is it that you find it necessary to run to your mother for these handouts? Why is it that you seem unable to live on what you earn?"

"There are taxes, Father, doctors' bills, tuition—"

His father waved his hand. "Everybody pays taxes. Everybody has doctors' bills. Frankly, Henry, your chronic inability to live on what you earn worries me. It is one of the reasons I have been hesitant to turn over the reins of the company to you, which some people think I should have done several years ago. Your seemingly improvident nature makes me wonder whether perhaps you have inherited your mother's lack of money sense. Is that it, Henry?"

"I'm sorry, Father," he began. "I'll try—"

"Or is it your wife, Henry? Is it her inability to control her spending that gets you into these financial embarrassments?"

He lowered his eyes. "No, it's not that."

"You're not a child, Henry. You're forty-two years old. We can speak man to man. Frankly, it is undignified for a grown man of your age to be running to his mother for handouts."

"It won't happen again, Father."

"You call them loans. Your mother calls them loans. But I see no evidence of interest having been paid on any of them, nor are there signs that any of these loans have been repaid. I suspect that you have begun to think of these advances of hers as outright gifts, with no strings attached. I am considering calling all of these loans of yours in, Henry. Calling them in, with interest. It might teach you a much-needed lesson."

"But, Father, I can't—"

"I'm considering it," his father said. And then, "Your daughter was in to see me yesterday."

"I know that, Father."

"She wants me to approve her plans to marry some inappropriate young man. A totally inappropriate young man."

"I haven't met him yet, Father."

"I told her that I thoroughly disapproved. I expect you to exert whatever parental pressure you possibly can against this plan of hers, Henry. I expect you—and Alice—to exert as much parental pressure as you can against this proposed marriage. Do you understand, Henry?"

He nodded.

"Good," he said. He gathered up the stack of documents on his desk, aligning their edges between his palms. "Drop the Magnin contracts on my secretary's desk on your way out, will you?"

A little later, Adolph Myerson placed a telephone call on his private line. "Mireille?" he said when she answered. "This is your grandfather calling."

"Yes, Grandpa," she said, thinking that perhaps he had had a change of heart.

"I have been doing a little checking on the housing project your friend Horowitz is putting up in Newark, Mireille. This is a million-square-foot project for the low-income and the elderly, most of whom, it seems, will be Negro. It seems that these buildings are being put up with many gross violations of the New Jersey Building Code. There are inadequate fire escapes, for one thing. There are no fire doors between the floors or between the two buildings, as called for in the contract. The list of Code violations is quite long, I'm afraid, and quite shocking, considering the sort of people he plans to have occupy these units. Shoddy work, all around. The New Jersey State Building Inspector is a friend of mine. I would hate to have to notify him of these shortcomings. Or to call this to the attention of my friends at the *New York Times.* . . ."

* * *

She had never seen Michael so angry. His lips were white, and his eyes blazed. "That bastard!" he said. "That shit bastard! He's trying to blackmail me! None of that is true! I'll sue him—that's what I'll do. I'll sue him!"

"Wait," she begged him. "My mother has a plan. She wants us for dinner tonight. It will be just the four of us—my parents, and you and me. She has an idea, some sort of plan."

It was a dinner party that never actually took place, where no one ever sat down for dinner.

Michael stood in the center of her parents' living room, his fists clenched. "He's bluffing. I know he's bluffing," he said.

Looking pale, her father said, "He isn't bluffing, Michael. I've known him, worked with him, for a long time. He's a man who's used to getting his own way."

"He'll do *any*thing to get his way," Mimi's mother sobbed. "Anything!"

"And you're telling me that your father would actually financially ruin his own son—throw you out on the street, as you put it—for letting me marry your daughter? *His own son?*"

"Please try to understand, Michael," her father said. "There's a portrait in my father's office that serves as a reminder to me of where I stand with him. It used to be a portrait of two men: my father, and my uncle Leo. When my father decided that it was time for Leo to leave the company, he had Leo's part of the portrait painted out. He can make people disappear."

"He'd do that to *his own son?*"

"He did it to his own brother, Michael. Why not to his own son? I can remember when that happened. Mimi's too young."

"What kind of a pantywaist are you, Myerson?" Michael shouted. "What kind of a lousy, lily-livered little cowardly pantywaist are you to let another man walk all over you this way?"

"Michael, please—"

"There are certain other circumstances," her father said quietly, glancing quickly at her mother. "There are other circumstances, Michael, that you're not aware of, and that Mimi's not aware of—circumstances that I can't go into here—that make it impossible for Mimi's mother and me to defy him outright. I have to ask that you accept that, Michael, that there are extenuating circumstances!"

"Impossible!" her mother wailed.

"*What* circumstances, Daddy?"

"I can't go into that."

"Well, I say you're both a bunch of lousy, fucking cowards!" Michael said. "Only a coward puts up with blackmail without fighting back!"

Her father was angry now. "I'm telling you that under the circumstances it can't be done!"

"Wait!" Mimi's mother cried. "Why won't anybody listen to my plan? I've got a *plan!*"

"Yes, let's listen to your mother's plan," her father said.

Mimi's mother rose from her chair, her drink in one hand, her face suddenly wreathed in smiles, and moved—almost danced—across the room to where Mimi sat. "Have an *affair!*" she said. "Why don't you two have a nice *affair?* This is nineteen fifty-seven, the year of contraception! There are lovely little devices a girl can use today! Don't look so shocked. When your father and I were going out, before we were married, there was only that little rubber thing that the man used, and we were never sure—"

"Alice, I really don't think—"

"Why not?" she said defiantly. "You and I had an affair before we were married, didn't we? Why can't she have . . . a lovely *affair?*"

"Alice, you've had too much to drink."

Suddenly her face fell. "What's wrong?" she said. "What's wrong with my plan? What's wrong with having an affair? People have them all the time! She could be fitted for a pessary."

"Sit down, Alice, please," her father said. "There is only one plan that will work. It's called patience. My father is eighty-seven years old. He can't live forever—"

"Oh, no!" Alice cried. "Because he *will* live forever. He already has lived forever. He won't die, and you know why? Because *he's too mean to die,* that's why! They're all too mean to die! Your mother's too mean to die! Your cousin Nate's too mean to die! They'll never die, any of them—as long as there's a way to torture us."

"Alice!"

"So go ahead: marry him! Forget the affair! Screw everybody! Screw this whole family!"

"Alice, for Christ's sake!"

"Are you going to hit me?" she said. "Go ahead and hit me! Hit me, Henry! I like it when you hit me!"

"I'm getting out of here," Michael said. "The hell with all of you. The hell with you, too, Mimi!" He started toward the front door.

"Oh, no . . ." She followed him to the door, and her mother moved to stop her, but her father held her back. Mimi followed him out the door, out into the corridor, into the elevator, down the elevator to the lobby, and into the street, clinging to his sleeve, whispering, "No . . . no . . . no . . ."

"Sorry, but I can't cut it with those people. Can't hack it," and he thrust his jaw sharply outward and flicked a lock of hair back across his forehead.

"Please, Michael . . . please . . ."

"Can't . . . can't . . . can't . . ."

On Ninety-seventh Street he headed east. She had no idea where he was going, but she still clung to his arm. His pace increased, as though he was trying to lose her, and she almost had to run to keep up with him, but she still clung to him; and when they reached the river, she thought for a wild moment that he was going to suggest that they both fling themselves into it from the embankment, even though a police squad car was parked nearby.

He stopped, refusing to look at her. "Don't you see?" he said. "It isn't going to work for us. Perhaps it never would have. Too much is going on in that family of yours that we can't control. It's over, kiddo. I won't say I don't love you. I will say I'll never forget this. You see, I can't even say good-bye, because I—I—" His voice broke, and he wrenched his arm from her grip, still not looking at her. "Now let me go," he said. "It's over." He reached in his pocket and pressed a wad of bills into her hand. "Take a taxi, and go home to that crazy-house you live in. Leave me alone now. I don't want to see you again for a long time."

"Then take back your ring!" she said.

"No! Keep the ring. You hear me? You give me back that ring, and I'll—I'll throw it into the East River! That's what I'll do—I'll throw the goddam ring into the East River, and that will be the goddam end of it for goddam everybody. The ring is yours. Now just get out of here and leave me alone."

She still has the ring, though of course she never wears it. She showed it to me once. "It's not a large diamond, is it?" she said. "Of course, at the time I thought it was enormous. I thought it was the diamond as big as the Ritz! Isn't it funny how, as you get older, things seem smaller than the way you first saw them?"

A few days later, her mother tapped at her door. "May I come in?" she asked. She stepped inside Mimi's bedroom and closed the door behind her. "I have some wonderful news, darling," she said.

Mimi lay dry-eyed on the bed, on top of the coverlet. She had cried her eyes dry of tears.

"Guess what, darling!" her mother said, sitting down on the bed beside her. "Your grandfather is giving you the most wonderful trip to Europe. You leave on Friday, so there's so much we have to do! You fly to London for a week, for lots of theatre, and then to Paris for another week. In Paris, you'll have tickets to all the couturier shows. Then you go to the south of France, and from there to Madrid, and from there to Florence and Rome. From there it's to Athens, and then to Istanbul, and finally to Geneva and Lausanne, and you fly home from Zurich. Isn't that wonderful? A real Grand Tour! It's his graduation present to you, so, you see, your grandpa's not all bad! You'll see everything, the museums, the castles, the cathedrals, and you'll be part of a lovely group—a very select tour group of young people your age, only twenty young people, from the best schools and colleges in the East! Eight whole weeks! I'm so thrilled for you, darling—envious, too. Because I've never been to Europe, never been anywhere . . . never. . . ."

In Paris, there was a letter waiting from her mother.

Dearest Mimi,   *Jul. 11, 1957*

> *I know that this has been a difficult time for you, darling, but believe me, things will seem better after time goes by. It is good, I think, to get away from things for a while, and let one's life come into focus. They say life is short, but life is really very long—too long, it sometimes seems— and you are still so young. Time turns all hurts to scars and in time the scars go away too! And I know that there are some things about our situation here that are difficult to understand, but believe me, there are reasons for everything, even though you may not understand what all the reasons are. Believe me, your Daddy and I want nothing but happiness for you—for the rest of your life.*
>
> *If you should see a pretty scarf or a pair of gloves, not too expensive, in Paris, please buy it for me.*
>
> *Daddy joins me in love. . . .*

And, in Madrid, there was a letter from her grandfather, which she read sitting on the steps of the Prado while the others in her group were inside, listening to a lecture on Velázquez.

My dear Mireille: *24 July 1957*

> *I trust this letter finds you enjoying your tour, and making many new friends and having many pleasant new experiences. Your grandmother and I have always found travel to be a broadening experience, and I am sure you will return home with a deeper understanding of the breadth and richness of our Western culture.*
>
> *I understand that your young man made a rather unpleasant scene at your parents' house that last night, and used crude language. That was of*

course unfortunate and, though it indicates a certain lack of poise and self-control, it was perhaps understandable under the circumstances. At least it will perhaps help you see why he never could have comfortably been made a part of the fabric of our small family.

Then, rather abruptly, his tone changed.

That day in my office, you spoke of love. I am an old man, Mireille, and I have had much experience with love. Will you trust an old man's experience? Love—first love—always seems the strongest. It can seem so strong as to be overpowering. But what that first love is, Mireille, is a test—a test of stamina, and of character. Though I am not a particularly religious man, I think that love is a test that God, or Life, or however you think of the force that impels us through this life, gives us and waits for us to pass —a kind of endurance test, if you will. Life is a kind of mountain journey, and the first love is the first crest in the path. But over that first crest lies another, and then another, until the mountain is scaled, and all the crests are conquered, and the journey is done.

"Bad news?" a male voice said. "You look a little sad."

"No, not really."

"I've watched you on this trip," he said. He was not bad-looking. "You always look a little preoccupied and sad."

"Well, I'm not. I'm not neurotic, if that's what you're thinking."

"We haven't actually met," he said. "My name's Brad Moore."

16

*E*DWEE has hit upon the perfect technique for gaining access to his mother's apartment while she is not in it. He literally frightens her out of her house. This morning, for example, he telephoned her to say that he needed to see her on a matter of urgent business concerning her future, needed to see her today, if possible.

"I'm sorry, Edwee. I'm busy today."

"Just for a m-m-minute, *M-M-Maman.*"

"I'm sorry."

"It's urgent, *Maman.*"

"Then tell me what it is on the telephone."

"It's something I have to show you, *Maman.*"

"*Show* me? You know I can't see. What is it?"

"Just a legal document that requires your signature. I'll show you where to sign."

"No! No! I'm not signing anything."

"I'm going to be in your neighborhood around noon. Let m-m-me pop by just for a m-m-m-minute."

"No! I'm going out at twelve. And stop stammering, Edwee! You only do it to annoy me."

"Where are you going? Perhaps we could m-m-m-meet."

"No! I'm having lunch with Rose Perlman. It's private." She had hung up on him.

Today, however, the plan had struck a slight snag. Patrick, the doorman, had greeted him with his usual cordiality and had been given his usual tip.

But George, at the front desk, had hesitated when Edwee asked for the key. "I'm sorry, Mr. Myerson," he said. "Your mother is indeed out, but she asked that no one be admitted to her apartment. And I'm afraid, sir, that she specifically asked that *you* not be admitted."

At first, Edwee's expression was one of extreme irritation, but quickly this changed to one of extreme sadness. "Oh, dear," he said. "Oh, dear, dear, dear. Isn't it sad to see how my poor, dear mother is failing?"

"She seemed perfectly fine this morning, sir."

"Oh, she is fine, physically. She has the constitution of an ox. But it's up here . . ." He tapped his head. "It's the old Alzheimer's, I'm afraid. You see, this is one of the symptoms of the disease. She says exactly the opposite of what she wants. She asked me to come by today at noon and obviously meant to tell you that I was expected, and that you were to let me in. Instead, she told you not to let me in. Sad, but what can we do?" He started to walk away.

"No, wait, Mr. Myerson. Now that you've explained it, let me give you a key."

"No, no—you mustn't do that, George. You have your instructions."

"Please, Mr. Myerson, here is the key."

His tip to George was larger than usual. In the elevator, he decided that he would keep this key and have a copy of it made before returning it. There are two entrances to the Carlyle, one on 76th Street and one on Madison Avenue. From now on, if further visits are necessary—which they may not be—he will simply use the Madison Avenue door, bypass the front desk, and go directly to the elevators like an ordinary hotel guest. There is always a way to do everything.

Now, in the apartment, Edwee has been joined by the elegant and urbane John Marion, Chairman of the Board of Sotheby–Parke Bernet, whom he has asked to meet him there. Crouched on the floor, at a safe distance, his mother's little dog barks at the two men incessantly. "She has some lovely things . . . lovely things," John Marion is saying over the dog's barks. "Every time I see this collection, I'm awestruck."

"Well, some things are better than others," Edwee says.

"As in any collection. She considered selling it, you know, after your father died—when I gather there were some difficult financial times. But I'm sure she's glad she changed her mind. It's much more valuable than it was thirty years ago."

"I'm sorry Mother's not here," Edwee says. "She was supposed to be, because I wanted her to hear your opinion. But apparently she forgot and went out." He taps his head. "The old Alzheimer's, you know. Oh, do be quiet, Itty-Bitty!"

John Marion nods sympathetically.

"Now, let me show you, John," he says, "what it is that troubles me about the Goya, if indeed it is a Goya." Using a slender silver pointer, and being careful not to touch the surface of the canvas, he begins to point to details. "If you'll notice these brushstrokes here," he says, "in the Duchess's lace overskirt, and here again in the mantilla, you'll notice a certain heaviness, a certain daubiness, that is quite uncharacteristic. The paint almost seems to have been smeared on, rather than brushed on, and as you know, Goya's brushwork was always light and quick. It was these details that first aroused my suspicions."

"Hmm," Marion says, peering closely at the painting.

"And then there is the angle of the left hand. It hangs at a rather awkward, clumsy angle, don't you think? The hand is not only in an awkward attitude. The flesh around her rings puffs out too much. Now notice the eyes. Do you see how they appear to be ever so slightly crossed?"

"Maybe the Duchess had puffy, awkward hands and crossed eyes," Marion says easily.

"Goya did many paintings of Osuna," Edwee says. "None of them show crossed eyes or puffy fingers."

"Could it be our Duchess had gained a bit of weight?"

Edwee's laugh is gentle and knowing. "If so, John," he says with a touch of patronage in his voice, "two other verified portraits of her, one painted immediately before, and another done very shortly after this portrait was *allegedly* painted, do not show it. But it is really the clumsy *positioning* of the left hand that bothers me the most."

"Even Goya may have had a bad day."

"As you know," Edwee continues, "Goya worked very rapidly. He could complete a portrait such as this one in two hours or less. Also, he never farmed out detail work, such as hands, to apprentices. And he was always particularly adept with hands."

"Hmm," Marion says again.

"Now, if you'll give *me* a hand," Edwee says, "let's lift Her Grace off the wall. There's something else I want to show you."

Together they lift the heavy frame from the wall and place it on the floor. "Let's turn it over," Edwee says, and they do so. "Now, as you know," he goes on, "Mother purchased this painting from Duveen, and Berenson authenticated it. Never mind that Spanish painters of this period were not Berenson's metier or field of expertise; that's beside the point. Let's grant that Berenson knew *some*thing about Goya's work."

"Well, yes . . ."

"And so, look here," Edwee points. "Do you need a glass?" He starts to fish his magnifying glass from his pocket.

"No, I can see fine."

"Then look at this. You'll see the handwritten words, 'Vrai—B. Berenson.' Someone like Charlie Hamilton, of course, could tell us whether this indeed is written in Berenson's hand, but it appears to me to be. But *look:* after the word *vrai,* there is a question mark! What Berenson actually wrote here was 'vrai?—B. Berenson.' "

"Well, I'll be damned," Marion says, looking at the handwriting closely. "I've examined this painting, front and back, at least a dozen times over the years and never noticed a question mark."

"The painting has been hanging here for nearly twenty years," Edwee says quickly. "It had gotten very dusty, particularly on the back, where these hotel maids of course never dusted it. The other day I was in here and took the painting down and began dusting around the signature with a camel's hair brush. That was when the question mark appeared, under the dust."

John Marion whistles softly. "I'll be damned," he says again. "Damned if I ever noticed that."

"Well, there it is," Edwee says. "Apparently Berenson was doubtful. What else could it mean? It was when I found the question mark under the dust that I decided I'd better bring you in on it, with your expertise, which, after all, is far greater than mine. I, after all, am only an art historian. You are an appraiser, and probably the finest in the world."

"Edwee, I don't know what to say," he says.

"Damn. I wish Mother had remembered this appointment with us today. She should be made aware, at least, that there's a problem. But Mother forgets everything anyway, so perhaps it doesn't matter. Now there's one other thing I ought to mention."

"What's that?"

"My sister, Nonie. She knew B.B. intimately and often visited him at 'I Tatti.' When I mentioned my suspicions to her, she recalled a conversation she had with him in the nineteen forties about this very painting. I want you to hear the details of this conversation from Nonie, who remembers it in some detail. May I suggest that you and I meet with Nonie at the earliest date convenient for the three of us?"

"Certainly. I'd be interested to hear what she has to say."

"Good. And once you hear what my sister has to say, then we'll decide how to proceed from there. You see, she was the only one in the family who knew B.B. My mother never met him, and neither did I. But Nonie knew him intimately, and he often confided things to her. Do you know Philippe de Montebello?"

"Of course."

"I wonder if we should invite Phil to our meeting, too. Mother has—tentatively—offered this painting to the Met. I'm sure you know how highly

I esteem the Met. I would hate the thought of the Met being given a picture that was a fake. Do you think we should invite Phil to our meeting, John?"

"I can ask him, if you'd like," he said. "But let me give you a little tip, Edwee. When you meet him, don't call him Phil. Philippe is a rather formal fellow who doesn't mind being called Count de Montebello. He is, after all, a French count."

"Yes, then let's ask him. In the meantime, I think we should keep this in strictest confidence. This city we live in is so prone to gossip. If the museum people, or, God knows, the press, heard so much as a rumor that this painting is a fake before we're sure it is, they would turn it down, and that would be . . . well, if it turned out that our suspicions were without foundation, that would be a great tragedy for the museum-going public of the city of New York. And I couldn't bear to have that happen. So until we meet with my sister and de Montebello, let's keep this matter strictly between ourselves."

"Certainly."

"I'll find out what my sister's calendar looks like and call you as soon as I know."

"Have you got the money?" he asks her a little harshly. "Have you got the cash?"

"Well, of course I don't have it in *cash*," Nonie says. "It will take a few days. You don't come up with sums of money like that in cash. Checks have to clear banks, that sort of thing. But the deal's been set, the money's been promised, and I'll have it for you in a few days."

"Your message on my machine didn't say nothing about promises. Your message said 'Have secured necessary funds.' *Secured.* Secured means secured."

"Surely you can be patient for a few more days, Roger."

"How long have I been patient with you, Nonie? Three weeks? A month?"

"Well, now it's only a question of days."

"How'd you get it, anyway?"

"I think I'd rather not say, Roger. Let's say it was a private business arrangement with an old friend."

"There's nothing funny about it, is there?"

"Funny? What do you mean, funny?"

"I mean, you got it in a strictly legit way, didn't you? I can't handle any money that wasn't got in a strictly legit way, you know. I don't want dirty money, narcotics money, stuff like that."

"*Narcotics* money! Honestly, Roger, where would I have access to something like narcotics money?"

"Okay. As long as you're sure it's strictly legit. I don't want any trouble with the feds."

"It is, I assure you, strictly legit, as you put it. Strictly." She pauses. "Can you come by for a drink tonight? Sevenish?"

"Sorry, I'm busy. Call me when you've got the money. And by cash I mean a certified or cashier's check."

"You're not being very nice to me, you know!" she says angrily. "You're not the only spot currency trader in town, you know!" And she slams down the receiver. And then, just in case he might be going to call her back to apologize for his rudeness, she takes the receiver off the hook and leaves it off.

But, she thinks, the trouble is, the question is: *Is* the deal she has struck with Edwee strictly legit? At first, Edwee's scheme seemed to her no more than a little harebrained, not actually dishonest, and if he was willing to pay her for participating in it, she would do so, in the spirit of nothing ventured, nothing gained. Who knew? The scheme might work and get him his precious Goya, and, up until now, she had not really cared whether the scheme would work or not. But suddenly she is not so sure. If it *does* work, will she have been a participant in some form of grand larceny?

Up to now, her only concern was whether Edwee would keep his end of the bargain. She has never entirely trusted Edwee. And so, this time, to ensure that Edwee will not try to wiggle out of his promise, she insisted that they put it in writing, as a letter of agreement, a contract between the two of them. Each has a copy, with both signatures. That way, if Edwee welches on his commitment, she can expose him for the fraud he is. That was *smart*, she thinks.

But the only trouble with *that* is, she reminds herself now, that if she exposes Edwee as a fraud, she will have to expose herself as a part of the fraud, and where will that leave her? Flapping in the high winds of some very embarrassing publicity. She wonders whether Edwee had perhaps thought of that, too, when he so willingly affixed his signature to the agreement she drew up in her best quasi-legal manner. Art fraud, she thinks. There has been a lot in the newspapers lately about art fraud. This, of course, involved art dealers who were passing off forgeries as original works. What Edwee is proposing to do is sort of the opposite. But is that art fraud, too? Is that just as reprehensible, even illegal? If the museum found out, could it come back to them—with a lawsuit, perhaps—claiming that it had fraudulently been prevented from receiving a piece of art to which it had been entitled? Could there be more than just unpleasant publicity? Could there be . . . legal action? Legal action involving millions of dollars?

Would it be like the Mayflower Madam? Would she go to jail? What would the press call Nonie Myerson—the Heiress Art Thief? The Goya Grabber? The Metropolitan Manipulator? A shiver of very real fear now chills her at the thought of the mess that she has let Edwee get her into.

Her best hope, perhaps, is that Edwee's scheme will *not* work. They are meeting with John Marion and Philippe de Montebello on Tuesday. She knows what she is supposed to say, and she is not too worried about that part of it. After all, as Edwee says, it *could* have happened, and there is no one in the world who could possibly prove, or stand up and swear, that it didn't. And Edwee has promised to pay for her performance, whether it works or not.

But what if it *does* work? What might happen next? And then, to top everything off, what if Edwee tries to wiggle out? How will she defend herself? She wishes she had consulted a lawyer, or some third party as a witness, before signing that contract, which could turn out to be as worthless as yesterday's newspaper.

Have I been tricked again? she asks herself, and another shiver of fear assails her.

She wishes, prays, right now that Roger is trying to telephone her from wherever he is, that he is sitting there, angry and frustrated by the repeated busy signal, prays that he is sitting wherever he is, just as uncertain and frightened as she is, but she still does not return the receiver to its cradle.

From Jim Greenway's notes:

I could not help noticing that Mimi did not quite seem herself today. When I was with her, she seemed a little distant and preoccupied, and from time to time I saw a small and quite uncharacteristic frown cross that lovely face of hers. Something, I think, is weighing on her mind—something that she is not willing, not yet, at least, to tell me about.

Of course, I'm certain that she's under a strain as the launch date of her new fragrance approaches. A lot of money has been invested in this, and I know how badly she wants "Mireille" to be a success. At the same time, the optimism about the success of "M" is running very high among the others in her office, where everyone seems confident that the "Man with the Scar" campaign is going to be seen as some sort of landmark in the advertising business. Mark Segal, her ad director, is positively giddy with excitement about it, and this excitement of his has had a trickle-down effect on every-one of the 16th floor, right down to the secretaries, the receptionist, and the boys in the mailroom.

We screened a rough cut of the first (redone) commercial today, and I must say I agree with Mark—that it's brilliant, fucking brilliant, as he keeps saying. There's something about the scar that does . . . *what*, exactly? It makes him, the model, look not really sinister, but somehow a little threatening, in a bedroomy sort of way. It gives his face a Paul Henreid sort of crookedness, and I kept thinking of Henreid lighting up two cigarettes at once for Bette Davis in *Now, Voyager*. It gives him a Bogey sort of face, the young Bogey, crossed with whatever it was that stirred women's vitals when George Raft appeared on the screen. Mark says the scar gives the model *"cojones"*—balls. Maybe that's it. But from watching the expression on Mimi's face, it was hard to tell whether she was pleased or not.

Meanwhile, Mark has come up with a publicity idea that strikes me as damned clever. It is sort of the "Does She, or Doesn't She?" idea from the old Clairol ads, but in this case it will be "Does He, or Doesn't He?"—does he, or doesn't he really have a scar? During the first few weeks of the campaign, Mark wants to do a publicity blitz that will focus on that question, to keep the public wondering about the scar and, naturally, talking about the ads and talking up "M." Of course, the success of this will depend on keeping the real Dirk Gordon under wraps for a while, but, considering what they're paying him, this should be no problem.

In the end, naturally, it will be revealed that the scar was in fact created by makeup—cosmetics from Miray, the company that can make women beautiful as easily as they can make a pretty-boy ugly! Brilliant, effing brilliant, as Mark would say. But, again, from her faraway look, it was hard to tell whether Mimi agrees or not.

And I know that Mimi is also very preoccupied with the details of her launch party, which will be on September 17. This will be a big, fancy affair at the Pierre, and the invitations are already at the printer, and the guest list is being drawn up. All the department store heads and all the buyers will be invited, of course, along with the editors and writers from the fashion press, plus the usual members of the Manhattan social zoo: Vreeland, Pat Buckley, Judy Peabody, Brooke Astor, Susan Gutfreund, and the rest. And there'll be the usual Big Question, which no one will know the answer to until the last minute: Will she or won't she show up? Jackie, that is. Half of Mimi's office staff, it seems, is working on the guest list, adding names, taking others off.

But I must say Mimi brightened up considerably when I mentioned that I'd like to interview some of the people whom the family call "the Leo cousins."

"Yes," she said emphatically. "Yes, I think you should talk to them, Jim. After all, it's no secret in the industry that there's one whole branch of my family that doesn't speak to the other branch. And, frankly, I'd like to know what's behind all this myself—*why* Grandpa had Leo's portrait painted out."

Then she made a surprising suggestion.

"What would you think," she said, "if I came along with you when you do these interviews? Would that cramp your journalistic style too much? Maybe you could be just the one to help me break the ice with them. After all, it's ridiculous for this sort of family feuding to go on for nearly fifty years! All the offending principals are dead, and surely it's high time that their offenses, whatever they were, should be forgiven. Maybe if I went with you, I could convince them that I'm not the ogre they've been brought up to believe I am. Maybe you could provide me with a toe in the door to these people who, after all, are stockholders of this company. Could I be a tag-along, Jim? What would you think of that?"

I told her I would be delighted to have her come along with me, that it would be my pleasure.

"I can give you all their names and addresses," she said. "I'm sure they're all perfectly nice people, though there's one who's not quite right in the head."

When I left her, she seemed in a much brighter mood, anticipating our trips to the various surrounding suburbs.

Why does it please me to be able to put her in a brighter mood?

Then, no sooner had I got back to my apartment than I had a telephone call from her Granny Flo, in a very agitated state.

"I've been invaded, Mr. Greenway!" she cried. "I've been invaded again! Edwee's been in my house again, I can smell him! I know how my own son smells, and I can tell he's been here again, snooping around. George, at the front desk, denies it, but I know he's lying. What are they trying to do to me, Mr. Greenway—all of them? George talks to me as though I'm teched in the head, as though I've lost my marbles. But I haven't lost my marbles! George talks to me like I'm a child—talks to me like someone telling a child there's no such thing as the bogey man. But there *is* a bogey man, and his name is Edwee Myerson! Edwee and someone else, because I can also smell another man! And if that isn't proof enough, there's the way Itty-Bitty's been acting, jumping all around, yip-yip-yipping, trying to tell me something's wrong, and then, suddenly, lifting her little leg against the leg of my chair and weeing! Itty-Bitty never does that unless something has been going very wrong. Help me, Mr. Greenway, help me. You're the only one I can trust. I'm surrounded by enemies! My own home isn't safe anymore!"

I asked her what I could do to help.

"Talk to Nonie," she said. "I think Nonie knows what's going on. Talk to Nonie, and see if you can get it out of her what they're trying to do, because Nonie isn't on my side, either!" Then, holding out the carrot at the end of the stick, she said, "Don't forget, there's a lot more things I could tell you, Mr. Greenway—a *lot* more! You've only just scratched the surface, Mr. Greenway, with the things I could tell you about this family!"

And so I called Nonie and asked to see her. She was polite, but a little cool. "Of course, I should be *delighted* to see you, Mr. Greenway," she said in her cultured-pearls voice. "But this week is just *not* turning out to be a *ruling* week for me. My poor calendar is simply chockablock. Call me next week, darling, and I'll try to set aside some time for you. . . ."

And so, inevitably and willy-nilly, it seems, I am being drawn deeper into the personal problems of this family in which at the beginning I had only a detached, professional interest.

And yet I don't find myself resenting this involvement. I am beginning to feel as though I am one of them.

17

I'*M JITTERY, MIMI,*" her mother says, twisting her rings. "That's the only way I can describe it. I'm jittery. I'm all a-jitter. Thank you, dear, for coming by. I told your Mr. Greenway that I just wasn't up to seeing him today."

"Well, he's not *my* Mr. Greenway, Mother," Mimi says. "And you don't have to see him at all, if you don't want to."

They are sitting in her mother's cozy living room in Turtle Bay, overlooking the private central courtyard with its fountain, leafy trees, and busy squirrel population. "Oh, I'll see him," her mother says, "because I know he wants to talk to all of us, and because I know you want us to talk to him. But not today, because I just feel so . . . jittery!"

"You look fine, Mother. In fact, you've never looked better."

"God love you for a liar! I know how I look. There are mirrors in this house, too, you know!"

Mimi looks into her mother's face and tries an encouraging smile. But it is true. In another year, her mother will be seventy, the beginning of old age, and Mimi must admit that her beautiful mother, the mother she once thought must be the most beautiful woman in the world, is looking old.

"What kind of a story is it, do you think, that he wants to write, Mimi?"

"I have only one theory when it comes to dealing with the media," she says, "particularly the print media, and that's be honest with them. If you're not, they'll just make up something. But I like this man. I think he wants to write an honest story."

"He'll want to ask me about your father, I'm sure. But that was so long ago—more than twenty years. I'm not sure I'm up to going back to all those memories, at least not today. Of course, they told us at the Ford Center there'd be days like this, when you just . . . can't seem . . . to . . ."

"What's wrong, Mother?"

Her mother's laugh is almost gay. "I want a drink, that's what it is! I want a drink, right now! A nice cold drink, with lots of ice, that I could nurse, the way I used to. My medicine. Liquid courage—that's all I want!"

"Deep in your heart, Mother, you know you don't."

"That's not true! Deep in my heart, I *do!* I keep a bottle, you know, right over there in that sideboard. They tell us to! Face your enemy, they say! Well, what would you say if I told you I'd opened that sideboard at least twenty times this afternoon and faced my enemy! But I've resisted, Mimi. I've resisted."

"Good," she says. "Good for you. I'm proud of you, Mother. Because you remember some of the things that happened."

"What things? What things happened? Oh, you mean on the airplane, going to California. Yes, I admit I was a naughty girl then—and thank God you were there to help me, Mimi. But other times I wasn't so bad, was I? I used to think of whiskey as my friend. It used to help me sleep at night. Now I have trouble sleeping, I can't—"

"Doesn't Dr. Bergler give you something?"

"Oh, yes. The valium. And Seconal, to sleep. But lately the valium doesn't seem to be doing what it did at first. And, with a Seconal, I sleep only three or four hours, and at two in the morning I'm wide awake, and thinking . . ."

"Thinking what?"

"Thinking that it wasn't like that when I could carry a drink to bed with me, and nurse it as I fell off to sleep, wonderful sleep! And I never had a hangover, Mimi. I never knew what a hangover *was.*"

"Not even that morning in California, Mother? You looked pretty sick to me."

"Well, that was different, I admit. That was my last fling. You might say that I did that deliberately, to prove . . ."

"To prove what, Mother?"

"Oh, you ask the same sort of questions they ask at the Ford Center. To prove that I could fail, they'd say! But you don't understand. After your father died, and I was all alone—with no real family left, and no real friends except my medicine, with you married—all my life I'd lived for your father, and for you, Mimi."

"Nonsense. You and Daddy fought like cats and dogs—and it was usually about your drinking."

"But we were *used* to it, that was the thing. We had our quarrels, yes, but we always made up afterward. You never saw the making-up part. There were happy times that you didn't see. No one ever saw the happy times. And there were other happy times you couldn't have seen because they were before you were born. *They're* what I'd like to tell Mr. Greenway about, those." Her mother rises and moves toward the sideboard at the corner of the room, and watching her, Mimi notices that her mother's footsteps are heavy and slow. She watches as her mother stoops and opens the cabinet door and looks at its solitary contents. "Facing my enemy," she says. And then, "What would you say, Mimi, if I said, 'Let's you and I have a drink right now'? What would you say?"

"I'd say, 'No thank you.' "

"What if I asked you to fix me a drink, the way you used to? What would you say?"

"I'd say, 'No, you can fix your own drink, Mother.' "

"And if I fixed one anyway, what would you do?"

"Nothing."

"Nothing?" Her mother looks at her narrowly. "And what would you think if you found out, after you leave tonight, that I've gone ahead and had a drink, or maybe more than one? What would you think then?"

"I suppose I'd sort of shrug, and think, Well, I guess the old girl doesn't have the guts to do it after all."

Her mother sits down hard on a small chair. "Then you don't really care," she says. "You don't really care what becomes of me."

"Caring has nothing to do with it, Mother. I loved you when you were drinking. I love you now. Please don't try to confuse my loving, and my caring, with what you decide to do with your life. The Betty Ford Center was your idea, remember? I didn't suggest it. I didn't try to push you into it. But I supported it because I thought it was something you wanted for yourself, to make you feel better about yourself. I'd watched you go in and out of other programs. I agreed with you that one more would be worth a try, that's all."

"You went out there with me! I was terribly touched when you offered to do that."

"Well, in retrospect, that may have been a mistake. Perhaps I should have let you go alone. After all, it was your idea."

"But the trouble is, I *don't* feel any better about myself. I feel just the same. If anything, I feel worse."

"If that's the case, that makes me very sad, Mother."

"I just don't know! I sit here, and I think, What difference does it make? I'm getting old, and perhaps I'm too old, now, to change, and even if I change now, what difference does it make? I behaved badly at your dinner party, didn't I? I made a scene."

"I understand that, Mother."

"I was cold sober, but I made a scene—the kind of scene I used to make when I was drunk, so what's the difference? And Dr. Bergler! I think they should call him Dr. *Burglar*, sitting there in his office for a hundred and twenty dollars an hour! What good does it do? Today, for the whole hour, we said almost nothing. I feel I've run out of things to say to him. For a while, I actually thought he might have fallen asleep in that overstuffed chair of his! Then, at the end of the hour, he suddenly said, 'Alice, do you feel responsible for what happened to your husband?' And, coming home in the taxi, I thought: Yes, yes I do feel responsible."

"That's silly, Mother. Daddy's only problem was a father who wanted absolute power over everybody, and when his absolute power was challenged, he turned mean."

"No, no, there was more to it than that. I did something very bad, way back in the beginning."

"What was that?"

"Guts. You talk about guts. I had guts in the beginning, believe it or not." She stands up again, closing the cabinet door, and begins twisting the rings again on her thin fingers, moving slowly around the room. "More guts than was good for me, you might say. I said to Henry, 'If you don't confront him with this, I will!' And that took guts."

"What do you mean?"

Her mother pauses by the window, parting the glass curtains with her fingertips. "There's one squirrel out there who chases all the others. I watch him every day. He's always chasing the others, from branch to branch, from tree to tree. All the other squirrels must hate him. I was like that, in the beginning."

Mimi says nothing, waiting for her mother to continue.

"You see, I was young, and I was naive, but I was ambitious, and I loved your father. I was ambitious for him. To me, he was a kind of genius—a genius whom his father refused to recognize. All he gave him in the company was lots of money, and lots of titles—vice-president in charge of this or that—but no authority, and no responsibilities. We lived well, your father and I, in those days, but you don't remember any of that. We didn't always live in that awful apartment on Ninety-seventh Street. We lived in *style*, at Eleven East Sixty-sixth Street, just a few doors from the Park. You don't remember Eleven East Sixty-sixth Street, because you were just a baby, barely a toddler, when we had to give that up, but it's still there. I walk by it now and then. I notice many doorbells by the entrance, so it must have been broken up, but in nineteen thirty-seven, when we were first married and your grandfather bought it for us as a wedding present, it was all ours: four stories, plus the basement, with an elevator, and a pretty garden in the back. For parties, we'd cover the garden with a tent, a yellow tent!"

"Why have I never heard about any of this before?" Mimi asks.

"It's your Mr. Greenway, I suppose. Calling up and stirring up all these memories, things I've been trying to forget. And I was—like that squirrel—always goading your father, pushing him, saying, 'Stand up to your father. Make him give you some responsibilities in the company! Force him to recognize your talent!' But Henry kept telling me, 'Just be patient. Be patient, these things take time. Rome wasn't built in a day,' he'd say, but I wasn't patient. And after you were born, I grew even more impatient, because now we were a family, with our child's future to consider. Can you understand that, Mimi?"

"Of course."

"And one day he came home from the office, very upset, and when I asked him what was the matter, he told me. It was something he'd suspected for a long time, and he'd found evidence to confirm it. The company had Mafia people on the payroll. They were using these people to intimidate the competition—to misdirect overseas shipments at the piers, to shoot holes in the tires of distributors' trucks, to hijack competitors' orders. There was even the possibility that there had been a murder. It was Revlon that Miray was after, mostly, because Revlon was the upstart and becoming their biggest competition. I said to Henry, 'Here's your chance! Go to your father and tell him what you know! Tell him that if he doesn't give you the kind of position and the kind of responsibilities you *deserve*, you'll go to the police! You'll go to the FBI! You'll go to the press! *Make* him turn over the company to you!' But Henry said, 'No, no, that isn't the way to do it.' He said that it was mostly his uncle Leo who seemed to have gotten the company into this mess, and that his father was already working on ways to force his uncle Leo out, and that if everybody would be patient—patient!—things would all work out in the end. And that's when I said, 'Well, if you won't confront him with what you know, *I will!*'

"Your father begged me not to, but I was so positive that this was the way to get *both* of them out—his father *and* his uncle Leo—that that's what I did.

"Your grandfather was furious. I'd never seen him so angry. He called me a blackmailer, and worse things than that. He called me a meddling *yenta*. He accused me of interfering with his company's business. He said he could never respect a man who'd let his *wife* interfere at her husband's place of employment. He denied everything that Henry knew was true and said that I was nothing but an interfering, busybody wife. He threw me out of his house, told me he never wanted to see me again. It wasn't until years later— you must have been about seven—that he would speak to me or have me in the house. Then he suddenly invited you and me to tea—do you remember that?—and I thought maybe he'd forgiven me. But I was wrong.

"But that was the beginning of everything, when everything started to go wrong, because of what I'd done. He punished Henry terribly for what I'd done. Was I wrong to do it, Mimi?"

"Knowing Grandpa as I did, yes, I would have to say yes, Mother, it was wrong."

"But at the time I didn't think so! I thought it would help my husband—help him command his father's respect. But obviously it didn't work. That was when the money began to . . . go. There were other things. That was when I began to drink. I drank because I was miserable. Then the house, Eleven East Sixty-sixth Street, went. And we couldn't afford anything anymore, no more parties under the yellow tent. We couldn't afford to entertain our friends because there was never enough money, and our friends couldn't understand it, and they began to think—I heard someone say this—that your father and I were 'peculiar,' and they stopped entertaining us. And so everything bad that happened was because of what I did. And so Dr. Bergler hit on something, didn't he? I do feel responsible."

"I think you just didn't realize the kind of man you were dealing with," Mimi says.

"I've never told anyone about any of this," her mother says. "I've never even told Dr. Bergler. Maybe I'll tell him in our next session. At least that will give us something to talk about!"

"Yes."

"Do you remember that young man you wanted to marry, Mimi—Michael Horowitz? Do you remember how your grandpa put a stop to *that?* Maybe if I hadn't done what I did, that would have worked out differently, too."

"I don't think so."

"He was so in love with you, Mimi, I could tell. Didn't you say he went to Choate? And you were in love with him, too. But your daddy was right about that one, too. He said, 'Patience, be patient,' or something like that —and less than three years later Old Moneybags was dead!"

"Yes."

"And I remember how helpful Michael Horowitz was to us after your grandpa died, when it turned out Old Moneybags had hardly any money left! It makes me smile, when I read in the papers about how rich Mr. Horowitz has become. If your grandpa had known that was going to happen, he might have whistled a different tune. Do you ever see Mr. Horowitz anymore?"

"Oh, yes. From time to time."

"Isn't it ironic how life works out? It's thanks to him, really—and of course to you, Mimi—that we're all rich again. Here I am, coming toward the end of my life, and rich again! I had a real estate agent call me just the other day and tell me he could get four million for this house! He said it was the prettiest house in Turtle Bay! Yet I wouldn't have had it if it hadn't been for what he did, first, and then later, what you did for Miray. Isn't life funny?"

"Yes, it is."

"And now you have your wonderful Brad. He's made you wonderfully happy, hasn't he, dear?"

Mimi says nothing.

"So everything works out for the best. And now I have my wonderful grandson, Badger. So handsome! And such a *good* young man, too, isn't he? Badger is the future. That's what I must think about now—the future, not the past. Oh, Mimi, isn't it wonderful to sit here on a summer afternoon and think about the future? I feel so much better, dear, for having talked to you! Thank you for coming over and helping me get all these things off my chest. My jitteriness is gone now, Mimi. My jumpiness is gone, just for having talked to you. And . . . guess what? I don't want a drink now, Mimi! I don't think I'll ever want another drink as long as I live. I've got half a mind to throw that bottle of whiskey out the window and into the courtyard." She laughs brightly. "But then they'd . . . have me arrested for littering. That would be just my luck, wouldn't it? Arrested for littering? But I do think I'm getting my guts back, Mimi. I'm going to try, anyway. I'm going to try, so hard."

Mimi rises and moves toward her mother, who is still standing by the window, and puts her hand on the soft portion of her mother's upper arm. "Mother, *dear*," she says.

"I'm fine, now," her mother says.

From the notes:

Driving up to Westchester in the back seat of one of Mimi's big company cars today (one of the perks of doing a story on the beauty business is that wherever you want to go, to tour a factory or visit a lab, they send a limo to take you there), I did a stupid thing.

Mimi seemed a little preoccupied, the way she's been for the last couple of days, and our conversation was mostly small talk—how the Bronx keeps creeping northward, that sort of thing. But, sitting beside her in the closed quarters of a back seat, the thing I'd never noticed about her before was how wonderful she *smelled.* I'd never been with a woman who smelled as good as she did. Finally, I commented on it.

She laughed that ripply, pebbly laugh of hers and told me that she was wearing her new fragrance.

Christ! She must think me an unobservant ass! What else would it have been?

Our destination was a rather pretentious house in Scarsdale, one of those stucco-and-exposed-beam jobs, with a brass carriage lamp at the foot of the drive and a cast-iron blackamoor holding out a ring for a hitching post. Even before ringing the doorbell, I knew it would produce musical chimes. (It did.) Before we got out of the car, Mimi said, "Do me a favor, Jim. Kiss my left shoulder . . . for luck. It's got to be the left one. Do you mind? I'm superstitious."

By now, I had the explanation of what I had witnessed that night with Felix. And if, when I touched my lips to her shoulder and drank in that heady perfume again, I squeezed her arms a little too tightly and pressed my body a little too close to hers, she seemed not to notice, probably because her mind was on other things.

Our hostess, Louise Bernhardt, turned to be a pleasant enough woman, slender and elegantly suburban-looking, with frosted hair, given to chunky silver bracelets, though she was quite taken aback when she answered the door and realized that the woman I was with was the famous Mimi Myerson. But Mimi carried it off beautifully. "Cousin Louise," she said, and gave her a little peck on the cheek. "I've wanted to meet you for years. Isn't it silly that whatever it was that divided this family has gone on for nearly two generations, when no one even remembers what the thing that divided us was? One of the things I'm determined to do is to bring the scattered members of the family together again."

As an interview subject, however, Mrs. Bernhardt was not very helpful. When I got around to what I call The Big Question—how Adolph Myerson was able to force his brother out of the company when they were fifty-fifty shareholders of its stock—her answer—honest, I think—was:

"I just don't know. As you say, Adolph couldn't have *voted* my grandfather out, since they were equal partners. It all happened before I was born, of course, and my grandfather would never talk about it. All I know is that he was very bitter. As children, we weren't even allowed to utter the name Adolph Myerson in his presence. Sorry, Mimi," she said with a nod in her direction.

"That's perfectly all right."

"And here's another mystery," I said. "After Leo left the company in nineteen forty-one, and for the next eighteen years until Adolph died in nineteen fifty-nine, Leopold Myerson's office was maintained at the company headquarters."

"I didn't know that."

"Nothing in that office was changed. It was kept exactly as he left it. The building staff cleaned it and dusted it, but no one else ever occupied it or sat at your grandfather's desk. It sat empty for eighteen years. After a while, people in the company began referring to that empty office as 'the *other* Mr. Myerson's office.' It was almost as though your grandfather's office was maintained as a kind of shrine. But that doesn't make any sense, does it? Why, I wonder?"

"I simply have no idea."

"Neither do I," Mimi said.

"Can I offer you some tea? Lemonade? A drink?"

"Did your father ever mention any of this?"

"My father died in nineteen sixty-two when I was a very little girl."

"Coincidence—that was the year Mimi's father died."

"Well, yes. I was eight years old." She stood up and fished for a cigarette from a silver box. "Does anyone mind if I smoke? We're the last persecuted minority, we smokers! You see, my father was murdered. I thought perhaps you knew that."

"No, I didn't."

"Yes. His body was found in the Saw Mill River. He'd been strangled with a bicycle chain. I can speak dispassionately of all this, because I barely remember him. My mother remarried not long afterward, and it was my stepfather whom I grew up calling Daddy. The murderer was never found. The presumed motive was robbery. He was known to carry large amounts of cash, and his billfold was missing, along with a gold watch and a couple of rings he wore. Are you sure I can't offer you some tea?"

After that, it was clear she had little else to offer, and for a while she and Mimi chatted about the family: Louise's children, and what they were doing in school, Louise's two brothers, their wives, and their children. Then it all at once became clear that Mimi had another reason for wanting to accompany me on this journey. It was not just to have a clubby reunion with a long-lost second cousin, and at first I was annoyed with her for not coming clean with me. But I forgive her because at least now I know what her recent business with Horowitz has been all about.

"I know Michael Horowitz has approached you about your Miray stock," she said.

"Yes. He was here to see me the other day."

"And I'm sure he made you an attractive offer, but I think there's something you ought to know. Though Michael hasn't announced anything, we're quite sure that he's in the first stages of an unfriendly takeover attempt. Do you know how these things work, Louise?"

"Not really. But my husband, Dick, is a lawyer, and I'm sure he'd know."

"Let me explain to you, very briefly, how these things work. Someone like Michael begins by singling out a company whose assets are worth a good deal more than the purchase price of its stock—a company like ours, for instance. He then borrows money and begins buying up stock. Let's say he's successful and acquires majority control. The first thing he must do is to repay his loans, and this can only be done by liquidating the company's assets, turning them into cash or other tax-deductible items. People like myself must also be paid off—with so-called golden parachutes, often costing many millions of dollars. In Wall Street, these are called 'opportunity costs,' and they're all tax-deductible. It's our tax laws that make these take-over opportunities so attractive. After these costs, and after disposing of any divisions of the company that show a trace of red ink, the acquisitor takes what's left, which usually doesn't amount to much more than a prestigious name. Or a new company that's saddled with debts to the past, instead of one dedicated to serving its customers and stockholders in the future. The result of these takeovers is nearly always a contraction, rather than an expansion, of a company's worth. So, while I'm sure Michael's offer may seem very attractive to you today, I'm asking you to think of the future of our company, and what it could mean for your children, and the generation after that, because by then, if Michael is successful, there'll be no more Miray Corporation as we know it today.

"I'd like to make one more point. Michael Horowitz is a deal-maker—a very good one, and a very successful one, I grant him that. He takes old rental buildings and turns them into condominiums. He takes defunct hotels in Atlantic City and turns them into casinos. He's after us because he sees a chance to make a deal. But what he does has nothing to do with what we do. While our company doesn't like to see red ink on the bottom line any more than anyone else does, we're not a deal-making business. We're called a glamour industry, and every now and then I like to remind the people who work for us what the word *glamour* means. It's an old French word that means, literally, bewitchment. We're in the magic business. We're in the business of casting spells. We don't simply sell beauty products; we also sell mystery, excitement, fantasy, and fun. If we deal at all, we deal with intangibles, such as hope and laughter and love and what makes the heart skip a beat. We wouldn't be where we are today if we didn't believe in make-believe and let's-pretend, in people having fun and feeling happy. Is there a deal-maker in the world who believes in make-believe? I don't think so."

I must admit I was impressed with her little speech.

"Frankly, I was tempted by his offer," Louise Bernhardt said after a moment. "And I should tell you that my husband wants me to take him up on it. Three children who'll be in college all at once, I don't need to tell you what that means. On the other hand, I did promise my grandfather that I'd never sell. He made us all promise that we'd never sell."

"Your grandfather was foresighted," Mimi said. "And obviously I can't tell you what your decision ought to be. But I will ask you this. We have a plan, which we'll announce at a stockholders' meeting, and put up for a vote, by which we can not only thwart the Horowitz takeover but which also, in the long run, could make all of us stockholders a good deal better off. Will you put Michael off until we've all met and we've outlined our plan? This may not be easy, because Michael is a very forceful persuader, and I'm sure he'll keep upping his offer. But I do ask you to sit tight until we have our meeting and outline a counterproposal. That won't be long."

"That seems a fair enough request," Louise Bernhardt said.

"Thank you. I'm sure you won't regret it."

"There was one thing that Mr. Horowitz said that puzzled me," she said. "Your son's name came up, and he said, 'He's the one I'm after.' What do you suppose he meant by that?"

Mimi shrugged. "Meanwhile," she said, reaching in her bag, "I have a little gift for you, Louise—may I call you Louise? This is a five-ounce bottle of a new fragrance we'll be introducing next month. And this is the companion men's cologne—I'm giving you a bottle of the splash-on as well as the spray since I didn't know which he'd prefer—that your husband might like to try. We're having a launch party for these on September seventeenth at the Pierre, which ought to be fun. I'll see that you get an invitation."

"*So,*" I said as we drove back to the city in her car, "*that* was why you wanted to come along with me today."

She laughed the ripply laugh. "Not a word to anyone!" she said. "Promise me. Not a word to anyone until we're ready to announce our proposal to the stockholders. Then I'll tell you everything." She was in high spirits now and did not want to talk about takeover bids. "Listen," she said. "I've got it all figured out. If the Mafia was involved with the company back in the thirties, as Mother says it was— back then, a lot of companies were— and if Leo was behind all that, as Mother says he was, then I'm sure his son Nate was involved in it, too. Nate, being the son, was probably the bag man, and Leo was the behind-the-scenes, mastermind one. So, here's the script. Grandpa forces Leo out of the company in nineteen forty-one, right? Suddenly the Mob is out of a big hunk of business, right? They're not pleased. They go after the bag man to try to get that business back. Maybe Nate even still owes them money for the last job they did. Nate's caught in a bind. He tries to put them off with promises. But the Mob gets impatient, the natives get restless. Pretty soon, it's put up or shut up, and by nineteen sixty-two they've had it with Nate. Okay, cut to the chase! They get out a contract on Nate, and he's bumped off! I mean, strangled with a bicycle chain and thrown in a river! Did you ever hear of anything that sounded more like a gangland-style killing? What do you think . . . ?"

She went on with elaborations and variations on this hypothetical script all the way back to 1107 Fifth Avenue.

Granny Flo Myerson (interview taped 8/30/87):

I'll tell you *exactly* how my husband got rid of Leo. It wasn't easy, I'll tell you that. It wasn't easy because Leo was dumb. Smart people are easier to deal with than dumb people. A smart person would have seen the handwriting on the wall—*Mene, Mene, Tekel, Upharsin,* as it says in the Book of Daniel. But Leo was too dumb to see that he'd been weighed and measured and found wanting.

How? My husband used psychological warfare, that's how. Ever hear of psychological warfare? I know all about psychological warfare because I was taught by a master, my husband. Psychological warfare means warfare of the mind. It means working on the mind. There's nothing illegal about it. It's not like germ warfare, you can't get arrested for it. What did Adolph do? Let's just say he worked on Leo's mind to get him out. You see, Leo was a bad person. He did bad things. I think I told you Leo was handsome, but he had a cleft chin. Beware of a man who has a cleft chin! *You* don't have a cleft chin, do you? No? Well, thank goodness for that! A man with a cleft chin has a cloven hoof for a heart. That was what Leo had.

Oh, but back to the psychological warfare. It was really something. I don't remember all the exact details of it, though I suppose I could if I tried. It was all in Adolph's diaries, but they're gone now—gone with the wind, as they say in the movies. I just remember it was done step by step. That's the only way to do it, step by step. Some of it was not too nice, perhaps. Some of it might not look too nice if you read it in the papers, and you write for the papers so maybe I'd better button my lip. Let's just say that Jonesy helped. Jonesy was my husband's secretary. Jonesy was secretly in love with my Adolph. She'd have done anything for him. I think painting Leo's face out of the portrait was Jonesy's idea. That was a part of it. That was the final straw that broke the camel's hump, right across his neck. That was the sword of Diogenes. That was the end of Leo.

Why did they keep his office there? I'll give you the answer in four little words. *Psy. Chol. O. Gy.* Adolph kept that empty office there as a reminder to anyone else in the organization who might forget who was the boss. That empty office was there to say a warning: "This could happen to *you!*"

Now tell me what you've found out about Edwee. There're a few things I know, a few things I could tell about Edwee that he wouldn't want to see in print. Oho! But I need to know what he's up to before I decide whether to bring out my heavy ammunition. . . .

"I need to see you, kiddo," he says. "It's important."

"I really don't think there's anything more we need to say to each other, Michael," Mimi says.

"But there is. A lot."

"What, for instance?"

"Well, for one thing, I owe you a long-overdue apology."

"Really? What for?"

"Your grandfather. I used to think he was an anti-Semitic, despotic old bastard. But it turns out that he really wasn't such a bad guy after all."

"What makes you say that?"

"I've been reading his diaries," he says. There is a silence from her end of the connection. Then he says, "They've just reopened the Rainbow Room. It's been done over just like it was in the good old days. What about that, kiddo, for old times' sake?"

✿

18

*A*T the Hotel Grande Bretagne in Athens, there was another letter waiting for her from her mother.

Mimi dear—   *Aug. 1, 1957*

I don't want to upset you, dearest, but there is something that I thought you ought to know. Your grandfather has been failing badly in the last few weeks, and we are all quite worried about him. He has suddenly lost a lot of weight, and his color is bad, and yet he refuses to see a doctor or to admit that anything might be the matter with him. I also fear that his mind may be going. On Sunday, at tea, he seemed to have trouble remembering my name, and at one point addressed me as "Ruthie," which was the name of a younger sister of his who died in the typhoid epidemic of 1884! It is terribly sad to see him like this, but your father and I do not know what to do, except to remember that in two more months he will be eighty-eight years old. . . .

Meanwhile, he insists on going to the office every day, though your father has been urging him to take a rest or perhaps a holiday. And of course he refuses to turn over any of the responsibilities of running the company to your father, which he really ought to do at this point. As your father points out, the company is really too big and complex an operation now for one man to run it single-handedly, the way your grandfather has always run it. Your father greatly fears that management details are being overlooked, and that decisions that ought to be made are not being made. But at this point your father's hands are tied.

Your Granny Flo has been spending the month of August at the Bar Harbor house, but next week, at my urging, she has promised to come back to the city and look in on him.

I hate to worry you with all this, Mimi, but I thought you should know, just in case something should occur which might mean you'd have to cut your vacation short. Of course for your sake I hope and pray that this won't happen.

I read in the National Geographic *that they sell natural sea-sponges in Greece. If you see any, and they are cheap, would you pick up a few for me? I am thinking of the little tiny ones that I can use for applying makeup. They would be lightweight, and you could tuck them into the corners of your luggage. . . .*

"Hypocrisy!" she said to Brad Moore after reading him the letter. "Did you ever hear such hypocrisy?"

"Hypocrisy? She just sounds worried because your grandfather's ill."

"This is the same mother who, a few days before I left for Europe, was screaming that Grandpa was too mean to die. She *hates* Grandpa! Now she's acting all worried because he's a little sick."

"Sometimes, when they're angry, people say things they don't mean. They say they don't care about people. But then, when things get down to the wire, they care."

He was like this, that cautious, thoughtful, Harvard Law School mind that always looked at both sides of every question. They were sitting in the central, glass-roofed courtyard of the hotel, sipping Coca-Colas. He would begin a statement with "On the one hand. . ." and then end it with "But then, on the other hand . . ."

"Stop being Mr. Lawyer," she said to him. It had become one of their little jokes.

"Is he very rich, your grandfather?"

"Oh, yes. At least to hear him tell it. People ask him how he can afford to live the way he does. Three big houses. A yacht. 'A hundred million dollars' worth of the best gilt-edged stocks in America,' he says." She giggled. "Modesty is not one of my grandfather's strong points."

"But, you see, that could be one of the reasons why your mother feels the way she does about him now. When he dies, I suppose your family will stand to inherit quite a lot of money. With that money will go an even bigger amount of guilt—over the unkind things she's said about him in the past.

Want to make a bet? I'll bet when your grandfather dies, your mother is going to be one of the noisiest mourners at his funeral."

"Hmm," she said thoughtfully, stirring her Cola-Cola with her straw. "They never give you enough ice in these countries, do they. Mine's already melted. My Coke's warm already."

"I've had some relatives who were pretty rich," he said. "There was an uncle who left my mother some money in a trust. But, on the other hand, we're New Englanders, you know. We believe in living only on the income from our income. That's why you and I didn't meet earlier on this trip. You've been up there in first class on all the planes, and I've been back in steerage with the peasants."

"When my grandfather spends money, he doesn't believe in cutting corners."

"New Yorkers and Bostonians. They're a different species, I sometimes think. Or are they? What do you think?"

"I don't know. You're the first Bostonian I've ever met."

They sat in silence for a while, and then he said, "I was sent on this trip to get over a love affair."

"Really?"

"She was a New York girl. At least, Long Island. Not that that's important."

"And have you got over her?"

"Yes. And you know why? Because now that I've had time to think about it, I realize it wasn't love. It was only sex, and love isn't just sex. I mean, on the one hand, I agree that sex is important—it is. But on the other hand—"

"Now, Mr. Lawyer—"

"I'm serious. Someone you love has to have more than just sex to offer, don't you think? I mean, don't there have to be other qualities like intelligence, and sensitivity, and a real interest in the other guy's life? This girl had none of those things. You know what she was like? She was like one of those Stately Homes we toured in England—a beautiful facade, but no central heating."

"Oh, Brad!" she laughed. "I like that!"

"Nice to visit, but you wouldn't want to live there."

"I know what you mean, *exactly.*"

"That was Barbara."

"Barbara?"

"That was her name, Barbara Badminton."

She almost squealed. "I know Barbara Badminton! She was at Miss Hall's!"

"Were you at her coming-out party?"

"No!"

"Well, if you know her, would you say she was particularly . . . intelligent?"

"No! She tried to copy my answers in chemistry quizzes."

"Then I gather you two weren't exactly friends."

"Hardly. In fact, I disliked her intensely." Then she said, "I'm sorry. I shouldn't have said that. She was your friend."

"Not anymore. I'm able to see through her now. All it was, was sex."

Mimi said nothing.

"That would have been like her, to cheat on a chemistry quiz. She cheated on other things, too. You see, I found out that I wasn't the only one she was involved with. In terms of sex."

"No," she said quietly, "that really doesn't surprise me. I might as well tell you, I really didn't like Barbara Badminton, and she didn't like me. Part of it was that I was on a scholarship at Miss Hall's. That put me in a different social class from people like Barbara. Also, I was—or, rather, I am, Jewish. That makes a difference to people sometimes."

"Not to me," he said.

"And then, my family being in the beauty business—that made a difference to someone like Barbara, whose father is the president of some bank. But I've never been ashamed of the beauty business. It's a fascinating business, very ancient, and I've done a lot of reading about it. For instance, did you know that in China, as long ago as three thousand B.C., women used nail polish? It indicated rank. Dark red and black were the royal colors, and women of lower rank were restricted to paler shades. Nowadays it's all tied in with fashion. Did you know that cosmetics colors depend on the hemline? A few years ago, when Dior introduced the New Look, and hemlines dropped, nail and lip shades became very deep and dark. This was because, when a woman couldn't show her legs, she wanted to draw attention to face and hands. Now that hemlines are up again, we've got the Pale Look in lipsticks and nail polishes. When I was at school, I drew up a chart showing how hemlines dictate cosmetics colors and sent it to my grandfather. But of course at home nobody pays attention to me because I'm just a *girl*. But I'm boring you with all this, aren't I?"

"No, no," he said. "Go on. This is fascinating."

And she realized all at once, sitting there, that one reason she liked Brad Moore so much was that he was one of the first people she had ever known who actually *listened* to her.

"I love listening to you talk," he said, echoing her thoughts.

"Do you really?"

"Oh, yes!"

And now another silence fell between them, and suddenly Mimi felt that something else was happening. At first, she wasn't sure what it was. "I don't quite know how to say this, Mimi," he said at last, "but I like you—very much."

"Thank you," she said, and was immediately not sure that this was the appropriate thing to say. "I like you, too," she added.

"Very much," he said. And now the air between them was somehow emotionally charged, and a kind of current seemed to have quickened between them. Suddenly their conversation became full of pauses, and everything that each said seemed to carry a secret innuendo, or double meaning: On the one hand, it said. But on the other hand, it also said.

"What is it this afternoon?" she said. "The Parthenon, I guess."

"Yes. Optional. That's one thing I like about this tour. Everything is optional. . . ."

"The Parthenon will still be there tomorrow, I suppose. . . ."

"Yes. . . ."

"The Parthenon is one of those things you can always trust to be there. Like you can trust the Leaning Tower of Pisa not to fall down."

"Yes."

"I have a fine view of the Parthenon from my room," he said. "Can you see the Parthenon from yours?"

"I don't . . . know. I didn't . . . look."

"A fine view. Would you . . . ?"

"All right. . . ."

His room on the fifth floor of the hotel did indeed face the Acropolis, and they stepped out onto the small balcony to look at it. "There it is," he said softly. "It's been there for twenty-four hundred years. And it only took nine years to build."

"Only nine?"

"Only nine."

"Do you . . . know a lot of facts like that?"

"Some," he said. "A few."

"So do I. A few. I know . . . I know the atomic weight of nitrogen."

"Fourteen point zero-zero-seven."

"That's right!"

"Chemistry," he said. "There can be a chemistry between two people, don't you think? Positive and negative forces . . . that attract."

"Yes."

"Should there be sex before marriage, do you think? What do you think?"

"I don't know. I've never—"

"On the one hand—"

"But then, on the other hand—"

But this was no joke now, and neither of them laughed. She felt his arm circle her waist. "I like you—very much," he said again.

As he drew her to him, she whispered, "Brad, there are some things I don't know very much about. Do you understand?"

She felt him nod, because she had still not looked into his face, and when she did she saw that a thin line of perspiration beaded his upper lip, and somehow this sign of his insecurity reassured her. It would be all right. "Do you have a . . . you know, a thing?" she said.

He nodded again. They parted the curtains with their hands and stepped back into the room, and he kissed her there.

"You'll have to tell me what to do," she said.

But that, of course, had not been necessary. Is it ever? A girl from Manhattan, a boy from Boston, a boy with a head for dates and arguments, and a girl with a head for figures, a girl who thought her heart was broken, a boy who thought he had lost his last illusion—positive and negative forces. There are only a few things that can happen to human beings under these circumstances when you are four thousand miles from home.

In Istanbul, there was another letter waiting from her mother.

Darling—   *Aug. 9, 1957*

Guess what? There is good news about your grandpa. He looks ever so much better, his color is better, and he seems much better in spirits. I think it was Granny coming down from Bar Harbor that did it, and for once maybe they'll both thank me for having a good idea. Granny says that she thinks that when she goes away he works so hard that he forgets to eat! She's going to spend the rest of the summer with him in New York, and see that he gets three good meals a day. I know you'll be relieved to hear this.

Of course we all wish that he'd ease off a bit at the office, and not insist on supervising and overseeing every tiny detail that goes on. Miray is launching a new polish/lipstick shade for autumn, with an amusing name, "Candied Apple," and your daddy says that the office these days resembles the War Room at the Pentagon, what with all the charts, sales projections and quotas that keep changing daily. I'm sending you some samples of "C. A." separately, and hope the package will make it to you through the Turkish Customs. It's really a very pretty shade. . . .

And guess what else? Your grandpa actually seems to be mellowing a bit in his old age. The other day, he suddenly asked, "What do you hear from Mireille? I miss her." What do you think of that? He said he misses you! So I think it would be awfully nice, dear, if you wrote him another letter soon. I know you wrote to thank him for the trip, but I think he'd appreciate hearing from you again with all your news, the sights you've seen, the people you've met, etc., etc. Do me a favor, and do this.

*How is your wardrobe holding out? Are you getting good mileage out of
your black ballerina . . . ?*

"Mireille," he said. "That's a lovely name. I didn't realize that was your
real name—Mireille."

"Oh, yes. I was named after my grandfather's Miray Corporation. I think
my parents named me that hoping it would make him treat them better. At
school, they used to tease me about being named after a nail-polish company, so I decided to be called Mimi."

"Will he like me, do you think?"

"Well," she says, settling into the banquette beside him, "where are these
alleged diaries?"

"Hell," he says, "you didn't expect me to bring them with me, did you,
kiddo? There're over forty-five volumes, covering almost fifty years of business and personal history. They fill a good-sized suitcase. Did you expect me
to lug that over here and spread out all those books on a table at the
Rainbow Room?"

"I thought that was the purpose of this meeting, Michael."

"One of the purposes. Just one of them."

"Then I assume you'll have them sent over to my office by messenger in
the morning?"

"Hold on," he says, holding up one hand. "I'm not so sure. That's one of
the things we're going to have to discuss. Let's have a drink, and we'll
discuss that."

"But I promised Jim Greenway he could look at those diaries for his
research—that is, if they really exist."

"Oh, they exist all right. But first tell Pablo here what you want to drink.
I'll have my usual, Pablo," he says to the captain who is standing over them.

"A dry martini," Mimi says. And then, when the captain has disappeared,
she says, "I don't need to tell you, Michael, that these diaries, if they exist,
and if they were written by my grandfather, do not belong to you. They
belong to my family. Legally, they are part of my grandfather's residuary
estate, as it's called. I don't know how you managed to obtain them, but
they are not your property."

He gives her a sideways look. "Did I say they were?" he says. "But what's
that they say about possession? Nine tenths of the law? Something like
that."

"Then may I ask, if you don't intend to turn them over to me, what you
intend to do with them?"

"Hold on," he says. "Will you please just hold on? I said there are things we need to discuss. We can discuss these matters, one point at a time, if you'll just simmer down and stop talking about who legally owns what. Thank you, Pablo," he says as their drinks arrive. He lifts his glass. "Here's looking at you, kiddo," he says.

"Thank you," she says. "Now let's have our discussion. Point by point, as you said."

"Okay," he says. "Well, to begin with, there's a lot in those diaries that's pretty boring stuff. Detailed descriptions of how they came up with the names of certain products, advertising strategies, promotional plans, sales figures—stuff that wouldn't interest anybody but a student of corporate history."

"Which is exactly what Jim Greenway is writing. A history of the company."

"I'd say maybe seventy-five, maybe eighty percent of what's in those books is stuff like that. But the point is that when your grandfather kept those diaries, he put in everything that happened. Everything."

"Jim is also interested in personal material," she says.

"Some of it is very personal. Intensely personal. As I said on the phone, there are things in there that changed my opinion about your grandfather completely."

"Such as?"

"As I read through them, I realized—I couldn't help but be struck by how deeply he cared about his family. Not just about his own reputation as a big shot, but his family's, how concerned he was about all of you, about his children, their safety, their well-being, their happiness, how protective he was of everyone. How he worried about them, how he tried to protect them."

"Protect them from what?"

"As I read some of these . . . more personal entries, I realized that this wasn't a bad guy at all. He was a man whose children's safety came first."

"But safety from what?"

"From forces, from people, who could have caused them great harm, great unhappiness. I guess what I'm trying to tell you, Mimi, is that there are things in the diaries that I'm pretty sure you wouldn't want your friend Greenway to read about or know about. By the way, where's your husband tonight?"

"In Minneapolis on business. But go on about the diaries."

"Does he know we're having dinner tonight?"

"I don't see why that matters. I'll be talking to him in the morning. Please don't change the subject, Michael."

"Well, as you can imagine, there's a lot about your father in the diaries—things I don't think you'd want Greenway to know."

She says nothing.

"As well as living people—people you wouldn't want to hurt. Your mother, for instance."

She hesitates. "Her drinking problem, I suppose."

"Well, yes. And your aunt Nonie."

"Nonie is—well, Nonie sometimes takes things from stores that she hasn't paid for. It only happens when she's upset about something, and it hasn't happened for some time, but—"

"And your uncle Edwee."

"Edwee's penchant for little boys, you mean? Nothing new."

"Your grandfather had to deal with all those problems, and he dealt with them as best he could, to protect his children and his family. There was a blackmail attempt from Florida, for instance."

"Involving Edwee? I've heard whispers about something like that over the years. No big deal."

"But there were some other things," he says quietly. "Even worse things. Things that had to be covered up. Things that your grandfather was forced to deal with. And did deal with."

"What, for instance?"

"For instance, a criminal manslaughter case," he says.

"That was my father's cousin Nate—Leo's son. I know all about that. Please tell me something that I didn't know already."

"No," he says. "It wasn't your father's cousin Nate. Nate died in nineteen sixty-two. This is a case that goes back to nineteen forty-one, the year Nate left the company—and the year coincidentally when the diaries end. The criminal is still very much alive. You see, what I'm trying to tell you, Mimi, is that there are entries in those diaries that I don't think you'd *want* to know about, and that *I* don't want you to know about." He covers her hand with his, and she allows it to rest there a moment before withdrawing hers. "And the reason I don't is because I care about your family, too, believe it or not, and don't want them hurt. And the only reason I care about your family, of course, is because I care about you and don't want you to be hurt."

Suddenly she finds herself becoming annoyed with him. "Oh, for heaven's sake, Michael, cut out this cat-and-mouse game. Everyone knows it's a game you play very well. You don't need to show off for me."

"I think those diaries should be destroyed," he says. "Too many people could be hurt by what's there. Including you. I'd like to ask your permission to destroy them."

"I think," she says, "that I should discuss this with my husband, who also happens to be my lawyer—after we've examined these diaries, which, in any event, are my property."

"Tell me something," he says. "Did Brad ever know about you and me?"

"What has that got to do with this discussion?"

"Rather a lot, I'm afraid. I don't mean about when we were supposed to be engaged. I mean later. I mean Riverside Drive. I mean the way you straightened my sock drawer. I mean the cranberry juice, and the Kellogg's bran flakes. I mean the days of the little white stars, the days when I was trying to make some sense of that crazy mishmash that turned out to be your grandfather's estate, the days of our brief reencounter with one another, the days I called our *Strange Interlude* days."

"Are you implying *that's* in Grandpa's diaries? How could it be? He was dead by then. You're really trying my patience, Michael. Please stop this. I really think I want to go." And, flipping her napkin on the table, she starts to rise, but, gently pressing her arm downward, he restrains her.

"Do you love him, Mimi?" he asks. "Did you ever love him?"

"Brad and I have been happily married for nearly thirty years."

"That's not an answer, is it?"

"It's *my* answer. Now, please—"

"And—happily? He has a girlfriend, you know."

"Nonsense."

With the tip of his left forefinger, he pulls down the lower lid of his left eye in a European gesture of disbelief. "I saw him with her at Le Cirque," he says. "So did you."

"It's nothing serious. It's just a mid-life fling."

"And what was it that we had? A youthful fling? Was that all it was? Why do I remember how you liked your tea?"

"I really don't know what you're talking about."

"Half a lump of sugar with your tea. You told me that at your grandfather's house they always gave you one lump, because that's what you'd been told to ask for when you first went there as a little girl. But you really preferred just half a lump, and a slice of lemon. Do you remember when I brought you tea in bed on Riverside Drive—with half a lump and a lemon slice? What you said then?"

"What I said then has absolutely nothing to do with why I met you here tonight. And I'm not going to listen to any more of this drivel."

"And Paul Anka singing on the radio, 'Put Your Head on My Shoulder'? That was your favorite song."

"Michael, you lured me here tonight with a promise to show me my grandfather's—allegedly—all-revealing diaries. But you haven't produced a single page. What's going on?"

"Oh, I could show you plenty of pages. Just not all of them."

"Oh. So now I think I get it. If I want to see these diaries—which may or may not even exist—I have to come up to your place to see them. Right? Is this the old come-up-and-see-my-etchings approach? Really, you disappoint me. I would have expected something a little more original from the great Michael Horowitz. Now I've really got to go."

"In the old days, you trusted me, Mimi. You needed me then. You said you loved me."

"I may have been vulnerable then. I'm not vulnerable now."

"Why do you take everything I say as a kind of threat? Even loving things. Do you remember, when you first came to my apartment, you wore my ring?"

"I may have been foolish then. I'm not now. I'm as tough as you are. Now—"

"Do you still have it—the ring?"

"Irrelevant question! Now let me go."

Once more he makes the gesture with his lower eyelid. "Sure you do. Don't lie to me, Mimi. You were always a lousy liar. I know you kept it so you'd always remember me."

"And you're turning into an absolute pest. Now let go of my arm. Do you want me to make a scene? I can, you know."

Still holding her arm, he says quietly, "I just want you to hear me out. In the old days, you always believed in hearing the other guy out."

She relaxes slightly. "Then will you please tell me something?" she says. "Why have you suddenly come back at me after all these years? Why are you trying to break me down? It doesn't make any sense—no sense at all. Everything we had was over long ago. Why have you suddenly come back at me, thirty years later, stirring things up again? What the hell do you want? Why?"

"It's pretty simple," he says. "You were the first *nice* girl I'd ever met. Who was I? A caterer's kid from Queens. But you were the first *nice* girl. You still are. I've had a lot of girls since then, I admit that. I know my reputation—the Romeo of Real Estate, and all that crap. But there's never been another *nice* girl. And all these years I've waited—waited until I was rich enough—richer than the Myersons ever were—rich enough to come back and claim you, to come back again and have what we had again, the little white stars, because those were things I'd never had before and, believe me, I've never had since with anyone. That's why I'm back: because I find you just as beautiful and desirable as ever, even more so. Your *fah-nee, fah-nee face*, remember? That's why I'm back: to have those things again, before it's too late for both of us."

"The operative verb is *claim* isn't it? You've come back to stake a claim on me. Well, you can't. Because I'm not some piece of real estate! I'm not one of your co-op apartment houses. I'm not one of your hotels. I think what you really want is to control me, to own me, but nobody owns any-

body. You want to control me by saying you have incriminating evidence
about my family in Grandpa's diaries. That's called blackmail, Michael. And
I'm not going to be blackmailed, and I am not going to be controlled. I am
not for sale!"

"I want you back," he says simply, "because I love you."

"I don't think so. I think you want me back because I'm the only game
you ever lost, the only deal you didn't cinch. I think your poor little male
ego has been bruised all these years."

He shakes his head slowly back and forth. "Why don't you admit some
things?" he says.

"And why are you making these threats? Because that's what they are—
threats. Criminal manslaughter! Just who the hell are you talking about,
anyway?"

He hesitates. "Your mother, perhaps?"

"That's a lie! Mother was hundreds of miles away when Daddy died.
You've been talking to Granny Flo, haven't you? You've been talking to all
my relatives, trying to get them to sell their stock to you. I know what
you've been up to, and it's not going to work. If you think you hold some
trump card against me, you've picked the wrong opponent. And if you've
been listening to what Granny Flo says, you're even crazier than she is."

"I'm not talking about your Granny Flo, and I'm not talking about your
father. I'm talking about stuff that's in those diaries, and I'm talking about
stuff that could damage living members of your family. But I'm not going to
tell you anything more. I've told you more than I wanted to already."

"More threats. More bullying. That's all you are, Michael, is a bully.
That's all you ever were."

"You didn't use to think so, did you, kiddo? Remember?"

"And stop calling me kiddo. I'm not a kid anymore, in case you hadn't
noticed."

"How can you have forgotten, when I remember everything?" He inches
closer to her on the banquette. "Why can't you be honest with yourself? Do
you remember the day we drove out to the new house I was building in East
Orange? Do you remember walking through the empty rooms, telling me
where I should put the piano? What color I should paint the walls of the
den? Chinese red, you said—a nice lipstick color. And cafe curtains. The
year was nineteen sixty, and cafe curtains were the big thing. Why do I
remember all of this? The things you said you'd do if the house were yours?"

"Ancient history. I haven't thought of that for years."

"And do you remember we walked out onto the terrace, where the pool
was going to be, and you looked across at the city skyline, and you said that
was exactly where you'd like to keep New York—miles away, on the other
side of the river? And you told me that you'd like to live in that house with

me, told me that you were free now, and were ready to divorce Brad and marry me. Do you remember any of that? I remember, because you told me that you'd always loved *me.*"

"I remember," she says evenly, "that it was a terrible time for me. Grandpa had just died, my father was at his wits' end trying to pick up the pieces of the company, and everything in the family seemed to be falling apart, and you seemed to be the only one—"

"The only one who what?"

"The only one who seemed able to make any sense out of the shambles Grandpa had left things in. It was a terrible time, and I was frightened, irrational, not knowing what was going to happen. I was weak then—at the weakest point in my life. I'm strong now. You were useful to us then. You're not useful now."

"Yes, irrational. Don't you think I saw that? That's why I said no—no, because you'd made your choice of husbands. And I didn't want to be called a home-wrecker."

"Yes! So pious, weren't you? Mr. Goody Two-Shoes! But now that you're so rich and powerful, you think you have a perfect right to try to wreck any home you want! Well, you can't wreck mine!"

"Ah," he says. "So that's it. You're still angry at me because I rejected your proposal."

"You son of a bitch. I won't even dignify that comment with an answer."

"But how can I be a home-wrecker now? Your home's already wrecked, isn't it?"

"That. Is. Not. True," she says through clenched teeth, making each word a sentence. "Now let me—"

"I want you back because I think that now you're able to make a sensible choice between Brad and me."

"The only choice I'm making is to leave this restaurant. If you have property belonging to my family, I'll sue to get it back. If you have plans to take over my company, I'll see you in court on that matter, too. Understand one thing, Michael. Nothing about me or my life belongs to you. Is that quite clear? Now I think I'm ready to make my scene. Ready? Here goes. *Waiter!*" she calls.

"And because I think you're the mother of my son."

She quickly reaches for her drink and, in so doing, overturns her half-filled cocktail glass. Both of them watch as the pool of clear liquid spreads across the white tablecloth, Mimi's expression frozen.

"Be honest, Mimi," he says softly. "You have something that I want. I have something that you want. Why don't we both admit that what we've both always wanted is each other?"

* * *

"Dearest Mother," she had written when the little party of summer tourists arrived at the Hotel du Palais in Lausanne late in August of that year:

I feel a little strange writing to you to ask you the question that I am about to ask you, but there is no one else whom I can ask, and so I am asking you.

There is a young man I've met who is in our tour group. His name is Bradford Moore, Jr., and he is from Boston, Mass. He is 24 years old, 6 ft. tall, with dark brown eyes and dark brown hair, and he graduated in June from Harvard Law School. This fall, he will start working with a N.Y. law firm downtown. He is nice, and pretty funny, though in a serious sort of way. For instance, he says that his real name could be Bradford Moore IV, but he thinks all that II, III, and IV business is pretty silly, so he settles for the "Jr."

Those are the vital statistics. I like him very much. But the important thing is that he has asked me to marry him.

Now this is the hard part, Mother. As you know, I was planning to start at Smith in September, and I have my scholarship and everything. I was really looking forward to college, and I told Brad that, but he doesn't want to wait four more years. He says he is too much in love with me to wait four years, with me in Northampton and him in N.Y.C. He says four years is too long to wait, and he wants us to be married as soon as possible, if my family approves.

Now here is the question, which is really two questions. For one thing, he isn't Jewish. In fact, one of his grandfathers was the minister in the First Congregational Church of Concord, Mass., for several years. He says it doesn't matter to him that I'm Jewish, if it doesn't matter to me, or to my family, that he isn't. Several of the partners in the law firm he'll be joining are Jews, and he likes them very much. He likes and admires the Jews. But —what do you and Daddy think? More important, what will Grandpa say?

Now the second question, which is really the most important question to me. He says he is in love with me, but I don't know whether I'm in love with him because I'm not sure I know what being in love means. I thought I was in love with Michael H., but this feeling of mine now is so different! I mean, I like everything about him. He is so nice, so kind and thoughtful, and I love being with him. I like being with him better than any friend I've ever known, just because he is so nice to be with. We laugh at the same things, and we talk and talk and talk. Is that what being in love feels like? Mother, what is being in love? You and I have never talked much about what being in love is, what it should feel like, how you and Daddy felt about each other when you were married. What did you feel, Mother? What was it like for you? What should it be like for a woman? What should she feel? Mother—what is love like for a woman? Please tell me, if you know.

I admire him, too, Mother. He is wonderfully ambitious and says his goal is to be a Justice of the United States Supreme Court. You see, I like and admire everything about him, and he is simply the nicest person I have ever met, and I think you will think so, too, when you meet him, but first, before I give him any answer, I need to know these other answers, and you are the only person in the world I can think of who can answer these questions for me. Please write to me here, or in Zurich, as soon as you can. . . .

Her answer was a long cablegram from her mother.

DARLING YOUR DADDY AND I SO EXCITED ABOUT YOUR NEWS. THIS IS THE MOST WONDERFUL THING THAT COULD HAPPEN TO YOU AND YOU MUST SAY YES. DO NOT WORRY ABOUT SMITH ETC. BECAUSE WHY IS COLLEGE EVEN IMPORTANT FOR A GIRL LIKE YOU. COLLEGES LIKE SMITH ONLY TURN GIRLS INTO BLUESTOCKINGS ANYWAY. SO EXCITED I CALLED YOUR GRANDPA IMMEDIATELY AND TOLD HIM THE NEWS AND HE IS THRILLED. HE KNOWS THE MOORES OF BOSTON WELL. DOESN'T REALLY KNOW THEM BUT KNOWS WHO THEY ARE AND WHAT THEY REPRESENT. A FINE OLD FAMILY. DARLING LOVE IS THE BIRD IN THE HAND AND THE RIGHT MARRIAGE IS THE MOST IMPORTANT THING IN ANY WOMAN'S LIFE ALWAYS BEAR THAT IN MIND. WHEN YOU COME HOME GRANNY AND GRANDPA WANT TO HAVE A LITTLE TEA TO MEET HIM. OH HOW LUCKY YOU ARE DARLING. YOUR DADDY WILL PROBABLY KILL ME FOR SENDING THIS LONG CABLE BUT IT'S TOO IMPOR-TANT FOR A LETTER. LOVE AND HUGS AND KISSES AND CONGRATULATIONS. MOTHER.

N

19

Naomi Myerson (interview taped 9/5/87):

My relationship with my father? Well, let's put it this way, dear boy. I was his mascot. I was his logotype. You know the little girl on the bottle of Miray baby shampoo? That's me, taken from a photograph when I was eight weeks old. My third husband, who was a lawyer, used to say that I should have demanded a royalty for the use of my likeness on a commercial product. Just think of it. If I'd been paid a royalty of just two cents on every bottle of Miray Baby-Sham that's been sold since the product was introduced, I'd be the richest member of this family—instead of what I am, the poor relation. But when I was eight weeks old, I was hardly in a position to demand a royalty, was I? I was exploited, my third husband said. I was the youngest victim of exploitive child labor in the history of commerce.

I was also my father's guinea pig. When I was nine or ten years old, my father was expanding heavily into hair-care products. He had read somewhere that if a straight-haired person's head was shaved, the hair would grow back curly. My hair was always straight, and so my father had my head shaved to see if the theory was correct. My head wasn't just shaved once. It was shaved seven, eight, maybe ten different times, and each time the new hair began to grow back it was sent to his labs to be analyzed for signs of curliness. You see, he hoped that this experiment would help the scientists and technicians in his labs come up with an ingredient that would give a woman permanently, naturally curly hair. My hair always grew back as straight as before. But in the meantime, I was the only fourth and fifth grader at Spence who wore wigs. During recess, the other girls were always pulling my wigs off and hiding them. Were there psychological scars as a result of this experiment? I leave it to you, dear boy, to answer that question.

Other than in that hair experiment period, my father paid very little attention to me. Everything was focused on the boys. My brother Henry was supposed to take over the company. Edwee, in Father's grand design, was to be the first Jewish President of the United States. I needn't point out to you that this didn't exactly happen, nor is it likely to. My father's will told the whole story of how he regarded me. When my father died, my mother was left thirty percent of his Miray shares. My brothers, Henry and Edwee, each got twenty-five percent. Mimi was left fifteen percent, and I was left exactly five percent. You can imagine that I was in a state of shock when the will was read, and I realized how cruelly I'd been shortchanged.

And that's not the worst of it When my brother Henry died—unexpectedly—he left a third of his shares to Alice and two thirds to Mimi. That little maneuver made Mimi the largest family stockholder in the company. Next came my mother, then Edwee, then Alice, and then, right down at the bottom of the ladder, as always, me. And there's even worse to come! You might say that five percent of my father's Miray shares would be worth, today, quite a nice piece of change, and you'd be right. They would—if I could ever get my hands on them! But no, the others all got their shares outright, but mine were locked into an irrevocable trust, and all I'm allowed to touch is the income from it. And since Mimi believes in keeping dividends small, and in plowing earnings back into the company for research and development and blah-blah-blah, that income is pretty damn small. And who are my trustees, whom I must go to groveling for every extra penny I might need? In addition to two bozos at Manufacturers Hanover, my trustees are my mother, Edwee, and Mimi—who inherited her trusteeship from Henry. My trust runs until the year two thousand, and if I die before then, who gets my shares? According to my father's will, they're to be divided equally among any surviving grandchildren. But there's only one surviving grandchild, and that's guess who? Little Miss Mimi. Mimi is going to inherit all my shares! Do you begin to see the reasons for my bitterness?

Even if my mother were to die tomorrow, and leave half her shares to Edwee and half to me (and there's no guarantee she'll do that), I'd never have the position and the clout in the company that the others, particularly Mimi, have. If I'm lucky, Mother will leave a little to me, a little to Edwee, a lot to Mimi, and a lot to Mimi's son, and I'll be screwed again.

That damned trust! There they sit, on all the money I have in the world, and whenever I try to wheedle a few pennies out of them, they get together and practice saying no to Nonie. They've gotten very good at it: "No, Nonie, no, no, no, no, no."

And let me tell you one more thing, confidentially. Should I ask you to turn off your machine? No, because this is true, this is a fact. The fact is that I could have run the company just as well as Mimi has. Every idea she's had could have been my idea. This new fragrance line of hers, for instance. I'm an expert on fashion, and an expert on fragrances. I could have developed that. I could probably have done it even better. What would it have been like if the new fragrance had been called Naomi, and not Mireille? Would it have been different? I say yes. Would it have been better? I say yes! If you ask me, Mimi's new fragrance is much too *herbal*. Want to bet her new fragrance will bomb? I'm betting on it.

But of course I never had the position and the clout in the company that Mimi had when she struck—pounced on the company—when the iron was hot, after Henry died. But I never had anything, never had zilch, never had zip, with my miserable five percent from my father's miserable will. "To my beloved daughter, Naomi," my father's will said. Ha! He could have said, "To my beloved Baldie." That was what they called me at Miss Spence's School. "Baldie. Baldie Myerson."

My relationship with Edwee? Well, Edwee is interested in lots of things that don't particularly interest me. He's interested in art, for instance, and antiques. You've seen Edwee's house; it's like a museum! As you can see from my apartment, I like modern things. My apartment is almost high-tech, don't you think? I don't like musty old books, old paintings, old rugs, and all that. In fact, you've just given me an idea. Maybe you can help me. Edwee has this plan, this scheme, which he wants me to help him with. I need a witness. I need someone to witness a private agreement he and I have made. Now, do turn off that machine, because what I have to show you is *strictly* confidential. . . .

That was when I learned about Nonie's involvement with Roger Williams, and about Edwee's plot to gain possession of his mother's Goya.

I was appalled by what she showed me. How, I wondered, could I possibly help her as a "witness" to this pathetic document she and her brother had signed, and how could I be a participant in this crazy, possibly illegal, maneuver that she and her brother were about to embark upon together?

And yet, at the same time, I was swept by a sudden wave of pity for her. As I read, and reread, the document, not knowing what to say to her, I sensed that this was a frightened, even desperate, woman. She was also a woman who, despite her slimness, her stylishness in a dark green Adolfo suit, her gold rings and bracelets and careful *maquillage*, was not young. Though no one knew Nonie Myerson's exact age, she had to have been born around 1920 and therefore must be in her late sixties. She had become, I knew, a creature of the evening hours and rarely ventured out of doors in broad daylight when shadows would etch the cat-scratch lines about her ears and eyes and mouth. Even today, though her apartment faces an expansive view of the East River, all the curtains in her rooms were drawn to exclude the sunlight, which had become her enemy, and to preserve the pink lamp-glow of twilight in her house.

She watched me intently as I studied the sad little letter of agreement with its "whereases" and "to wits," and, as though sensing my thoughts, she said urgently, "Don't you see? I've got to have *something*. I can't go through the rest of my life being nothing more than Adolph Myerson's daughter. Help me, dear boy. *Aidez-moi.*"

"I just don't see," I said finally, "how my being a witness to this could be of any help to anyone."

Her eyes narrowed slightly. "It could help, believe me."

"And you want me to add *my* signature to this?"

"That won't be necessary. It's enough that you've seen it, and know about it. That could help me, later on. And later on, it could also help you. You see, if Edwee plays straight with me, you can forget you ever knew about this. But I think he may be planning to double-cross me. If he tries to double-cross me, you could put that in your story—everything. You could ruin him."

In Mimi's Fifth Avenue apartment, the telephone rings distantly and, distantly, the call is picked up. A few moments later, Mimi's butler, Felix, appears in her living room with tea: a silver teapot, a china teacup and saucer, a folded napkin, and three slices of cinnamon toast in a silver rack, on a silver tray.

"Who called, Felix?"

Felix places the tray on a small table beside Mimi's chair. "It was another of them, I'm afraid."

"Another of them?"

"There have been quite a few of them lately, madam. The telephone rings, I answer it in my usual way, and the caller immediately hangs up, breaking the connection. It is most annoying, if I may say so."

"Really? How many of these calls have there been, Felix?"

"As many as six or seven a day, madam. Usually in the evening, or on weekends, like today."

"I see."

"May I suggest," he says, "that madam might consider having her private number changed?"

"Yes," she says.

"Shall I call the telephone company business office on Monday morning and have that taken care of?"

"Well, let me think about it," she says. "It's such a nuisance having to give out a new number to everyone you know."

"Yes," he says. "But may I suggest that someone is becoming quite a nuisance to you?"

"Yes. Well, I'll think about it, Felix."

He hesitates beside the tea table, adjusting the tray so that it sits at a slightly more convenient angle for her. He clears his throat, fussing unnecessarily over the angle of the tray. "There's one more thing," he says. "If I may speak to you."

"Certainly," she says. "What is it, Felix?"

"When I was preparing Mr. Moore's suits to go to the cleaner's this morning, I found a letter in his jacket pocket. I thought perhaps that you should see it."

"Oh?" she says. "Why would I want to see it, Felix?"

"I'm not suggesting that you would *want* to see it, madam. I'm suggesting that perhaps you *should* see it. There's a difference between want and should."

"I take it," she says, "that you have read this letter, Felix."

He says nothing, merely bows slightly.

"I don't really enjoy reading other people's mail."

"It did occur to me," he says, "that there might be a connection between this letter and these telephone calls."

"I see," she says again.

"Suppose," he says, "that I just leave this letter with you, and madam can decide to do with it what she wishes." He withdraws a blue envelope from his vest pocket and places it beside the tea tray, address side down.

"Thank you, Felix."

He bows again and discreetly leaves the room.

Mimi fills her teacup and, for a moment or two, gazes at the back of the envelope, which is blank, revealing no information. Then she slowly picks the envelope up and turns it over. It is addressed, in a rounded, rather schoolgirlish hand, to his Wall Street office and is marked "Personal—Confidential," with the dots over the *i*'s in "Confidential" indicated by little circles. She sees that the envelope is postmarked "New York, N.Y. 10010," revealing that the sender posted her letter somewhere in the Chelsea area.

All Mimi's principles are under assault as she balances the envelope between the thumb and forefinger of her right hand. In the 1970s, when her son, Badger, was at boarding school and college, there were several friendships that appeared to be of a dubious nature, and the parents of his contemporaries traded horror stories of incriminating letters, publications, seeds, and powders uncovered in laundry sacks, at the bottom of closets and dresser drawers, stuffed into innocent-looking tennis shoes, and found in other hiding places during clandestine searches of children's rooms: the copies of *Playboy* and *Penthouse* stuffed under mattresses and sofa cushions, the tubes of airplane glue in the desk drawers of boys who had no interest in model planes, the yellow, lozenge-shaped capsules in Benzedrine inhalers. It was her duty as a parent, her friends had told her, to ferret about among a teenager's possessions looking for such objects: "You have to know what's going on!"

But Mimi had always resisted this. It had something to do with her son's honor, and with her own honor, with her own sense of self-respect, and his. She had always congratulated herself on her refusal to invade Badger's privacy, and, after all, he had turned out all right. But now she knows that the undertow of temptation is too powerful, and she feels herself sucked inexorably into the murky waters of duplicity—inexorably, and excitedly, too, for there is always a little thrill, an adrenaline rush, when one knows that one is about to do something that one knows is a little naughty.

Here goes my image, Mimi thinks. Here go my pious principles. "Aloe-eyed, long-legged, alabaster-skinned Mimi Myerson," *Time* magazine had written of her in a cover story a year or so ago, "is something of an anomaly in the beauty business—a straight-shooter and a square-dealer in an industry noted for its cutthroats and charlatans. Even her stiffest competitors acknowledge, begrudgingly, her track record of integrity. She applies the same rules of candor and scrupulous fairness when it comes to managing her household and family, which includes poised and polished lawyer husband Bradford Moore, and their son, Brad Moore III, known in the family as Badger. 'Mom's always on the level,' says Redford look-alike Badger Moore." At the same time, a famous astrologer had told her, "You are a woman with a sunny exterior that hides a dark side. Two forces do battle within you, Gemini: a desire to please the crowd, and a killer instinct. When you do not achieve what you want with honey, you are capable of employing vitriol."

Mimi almost giggles, recalling these two analyses. Well, she thinks, here goes Miss Perfect Parent and Miss Perfect Wife, and welcome to the dark side. But, after all, turnabout is fair play. Didn't Brad humiliate me by showing up at Le Cirque with that woman, causing the captain to phone and apologize for seating us in the same room, forcing me to tell a lie in order to explain the situation? He sho-nuff did. Yassuh. And am I any more unprincipled than any other woman who has reason to believe her husband is cheating on her? I sho-nuff ain't. And, finally, is there any reason why a woman who employs a butler shouldn't be entitled to know as much about her life as her butler knows? As Diana Vreeland once said, "Husbands are replaceable. A good butler is to be treasured above jewels."

She removes the letter from its envelope, unfolds it carefully on her lap, and reaches for her teacup, feeling quite justified, even happy.

The letter is written on rather florid blue stationery, embossed with the single initial "*R*," the curling serifs of the monogram entwined among a scattering of blue and yellow daisies. Piss-elegant, Mimi thinks. The *R*, of course, could represent either a last initial or a first. Ruth. Rowena. Rachel. Rebecca. Roberta, or something cutesy-pie like Rusty. "My dear Bradford," she begins.

Bradford. No one, to Mimi's knowledge, has ever called Brad Bradford except his mother, and then only when she was angry with him. There is something about the letter's opening that is vaguely challenging. She reads on:

> *You told me before you left that you intended to use some of your time during your trip to Minneapolis to do some serious thinking about what you see as the future for you and I. . . .*

A mistress, Mimi thinks, should not, after all, be expected to have full command of the King's English.

> *But this statement of yours has left me wondering why you feel that it is up to you to decide what our future is to be. Am I not entitled to be a part of any decision that involves our future jointly? Where do I stand in this decision-making process? Don't I count, too?*
>
> *You've told me many times that you loved me, and that your marriage was an unhappy one. . .*

Oh, God, Mimi thinks.

> *. . . but where does that leave me? It leaves me waiting for you to decide what our future is going to be, which does not strike me as very fair. Bradford, I am not the sort of woman whom you can just toss her out like some used toy or plaything when you decide you've had enough of her. I am not the sort of woman whom will be just sitting here and waiting for you to tell her what your decision is going to be!!!! I have rights in this situation too, remember, since we both went into this together with our eyes wide open, and both knew that there would be risks involved on both sides. This is why I want you to have this letter before you leave for M'pl's*

to do your deciding, because while you are gone I intend to do some deciding too.

You did not—on purpose?—tell me how long you would be staying in the Land of 1,000 Lakes, or when you would be back, or even which hotel it was that you would be registered at. Are you planning to hide out on me? That is not fair, either, because while you are deciding everything there is no way I can be a part of the decision-making process. In case you have forgotten it, I am a human being too. I have feelings too. I have pride too. I have self-respect, and I have the same right to demand the self-respect of the man I love, or thought I did.

So let me just tell you what I will be deciding while you are off deciding what is going to happen to you and I. I am going to be deciding, if your decision isn't the one you have led me to expect, whether to go to that wife of yours and tell her exactly what has been going on!!!! I know who she is and how to get in touch with her, and if you plan to throw me out like one of your used condoms, and flush me down the commode, you will be very sorry that you did not treat me with the same self-respect which I treated you with.

Sorry to be so blunt, but "decisions" are not a one-way street when it comes to you and I.

Sincerely yours,
R.

P.S. Don't tell me that you are a lawyer and these things take time. How much time does it take to say, "I want a divorce?"

Mimi puts down the letter with a little sigh. If there is any consolation here, she thinks, this "R" sounds like a perfectly dreadful woman. If, after all these years of marriage, she knows Brad Moore at all, this woman could not possibly make him happy. There are a few unanswered questions in this letter, of course, other than the identity of the sender. "Risks involved on both sides," for instance—what does that mean? She can see how there would be risks involved for Brad, but what risks were there for "R"? "Like one of your used condoms." If they have been practicing birth control, this indicates a younger woman, who must be the woman she saw him lunching with at Le Cirque. Or else he is worried about AIDS, and which is worse? "You've told me many times that you loved me." Well, she thinks, another man just told me that he loved me—just yesterday, in fact.

At first, her impulse is to tear the letter into little scraps, toss them into the fireplace, and light a match. But, on second thought, she decides against this. She refolds the letter, replaces it in its envelope, and places it in the pocket of her silk caftan.

In the distance, the telephone rings again, and Mimi feels the muscles of her throat grow tense. Presently Felix appears at the doorway and says, "Mr. Moore calling from Minneapolis, madam."

She rises and moves into the library to get the phone. "Hello, darling," she says brightly, trying to keep her tone easy and light. "How's the Sturtevant business going?"

"I think we're finally about to hammer out a settlement," he says. "Thank God."

"Oh, good!"

"If we settle before ten o'clock tonight, you'll be reading about it in tomorrow's *Times*. What've you been up to?"

"Oh, the same old thing: working on the launch party for Mireille at the Pierre, getting the invitations out. Facing the same damn nuisance of who wants to be seated where, and with whom, and who refuses to sit at the same table with whomever—all that nonsense. Doing the advance publicity for the mystery man-with-a-scar. We're going to air the first three commercials at the party, and the mystery man will mysteriously *not* be there."

"Everything fine at home?"

"Oh, yes. Except . . ." She hesitates. "Except we've been getting a lot of funny hang-up calls. No heavy breathing, or anything like that. The phone rings, Felix answers, and then—click! Whoever's calling just hangs up. It's been driving poor Felix crazy. If this keeps up, do you think we ought to have this number changed?"

He is silent for a moment. Then he says, "Well, perhaps—if it keeps up." Then, "It looks as though I'm going to be able to make the five o'clock home tomorrow night. I'm booked on it, anyway, and I've got my fingers crossed."

"Good," she says. "Wonderful. Because I've missed you, darling." Then she says suddenly, "Have we had a happy marriage, darling? Have we?"

"What?"

"Have we? Have we had a happy marriage?"

"That's a hell of a question to ask me out here in the Gopher State!"

"I don't mean a *perfect* marriage, because I suppose no marriage is that. I just mean a happy, reasonably happy marriage. I was sitting here alone this afternoon, missing you, and just sort of started asking myself that. Has it been a reasonably happy marriage? Has it been happy for you, darling?"

"Of course it has."

"I thought so," she says. And then, "I love you, Brad."

"I love you, too."

*   *   *

Almost immediately, the phone rings again, and Mimi picks up the receiver in the middle of the first ring, before Felix can answer on his extension. "This is Mrs. Moore," she says pleasantly. There is a little sound at the other end of the connection, a small gasp or gurgle. "Yes?" Mimi says. "May I help you?" Then there is the click, and the line goes dead, followed by the hum of the dial tone.

20

THE LAST WILL AND TESTAMENT of Adolph Myerson was read on December 9, 1959, in the East 42nd Street offices of George Wardell, Sr., whose law firm, Wardell & Wardell, had represented Mimi's grandfather for the last twenty-five years of his long life. He had died five days earlier, at the age of eighty-nine, in his suite at the Mark Hopkins Hotel in San Francisco, where he had gone to preside over the opening of a new Miray boutique at Saks Fifth Avenue, just off Union Square. There was every indication that his end had been peaceful. He was found, clad in his pajamas, in his bed by the hotel's morning maid. The maid reported that there was a trace of a smile on his lips. She wanted the family to know this.

Gathered at the reading of the will, in addition to the senior Mr. Wardell, were the immediate heirs of the deceased: his widow, Fleurette Guggenheim Myerson; his two sons, Henry and Edwin; his daughter, Naomi Myerson; his daughter-in-law, Alice; his granddaughter, Mimi; and Mimi's new husband, Bradford Moore, Jr. All, including the widow, were doing their best to appear composed and businesslike.

The first matters to be disposed of were the deceased's shareholdings in the Miray Corporation. "To my beloved wife, Fleurette, thirty percent of all shares owned by me . . . to my beloved sons, Henry and Edwin, each twenty-five percent . . . to my beloved granddaughter, Mireille Moore, fifteen percent . . ."

"Where am *I?*" Nonie had suddenly cried out. "What happened to me?"

"And to my beloved daughter, Naomi, five percent. . . ."

The response to this had been a shriek. "Five percent!" Nonie had cried. "Is that *all?*"

"Please, Naomi," George Wardell had said. "A paragraph in the will deals with your special situation. It is the next paragraph. Let me read it to you. 'For reasons that will be well understood by my daughter, and having to do with her mercurial nature and temperament and record of marital instability, this unequal distribution of shares is made. It in no way reflects any diminished love or affection on my part for my daughter."

"That's a lie!" Nonie sobbed. "He always hated me! It was always the boys . . . the boys . . . the boys. . . . He didn't have *their* heads shaved!"

George Wardell then continued with the details of the trust in which Nonie's shares were to be held, how this trust was to be administered, the appointment of trustees, the eventual dissolution of the trust in the year 2000, and the distribution of the trust's shares at that time, when, as nearly everyone in the room knew, Nonie Myerson would be eighty years old. Throughout all this, Nonie sobbed uncontrollably, while the others in the family made soft clucking noises, intended to comfort her.

"Punishing . . . punishing . . . ," Nonie sobbed.

"You brought this on yourself!" her brother Edwee hissed.

George Wardell then went on to read the list of specific cash bequests to various charitable and cultural institutions: "To Mount Sinai Hospital, New York City, the sum of ten million dollars to be used to create and endow the Adolph H. Myerson Memorial Pavilion for Dermatology Care and Research; to Harvard College School of Business, the sum of ten million dollars to establish and endow the Adolph H. Myerson Memorial Chair of Industrial Cosmetology; to the New York Animal Hospital, the sum of five million dollars—"

"*Animals!*" Nonie cried. "He never gave a damn about animals!"

"He loved Itty-Bitty!" Granny Flo snapped. (The present Itty-Bitty is one of a series of Itty-Bittys who have shared the Myerson household over the years.)

"To the Boy Scouts of America, the sum of five million dollars; to the American Red Cross, the sum of five million dollars; to the New York Metropolitan Museum of Art, the sum of five million dollars. . . ."

There followed a list of smaller bequests to longtime employees and servants, the last of which was a gift to Miss Iris Jones—the loyal Jonesy, who had been his private secretary for forty years—of a thousand dollars.

When he had completed his reading, George Wardell placed the document flat on his desk, removed his glasses, cleared his throat, and frowned. "I think I should tell all of you," he said, "that there appears to be a problem involving the distribution of some of these cash bequests."

"What sort of a problem?" Edwee wanted to know.

"Upon reviewing your father's estate over the past few days, it appears that there are insufficient funds with which to carry out these bequests of his. This is unfortunate, because—"

"Insufficient? How insufficient?"

"Your father kept his books in a somewhat unorthodox fashion," Wardell said. "It has been very difficult for us to determine exactly how much cash is in the estate. But from what we have determined thus far, it would appear that your father had somewhat grandiose notions as to how large his estate would be at the time of his death. Yes, I'm afraid, somewhat grandiose."

"How much is there?" Edwee wanted to know.

George Wardell paused, pinching the bridge of his nose between his thumb and forefinger, and looked down at a slip of paper on his desk. "From what we can determine thus far," he said, "from examining the statements of banks and brokerage houses where your father had accounts, it would seem that the cash value of the estate is exactly fourteen thousand, three hundred and eighty-seven dollars and twenty-six cents."

There was a collective gasp, followed by a stunned silence, throughout the room.

"Of course, it is possible that, as we continue our searches, more funds will turn up. But, thus far, we have found nothing."

"What about the hundred million?" Edwee shouted. "He used to say that he had a hundred million dollars' worth of the best gilt-edged securities in the world!"

"Upon examining the contents of four separate safe-deposit boxes that we know he kept, we have found certificates for stock in many different companies, but most of these, I'm afraid, went out of business a number of years ago. For instance, he owned ten thousand shares of something called the Pittsburgh Municipal Streetcar Company. Pittsburgh Municipal declared bankruptcy and went out of business in 1933. I've prepared a full list of the securities he owned but, I'm afraid—"

"Worthless!" Nonie sobbed.

"At some point in time, these securities may have represented an investment of a hundred million dollars, or thereabouts, on his part. But, today, I'm afraid—"

"Worthless! Worthless pieces of paper!"

"Yes, I'm afraid so. Yes." He paused again. "Meanwhile, there are, of course, other assets in the estate. There is the Miray manufacturing plant in Secaucus. There are the two distribution warehouses in East St. Louis and in Burbank, California. And there is the value of the inventory presently stored in these warehouses, and the products in Secaucus that are ready for sale. All this—equipment, supplies, office furnishings—will be taken into account when we compute the book value of the shares of Miray stock each of you now owns. That will take some time. Meanwhile, unfortunately—"

"Unfortunately what?"

"Unfortunately, against these assets there are some rather heavy liabilities. During the last twenty or twenty-five years of his life, it seems, your father borrowed rather liberally—too liberally, it would now seem—from various banks, brokerage houses, insurance companies, and other financial institutions. These outstanding debts, unfortunately—"

"How much?" It was Edwee again.

"Right now, we are talking about a figure between eighty and ninety million dollars."

There was another collective groan around the room.

"And, of course, there is no guarantee that other debts won't surface as we move forward in time. No, unfortunately, no guarantee. We are talking only of the state of affairs at this particular point in time."

There was silence now, and none of the members of the family seemed able to look at any of the others.

It was Henry Myerson who broke the silence. "This whole thing is inconceivable to me," he said. "How in God's name did this happen, George?"

"Straighten your necktie, Henry dear," Granny Flo suggested.

"I was never privy to your father's business decisions, Henry," George Wardell said. "I only served as your father's legal counsel. My specialty, as you know, is trademark law."

"Your necktie, Henny-Penny," Granny Flo said, tapping her collarbone. "It's all twisted and funny."

"Tell me something," Henry continued. "How much of this Miray stock we've just inherited is being used to collateralize these loans of his?"

"That's another thing," Wardell said. "Another most unfortunate thing. Quite a lot of it has been used that way. Most of it, it seems."

"So the banks own us."

"My God!" Nonie screamed. "First you tell me that I got only five percent, and then you tell me it's five percent of nothing!"

"Now listen, Nonie," Henry said. "There are more important things to discuss here than who got what. We've got a company to run. We've got a payroll to meet, for one thing."

"Yes," George Wardell said. "There is a payroll to be met on the fifteenth of this month, which I don't need to remind you is only six days away. One hundred and fourteen thousand dollars will be needed for that. Yes, Henry, I agree that meeting this payroll must be one of your very first concerns."

"How would he have met it if he had lived, I wonder?"

"That, Henry, I do not know. It's one of the questions I've been asking myself as I've been going over the estate. Your father was a very shrewd businessman, but also a very secretive one. He carried his entire business, as they say, around with him in his head." George Wardell chuckled softly, as though he had made a little joke, but there was little mirth in the chuckle.

"Those loans will have to be extended—somehow," Henry said. "Also," he said, looking around the room at the others, "all of us are going to have to make some deep personal sacrifices."

"Don't talk to me about sacrifices!" Nonie said. "I have nothing to sacrifice! I'm penniless. I'm a pauper, now."

"Listen to me, all of you," Henry said, sitting forward in his chair. "If I'm going to run this company, I'm going to need sacrifices from all of you—personal sacrifices, or there's going to be no Miray Corporation left to run, and nothing left for any of us. I'm talking about personal funds—stock portfolios, savings accounts. I'm going to need your help. Are you all behind me, or are you not?"

"We're behind you, Daddy," Mimi said.

"Well, I'm not!" Nonie said. "Count me out!"

"Nonie, this is a crisis," he said. "Don't you understand? It seems to me you've always lived pretty well. Think you could do without your butler, Nonie? Think you could do without your personal maid? Without your private secretary? Without getting your hair done every day?"

"You're asking me to give up my private *secretary?*"

"You're talking like a damned fool, Nonie," her mother said.

"As for the widow," George Wardell said, "Mrs. Myerson has inherited, outright, three important pieces of property—outright and, fortunately, unentailed. There is the house on Madison Avenue, the house in Bar Harbor, the house in Palm Beach—plus, of course, the yacht. These pieces are of not inconsiderable value, and there is also the value of their contents—antiques, Oriental rugs, the art collection, jewels, and so on."

Granny Flo, who had been working on her needlepoint throughout most of this, suddenly put down her stitchery and looked up. "My Guggenheim trusts," she said sharply. "Where are they?"

"Subsumed, I'm afraid. Dis—"

"I had a trust from my father and grandfather, and from each of my uncles!"

"I realize that. But, you see, Mrs. Myerson, you gave your husband your full power of attorney in 1936. The following year, he appointed himself your sole trustee. The funds in those trusts appear to have been dissipated, I'm sorry to say."

"Dissipated! Stolen, you mean! Robbed blind! I might have known it! All those pieces of paper he was always getting me to sign!"

"Most unfortunate, yes."

Granny Flo slapped her needlepoint canvas with the back of her hand. "So. I'm left with three big houses, and no money to run them on."

"That would seem—"

"Where did it go? What did he spend it all on?"

"On maintaining, it would seem, your somewhat opulent life-style."

"Opulent," she snorted. "Well, I'm fed up with opulence. I've had it with opulence up to *here*," and with her index finger she drew an imaginary line just beneath her chin. "With opulence and a quarter, you can get a free ride on the bus! So that's where it all went—on opulence. All through the Depression, when everyone else was tightening their belts, nobody could understand how we were able to live the way we did. The Magnificent Myersons! Ha! The Magnificent Mr. Myerson was just raiding his wife's trusts. Well, I'll tell you what I want to do, George. I want to unload all that stuff. Right now. All of it. Unload Madison Avenue; I never liked that house, anyway. Unload Bar Harbor. I hate Bar Harbor—those snobs. They came to our parties but never invited us back. Unload Palm Beach; I hate Palm Beach even more than Bar Harbor, if that's possible. Down there, they wouldn't even let us inside the Everglades Club because we were 'of Hebraic extraction.' Unload the damn yacht. I tossed my cookies every time we went out on it. Unload everything. All I need is a little apartment, big enough for Itty-Bitty and me. I'll tell you what I want you to do, George. There's this hot-shot young real-estate man in town—Michael Something. Mimi knows him."

"Horowitz," Mimi said.

"That's him! Michael Horowitz. They say he could sell umbrellas in the Gobi Desert. Call him. Tell him I want to unload everything, as fast as I can, and for as much money as I can get. Tell him Miray has a payroll to meet in six days, so there's no time to waste. Got that? Get this Michael Horowitz for me." She stood up abruptly to her full stature, which, for Fleurette Myerson, was not very tall. "I don't know about any of the rest of you," she said, "but I'm going home now. I'm going home and start putting price tags on everything. Good-bye." She gathered up her needlework and marched toward the office door, opened it, and closed it with a slam behind her.

After her departure, George Wardell replaced his spectacles on his nose and looked about at the others. "I'm afraid this hasn't been a very happy meeting for any of us," he said quietly. "All this, coming on top of your natural bereavement—"

"Bereavement!" Nonie said. "I'm glad he's dead. Now we all know what a bastard he was."

* * *

"Well," Brad said to Mimi as they sat having a drink, "at least we still have each other." They had crossed the street to the Biltmore's Under-the-Clock bar after leaving the lawyer's office, and a string quartet was playing "Zegeuner." "I may not have married an heiress, but I married the prettiest, smartest girl in New York, who makes me very happy." He touched his cocktail glass to hers. "I'm doing all right downtown. Next year, I expect to be made a partner—old Walrus Waldenmeier has hinted at it. I'm happy, I'm in love, we're together. We'll survive."

"I felt sorriest for Aunt Nonie. She's always been a frustrated tycoon. Or tycooness. Is there such a thing as a tycooness?"

"I felt sorrier for your father, taking over a company that's eighty-plus million dollars in the hole."

"Don't worry about Daddy. Now that he's finally been given his head, I think he'll show strengths that will surprise you. He'll pull the company out of this. You'll see."

"This reminds me of one of my uncles," he said. "One of my Bradford uncles in Boston, Uncle Reggie. Everybody assumed that Uncle Reggie was pretty rich. Since he and Aunt Abby had no children, everybody sort of hoped, you know, that when Uncle Reggie died, each of us would get a little something. Well, when Uncle Reggie died, there was nothing. Nothing. What had he been living on? On air, it seemed, and credit. He owed everybody in town. Aunt Abby kept insisting that he must have had a lot of money hidden away somewhere. She became convinced that he must have had the money pasted under the wallpaper of his house, so she had all the wallpaper stripped throughout the house. They stripped off layer after layer of wallpaper, looking for a layer of thousand-dollar bills. Of course they never found anything. They ended up with nothing but a paperhanger's bill."

"Fourteen thousand, three hundred and eighty-seven dollars and twenty-six cents. That's all Grandpa was worth. How much will old Wardell's bill be for all of this, would you imagine?"

With a finger, he scooped the olive out of his martini glass and popped it into his mouth. He scratched his head. "Well, speaking as a member of the legal profession," he said, "my guess would be that Wardell's bill will be roughly fourteen thousand, three hundred and eighty-seven dollars and twenty-six cents."

She laughed. "Dear Brad," she said, "that's what I love about you. You can make me laugh. Even in the face of disaster, you can make me laugh."

"I had to hand it to your Granny Flo. I think she plans to help the company out in any way she can. That thing she said about Miray having a payroll to meet. You say you know this Michael Horowitz character?"

"Oh, yes."

"Is he the right person to handle her property, do you think?"

"Yes," Mimi said. "He probably is."

21

*M*Y *FATHER* did a very brave thing," Mimi is saying. "In retrospect, given hindsight, it may not have been the wisest thing to do, but, at the time, *something* had to be done, and what he did took courage. He acted decisively, and he acted fast. I was terribly proud of him at the time.

"If you talk to others in the industry, you'll hear them say that Henry Myerson took a deeply troubled company and drove it virtually into bankruptcy. But that's not a fair appraisal of what really happened.

"To begin with, you have to understand that this is a business where newness is everything. You've got to keep introducing new things—new nail and lip shades, new creams, new fragrances. This year's new nail shade may not be all that different from last year's, but at least it has a new name, and looks a little different, and seems new. My grandfather understood this, and the Revsons understood it—they learned it from Grandpa. The Lauders are just now beginning to understand the importance of newness. I mean, Estée came out with something called Youth-Dew twenty-five years ago—a perfectly good fragrance, with a nice name. But when Estée introduced Youth-Dew, her market was women in their thirties and forties. That's the major market for all of us. This is a business about women—and men, too—wanting to stay looking young longer. And it's in their thirties and forties that Americans start worrying about losing their youthful looks and begin turning seriously to perfumes and cosmetics for help. We have to grab our customers during those golden years. But the trouble with Youth-Dew today is that women who started using the product twenty-five years ago are now in their fifties and sixties, and let's face it, Youth-Dew today is considered an old ladies' scent. Over at Lauder, they realize they're losing their younger market, and so now they're busily developing new products to try to recapture this market. You've got to keep moving forward in this business. You can't just sit back and enjoy the success of a certain product. And you can never go backward.

"But to get back to my father, and what he did, or what he tried to do. First of all, you have to remember that among the other tremendous problems he inherited was what we still refer to here as the Candied Apple Fiasco. Whenever we sense some sort of a problem brewing with a product, we still say, 'Beware of the Candied Apple!' Or, 'Is there a Candied Apple in the woodpile?' Candied Apple was a lip and nail shade that my grandfather introduced a couple of years before he died. It was a disaster. Who knows why? Sometimes there's no clear answer to why a product, or a color, just refuses to catch on, but Candied Apple was one of these. It just didn't fly, as we say in the trade. I still think the name is kind of cute, and the color was . . . well, it was the color of the candied apples they sell at carnivals. The shade seemed to have a lot of fun things going for it. The ads were full of roller coasters and merry-go-rounds and Ferris wheels. But the shade just would not move off the shelves. Maybe the name wasn't sexy enough, wasn't sophisticated enough. Maybe it sounded too gloopy and teenagey. Maybe the name reminded women of the acne set. Maybe it sounded too *digestive*. Who knows? But, whatever it was, the customers, as we say, stayed away in droves. Candied Apple was the Edsel of the cosmetics business.

"My grandfather blamed my father for the failure of Candied Apple, which was really unfair. My father had nothing to do with developing the shade, and the name was my grandfather's—the names were always his. But what happened was that, when they were spot-testing the products, my father brought some samples home to Mother, and Mother *loved* Candied Apple. She loved the color, and she loved the name. My father passed this fact along to my grandfather, and as a result of this one-woman sampling of public opinion, Grandpa immediately decided that Candied Apple was going to be the hit of all time. He immediately upped the advertising and promotion budget. He hired extra salesmen. He quadrupled the production order. And then, when Candied Apple fell flat on its face, he blamed Daddy for the enormous production overrun. That was the way Grandpa's mind worked. He could never take the blame for any business misjudgment *himself*. It had to be someone *else's* fault. In the case of Candied Apple, Daddy became the scapegoat—just for passing along the word that my mother liked the shade!

"It was ridiculous, it made no sense. As you know, my grandfather never had a very high opinion of my mother, never thought she was good enough for his precious oldest son. Why did her vote have so much weight in this particular matter? Who knows? Maybe he was looking for an omen of good fortune, and that was it. In this business, we're always looking for omens, portents. Charlie Revson would never hire anyone if the number on his license plate added up to thirteen. I'm superstitious, too. Why am I having my launch party for Mireille on the seventeenth? Because an astrologer told me that this would be the most auspicious date for me!

"Anyway, I won't say that the Candied Apple Fiasco was the sole reason for the horrible state of affairs the company was in when Grandpa died, but it certainly hadn't helped. And among all the other problems my father inherited when he took over the company were thousands and thousands of unsold tubes and bottles of damned Candied Apple sitting around in Miray warehouses, gathering dust, where they were already beginning to call it Rotten Apple. It wasn't just a question of changing the name and reintroducing the shade as something else. That's often done in this industry. Candied Apple had been given very distinctive packaging: each lipstick tube had a bright red apple on its cap, and the top of each polish bottle was also an apple shape. So, part of Daddy's plan to rescue the company in its emergency situation was to try to unload the Candied Apple overstock, to get rid of the loser. It made good sense to me at the time. Of course, I was desperately young then—barely twenty—and not very clever and knew none of the things about the beauty business that I know now. I was a babe in the woods, and I adored my father. To me, he was the handsomest, smartest, bravest man in the world—the knight in shining armor who was going to charge forth and save the company single-handedly. As I say, given hindsight and what I know now, I would probably have to revise that opinion. Daddy made one fatal mistake. What he tried didn't work, but it was a brave try.

"And you have to remember that, over the years, my father had been given fancy titles but no authority, no real power. All the final decisions were made by my grandfather. There are subtleties in this business that maybe my father hadn't grasped, but then how could he have? No one had ever consulted him on anything. My grandfather may have been a tough administrator, but he was a lousy teacher. After Grandpa died, Daddy had about two days to learn everything there was to know about the beauty business!

"Meanwhile, I'll always have to give Granny Flo credit for coming forward the way she did. God knows, without her help, we wouldn't possibly be where we are today. For all her orneriness, for all her contrariness—for her blow-ups like the one at my mother the night of my party—I have to forgive her and remind myself what she did at the time of that crisis, in 'fifty-nine and 'sixty. She proved herself to be a real stand-up lady. At the time, she had more guts than anybody.

"She immediately put all her properties up for sale, and the timing turned out to be just right. Madison Avenue was already becoming commercial north of Fifty-seventh Street, and Madison and Sixty-first is now an office tower. I have to give Michael Horowitz credit, too; he handled that sale brilliantly. His negotiations for the air rights over that corner piece were fantastic. He also made a beautiful deal for 'Merry Song,' Granny's place in Bar Harbor. Where 'Merry Song' used to stand, there are now four hundred and fifteen time-sharing condominiums, a shopping mall, and a marina for medium-sized boats—tacky-looking, but very profitable. Of course, Michael took his commissions on all these deals. He wasn't just doing this out of the kindness of his heart, but all these were good deals for Granny, and Granny turned over almost all the profits to my father, to help him keep the company from going under. I remember seeing her sitting there, at her desk in the little apartment she moved to at Thirty Park Avenue, just writing out these enormous checks!

"The yacht, *Mer et Son*, was more of a problem. It was something of a white elephant. The Arabs and the OPEC boys hadn't come into the market yet, and nobody wanted a big boat like that. Also, Granny and Grandpa hadn't been invited to join the Northeast Harbor Fleet Club, so *Mer et Son* had been lying at anchor for several years in the little cove at the foot of Granny's lawn. Her hull had become badly silted in, and she was covered with barnacles, and she was listing badly. She looked like hell, and she was probably filled with rats. Finally, Michael was able to make a deal with the U.S. Navy, who agreed to take her over as a training cruiser. No big profit there, of course, but there was a tax deduction, which was helpful.

"The *real* white elephant was 'Ma Raison,' the Palm Beach house. It's the biggest house in Palm Beach, you know. It was Grandpa's final folly. Back in 1960, it went on the market for twenty-two million, but there were no takers. I mean, that house is just too big for *any*body . . . or almost anybody. The zoning laws down there prohibit that property from being broken up and developed. It can't be put to any commercial or public use. At one point, Michael came up with a scheme to present the house to the U.S. Government, as a winter White House for presidents or visiting foreign VIPs. The government didn't want it. The upkeep was too much. Over the years, we've kept dropping and dropping the price, but still nobody wanted it, and meanwhile the taxes were staggering. It sat there for over twenty years, minimally maintained, looking shabbier and shabbier. And there was another problem with that house. Its central bell tower, which has a beacon on it, was on the main flight path into the West Palm Beach airport. This made 'Ma Raison' not just the biggest place in Palm Beach. It was also the noisiest. Right around five o'clock, when you'd think it would be nice to go out for a quiet drink on the terrace, the big jets would start piling in from the north. You couldn't hear yourself think.

"Meanwhile, we kept lowering the price. Finally, a couple of years ago, when the best offer we had was four million, Michael Horowitz offered four-point-two and bought it himself. God knows why he wanted it. He got it at a distress-sale price, of course, but four-point-two is better than nothing, and Granny is relieved of those god-awful taxes. And do you know what our smart little sometime friend Michael was able to do? He began putting pressure on the boys at the airport and got them to change their flight-approach pattern. You can do that sort of thing if you're as rich as Michael Horowitz.

"But I keep digressing from what my father tried to do. . . ."

The first stockholders' meeting of the Miray Corporation, with Henry Myerson as its new head, was held two days after the reading of Adolph Myerson's will in the boardroom at Miray's offices on Fifth Avenue. Only five members attended: Edwee, Nonie, Mimi, Granny Flo, and Henry himself. The Leo cousins, who had been notified of the meeting by telegram had not bothered to attend. Since the departures of Leo and Nate from the company in 1941, the cousins had never bothered to attend stockholders' meetings, and, today, they were of course unaware of the special gravity of the situation. The five Myersons sat around the big table, while Henry presided from the oversize chair that for nearly fifty years had been the royal seat of the company's founder.

"I don't need to remind you all of the crisis we face," Henry began.

"Henny-Penny, your tie's *still* crooked," his mother put in.

"Mother, *please*," Henry said, almost angrily. "Your tie would be crooked, too, if you'd spent the last two days and two sleepless nights trying to make some sense out of the mess this company's in!"

"Well, at least sit up straight," Granny Flo said. "Don't slump. Your father never slumped."

"We face a crisis," Henry continued, his face visibly perspiring, though the temperature outside had dropped into the teens and, among the emergency measures Henry had already ordered, the office thermostats had been lowered to sixty-five. "We face a crisis, and I'd like to outline to you the emergency measures I've already taken. The office staff here is being reduced by twenty-five percent, starting with those most recently employed, and the employees affected have already received their notices. The Miray sales staff in the field is being reduced by another twenty-five percent. Executives who have formerly enjoyed private secretaries will from now on use the services of the steno pool. The company employs a fleet of eleven limousines. This fleet is to be discontinued and the vehicles sold. From now on, executives will use local taxis to get about the city on business. Strict restrictions will be imposed on all business travel, and executives who have previously used first-class air travel will from now on fly economy. Similar restrictions will be applied to all business entertaining, lunches, and so on. The order for the Gulfstream corporate jet that my father placed five months ago has been canceled. Other cost-accounting measures, never imposed in my father's day, have already been put in place by me, including plans to lease out some five thousand square feet of unneeded office space on the northeast corner of the sixteenth floor. I have placed myself in charge of cost accounting. Finally, I have asked all staff at the executive level to volunteer to accept, at least temporarily, a twenty percent cut in salary. Needless to say, I was the first executive to so volunteer."

There was a polite round of applause.

"But I don't need to tell you," he went on, "that all these measures will have roughly the effect of applying a Band-Aid to a gunshot wound in the head. Other, much more drastic measures will need to be taken if we're going to survive as a corporate entity. These are the measures that I'm going to ask you to vote on here today."

There was a suspenseful silence. "Well, tell us what they are, Henny," Granny Flo said, tightening a knot in her needlepoint.

"What I'm going to propose to you is a three-point program," he said. "First, I'm going to ask you to agree that all dividends on Miray stock be discontinued for an indefinite period of time, until this company begins to show some black ink on the bottom line."

There was a collective groan around the conference table, but there was also a general nodding of heads.

"Second, I ask your permission to begin immediate negotiations with all banks and financial institutions with whom we have loans, seeking to extend these loans at, naturally, the most favorable rates they can give us."

There was more nodding of heads.

"And, finally," he said, "the most drastic measure of all. Believe me, I've given this idea a great deal of long, hard thought over the past two days, and I've come to the conclusion that this may be the quickest, most effective— maybe the only—way we can salvage this company from its present predicament. What I am proposing is an entirely new marketing strategy for Miray products. As you know, under Adolph Myerson's leadership, Miray positioned itself gradually in an upscale, specialty-store market, working with such upscale outlets as Saks and Magnin's and Neiman's. On the other hand, when Miray began its corporate existence back in nineteen twelve, our products were distributed solely through lower-priced and discount outlets—the dime-store chains and neighborhood drugstore and foodstore chains. It was this marketing strategy that got Miray off the ground in the first place, years ago. Ladies and gentlemen, I am saying to you that Miray, unfortunately, finds itself in that same position today—back at the ground floor, reentry level, back at square one. I am saying that, if we are to survive and prosper as we once did, we must reposition all our products in a downscale market. We have a prestige name. In a downscale market, I believe we can compete successfully with such brands as Cutex. As most of you know, one of the biggest problems facing us right now is a huge warehouse inventory of a shade called Candied Apple. As most of you know, Candied Apple has failed, dismally, to attract the upscale market that the shade was conceived for. I believe that, in a downscale market, the shade will be successful. This will mean slashing our suggested retail prices, of course, but it will also rid us of an enormous, and expensive, overstock, and at a profit. I suggest that this new retail tactic be applied to all Miray products. With Candied Apple, the upscale market appears to have abandoned us. By repositioning ourselves in a downscale market, I believe we can rebuild the kind of success that my father built. We are going back to our roots, as it were— our humble roots. But they are also proud roots. They are honorable roots. They are roots from which we grew to be one of the leaders in the industry. They are roots from which we will grow again, and continue to grow. Like the proverbial South, we will rise again. Ladies and gentlemen, I ask you to approve this proposal. As I said at the outset, it is a drastic one. At the same time, as I see it here today, it may be our only hope."

There was silence around the table. Finally, Granny Flo said, "It's as bad as that, then."

"It's as bad as that, Mother."

"I say bravo, Daddy," Mimi said softly.

"Well, then," Henry said. "There you have it, my three-part proposal. Shall we vote on each of the three parts separately, or on all three together?"

"Together!" Granny Flo snapped.

"Then how do we vote—for or against?"

"For," said Granny Flo without dropping a stitch.

"For," said Edwee.

"For," said Mimi.

"Against!" said Nonie loudly.

"Then," Henry said, slumping further in his chair, "my proposals have been accepted by a ninety-five percent majority."

The next day, in Philip Dougherty's Advertising column in the *New York Times*, there was the following headline:

MIRAY MARKETING SWITCH
STUNS INDUSTRY

In a surprise press conference at the Fifth Avenue headquarters of the Miray Corporation, Mr. Henry Myerson, Miray's 43-year-old new President and Chief Executive Officer, announced a startling new marketing strategy for his company, makers of a long line of luxury cosmetics, beauty, skin, and hair-care products.

Miray, long available only at the counters of select specialty and department stores in major cities, will from now on reposition its products in the cheaper retail and discount outlets across the country. "We've become too much of a snob name," Mr. Myerson said. "There's another, bigger market out there eager for quality products, and we intend to go after that." Industry analysts announced themselves "stunned" by the latest Miray move. It is the first time in industry history, as far as is known, that a prestige name has chosen deliberately to downgrade itself.

Amid rumors that Miray may have found itself in fiscal turmoil following the recent death of the company's 89-year-old founder, Adolph Myerson, the younger Mr. Myerson, who is Adolph Myerson's son, assured reporters that such rumors are without foundation. "The company's in great shape," Mr. Myerson said. "It's just time for the next generation to take us over and head us in some promising new directions." Miray, a privately owned corporation whose shares are held by immediate members of the Myerson family, is not required to reveal information pertaining to its financial status. However, some dismissals of company personnel are known to have taken place in recent days, and a recently introduced lipstick and eye-shadow [*sic*] shade is known to have had disappointing sales. The shade, called Candied Apple, was launched with great fanfare in the fall of 1957, to a poor box office.

"It's just a case of the new broom sweeping clean," said Henry Myerson, referring to the employee dismissals. "I'm the new broom."

Meanwhile, spokesmen within the industry remained skeptical about the wisdom of Miray's about-face reversal in sales strategy. "It's like taking Tiffany and turning it into J. C. Penney," said one. . . .

"It was a disastrous move," Mimi says. "Bold, but disastrous. I know that now. I didn't then. What it did was to almost completely destroy the prestige and respectability and credibility of an old-line name. Years had been spent building loyalty and goodwill among a certain class of well-heeled customers. All that went out the window overnight. How does a woman feel, who's been used to paying twelve dollars for a lipstick at Saks, when she sees the same lipstick for sale for a dollar nineteen at Walgreen's or Kmart? She feels angry. She feels cheated. She feels as though someone she'd trusted as an old friend for years—or a lover, or even a husband, I suppose—had been betraying her all along. She feels disgusted. When Daddy decided to give up the carriage trade and go mass-market, he lost whatever we'd had in terms of customer loyalty. You just can't turn back the clock in this business. Perhaps you can't do it in any business.

"Meanwhile, there were several things that could have been done with the Candied Apple overstock. It could have been sold in Europe, or in Japan, or any number of Third World countries. It could have been turned over to a wholesaler and sold under a new label. Or, after a suitable period of mourning, and using the same packaging, it could have been reintroduced under a new, sexy name—Apple of Eve, or Apple of Temptation, neither of which is all that bad, come to think of it.

"And we had other products that were all doing very well in the specialty-store market. There was no need to tie everything in with the one failure of Candied Apple. But it was as though my father was obsessed with the failure of that one line—perhaps because Grandpa kept saying it was all his fault. So my father decided to have a fire sale on everything, even the products that were popular and profitable. Disastrous. Given hindsight, I see now that Daddy's problem was more than inexperience. He was naive, an innocent, a babe in the woods.

"Other problems developed—the Leo cousins, for instance. When their Miray dividends stopped coming in, they understandably wanted to know why. They brought in their lawyers. When the lawyers learned about that little December stockholders' meeting, they claimed that the vote taken there in favor of Daddy's plan was illegal. The cousins, after all, held fifty percent of the outstanding shares, and a failure to vote at such a meeting is counted as a vote *against* the proposal, whatever it is. Daddy had never heard of such a rule and neither had any of the rest of us. So, since they hadn't voted, the cousins claimed that they had actually voted against Daddy's proposal. Technically, they were right. And they claimed that Nonie's negative vote was actually the swing vote—that Daddy's proposal had actually been defeated by a majority of the sharcholders. That's when the lawsuits started coming in, charging mismanagement.

"Poor Daddy. During those two short years he had as head of the company, most of his time was spent defending those lawsuits. He grew more and more discouraged and depressed, and the red ink kept pouring in—redder than any red that had been bottled as that goddamned Candied Apple! Thank God for Granny and, I suppose, thank God for Michael. . . .

"Those two years were terrible years for Daddy. He aged terribly. I watched as my handsome father's thick, dark head of curly hair grew completely white. I watched his fine, athletic figure develop a stoop. In those two years, he seemed to age twenty. Brad and I watched this physical disintegration of his feeling helpless. And my mother was . . . well, drinking more heavily than ever. No help to him at all. Several times I went to him and said, 'Is there anything I can do to help, Daddy? Can I help?' But he'd just look away from me, and say, 'No . . . no. . . .'

"And then he . . . well, if it's true that he was a . . . you know, a suicide . . . then those two years were enough to do it, I suppose. I don't know. Perhaps. He tried to turn back the clock, and he failed. In the end, he knew he'd failed."

"Itty-Bitty has to go to the doctor," her Granny Flo said on the telephone. "He has something called a plantigrade wart, the vet calls it, on his poor little left front foot, and it's hurting him so. At first, I thought it was just a little blister, from the hot sidewalks, perhaps, but the vet says no, it's a plantigrade wart. He needs to see a specialist. And the only dog pediatrician we can find is way up in Mount Kisco."

"A pediatrician?"

"Yes. Who works on doggies' feet."

"Oh. I think you mean a podiatrist, Granny."

"That's what I said. And, meanwhile, Mr. Horowitz has some leases he wants me to sign on the Bar Harbor lots. I was going to go up to Mr. Horowitz's house to sign them—they need to be in the lawyers' hands first thing in the morning—but now Itty-Bitty and I have to take the one-ten train up to Mount Kisco. Would you run up to Mr. Horowitz's place and fetch those papers for me, Mimi? I asked your mother, but she says she's not feeling herself today. You know what that means. She's pickled again. I'd ask your father to do it, but he's so busy."

"Tell you what," Mimi said. "Why don't you run over to Michael's place, and I'll take Itty-Bitty to Mount Kisco?" She was rather pleased with the fact that, during all these family negotiations with him, she had not had to come into direct contact with him.

"Oh, no, that won't work," her grandmother said. "Itty-Bitty will want me with him. If the doctor has to operate or something, Itty-Bitty will want me there."

"Why can't he send a messenger?" she said, trying to think of some way to avoid this encounter.

"Won't you do me this little favor, Mimi? I wouldn't ask you if it weren't so important. He lives on Riverside and Eighty-first. It shouldn't take but a few minutes. Are you that busy?"

"No, of course not, Granny. I'll be glad to do it."

"He doesn't trust a messenger. They come on bicycles. This is too important for a bicycle."

"Give me his exact address," Mimi said.

"Hi, kiddo," he said, greeting her breezily at the door of his apartment as though more than two years had not passed since they had last seen one another. He was dressed in jeans and an open shirt, a loosened necktie slung rakishly over his shoulder. He immediately handed her a fat manila accordion envelope, and for a moment, she thought he was not even going to ask her in. Then he said, "Care to step in for a minute? See my place?"

His apartment was clearly designed to draw an appreciative gasp from a visitor, which was exactly what Mimi did when she entered it. The floor of his huge, cathedral-ceilinged living room was covered, wall to wall, with deep-pile white carpet, and the room was furnished with oversize white sofas and chairs, plumped up with dozens of big white toss pillows. Every surface that was not white was mirrored: mirrored walls, doors, table tops, and lamp bases. An elaborate track- and recessed-lighting system had been installed in the ceiling, and tall, floor-to-ceiling sliding glass doors across the entire west-facing wall opened out onto a wide terrace planted with hedges and fruit trees. Mimi could not help noticing that the trees and hedges were artificial —good artificial, but still artificial. Beyond, there was a sweeping view of the Hudson, the New Jersey Palisades, the towers of Fort Lee, and the twin towers of the George Washington Bridge.

"It's beautiful, Michael," she said. "Not just beautiful, spectacular!"

He laughed. "Michael Taylor, San Francisco. He's the climax decorator out there. He asked me, 'Do you want an old-money look or a new-money look?' I said, 'What's wrong with a new-money look? After all, that's what it is. Why pretend it's anything else?' We knocked out walls all over the place. This room used to be four smaller ones. Taylor likes built-ins. Everything's built in. Here's the entertainment center." He opened a pair of mirrored doors. "TV, stereo, tape deck, concealed speakers." He opened another pair of doors. "Here's the communications center. It's all computerized. Ever see one of these? Brand-new from Sony—a cordless phone." He swung open a third pair of doors. "Here's the wet bar—refrigerator, ice-maker. The ice-maker makes ninety pounds of ice a day. Why would I need ninety pounds of ice a day? Hell, I don't know, but Taylor wanted me to get it." He moved around the room, opening and closing doors of built-ins. "Anyway, I'm building a house in East Orange that's gonna make this place look like a dump. I may not be the richest guy in New York yet, but I'm on my way. Can I fix you a drink?"

"No, thanks. I can only stay a minute."

"Sit down," he said. She sat down on the edge of one of the oversized sofas, with the thick manila envelope in her lap, and he sat opposite her, leaning forward, his elbows on his knees, his chin on his fists. She saw that he had acquired a gold Rolex watch. He studied her intently for a moment, then tossed the wayward lock of sandy hair back across his forehead, jutting out his lower jaw in the same motion. "You're looking good," he said. "Marriage agrees with you, I guess."

She smiled, and tapped the manila envelope with one finger, and glanced at her own watch.

"I read about your wedding in the *New York Times*," he said. "It was in the Society pages. I guess if you'd married me, it wouldn't have made the Society pages. 'From an old Boston family,' the *Times* said. That must have pleased your grandfather."

"We're all terribly grateful for what you're doing for us, Michael," she said.

"Nothing to it," he said. "That's what I do best—real estate deals. But something's worrying you, kiddo. I can tell. There are little worry lines around your eyes. What is it?"

"I admit I was a little nervous about coming to see you today," she said.

"I think there's more to it than that. That's why I asked your grandmother to send you up here today."

"So. Sending me here was *your* idea. I should have guessed it."

"I wanted to see how you were taking all this. You look worried. You look scared."

"Scared? Well, it was kind of a shock to all of us, when we discovered the way Grandpa left things in his will."

"Tell me something," he said. "Do you think what your grandmother's doing, what I'm helping her do, is really going to help that company?"

"Well, I gather what's needed right now is capital, and—"

"What does your husband think? He's supposed to be a hot-shot lawyer."

"Brad's from New England. He's being very stoic about it."

"A cold fish, you mean?"

"No. He's very optimistic, actually. He makes a joke out of a lot of it—the legal fees, and so on."

"A *joke?* I wish I could see anything funny about the situation. I think your company's in more trouble than any of you may realize. I think what your grandmother is doing is great, but I think all she's doing is sticking her little pinky in the hole in the dike—a hole that's going to keep getting bigger."

"Really, Michael?" she said. "Now you really are scaring me."

"Have you ever thought of running that company yourself? You could do it, you know."

"Me? But it's Daddy's company now, and—"

"I always thought you were the smartest one in that family. I always thought you were the best of that whole lot. You've got brains, and you've got taste. Me, I've got no taste. This"—he gestured around him—"this isn't my taste. This is Michael Taylor's taste. But you've got everything that it takes. You've got beauty, brains, taste, and class. Anyway"—he jumped to his feet—"you've gotta run. But think about what I've said. From what I know of what's going on, your family's in a very no-joke situation. There's more needed than sticking the little finger in the dike."

He walked her toward the door. Suddenly, at the door, he drew her toward him and, roughly and a little clumsily, kissed her hard on the mouth. "For old times' sake," he said, releasing her. "Now beat it, kiddo. I've got work to do. But think about what I've said, and call me if you need me."

All at once she was out the door, and the door had closed behind her.

22

IT HAS BEEN DECIDED that this afternoon's meeting should take place at Nonie Myerson's apartment at 200 East 66th Street. It is a little more convenient to Philippe de Montebello's museum than Sutton Square, and Mr. de Montebello's schedule is, of course, tight. Even more convenient, in terms of distance, would have been the Carlyle, but Edwee could not be certain that his mother could be got out of the place in time for the gathering, and besides, de Montebello has already examined the painting several times in the past, so the venue of the meeting does not really matter all that much.

Now everything is in readiness, and Nonie has placed a pad of yellow legal cap and freshly sharpened pencils at each corner of her glass coffee table, in case there is a need for notes to be taken. She has efficiently thought of everything, including a silver carafe of ice water and four glasses on the table, all very businesslike. The tall and dark and startlingly handsome Philippe de Montebello arrives punctually on the dot of three, looking, as always, like the European aristocrat he is. John Marion arrives one or two minutes late, and of course Edwee and Nonie have been there well in advance.

After the customary pleasantries, Edwee opens the proceedings.

"I'm sorry, Mr. de Montebello," he begins, "but my mother won't be joining us this afternoon. She had promised to be here, but when I called her a few minutes ago to remind her of this meeting, she had forgotten about it completely. In fact, she was still in bed! It's so sad, the way her mind is going." He taps his forehead. "It's the old Alzheimer's, I'm afraid."

"She seemed very alert when I saw her a couple of weeks ago," Philippe de Montebello says.

"Oh, she has some good days," Edwee says, "but fewer and fewer of those as time goes by."

"More bad days than good days now," Nonie says.

"Many more," Edwee says.

"She even has trouble remembering your name," Nonie says. "The other day she referred to you as Mr. Monticello."

"Or sometimes it's Montecarlo."

"Or Montessori . . ."

"Sad," Edwee says. "But the main thing is that my sister and I know that Mother has had discussions with you about her collection, and that she has proposed turning over certain items to the Metropolitan—whichever items you might wish. Let me say that we are absolutely delighted."

"Thrilled," Nonie says.

"In fact, my sister and I have been urging her to do something of this sort for some time. It was at our instigation, really, that Mother sought you out. Our reasons are partly altruistic. We are New Yorkers, born and bred, and our affection for the city's cultural institutions runs deep. New York has been kind to us, you might say, and we want to repay the people of this city by offering whatever we can to its greatest, most important cultural institution of all, your Metropolitan Museum."

"My earliest memories as a little girl," Nonie says dreamily, "are of being taken to the Met by my nanny, and of walking through those galleries, and of marveling at the concentration of sheer beauty assembled under that one roof. I remember I cried when my nurse told me it was time to go!"

"But there is another reason why we've been urging Mother to dispose of her collection—to offer it either to you, or to someone else—that is more pressing, and more practical."

"She can't even see the paintings anymore," Nonie says.

"Yes, sad about her eyesight," de Montebello murmurs.

"But the more practical reason," Edwee continues, "is taxes. If something should happen to Mother—and, alas, she's not getting any younger—and the collection went into her estate, and were to be taxed as part of it, the tax effects on her estate could be disastrous."

"Disastrous," Nonie echoes.

"I understand," de Montebello says. "This is a nice little jade elephant," he says, picking it up. "Very nice."

"Mmm," Nonie murmurs.

"Therefore," Edwee says, "as our mother's only heirs, we feel that her collection—or as much of it as you're willing to accept for the Metropolitan—should be donated as quickly as possible. To eliminate the tax threat. It would make my sister and me very sad to see those paintings put on the auction block to pay the taxes."

"Aren't there other heirs? What about Mimi and Mimi's son?" de Montebello says.

"I meant her *direct* heirs," Edwee says. "Now, I'm sure there are some pictures in the collection that you'd be willing to accept, while there are others that you might decline."

"Well, she has several very nice things," de Montebello says noncommittally.

"Which brings us to the Goya," Edwee says. "For years, her Goya portrait of the Duchess of Osuna has been considered sort of the flagship painting of Mother's collection. And, assuming that the Goya is one of the paintings you might want to acquire, we are naturally anxious to be sure that the provenance of the painting is authentic and unclouded, that there are no doubts about its . . . authenticity."

"Authenticity?" says de Montebello, sitting forward in his chair. "What makes you question its authenticity, Mr. Myerson?"

"John?" says Edwee to John Marion. "Suppose you tell Mr. de Montebello what you noticed when you and I examined the canvas the other day. Or do you prefer to be called Count de Montebello?"

"Mr. is fine," de Montebello says.

"Well, actually it was Edwee who noticed it," Marion says. "It was damned strange. I've examined that painting dozens of times, front and back, over the years, and never noticed anything odd about it. But when we took it down the other day, there was a question mark after Berenson's verification of it."

"The painting had gotten very dusty," Edwee says. "That's why no one noticed it before."

"Question mark?" says Nonie sharply. "What's this about a question mark?"

"Instead of 'vrai—B. Berenson,' it seems to say 'vrai?—B. Berenson,' " Marion says.

"You never told me about any question mark, Edwee!" Nonie says.

"Didn't I?" he says smoothly. "I must have forgotten to mention it to you, dear."

"That *is* odd," de Montebello says. "I examined the painting myself just a few weeks ago and didn't notice any question mark."

"Very dusty," Edwee says again. "That's why no one noticed it."

"*Very* odd."

"But, as you know," Edwee continues, "Berenson often verified paintings for Duveen about which he had doubts, particularly if Duveen thought he might lose a sale if he didn't have Berenson's imprimatur. Berenson *tried* to be scrupulous, but sometimes Duveen wouldn't let him be. Frankly, I'd always had some misgivings about our Goya—the awkward position of Osuna's left hand, for instance, and a certain *daubiness* in the execution. . . ."

"I was never struck by any daubiness," de Montebello says.

"Well, as an art historian, there was something about this Osuna that bothered me. Let me just say that. But when we discovered the question mark—"

"*Who* discovered the question mark?" Nonie asks.

"We—"

"It was actually your brother who pointed it out to me," John Marion says. "But it's definitely there."

"Actually, I wouldn't have given a second thought to the question mark; even the greatest art authorities sometimes have doubts. And none of this would be worth our discussion today, if it weren't for something my sister recalled the other day. My sister was an intimate friend of Berenson's, you know, and often visited B.B. at 'I Tatti.' Nonie, tell Mr. de Montebello about the curious conversation you had with Berenson that day."

This is the cue for Nonie's performance. She sits forward in her chair, smooths the skirt of her new Dior, folds her hands in her lap, and begins.

"It was in the spring of nineteen thirty-nine," she says. "It was a lovely day, and the hills around Settignano were glorious. B.B. and his darling Mary had invited a group of us to 'I Tatti' for luncheon. I was married to Erik Tarcher, my second husband, the actor, at the time, and we drove up from Florence in a rented Fiat. As I say, the day was glorious, but the mood at the luncheon was a little tense. It was nineteen thirty-nine, and the lights were already beginning to go out all over Europe. B.B. was very tense about reports of what was going on in the countries to the north of him. Berenson was Jewish, you see, and there were disturbing reports from Germany and Austria. We talked about these through much of lunch. . . .

"I remember it so vividly. Greta Garbo was there—darling Greta, with her friend George Schlee. Needless to say, George's wife Valentina was *not* there. The Duchess of Windsor was there—darling Wallis. Did you know Wallis, John?"

"Certainly. We handled her jewelry sale in April."

"Of *course*. How could I have forgotten that? The Duke was not there. Wallis explained that David had an attack of hives and couldn't make it. But, if you knew Wallis, you know that David's attack of hives wasn't going to keep *her* from a party. She loved any kind of party. Goodness, how hard that poor woman worked trying to keep that sad little man amused!"

"Get to your conversation with B.B., Nonie," Edwee says, with a slight edge to his voice.

"And Lady Diana Cooper was there—dear Diana—and Duff. That was the little group, nine of us. Greta and George, Wallis, the Coopers, the Berensons, and Erik and myself. The table had been set for ten, of course, and I remember that B.B. joked that we would keep the empty chair at the table in David's honor, like the empty chair for Elijah at a seder. He was such a darling man, B.B. Wallis laughed and laughed at that!

"After lunch, B.B. wanted to show Greta his art library. She'd never seen it, and was eager to. I, of course, had seen it dozens of times. So, while they were doing that, Wallis and Diana and I took our coffee cups and strolled out into the garden, while Erik and Duff and George and Mary stayed behind, talking politics. I'm sure you remember B.B.'s famous green garden: it was built on terraces sloping down the hillside, away from the house. B.B. was terribly proud of it. We found a seat on a garden bench, and presently B.B. joined us there. I made some sort of casual remark about the lovely day, about the intense greens of the poplars and cypress trees, and said that the colors reminded me of the greens in the sleeves of the Duchess of Osuna's gown in my mother's Goya.

"An absolutely stricken look came across B.B.'s face. I have never seen a man wear a more stricken look. He grasped my elbow. 'The Myerson Goya,' he whispered. 'I begged Duveen not to force me to verify that picture. It is most assuredly a fake. It is the worst deception I have ever committed in my life. I pleaded with Duveen not to force me to do this! But Duveen insisted that he must have this sale. The world was in a Great Depression, the art market was in disarray, and he needed the money. He pointed out that I needed the money, too—and it was true! There were doctors' bills for an illness of Mary's'—poor Mary would die, you know, a few years later—'and he threatened to withhold other commissions that were due me if I did not do as I was told. And so I succumbed to the devil Duveen, may he twist eternally in his grave! Dear Nonie, I am so ashamed of what I have done. Can you ever forgive me? Can your mother ever forgive me?'

"I was stunned, of course. I didn't know what to say. Wallis was the first to speak. 'Are you certain it's a forgery, B.B.?' she said. 'Absolutely,' he said. 'It is a nineteenth-century forgery. Duveen knew this, too. He knew the painting's provenance.' I said, 'I must tell my mother.' 'Yes,' he said with tears in his beautiful eyes, 'I'm afraid you must.' That was when Wallis reached out and touched my hand. Wallis was always such a kind, sweet soul. 'Don't,' she said. 'Don't do that. It would hurt your mother too much to know that she has been deceived. It would also hurt our dear friend B.B.'s reputation if word got out that he had knowingly taken part in this deception. Don't tell your mother, Nonie, for everyone's sake. What difference does it make, after all? Your mother's happy with her painting. Let sleeping dogs lie.'

"Diana agreed with her. 'Wallis is right,' she said. 'You must never tell her. Too much hurt would be caused by telling her now. Promise us you'll never tell her.' And so that's what I promised them, my dear friends Wallis and Diana, years ago. And I've kept that promise to this very day. And when I made it, dear B.B., who was weeping now, bent over me and kissed my forehead, and whispered, 'Thank you, blessed Nonie.' "

"And so," Edwee says, after a little pause to let Nonie's performance sink in, "that is the cause for our concern. We don't want the Metropolitan Museum to be saddled with a costly fake—the embarrassment, the horrid publicity, if it turned out, later on, that the museum had been deceived too. We felt you should know this now, for your sake."

"Tell me something," Philippe de Montebello says. "Did Berenson mention anything about placing a question mark after his verification?"

"To him, there was no question about its being a fake at all! He said it was *unquestionably* a fake!"

"I see," he says, rising from his chair. "Very interesting. Obviously, I'll want to have another look at the painting. And I'd like to bring along some of the museum's curatorial staff when I do."

"Of course," Edwee says. "That will be no problem. Do give Mother a call, and set that up. Poor Mother, of course, may have no idea what you're talking about, and what you all are doing there. But I'm sure she'll let you have another look."

"Well," Nonie says when the other two have gone, "how'd I do?"

"I think," Edwee says carefully, "that we may be going to pull it off. That 'blessed Nonie' business was a bit much, perhaps. But otherwise . . . yes, you did a satisfactory job."

"By the way, where did this question mark come from? Never mind. I don't want to know. I've done my job. Everything I was supposed to do. Now where's my money?"

"You'll have it in a few days," he says.

"How many days?"

"A few. These things take time. Don't be greedy, dear. And de Montebello's right: that *is* a nice jade elephant. So *familiar*-looking, too."

"There's one thing I don't understand, Mimi," I said to her one afternoon when we were chatting in her office. "All those years before your grandfather died, before it turned out that the old man had squandered most of his money, and your grandmother's trusts as well, your father earned a good salary with the company—well into six figures, which was good money in the forties and fifties. And yet, when you were growing up, you say your parents never seemed to have any money. You were sent to Miss Hall's school on an academic scholarship, for instance. Why was that?"

"That," she said thoughtfully, "is the sixty-four-million-dollar question. If you can find the answer to that one, I'd love to know what it is. I've never understood it, either."

"Your grandmother blames it on your mother's extravagance."

"That isn't true. My mother wasn't extravagant. We lived very simply. She did her own housework, her own cooking. When she went to the market, she always had a purseful of Green Stamps to paste into those little books. Her clothes, and mine, were always bought at sales. My grandparents were the ones who lived extravagantly."

"Was your father a . . . gambler, do you think?"

"Not that I was ever aware of. Wouldn't you think, growing up as an only child in that household, I'd have noticed it if he was? Wouldn't I have noticed it if he'd been always at the racetrack, or on the phone with bookies, or whatever? All he ever did, as I remember it, was go to the office in the morning and come home at six o'clock for dinner. They didn't even have friends in for bridge. Daddy wasn't a drinker. My mother, of course, was— or is, I should say—an alcoholic. That's probably what Granny was talking about—the drinking. But that wouldn't have been enough to do it. One person couldn't possibly drink a hundred thousand dollars' worth of whiskey a year, could one? She even shopped for discounts at the liquor store. My father's finances were always a mystery to me. They still are. After I married Brad, he couldn't understand it either."

"Would your mother know the answer, do you think?"

She hesitated. "Yes," she said at last. "Yes, I think she does. In fact, I'm sure she does. But do me a favor, Jim. I don't want to try to influence the way you write your story, but I want to ask you an important favor. When you interview her, don't ask her that question. As I say, she's a recovering alcoholic. She's been sober since the middle of May. In fact, her four months' anniversary is coming up soon. Emotionally, she's still in a very fragile state, as you saw that night at dinner at my house. If you ask her that question, it will upset her. I know it will, because I made the mistake of asking her the same question when I went out to California with her in May, to check her into the Betty Ford Center. It set her off. It could set her off again. She's like a ticking bomb on that particular subject. So, when you talk to her, be gentle, Jim. She's trying, now, to live each day in the present. Don't try to draw her out too much about the past."

"I'll try not to, then."

"I trust you," she said. "I don't know why, but I trust you."

* * *

"Evil forces," her mother said. "There were evil forces in the world. They ruined your father's and my lives, like a curse." They were sitting side by side in the first-class compartment of the wide-bodied United Airlines jet to Los Angeles that day in May.

"What sort of evil forces, Mother?"

"I said evil forces! Evil people," Alice Myerson said. "What more do you want me to say? Leo died, but then there was Nate. Then Nate finally died, thank God, but then it was too late."

"Nate?"

"Nate. Your father's cousin Nate! I don't want to talk about this anymore, Mimi!"

Mimi had changed the subject. "I'm so glad you've decided to do this, Mother," she said. "I'm terribly proud of you."

"Decided to do what?"

"The Ford Center. You're going to feel so much better about yourself."

"I'm going to try."

"I know you are, Mother."

"I'm going to make it work."

"I know you are," and Mimi had squeezed her mother's hand.

But, about an hour out of La Guardia, Mimi got up to go to the ladies' room, and when she came back, her mother's tray-table was down and she had ordered a double Scotch.

"Oh, Mother," she said softly. "Please don't."

"Don't worry," Alice said. "I'm not going to get drunk. I just need a little liquid courage. This is a big step I'm taking, and I need a little bit of liquid courage to get me there."

Mimi said nothing but closed her eyes and pretended to sleep. The captain announced over the loudspeaker that they were passing over Indianapolis or St. Louis, or some other dim place, and presently, through half-closed eyes, Mimi saw her mother wave her finger at the flight attendant—a slenderly beautiful black woman with sleek, ebony hair pulled back tightly in a bun—and say, "Two more Scotches, please," in her most ladylike voice.

"Why, sure, honey!"

Mimi is not sure how many more drinks her mother had ordered after that because, somehow, she had genuinely managed to sleep. But she remembers waking to hear the cockpit announce that passengers seated on the right-hand side of the aircraft would have an excellent view of Pike's Peak, and she remembers her mother poking her in the shoulder and saying, "Wake up! Wake up! You're only pretending to be asleep. Pike's Peak!

Don't you want to see Pike's Peak?" Across the aisle from them, a business-man in a grey suit, doing briefcase work in his lap, stared momentarily at Alice, then tapped the papers in his lap with the head of a pencil. "Two more Scotches," Alice had called to the flight attendant.

The flight attendant had eyed her dubiously. Returning with the pair of miniatures, she had said, "This will be last call, ma'am."

"Last call? What do you mean last call? We're only halfway there. We're only at Pike's Peak!"

The flight attendant's smile had been intense. "Last call for you, ma'am," she had said.

"Why do you think I fly first class? With a first-class seat I'm entitled to as many drinks as I want!"

"I'm sorry, but FAA regulations permit us to use our discretion and refuse service to any passenger who appears to be intoxicated."

"Intoxicated! Mimi, am I intoxicated?"

Mimi, her eyes still closed, her head back on her seat, said through clenched teeth, "Yes."

"This is outrageous! The president of this airline will hear from me about this! Do you realize who I am? Which airline am I flying?"

"This is United Airlines flight one forty-two," the flight attendant said.

Across the aisle, the grey-suited businessman snapped his briefcase shut, rose, and moved his seat to one that was vacant two rows behind them, in the smoking section. Mimi heard him mutter, "Drunken bitch."

"What did that man just say to me?" Alice said. Then she said, "Well, luckily for you, Miss Last Call, or whatever your name is, I happen to have brought my own bottle," and she reached into her purse and removed a silver flask.

"I'm sorry, ma'am, but FAA regulations prohibit passengers from drink-ing alcoholic beverages from their own supplies," and she reached for the flask.

"Don't you dare touch my flask!" Alice had cried, clutching it to her bosom. "This is *mine*. It is a sterling-silver flask given to me by my late husband, Henry Myerson! And do you know who *he* was? Only the presi-dent and chief executive officer of the Miray Corporation, that's all! Ever hear of the Miray Corporation? And do you know who this young lady with me is? Only the *present* president of the Miray Corporation, my daughter, Mimi Myerson. She was on the cover of *Time!*"

"Please serve her the drinks she wants," Mimi said to the stewardess. "It's the only way."

"I'm sorry, ma'am, but FAA regulations do not permit—"

Then Alice apparently changed her mind. "Never mind," she said. "Just bring me a Coca-Cola."

"Certainly, ma'am."

But when the flight attendant returned with the glass of Coca-Cola, Alice had taken it and then poured its contents onto the carpeted floor of the plane beside her, retaining the ice cubes with her fingers. Then she refilled the ice-filled glass with whiskey from her flask. "Thank you *very much!*" she had cried, triumphant.

"I'm sorry, ma'am, but I cannot permit—"

"Look at her!" Alice cried. "Look at Miss Last Call! Look at her nails! Look at her lipstick! She's not even wearing Miray products! She's wearing some cheap stuff, I can tell. Typical nigger!"

The flight attendant stared at Alice for a moment with expressionless eyes, saying nothing. Then she turned and walked toward the front of the plane, opened the door to the cockpit, stepped inside, and closed the door behind her.

"There!" Alice cried out to no one in particular. "That got rid of Miss Last Call!"

Beside her, Mimi closed her eyes again.

Presently, the cockpit door reopened and the stewardess reemerged, followed by a tall young man in a dark blue uniform with three gold stripes on his sleeve.

"Do we have a little problem here?" he said in a pleasant voice.

"Yes! We certainly do! Your stewardess tried to steal my priceless heirloom antique sterling-silver flask!"

That was when Mimi left her seat and walked back to the middle of the plane where there was a telephone.

These air-to-ground telephones are gadgets, at best, and have a long way to go before they are satisfactory media for human communication. Making a call involved inserting a credit card, then listening to a computerized voice repeating, "Please . . . wait . . . for . . . the . . . dial . . . tone," again and again. The dial tone sounded, then disappeared, then sounded again, and disappeared again, as the robot's voice continued to instruct the caller to please wait. Finally, when Mimi had a recognizable human voice, which could have been a man's or a woman's as it bounced across the scarps of the Sierra Madre Mountains, at the other end of the connection, Mimi had to shout into the receiver to make herself heard. "Is this the Betty Ford Center?" she had shouted. "Is this the Ford Center?"

"What? Who is this?"

"It's Mimi Myerson," she yelled. "I'm Alice Myerson's daughter. We're on the plane. My mother is drunk."

"What? I can't hear you."

"My mother, Mrs. Myerson, is drunk! What should I . . . ?"

"No. Not if she's drunk. She can't register here unless she's sober."

"Then what should I do?"

"No . . . sobriety to register . . . hotel . . . Los Angeles or Palm Springs. Bring her here tomorrow," she heard the distant, crackling voice saying. "Sobriety . . . condition at admission. Do you want us to . . ." But the rest of the conversation became unintelligible.

"I'll call you from Los Angeles!" Mimi said, and replaced the headset.

And when she parted the curtain to return to the first-class section, she saw her mother. She was kneeling on her seat now, her arms across the back of it. She had taken off her blouse and was cupping her breasts in her hands, saying to the grey-suited man behind her, "Don't you like my tits? What's the matter with my tits? Don't you think I have pretty tits? Don't you think my tits are as good as Marilyn Monroe's?"

The stewardess and the young first officer were struggling with her, trying to cover her shoulders with a blanket, and the stewardess was saying angrily, "Cover yourself up, woman!"

The grey-suited man was on his feet. "May I please change my seat to tourist class?" he said.

"I'm sorry, sir. Economy class is completely full."

"How much more of this shit do we have to put up with?" the man said. "I demand a refund on this ticket!"

"You can take that up with the passenger service agent when we reach Los Angeles, sir."

"Refund!" Alice cried. "I'm the one who should be entitled to a refund! For abuse, mistreatment, insults . . . party poop!"

"She's my mother," Mimi said. "The best thing to do when she's like this is to ignore her."

"Ignore me? Why should I be ignored? Because I was an unwanted child? Is that it? Because my mother didn't want to have me because she was afraid I'd spoil her famous figure? Because I was supposed to be an abortion, but it was too late? That's true! She told me so! Afraid I'd spoil her famous figure! Well, what do you think of these tits of mine? Party poop! This old party poop is trying to pretend he doesn't think I have great tits!"

"Cover yourself *up*, woman! Ain't you got no *shame?*"

"If you'd served her the drinks she wanted, this wouldn't have happened," Mimi said. "Anyone who's dealt with alcoholics knows that."

"Our FAA regulations state—"

Eventually, they had been able to subdue her, strap her in her seat belt, and cover her upper body with a blanket, because she refused to put on her blouse. Throughout the rest of the trip, though, she continued to scream and shout and sob, while Mimi sat rigidly beside her.

When they were finally parked at the jetway at LAX, the captain announced, "Will all passengers please remain seated, and with their seat belts fastened, for just a few more moments while we attend to some airport business."

That was when two uniformed airport policemen (the captain had apparently radioed ahead about the problem) boarded the plane, moved quickly to where Alice Myerson was seated, and, showing remarkable teamwork, snapped handcuffs about her wrists, and carried her, kicking and screaming, out of the plane and down the jetway.

And so Alice had not spent the night in a hotel. She had spent it in the drunk tank of the Los Angeles County Jail, and Mimi had spent it in an anteroom outside, waiting for it to be morning in New York, when she called her husband and arranged for a local lawyer to handle her mother's bail and release and to apply whatever leverage was possible to persuade the reporter from the *Examiner* who covered the police blotter not to publish a story about the episode on Flight 142.

It was early afternoon before all arrangements had been made and Mimi and Alice were able to enter the hired limousine that was to drive them over the mountains to Palm Springs.

Beside her, in the back seat, Mimi's mother was a huddled, disheveled, red-eyed figure.

"It was all *your* fault, you know," she said once. "You got me started thinking about all those things long ago. You started it."

But Mimi, who had had no sleep the night before either, said nothing as the big car made its way down out of the mountains toward the desert valley floor below.

Finally, her mother said, "I'm sorry," and began to cry.

23

*Y*OU'VE GOT TO DO SOMETHING about your mother's drinking," Brad said to her. This was in the summer of 1960, during her father's first year as the company's new president. "She called me at the office this afternoon, and I couldn't make head nor tail out of what she wanted. When she's drunk, she gets belligerent. The first thing I knew, she was shouting at me and calling me foul names. I finally had to hang up on her and tell my secretary not to put through any more calls from her."

"Everybody's tried everything," she said. "I used to pour her liquor down the drain, but she just found cleverer places to hide her whiskey. I tried to close her charge account at Sherry-Lehmann, and she just went to another liquor store. We had a doctor prescribe something called Antabuse; it's supposed to make you deathly ill when you take a drink. But she wouldn't take the pills. I've tried to get her to join Alcoholics Anonymous, but she won't attend the meetings. I've tried calling her early in the morning, and have had friends call her, to catch her during the hangover period, to give her pep talks. It doesn't help. I even went to a group called Al-Anon, which is supposed to be for the families of alcoholics. But all those people seem to do is sit around and hold each other's hands—and pray."

"Well, somebody ought to do something."

"What else is there to *do*, Brad? Tell me."

"What she's doing is ruining her reputation."

"But she just doesn't care about her reputation, don't you see?"

"They're even talking about it at my office. Those girls at the switchboard —they know what's going on."

"Or is it *your* reputation you're worried about? Is that it, Brad?"

"I just wish you'd do something about it."

"You wish *I'd* do something?" she said, suddenly angry. "Why must it be me? Why is she suddenly all *my* responsibility?"

"She's not *my* mother," he said. "My mother doesn't behave that way. My mother's not a drunk."

"Oh, no," she said, letting her voice fill with sarcasm. "Of *course* not. Because *your* mother's a real New England *lady*. That's what you're saying, isn't it? Your mother's a proper Boston Brahmin, and my mother's a drunken slut. Is that what you're trying to say to me?"

"Skip it," he said. "Let's see what's on TV."

"No, I won't skip it, Brad. I want to know what it is exactly that you're trying to say to me."

"All I'm saying," he said, "is that I can't understand what it is about you people that makes you feel you don't have any control over your lives."

"Now wait a minute," she said. "Just what do you mean by 'you people'? Do I detect a faintly anti-Semitic slur here?"

"Of course not. But I was brought up to believe that if there was a problem in a family, there was usually a solution to it, and someone in the family took charge. And I'm saying that if you don't do something about your mother's drinking, nobody will. Your father doesn't seem able to control her. He doesn't even seem to try."

"My father happens to have more important things on his mind right now!"

"Then that leaves you, doesn't it?"

"Oh, yes," she said. "That leaves me. But what about you? Have *you* offered to do anything to help? Of course not."

"As I said before, she's not my mother."

"Have you offered to help in any *other* ways? Everybody else in this family has been making sacrifices. Look what poor old Granny's doing! Even Edwee's loaned Daddy money, but what have you done?"

"Edwee didn't loan him any money. All he did was purchase a few more shares of Miray stock."

"It amounts to the same thing, doesn't it? Cash? That's what the company needs now, isn't it? Even Nonie's been making sacrifices. She's fired her servants, she's looking for a smaller apartment. But we haven't done one damn thing!"

"We?"

"*You*, then. I don't have any money. But you seem to be doing all right. But I haven't seen you offering to write out any checks!"

"I don't know anything about the beauty business. I don't want to get involved in it. I have my own career to worry about."

"Oh, of *course!*"

"And our livelihood, yours and mine."

"Of *course*. Why don't you come right out and admit it, Brad? You find the beauty business a little *common*, don't you. Not quite tuned to your fine New England taste. *You—you're* down at Sixty-seven Wall Street with all your *Social Register* snobs!"

"Well, if you're so hot on helping out your father, why don't *you* do something?"

"What could I do, besides offer to take over the company and run it for him? Which I could probably do, by the way. I know a few things about the business. But I hardly think he'd take kindly to that suggestion. Do you?"

"You could do *something*."

"Like be a saleslady at Macy's, you mean. Something—while you do nothing! No, I'll tell you why you won't do anything to help, Brad Moore. It's because you're a cold-blooded, cold-hearted New Englander—a cold-fish Yankee, long on pedigree but short on feelings. At least we Jews have feelings. At least we Jews pitch in and pull together and help each other out when the chips are down! You and your Puritan stoicism! Puritan selfishness is all it is!"

"Look," he said, "we shouldn't quarrel like this. Let's stop."

"I think I know what this is all about," she said. "When you married me, you thought I was going to inherit a lot of money. Now that it turns out I didn't inherit a lot of money, you turn on my family and start criticizing them."

"That's hogwash, Mimi, and you know it's hogwash."

"Is it? I'm not so sure. I think you thought it was okay to marry a Jewish girl as long as she was a *rich* Jewish girl. But now that it turns out she's *not* a rich Jewish girl, but a poor Jewish girl, it makes all the difference, doesn't it? Then you start criticizing, finding fault. Well, I apologize for the fact that the money you married me for failed to materialize!"

"Hogwash," he said again.

"Listen," she said, "speaking of 'you people,' I know how *you* people talk. A poor person who's an alcoholic is called a drunken bum. But if you're talking about a *rich* person who's an alcoholic, you say, 'Old So-and-So's been hitting the bottle a bit lately.'"

"Please, let's stop this, Mimi. You're getting into things that have nothing to do with—"

"You started this!" she said. "All I did was ask you how your day went, and you started in on my mother—whom I happen to love."

"Your mother pretty much managed to ruin my day!"

"See? There you go again!"

"Look, we're all under a strain," he said. "I know that, and fighting with each other won't help. And, you know, I was thinking. Maybe if we were able to make a baby . . . maybe that would help. What do you think? Shall we try again tonight? Without your . . . you-know-what."

"A *baby?*" she cried. "Are you out of your mind? You'd drag an innocent baby into this mess?"

"Maybe it would make us feel more like a family, you and me. Maybe it would help take our minds off . . . all the other business."

"You see? That's all you want. You want to put all of Daddy's problems out of your mind. You just want to forget about what's happening to my family. You want to get everything out of your sight, and out of your mind."

"Think about it, Mimi," he said, reaching out to take her hand. "Let's try—"

"No," she said, pulling away from him. "Don't touch me. I want nothing to do with a man as cold as you are."

He rose from the sofa and headed toward the door.

"Where are you going?"

"I'm going to spend the night at the Harvard Club."

"Good!" she called after him. "Perfect. That's the perfect address for you! Go to the Harvard Club. Go—and stay. Stay as long as you want. You can stay there forever as far as I'm concerned! Cold-blooded Yankee WASP bastard!"

The next morning, he returned and packed a suitcase, while she watched him wordlessly.

"You told me to call you if I needed you," she said. "I think I need you, but I'm not sure what I need you for." They were sitting in his huge, high-ceilinged living room on Riverside Drive. "I'm frightened, Michael. I don't know what to do."

He gave her a long, sideways look, saying nothing.

"They sent me away to school," she said. "To learn. I don't think I learned very much. Everyone says you're very smart. They say—"

"You're growing up," he said. "When I first met you, you were just a little kid with a broken skate lace. Then you broke my heart."

"I probably shouldn't have called you," she said. "I probably shouldn't be here."

"No, I'm glad you called me." He rose and crossed the room and sat down beside her on the sofa. "I think you need a friend," he said.

She studied her lacquered fingertips. "Yes, that . . . and perhaps something else," she said, choosing her words carefully. "Advice, perhaps. You've made a lot of money, haven't you?"

He smiled. "Yes, I've got to admit that's true," he said.

"People all over New York are saying you're a brilliant businessman."

He shrugged and spread open the palms of his hands in a Jewish-peddler-parody gesture. "Just schlepping along," he said.

"Please. I'm serious. I want you to tell me the truth. Is my father a brilliant businessman, or isn't he?"

"Golly, I—"

"I used to think he was. But now I'm not so sure. Since my grandfather died, I've tried to learn a little bit about this business. After all, I'm the only grandchild. Someday—who knows?—I *might* be in a position to take it over. But from what I've learned, I now think my father has made some very serious mistakes. And now there are all these lawsuits, charging mismanagement. Recklessness. Fiscal ineptitude. What do you think, Michael?"

He scowled. "I don't know anything about your dad's business," he said. "All I know is what I've picked up on the street. And, since I've become at least peripherally involved with your family, I've kept my ears open."

"And what have you heard?"

"Well, to be frank with you, most of what I've heard has not been good. People in the business are saying that this new merchandising strategy of his is suicidal."

"Yes," she said quietly. "That's what I've heard, too. I've read it in the newspapers. What's going to happen, do you think?"

He spread his hands again. "I don't know. How much longer can your grandmother keep pouring money into the company? She's going to run out of properties to sell at some point, you know."

"And that's another thing. I see all this money of Granny's going into the company. But I see nothing coming out. What's happening to those funds, Michael?"

"I have no idea. Why don't you ask him?"

"I've tried. I've tried to meet with him, tried to talk about it. But he's too . . . preoccupied. And the thing is, too, that I'm a woman. Women in this family—the whole female sex—have never exactly occupied a position of respect. But I'm thinking that if a man, a businessman like yourself, could talk to him, man to man, maybe he'd listen to you. Maybe you could help him, guide him. And also find out what's happening to Granny's money."

"Someone like me," he said flatly.

"Yes."

"It seems to me that if someone were to do that, it should be your husband."

"Brad is too . . . too preoccupied with his own career," she said. "He's been made a partner in his firm. There's been talk of him running for public office. Brad has ambitions of his own that have nothing to do with my family's business. Besides, Brad thinks that the beauty business is a little bit—"

"Too Seventh Avenue for his Christian taste."

"Yes, perhaps," she said lowering her eyes.

"You and he have had words on this subject, I gather."

"Yes. But what if you were to try to talk to Daddy?"

Suddenly he sprang to his feet and began pacing the white room, his hands thrust deep into the back pockets of his jeans, pacing and bouncing springily on the balls of his sneakered feet. "Why would he talk to me? Why would he listen to anything I had to say? I only met the guy once before."

"He has great respect for what you've been doing for Granny."

"What could I tell him, Mimi? What could I tell him without looking at the company's books? And why would he let me look at the company's books? It's a private company, you know, and he could simply tell me to go to hell. Why would he let me look at his company's books? Why would he let me look at a single balance sheet?" He continued pacing up and down the length of the white-carpeted floor, his shoulders hunched forward, pantherlike, or like a boxer sizing up his opponent in the ring. "No way," he said, pounding his right fist into the palm of his left hand. "No way he'd let me do that, Mimi. Now your grandmother, she's another story. She could ask to look at the books. She's entitled, after all."

"What would *she* be able to tell from looking at the books?"

"But *me?* No way."

She sat forward in her chair. "But would you at least *try* it, Michael?" she said. "For me?"

All at once he stopped pacing and stood in the center of the room gazing at her, his dark eyes seeming to grow wider and deeper. He tossed the sandy forelock of hair back from where it had fallen across his forehead and began to smile that slightly crooked smile, revealing the perfect teeth and the three dimples, one at each corner of his mouth and one in his chin. Pink spots of excitement lighted his cheekbones, and with her fingertips Mimi touched her own cheeks because she could feel them reddening as well.

"Well, if you put it that way, of course I will," he said. "For you, I'll do anything. For you, I want everything. For you, I want towers—yes, towers. Towers and minarets and spires, and palace gates, forests, shores and islands, gems and pearls and scepters and all the emperor's diamonds, and every brilliant in King Oberon's crown. You shall have temples and mosques and fountains, rings on your fingers and bells on your toes, fountains and waterfalls and tapestries and flowers and thornless roses from the spice islands, and . . ."

And as he spoke he moved around the room again, opening and closing doors of the mirrored built-in closets and cabinets.

"What are you doing?" she whispered.

"Turning off the stereo, turning off the computer terminals, turning off the telephone, so we can make love in the afternoon."

"Michael, I didn't come here for this," she said. But even as she spoke, she knew this wasn't true, because once again the air between them was charged, electric, the way she remembered it from nearly three years ago. The current in the air that separated them was so strong that it was almost tangible, a thick and ropy presence that seemed to draw her toward him, and her voice choked when she tried to speak. And she knew that this, yes, was of course what she had come here for, for this reason above all others, to see if this would happen again, and that all the rest had been just an excuse —an honest excuse, forgive me for that, she thought—for this, and now that it was happening again she was overwhelmed with desire for him, that overpowering Michael feeling.

His eyes were blazing now, and from her place on the sofa, she tried to stare him down with her own eyes, but his wide, smiling eyes defeated hers, and she looked down at the changeless pattern of the thick white carpet, feeling weak and not quite ill.

"I want to make you . . . happy," he said at last.

"Michael, I . . ."

He pressed a button, and the electric drapes across the wall of glass drew silently closed. One narrow shaft of sunlight remained between the closed drapes and fell directly into Mimi's eyes, and she raised her left hand to shield her eyes.

"Don't," he said. "Your eyes have little white stars in them when the sun shines in them. I want to remember this when you have to go. The sun in your polished-silver eyes."

"The world's gotten to be such a small place," she said.

"Yes. Here we are again."

"Is it . . . ?"

"Yes."

"Should we . . . ?"

"Yes."

"It isn't ended, then?"

"No."

"Can we?"

"We can. We must. I must. You must. You must," he said. "We can." And on noiseless, sneakered feet he moved toward her, took her out-stretched hand, and lifted her gently to her feet.

When it was over, his laugh was almost boyishly exultant. "I saw them again!" he said. "Little white stars—in my brain, when it happened! Did you see them too, darling?"

"Yes, I think I did."

"Little white stars!"

Soon he was asleep, and Mimi rose and moved about the mirrored half-darkness of his bedroom. In his bathroom, she found an oversized white bath towel and wrapped herself in it. Then she began exploring his closets, opening the mirrored doors and drawers and touching his things: the suits, the shirts, the racks of neckties, the tiers of shoes, the drawers of handkerchiefs, sweaters, socks, and underwear. Suddenly she was aware that he was awake again and watching her.

"Your sock drawer is a mess," she giggled.

He held out his bare arm for her, and she went to him again.

"You're the only girl I ever loved," he said. "You know that, don't you? You're the only girl I'll ever love. At least I can finally have you for a little while. At least, for a little while, we can have each other. The way it was supposed to be."

"I love you, Michael."

Did I say that? she asks herself now. It all seems so long ago, and in another world entirely, and their affair only lasted two weeks—two weeks, at the most, was all it had been, give or take a few days. Two weeks, she thinks. That was the title (wasn't it?) of a novel, *Two Weeks*, yes, by Elinor Glyn, a steamy romantic novel of the 1920s, set in some mythical Graustarkian kingdom, in which the heroine and her lover rolled about on leopard-skin rugs in the lover's palace.

But there had been no leopard-skin rugs in her affair with Michael, and the palace had been only Riverside Drive. In her mind, now, the affair seems not only long-ago and passionate, but at the same time somehow banal. He seemed to bring out a domestic, housewifely side of her that she had not known existed. She had discovered, for instance, that he was a terrible housekeeper. His, or his decorator's, passion for built-ins was based on the fact that he used the built-ins to conceal his clutter. He hid his laundry under his bed. He stored his firewood behind the skirts of one of the big living room sofas. She bought him a laundry bag and made space in a closet in which to hang it. She found a sheltered corner of his terrace on which to stack the firewood. She took his suits to the cleaner's and, when they came back, saw that they were hung neatly in even rows, on matching wooden hangers, and in plastic garment bags. She dusted and lined up his shoes in their trees. She organized his tie racks, for he had a habit of hanging up his neckties without undoing their knots. She arranged his shelves of shirts and sweaters according to color and long-sleeve, short-sleeve. She paired and folded his socks. Though Michael employed what he called "my dusty lady" as a maid-housekeeper, dusting seemed to be the dusty lady's sole field of expertise.

Mimi cleaned out his medicine chest, discarding many empty tubes of toothpaste, cans of shaving foam and deodorant, spent razor blades, bottles of cologne and after-shave, and . . . bobby pins. She felt a slight twinge of guilt throwing out the bobby pins but decided he had no further use for them. Ancient prescriptions, long past their shelf life, along with an imposing collection of used Q-tips, also made their way into the garbage. He was, she discovered, a penny saver. A gallon jug was filled with copper coins. She counted and stacked these in paper rollers, took them to the bank, and exchanged them for bills.

She attacked his refrigerator, throwing out many objects of dubious age, identity, and odor, including a drawerful of what may have once been recognizable as species of vegetables but were now pulpy and discolored blobs. She bathed the refrigerator's interior with detergent and baking soda. In the process, she discovered that his eating habits were erratic, at best, and that he lived primarily on carry-outs—pizzas and Chinese food. She restocked his larder with health foods, his freezer with wholesome frozen vegetables, his refrigerator with fresh milk, eggs, fruits, and juices. He made jokes about her efforts to organize and systematize his household and life and told her she was "turning into a typical Jewish mother."

But the process of discovery and change was not at all a one-way street during those few weeks. In their lovemaking, he took her on a journey of discovery to a destination she had never known about before. He called it "little white stars"—an implosion of them from an inner, unexplored galaxy.

"Did you see them?" he would ask her.

"Yes . . . oh, yes."

They had never once spoken of Brad.

"I'm going to see your father tomorrow," he said.

"Thank you, darling."

"After that, how'd you like to drive over to East Orange and have a look at the house I'm building there?"

"I'd love that."

"Good. I'll pick you up at your house at four. You'll be my pick-up," he said.

In Henry Myerson's office, he took a seat opposite the company president's big desk.

"It's funny," Henry Myerson said, "that you should have asked to see me, because for the last few days I've had it on my mind to call and ask to see you."

"Is that so?" Michael said.

"Yes. It's occurred to me that you might be able to be of unique service to me, Mr. Horowitz."

"Well, that's what I'm here to offer you," Michael said. "To be of any service that I can."

"I know you by reputation," Henry said. "As a builder and developer—as well as what you've been doing for my mother."

"Excuse me, sir," Michael said, "but I don't think you realize that we've met before."

"Have we?" Henry said, looking flustered. "I'm sorry, but I don't recall—"

"About two and a half years ago, your daughter and I came to your house to tell you that we wanted to get married."

"Oh," Henry said, shaking his head as though to rid it of dusty memories. "Was that you? I'm sorry, but I didn't . . . forgive me, but that was a very emotional time for all of us, I'm afraid. Very emotional. I'm sorry I didn't connect the name—not an uncommon name, after all. And I'm afraid that meeting wasn't a very pleasant occasion for you, was it? Sorry about that."

"No, sir, it wasn't pleasant. It wasn't pleasant at all."

"Well, these things work out in the end," Henry said. "Mimi's happily married now. Fine fellow, Brad Moore. Lawyer downtown. He's made her very happy."

"Yes, sir. I'm sure of that."

"And you—I'm sure you're married yourself by now."

"As a matter of fact, I'm not."

"Well, then," Henry said a little lamely, "it's good to see you again."

"Thank you, sir."

"Now then," Henry said, and he rose from his chair, walked to his window, and stood looking out, his hands in his pockets, his back to Michael. "You're a builder, you're a developer, Mr. Horowitz."

"That's correct, sir."

"Primarily in New Jersey, I gather."

"I also have a project going up in Manhattan, on the Upper West Side."

"Good. Lots of development going on, on the West Side. Lincoln Center and all that."

"Yes, sir."

"I suppose—or at least I gather," Henry said, "that as a builder and developer, dealing with unions in the building trades and that sort of thing, you have occasion to do business, and come into contact with, people—men —who are members of what I believe is called the Cosa Nostra."

"I'm not quite sure what you mean by that," Michael said carefully.

"I mean, I've heard, I've read—and surely you have, too—that building contractors, in dealing with the unions and so forth, often have occasion to deal with some questionable types, people who at least have connections with the Mafia."

"Yes, I've heard that, sir. But I personally—"

"There's never been anyone you've suspected of being connected with any of this?"

"Well, I've had my suspicions, yes. But in my business, I try—"

"So at least you know who these people are. You see, Mike—May I call you Mike?" Henry Myerson went on, "This company faces a lot of problems right now—problems of transition, from old management to new. Most of these problems we're going to be able to deal with, I'm confident of that. But there is one problem, a persistent problem, that's not going to go away unless a certain individual is . . . eliminated."

"Eliminated?"

"Yes. This is an individual of no moral worth whatsoever, a scourge on society, a person society would be better off to be rid of. I've been thinking about this for some time, Mike. I assure you I'm a moral man and have never considered taking means as drastic as I'm thinking of to dispose of an undesirable, totally worthless person, a lowlife of the lowest possible order. But under the present circumstances—"

"You're talking of having someone killed," Michael said.

"Well, that's a rather crude way of putting it, but yes. And it occurred to me that someone like you, a developer, with your connections, might have access to—"

"Does this individual have a name?"

"Nathan Myerson."

"A relative?"

"In a sense, yes."

"Well, let me tell you this, Mr. Myerson," Michael said. "In my business, I've run across people whom I've suspected of Mafia ties—I won't deny that. But I've personally tried to steer clear of any of that. I don't want my business, or my reputation, tainted with any of that. Whenever I've had an inkling that a person I'm dealing with isn't straight, I stop doing business with that person. Immediately. I will not knowingly do business with those people."

"You couldn't even supply me with a name?"

"I'm afraid not, sir."

"I assure you, you'd be helping rid the earth of one of its worst scum."

"I'm sorry, I can't help you."

"There'd be money in it, of course."

"I'm sure there would be, but the answer is negative."

Henry Myerson turned from the window, spreading his hands. "Well, there was no harm asking, was there?" he said. "I thought there might be something you could do to help us."

"There is nothing," Michael said, getting to his feet. "There is nothing I can do, except to say, if anyone asks me, that I know nothing at all about a man named Nathan Rosenblum."

"Myerson. Nathan Myerson."

"The name is *Rosenblum*. The name of the man I remember discussing with you in your office today is Nathan Rosenblum. If I'm asked if we discussed a man named Myerson at this meeting today, I'll say no, it was Rosenblum. Do you understand? I'm doing this for your sake, Myerson, and for your daughter's sake."

"Mimi could benefit, greatly, in the long run, if this were done."

"I think I'll be the judge of that," he said.

In East Orange that afternoon, she had not noticed anything particularly different about him, except that he seemed to be talking unusually rapidly. They were walking around the grounds (or what one day would be the grounds) of his new house, but the grounds that day were not much more than mounds of excavated earth and rock, scattered with pieces of heavy building equipment.

"This will be a flagstone patio," he said, "leading off the glassed-in garden room. The pool goes here, and over there will be the tennis court. I may put in two tennis courts; I haven't decided yet. My landscape guy, Tommy Church, is pushing for two, and what the heck? There's plenty of room. There's five-acre zoning here, and I have fifteen. The courts can be lighted, because there are no neighbors within sight of this to complain. Tennis courts should be lined up north-south, did you know that? So the sun never gets in the players' eyes. The things a guy learns when he gets rich . . . Amazing. . . .

"Over here I'm going to put a greenhouse. Not a humongous greenhouse, just a fair-sized one to grow fresh flowers for the house. This whole hillside is going to be terraced, with fieldstone retaining walls, all the way down to the brook, and of course all this will be planted. And look at the view, kiddo! All of downtown Manhattan in my backyard, from the tip of the Battery—look! —up to and including the Empire State Building. And see over there, through the trees, that green shape? The Statue of Liberty! Those trees are coming down, so there'll be a better view of her. You should see it at night, the view. . . ."

Inside the house, which had been roofed over, the partitions between the rooms were still marked by bare upright studs and lintels, and they picked their way across bare floors scattered with sawdust and carpenters' nails.

"A piano would look lovely in that corner," she said.

"Hey! Great idea! Not that I can play a note. The room's big enough—forty by fifty. Off this hall, here, goes a powder room, and down the hall, there, will be my study. Here's the dining room. . . . Think the kitchen's big enough? And talk about organized. If you think you organized my kitchen in the city, this one's *really* going to be organized. There's going to be storage for everything. This will be for a walk-in freezer. In the center goes the appliance island: plenty of counter space, an eight-burner range, two double ovens, plus a microwave. Dishwasher . . . double sinks. Here," he says, leading them along, "is the butler's pantry. Hey, get me! I don't have a butler yet, but I've got a butler's pantry! In here: laundry room. Washer, dryer, lots more linen storage. Ceramic tile floor."

"A butler to polish your George the First silver every day. . . ."

In just ten years, he would declare this house too small for him and would be building an even larger one.

"You haven't said how your meeting went with my father this afternoon," she said, when they finished the tour.

"Not good," he said, avoiding her eyes. "He wouldn't let me look at his balance sheet. That's his right, of course. But without seeing that, there's nothing I can tell him."

"Oh," she said, trying to hide her disappointment. "Well, thanks for trying, anyway, Michael."

"Know something?" he said. "It was pretty funny. He didn't even remember me."

They moved outside again, where rutted, muddy tracks marked where his driveway would curve in, between tall stands of birches, from the street beyond. "Four-car garage," he gestured. "Heated, of course."

"It's going to be a beautiful house, Michael," she said. "It ought to have a woman for you to share it with."

He said nothing.

"Could it be me, Michael?"

His look darkened, and he tossed the sandy lock of hair back from his forehead. Finally, he said, "Sit down a minute, Mimi." He indicated a pair of carpenter's sawhorses. "There's something I've got to tell you."

They sat, and he said, "It can't be, Mimi, and for a couple of reasons. To begin with, I'm crazy about you. I think you know that. I have been since I first met you, and I probably always will be, but that's not really what I want to say. What I want to say is that you've made your choice of husbands, and I think you made the right one. How old are you now, Mimi? Twenty-two? You've got your whole life ahead of you, and the world's a beautiful place, and there are a whole lot of wonderful and beautiful things and places in it, and you wouldn't want to spend the rest of your life with a guy like me. Don't interrupt. Listen to what I say. Me? I'm all over the place—I'm here and there, one place to the next. Even with this house, I know I'll never settle down anywhere for very long. It's not me. I'm too restless, too ambitious. I'm not solid, Mimi. Your husband's solid. I need a woman who'll take care of me, pick up after me. You need a man who'll take care of you. That's the man you married. You knew what you were doing, and you did it.

"And let me tell you something else, kiddo. I'm Jewish, and you're Jewish, but there's a difference, and your grandpa saw that. Your husband's a goy, and that's important for someone like you. He can take you places and show you things that I never could. I'm not ashamed of being a Jew, but I'll tell you, Mimi, in this world we live in, being a goy is better. That's just a fact of life, and anybody with any sense admits that. I mean, you're blond but they're blonder. If life's a crapshoot, the goyim have the better odds. If life's a poker party, the goyim hold the higher hands—that's why the guy you married is a better choice than me. What's more, the guy has class and he has style—like you do, which is why you need a guy with class and style. Me? I have no style, and I have no class. I'm just a schlepper—an honest schlepper, maybe, but a schlepper just the same. The guy you married will give you a beautiful life, Mimi. I don't want you to schlep through life with me. An old New England family, it said in the paper. He can give you that; that's class on top of class. I can't give you that. Now, listen very carefully, because I'm going to tell you what I want you to do. I want you to call him at the Harvard Club—"

"How did you know he'd moved to the Harvard Club?"

"We live in a small town, Mimi. New York is a village. Everybody who's anybody knows where everybody else who's anybody is living. Call him at the Harvard Club, and tell him you're sorry about whatever you said or did that made him move out on you. Ask him to forgive you—I mean, *beg* him to forgive you. Tell him you love him, tell him you want him back, beg him to come home—I mean, get down on your knees and beg him! Because I'll tell you something else about this guy I've never met: he's *proud*. They all are, the goyim. I mean, I'm proud to be who I am, but he's prouder to be who he is. I want you to deliver a real performance, Mimi, appealing to his pride, his honor, his dignity, his sense of duty. Tell him you need him back because you can't live without him. He'll come back because, believe it or not, I know him very well, this guy I've never met. Because I know he loves you. If he didn't love you, if you hadn't hurt his pride, he wouldn't have moved to the Harvard Club. He'd have moved back to Boston.

"I want you to do this for me, kiddo. If you love me at all, you'll do it. If you want me to have any more respect for you, you'll do it, because I know it's the right thing, the only right thing, for you to do. You see, you deserve a guy who belongs to the Harvard Club—not me. Oh, kiddo, kiddo, it's so hard to say good-bye." She saw there were tears in his eyes.

Sitting outside his unfinished mansion, in the ragged ruins of his unfinished garden, Mimi's own eyes focused on banal objects—an idle Bobcat tractor standing ready to move more earth to shape his driveway, a pile of slate that would one day become a terrace, a stack of two-by-fours—and for a moment her own life seemed as broken and surreal as that broken and unfinished, almost lunar, landscape. She thought: How can I have let myself be hurt this way again? And by him. Again. Squeezing her eyes shut and making fists of her hands, she offered up to God, if there was a God, a great crimson promise and a prayer: *Dear God, if there is a God, I promise that as long as I live I'll never let myself be hurt this way again.*

Then she stood up. "We'd better get back," she said, patting smooth the creases in her denim skirt.

They drove back to the city in his car that afternoon, saying nothing. There seemed to be nothing more to say.

Was that me? She asks herself now. Was that naive girl me, nearly twenty-seven years ago? We can never go back to that place again, that much is certain. The past is too recent, too new, and it is also too long ago. We cannot remake ended things. She and Brad had been married less than two years then, and perhaps Michael had been right, it was too soon to end that. "Think it through," he had said, "you're not a child anymore." Yes, she had been angry, and hurt, and yes, she had thought: I will show him. I will show him that I can make this marriage work, and someday he will come back and be sorry that he did what he did then. And now he has, and he wants me again. I think. Or so he says. But he can never hurt me that way again.

She and Brad had settled on their wedding date: October 10, 1958. Her mother had come into her room, looking anxious. "Have you checked the calendar?" her mother asked.

"The calendar?"

"Yes, the calendar. Are you sure the date is . . . all right?"

"Of course it's all right. It's a Friday, and it works out well for both of us."

"But, I mean, it's still four months away. Have you checked your calendar, to figure everything out?"

"To figure *what* out, Mother?"

"Oh, Mimi. I'm talking about your *calendar.* You know what I mean. Your wedding night—he'll want to—you should check your calendar. To be sure the date's all right."

"The date is fine, Mother," she said.

That was the closest her mother had ever come to discussing love with her, or marriage, or the facts of life.

Is it possible, she had asked herself as they drove back to New York that afternoon, to be in love with one person as easily as with another? All she knew was that it was important, desperately important, for a woman to love someone, for a woman to be in love. Love was the prize, it was what one lived for, just to be in love. Without love, life had no meaning, no message. All her friends at Miss Hall's School had told her that. Then was it possible to be in love with two people at the same time? she asked herself. Perhaps, she had answered. Perhaps. Why not?

That, she thinks now, is how young I was.

It was two months after Brad moved back into their apartment that she discovered she was pregnant. "This cements us," he said.

24

NOW TELL ME what you think, Badger," Mimi says as she, her son, and Mark Segal, her advertising director, gather in her office. "Should we schedule our stockholders' meeting before or after the launch party on the sixteenth?" The launch party, scheduled for September 17, is now just ten days away.

"After. Definitely," Badger says. "All seven of the Leo cousins have been invited to the Pierre. Six have already accepted, and we're sending limos for all of them. If the seventh accepts, we'll be batting a thousand. We're going to give them the real red-carpet treatment at the party. They'll meet all the celebs—did I tell you Brooke Astor's accepted? So have Barbara Walters, and what's-his-name, her husband—"

"I think we've got a good chance at Liz Taylor, too," Mark Segal interjects. "I talked to her press agent this morning and told him it would be nice if she showed up, 'to sniff out the competition.' He liked the idea. Even if she doesn't like the fragrance, there'd be nice ink in it for us: 'Liz turns up nose at new Mireille scent.' 'The scent Liz Taylor loves to hate.' That sort of thing."

"Yes," Badger continues. "The cousins will meet all these people. It's going to be a real New York razzle-dazzle party, and all for sweet charity. And what classier beneficiary is there than the New York Public Library? Most of these cousins seem to lead kind of quiet lives, and they're going to be impressed by what they see on the seventeenth. They're also going to meet all of us, and they're going to be impressed by us—and the kind of company we run, and the kind of company they own. Then, on the heels of the whammo launch party, we'll call the stockholders' meeting. If the cousins come to that—and I'm betting they will—they'll be coming on a launch-party high."

"Of course," Mimi says carefully, "you're assuming that this launch is going to be a success. What if it fails?"

"What?" Badger cries. "You're thinking *failure?* Aren't we all thinking success right now? It's too late to think about failure now. Too much time and money have been committed."

"Badger's right," Mark says. "We've all got to try to think success."

"Two little words always come back to haunt me," Mimi says. *"Candied Apple.* It could happen again. We all know that."

"Candied Apple was long ago, and in another part of the forest. That was B.M."

"B.M.?"

"Before Mimi."

"Here's the first of the press releases that will go out about the party tomorrow," Mark says, and he hands out copies of the release to each of them.

They read:

NEWS FROM: THE MIRAY CORPORATION
666 Fifth Avenue
New York, N.Y. 10020

FOR IMMEDIATE RELEASE

For Further Information
Contact: Mark Segal
(212) 555-8919

LIBRARY GALA TO LAUNCH NEW MIREILLE FRAGRANCE

Twelve hundred notables from the worlds of business, fashion, entertainment, and society will gather in the Ballroom of New York's Hotel Pierre on Thursday evening, September 17, to sip champagne and nibble caviar for the launching of Miray's exciting new fragrance—"Mireille."

The gala evening, which has been completely underwritten by the Miray Corporation, will benefit the New York Public Library's New Books Fund.

Guests who have already accepted invitations to the event include Mrs. Vincent Astor, Mr. and Mrs. William F. Buckley, Diana Vreeland,

Steve Martin, Victoria Principal, Mr. and Mrs. Robert Redford, Si and Victoria Newhouse, Ricky and Ralph Lauren, Georges and Lois de Menil, Geraldine Stutz, Mr. and Mrs. Donald J. Trump, Barbara Walters and Merv Adelson, Dustin Hoffman, Michael Horowitz . . .

"Michael Horowitz is coming to the party?" Mimi says.

"He's bought two thousand-dollar tickets," Mark says.

"Badger? What do you think?"

"We can't really stop him from coming, can we? We can't turn down money for the library."

"I suppose not. But still . . . I don't like it."

They read on.

Elizabeth Taylor has also indicated that she may attend the "Mireille" gala "to sniff out the competition." Miss Taylor has recently been on national tour to promote a fragrance entry of her own.

"Should we mention the name of Elizabeth's fragrance?" Mimi asks.

"Hell, no. Why give her product a plug?"

Also attending will be various members of the Myerson family, who have been associated with the Miray cosmetics company for three generations. Hosting the black-tie evening will be the legendary Mireille "Mimi" Myerson, President and CEO of Miray, and her husband, Wall Street attorney Bradford Moore. . . .

"Do I have to be legendary?" Mimi says.

"I like *legendary*," Mark says.

"Brad may not be able to make the party."

"Really?" Badger says. "Why not?"

"You may have to be my co-host, Badger."

"Well, it doesn't really matter," Mark says. "Now here's release number two."

MYSTERY "SCARFACE" MODEL TO APPEAR
AT MIREILLE GALA

"Really?" Mimi says. "I thought the mystery was that he *wasn't* going to appear."

"Read on, please," Mark says.

Rumors have been circulating in the canyons of Madison Avenue, and in the beauty and fashion circles along Fifth and Seventh, concerning the identity of the handsome blond male model who will be used in print and television advertising for "Mireille," the exciting new fragrance being launched by the Miray Corporation later this month.

"Mireille" ads and commercials will feature the "Mireille Couple," promoting both "Mireille," the fragrance for women, and "Mireille for Men," a companion men's cologne. The "Mireille Woman" will be portrayed by the beauteous raven-haired model, 19-year-old Sherrill Shearson. But the identity of the male model remains a secret and has become something of a mystery that has kept industry insiders, who have managed to sneak previews of the campaign, guessing.

"He looks awfully familiar to me," says Jessica Rayford, casting director for Young & Rubicam, "and I have a feeling we've even used him here. But then there's this disfiguring, but kind of fascinating, scar across his cheek, his left cheek, that I don't recognize ever seeing on any model before."

The question admen and beauty bigwigs are asking: Is this a model with a real scar? Or is the "scar" merely the clever creation of Miray, the cosmetics giant? Is it real . . . or is it makeup? Does he . . . or doesn't he?

At the launching gala for "Mireille," to be held September 17 at New York's Hotel Pierre, guests will be introduced to the real "Mireille Man." Will the real "Mireille Man" please stand up? He will at the Miray gala, which benefits the New York Public Library's New Books Fund.

"Oh," Mimi says. "I think that's something of a letdown. I think I'd like it better if he didn't appear. Let's keep them guessing for a few more weeks —at least until the commercials have saturated. Don't you think so, Mark?"

"Now wait a minute," he says. "Just hold on. Let me set the stage for you a bit, okay? Okay: we're at the Pierre on the seventeenth. The guests start arriving at around seven. Cocktails are being served, and Glorious Food is doing their bit. The music is soft but lively, Bobby Short is doing his bit with Porter and Coward. Everybody is being sampled with Mireille, and the scent of Mireille is wafting . . . wafting"—he makes a wafting gesture with his hand—"while *le tout* New York is circulating and telling each other how *mahvelous* they look, the scent of Mireille is wafting through the air. At eight o'clock, the house lights dim. On the stage, the curtains part, and the giant screen comes down, and we air the first three thirty-second commercials, one, two, and three. Pause for thunderous applause. The house lights come up a bit, and that's the cue for the legendary Mimi Myerson—looking legendary, I hope—to make her entrance from the wings. 'Ladies and gentlemen,' she says, 'friends and competitors alike, may I present . . . the Mireille Woman!' Sherrill steps out from the wings, does a turn or two, and takes a bow. Applause, and exit smiling. 'And the Mireille Man,' Mimi says. The house lights drop altogether, and there's just a single spot left on the act curtain. Now, excuse me; I have to get into costume."

He turns his back to them, reaches for something in his briefcase, and places something on his face. Then he turns and stands. He is wearing an enameled white plastic mask, with holes cut out for eyes, and the contour of the mask extends downward in an irregular line across the left side of his face.

"My God!" Mimi cries. "*What is it?*"

"I admit I'm not as good-looking as pretty-boy Gordon," he says. "And the red beard doesn't do much for the outfit."

"But what in the world . . . ?"

"It's Michael Crawford's mask from *Phantom of the Opera.* We'll play *Phantom* theme music while our masked Dirk Gordon takes his bow."

"Oh, I love it, Mark!" Mimi exclaims. She jumps from her chair and runs to him and kisses him, smack on the acrylic mask.

"Bravo, Mark!" Badger says, pumping his hand at the same time.

"The crowd at the Pierre will go wild," Mark Segal says. "With frustration. Needless to say, the *Phantom* people are nuts for the idea."

Five full business days have gone by since Nonie and Edwee had their meeting with John Marion and Philippe de Montebello, and Nonie has heard nothing from her brother. She has tried repeatedly to call him, but all she has been able to reach is Tonio, his houseboy, who tells her that her brother is unable to come to the phone. Now she is trying a different tack. She got through to Gloria and suggested that the two of them "have a little girlie lunch" today. "It's time we got to know each other better, darling," she said. And, fortunately, Jacques, the captain, has seated them in the front room of La Grenouille, not in the back, because the people from *Women's Wear* keep track of who sits where. One way or another, Nonie intends to find out exactly what is going on.

"And how *is* Edwee?" Nonie asks, after they have ordered their drinks—a Perrier for Nonie and a Tanqueray (Gloria pronounces it Tan-QUARE-y) on the rocks for Gloria. "I've tried to call him several times, and all I get is that Jap houseboy of his."

"Actually, Tonio's not a Jap," Gloria says. "He's from the Philippines."

"It's the same thing, darling."

"Is it?" Gloria asks innocently. "I didn't know Japan was in the Philippines. Anyway, Edwee asked me to apologize. He's just felt so *punk* lately. He's just felt too punk to talk on the phone. He asked me to tell you that he'll give you a call in a few days, as soon as he's feeling a little better."

"I see," Nonie says. And then, "Oh, yes, I remember. He told me. Morning sickness."

"But he also feels sick in the afternoon. He really does."

"Edwee told me your little secret, darling."

"*Did* he?" Gloria asks, wide-eyed. "Did he *really?* He told me not to tell a living *soul,* especially—but then, if he's already told you, then I guess it's all right for us to talk about it, Nonie."

"I'm terribly excited for you, dear."

"Well, yes," Gloria giggles. "So am I, actually. It will be a whole new experience for me."

"Just think: there's going to be a little stranger."

"Actually, I'm very good with strangers," Gloria says. "I'm usually considered very good at making friends."

"I'm sure you are," Nonie says, not exactly sure she knows what Gloria means by this. Their drinks have arrived, and Nonie lifts her glass and says, "Cheers—congratulations to you both."

"But I'm going to have to go out and get a lot of new clothes for it," Gloria says. "That's what's thrown me for a loop."

"Well, friends have told me that during the first few months, you can usually get by if you have the seams on your regular dresses eased a bit."

"But I don't intend to gain any *weight,*" Gloria says.

"Oh, but you will, dear. You will. It's inevitable."

"Well, Edwee and I do eat out a lot. And there are a lot of good restaurants. So maybe I will. But I hope not."

"Yes. You should watch your diet very carefully."

"Oh, I *know.* But the thing is—the clothes. I've got to get a lot of summery-type things. All I've got now is a lot of New Yorky-type things."

"Summery things?" Nonie counts on her fingers. "Well, let's see. This is September. I suppose that could bring you up to June. When is all this going to happen, anyway?"

"Oh, any *day* now. Maybe next week."

"Next *week?* Surely you're not—"

"That's why I've got so much to do! After I leave you, I've got to go out and shop and shop and shop. I just hope they speak some English there."

"Where, in the stores?" But suddenly Nonie realizes that she and Gloria must be talking about two different things. She reaches for her glass. "My dear, what exactly are you talking about?"

"Edwee's and my little secret. Belize."

"Belize?"

"It's the most darling little tropical country, just off South America. We're going to have the sweetest little house there, right on the beach."

"I see," Nonie says. "You're taking a trip."

"I'm so excited, Nonie. I've never been outside the United States of America."

Nonie takes a deep breath. "And how long do you plan to be gone?" she asks.

"Oh, permanently. Didn't Edwee tell you that? We're moving there permanently. That's what's so—"

"I see," Nonie says, studying the little bubbles rising in her glass. "Edwee didn't tell me . . . the exact purpose of this move."

"It's his health," Gloria says. "Edwee's doctor's told him that he'll do much better in a tropical climate."

"There's never been anything wrong with my brother's health!"

"His doctors say—but, anyway, all he's waiting for is a certain letter, some sort of business he's involved in, and then, off we go! You'll come and visit us there, I hope."

"Edwee told me you were pregnant."

Gloria giggles again. "Oh, that turned out to be a false alarm. But we're still trying. Edwee really wants a son. He says we need a son to carry on the Myerson name."

"So," Nonie says. "It's Belize." She grips the stem of her glass but is afraid that her hand will tremble so violently that she will be unable to lift it to her lips. She looks at her watch. Then she says quickly, "Look, Gloria, do you mind if we make this just a drink, and not for lunch? I just remembered that I promised a friend I'd meet her plane at La Guardia at one-thirty, and it's quarter of. And you've got all your shopping to do. Do you mind terribly, darling?" She calls out to a passing waiter. "Check, please!"

Edwee is in fine spirits this morning. There is a faint, crisp scent of autumn in the air, but the sun is warm and the breeze is as light as Edwee's step, ruffling his long silver hair—in an attractive, youthful fashion, he thinks, as he glances at his image in the shop windows along Madison Avenue as he walks uptown, and adjusts the fresh red carnation in his buttonhole. God is in his heaven, Edwee thinks, and all's right with the world. This morning's letter from Philippe de Montebello had contained everything he could have asked for—well, almost everything. "Dear Mr. Myerson," it began.

> *I visited your mother on Thursday afternoon with four members of my curatorial staff, at least two of whom are considered experts on the Spanish painters of Goya's period. I must tell you that both my Goya experts are convinced that your mother's portrait of the Duchess of Osuna is authentic, and that the curious "question mark" you noted following Berenson's signature was added later, and in another hand.*

There had been a heart-stopping moment when Edwee read this sentence, but then he read on.

> *On the other hand, in light of your sister's account of her meeting with M. Berenson at his villa several years after your mother acquired the painting, and the fact that at least someone has questioned the authenticity of the painting, we feel that the position of the Museum must be to decline your mother's most generous offer. We hope that this will not disappoint your mother or yourself.*

Disappoint! Edwee thinks. Ho-ho! Ha-ha!

> *Needless to say, out of consideration for your mother and her advanced age and certain infirmities, I do not plan to tell her the precise reasons why we are declining her gift, since the reasons might cause her undue distress. Rather, I am writing her separately today merely to say that, while we deeply appreciate her offer, the Museum feels that it already has a sufficient representation of Goya's work, and that due to such considerations as insurance costs, shortage of hanging space, etc., we are respectfully declining her offer.*

> *Yours sincerely,*
> *Philippe de Montebello*

His mother, when he had phoned her this morning, had also seemed in an unusually chipper and cheerful mood and surprisingly willing to see him when he told her he had something he wanted to discuss with her. "Do come by, Edwee," his mother said brightly. "I'd love to see you. It's been a coon's age. I'll be right here all morning."

"Good morning, Patrick!" he said to the doorman as Patrick held the door open for him.

"Good morning, sir."

"Fine day, isn't it?"

"Yes, sir!"

"Good morning, George," he said as he passed the front desk.

"Good morning, Mr. Myerson. Your mother's expecting you."

All the way up to the twentieth floor, Edwee whistled a little tuneless tune.

"Come in, Edwee!" his mother called when he rang the bell. "The door's off the latch." As he opened the door to her apartment, the sheer glass curtains against her open windows billowed into the room from the westerly breeze, billowed like white sails on an open sea, billowed and flapped and gusted into the sitting room where she has been sitting, waiting for him, wearing her pearls.

"It is you, isn't it, Edwee?" she says.

"Yes, *M-M-M-Maman.*"

"Come in, come in."

Immediately, Itty-Bitty begins barking shrilly, crouching, her rear in the air, forepaws extended, barking, growling, snarling at him. But the minute Edwee steps from his mother's entrance foyer into her sitting room, he stops in his tracks. "Where is it?" he gasps.

"Where's what, dear?"

"The Goya! *Where is it?*"

"What Goya, dear?"

"There!" he screams, pointing at the empty wall, at the pale rectangle against the yellower wall, where it had hung. "It was right there! It hung right there! It's always been there! What have you done with it, Mother?"

"Well, you know I can't see," his mother says. "So I don't know what you're talking about, Edwee."

"What have you done with your Goya, Mother?"

"You see, you don't stammer when you don't want to," she says. "Sit down, Edwee. Would you like a cup of tea?"

"God damn it, Mother—what have you done with your Goya?"

"Don't swear, Edwee. It's rude. What are you talking about?"

"Your *Goya!* Where is it?"

"Goya?" she says thoughtfully. "You mean the painter, Goya? I've never owned any Goya, Edwee. I considered buying one years ago, but I changed my mind. Mr. Montecarlo, from the museum, was here the other day. He admired my Monet, my Cézanne, my little Renoir still life, my Degas dancers—but he never mentioned any Goya."

"You're lying, Mother! Don't try to pull that stuff on me! It was right *there!*"

"Well, whatever used to be there must be still there, because nothing's been moved out of this apartment since I moved in, so you must be thinking of something else, because I've never had any Goya. You must be thinking of something else."

"I am *not* thinking of something else!"

"The little Renoir still life maybe? As you know, I'm old, and you know I can't see."

"I think you *can* see!" he says. "And you know exactly what I'm talking about! Where is it, you bitch?"

His mother rises from the sofa to her full height and, touching her pearls, faces him. "If you've come here to be rude and nasty to me, Edwee," she says, "then I don't want to talk to you anymore. You can just go." She turns quickly and walks to her bedroom door, opens it, and closes it behind her with a small slam. He hears the bolt in the lock.

He runs to the door and begins pounding on it with his fists. "What have you done with it?" he screams. "What have you done with my Goya? What have you done with it, you stupid, senile, selfish, disgusting old bitch! I'm going to put you in a nursing home!"

"Get out of here, Edwee," he hears from behind the door. "Get out of here before I call Security."

He continues banging on the panel of the door. "Bitch! Bitch! Horrible old bitch that I hate!"

"I'm going to call Security."

He leans against the door. Near him, on the floor, Itty-Bitty still crouches, barking noisily, snarling, growling. Edwee steps toward her, and the little dog shies away, snarling and snapping angrily, but Edwee moves faster and seizes the little dog by its collar and its tail. While the little dog screeches and struggles in his grip, trying to bite him, Edwee strides to the open window and flings the dog out. The sheer glass curtains billow outward now, outward into the bright New York morning.

In the sudden silence that follows, Edwee Myerson leaves quickly.

He is well out of the apartment, well out of the Carlyle, when, perhaps ten minutes later, George from the front desk telephones Granny Flo Myerson to tell her the dreadful news.

Part Four

A HOMECOMING

25

I FINALLY HAD A CHANCE to speak to your uncle Edwee today," Brad says.

"Oh?" she says. She has momentarily forgotten what it was that he wanted to speak to Edwee about. They are sitting in the living room of the apartment at 1107 Fifth Avenue, having their customary before-dinner cocktail. On late-summer evenings such as this, Mimi likes to use as little artificial light in this room as possible, letting the sunset colors, reflected from the lake, refracted by the glass prisms, and echoed by the colors in the abstract paintings (the Morris Louis, the Youngerman, the Jasper Johns) supply the only flashes of color in the otherwise all-white room, adding to the room's feeling of floating in space above the park. "I forget," she says. "What was it you . . . ?"

"About this apparent interest in your male model—what's his name?"

"Dirk Gordon. Oh, yes."

"I'm a little worried about Uncle Edwee, Mimi."

"Really? Why?"

"Well, Edwee's never been exactly the most . . . stable person, has he? And when I talked with him today, I actually wondered if he was losing his mind."

"Seriously, Brad?"

"He was quite irrational—hysterical, almost. He went on and on about Granny Flo's having hidden a painting from him. Her Goya. He says she's taken it off the wall and is hiding it somewhere . . . from him."

"She's giving that painting to the Met. That's probably where it is. They've already collected it."

"No. He says he's had a letter from the museum, and he says that they don't want it. He says your grandmother had a letter to the same effect."

"That's strange. I thought they'd kill to get that painting."

"Anyway, now it's disappeared. And he wants us—or you, specifically—to get it back. For him. He kept referring to it as 'my Goya.' "

"That's ridiculous. It's always been Granny's Goya. Everybody knows that."

"And now you're supposed to find out where it is, and get it back."

"Well, I certainly have more important things on my mind right now than worrying about where Granny's Goya is."

"I told him that. That was when he really became irrational. That was when he began to threaten."

"Threaten? Threaten what?"

"I mentioned your male model. Edwee has—or at least *claims* he has—a pornographic videotape, featuring your model, Mr. Gordon. He says it could be potentially embarrassing to your Mireille campaign if he were to release it."

Mimi is silent for a moment. Then she says, "I see. Thank you, Uncle Edwee. I needed this."

"Could it be? Embarrassing to you?"

"Well," she says, "they say Joan Crawford made porno films before she became a star. They say they're collectors' items now. She lived it down. Vanessa Williams posed in the nude for Bob Guccione. She lost her title, but she bounced back. But right now . . . well, the timing couldn't be much worse, could it? If he's telling the truth. What do you think I should do, Brad? Oh, god damn you, Edwee!"

"Well," he says, "I've been thinking about it. First, there's the possibility that he's lying. There's the possibility that he's gone completely off his rocker. But I think we should face the possibility that he's got something. There are things we could do, legal steps we could take. We could bring in the FBI—this, after all, is a blackmail threat. But that could generate publicity. It could also take time. You don't have a lot of time before your campaign breaks—"

"A week and a half."

"We could demand to see the alleged tape. Or we could help him find where the damned Goya is—which is what he wants. Or we could simply call his bluff, and do nothing."

"Which do you think?"

"I told him that I refused to take his threat seriously unless I could see the tape."

"And what did he say to that?"

"He hung up on me."

"You see? I think he's bluffing."

"Perhaps. We'll see."

They sit in silence for a while as the room grows darker. Mimi reaches out and switches on a lamp. "Well, thank you, darling, for trying to help out with this," she says at last. "Thank you for putting up with this . . . this family of thieves and varlets that I seem to have. The Magnificent Myersons! We're quite a bunch, aren't we?"

"Oh, it's been worth it," he says with a small smile.

"Has it? Has it really, darling?" In the distance, the telephone rings, and presently Felix appears at the door.

"Mr. Michael Horowitz for you, ma'am."

"Oh, yes. I need to talk to him." She rises and steps into the library to take the call.

"Michael," she says. "Thank you for calling back."

"Hi, kiddo. Sorry to call you at home, but your message said it was important."

"It is," she says. "I'm calling to ask you a favor, Michael."

"You sound in a little better mood than you were in the last time I saw you."

"Actually, I'm not."

"Then shoot. What's the favor?"

"I see you've bought tickets to my launch benefit."

"That's right."

"May I ask why?"

"It sounded like a good party," he says. "And it's for a good cause."

"Is that all? Michael, please be honest with me. Let's be honest with each other. We used to be honest with each other. I know you've been buying up our stock. I know you've approached certain cousins of mine and offered to buy up their stock. You're trying a takeover, aren't you? There's already been talk in the industry about something happening at Miray. People have noticed the way our stock's been reacting. They're asking questions. They know something's behind it. It won't be long before the financial press gets wind of this, and when that happens there won't be anything that you or I can say or do about what they print. But do me a favor, Michael. At least give me a chance to make a counterproposal to my stockholders before you make your announcement. I mean, there used to be a certain amount of ethics and etiquette in business, didn't there? If we're going to fight, let's fight like ladies and gentlemen."

"Or like the lovers we used to be," he says.

"Please, Michael. I'm quite serious."

"You keep talking takeover, Mimi. I told you before: I'm buying Miray for my portfolio because I think it's a good company. I'm also buying International Harvester for the same reason. If that's made your stock go up, well, that's good for me, and it's good for you, too, isn't it?"

"Michael, I just don't believe you. Please be honest. I mean, you have every right to want to take over my company. I respect that right, it's a fact of life in today's marketplace. And I have every right to do what I can to stop you. But, please, don't use my party as some kind of forum to announce your intentions. I would consider that a very unkind and very unfair thing to do."

"I was planning to come to that party as a private individual," he says, sounding hurt. "Purely as a private individual. I wasn't planning to make any announcement there."

"Are you sure? Is that a promise? Because the focus of this party has got to be my new perfume—and my new ad campaign. And the library. That's why I'm giving it. The focus can't be turned to Michael Horowitz and his plans, whatever they are."

"Look," he says, "you're giving this party. You're the hostess. If my hostess doesn't want me at a party, I won't be there. That's all there is to it. I'll give my tickets to somebody else."

"Even your *presence* at the party could add fuel to the rumors, Michael. The press will be there. They could ask you questions."

"Don't you think I know how to handle the press? Anyway, I just told you. If you don't want me, I won't be there. I don't go to parties where I'm not wanted. I've just been disinvited, kiddo."

"I can't *prevent* you from going, Michael. It's just that I want everything to be perfect on the seventeenth."

"And I want everything to be perfect *for* you. But, frankly, Mimi, you disappoint me."

"Why?"

"Did you really think I'd use your party to make some kind of grandstand play, and steal your thunder? Did you really think I'd jump up on the stage, grab the microphone, and say, 'Ladies and gentlemen, you're looking at the next president of Miray'? Because if you thought I'd do a thing like that to you, you don't understand me very well, or know me very well at all, and that makes me kind of sad."

"But Michael, it's just that—"

"I'd never rain on your parade, Mimi. I thought you knew that. Frankly, the real reason I wanted to come was because I thought it would be fun to see you at *work*. That was the only reason, Mimi. Remember, years ago, I said I thought that you were the one who should run that company? I always sort of thought that my suggestion might have had something to do with what you're doing now, and the kind of woman you've become. Anyway, that's what I liked to think. And I just thought it would be kind of fun to watch you in action. That's all it was. Honest."

"But you see—"

"Haven't I always tried to help you and your family out? Have you forgotten all of that? I've always thought I had your best interests at heart. Even when it was only a broken skate lace."

What he is doing, she thinks, is what is known in the business as "credentialing himself"—reminding her of past services rendered and future favors owed.

"Then what about Grandpa's diaries?" she says. "Why are you holding on to them? Isn't it to put some kind of pressure on me?"

There is an audible sigh on the other end of the line. "Those damn diaries," he says. "Why would I want them? To hurt you? No. To prevent you from being hurt by some not very pretty things you'll find in them. I told you that. If you want them so badly, you'll have them. I'll have them wrapped and shipped over to your office in the morning."

"Well, in that case, Michael—"

"If there's one thing I am, it's a man of my word. I just didn't know you had such a low opinion of me, Mimi. That's what hurts."

"In that case, please come to the party, Michael. I apologize for what I thought."

"No, you've pretty much taken all the fun out of it for me, kiddo."

"Please. Please, I want you to come."

"No, no. . . ."

"Oh, please. I'm sorry." She realizes she is completely reversing herself. "Please come to the party."

"That you'd think that I'd get up on the stage, and—"

"I *don't* think that now."

"Well, I'll think about it."

"Please."

"You think I'm a really rotten person, don't you?"

"No, I don't! Please be there."

"I'll think about it," he says again. "You kind of hurt me just now."

She replaces the receiver in its cradle, wondering: Have I been manipulated? Has he bamboozled me again?

In the living room, she finds Brad standing at a window, looking out, one hand deep in his trousers pocket, the other holding his cocktail glass, and for a moment she is tempted to go to him, hook her hand into the space between his sleeve and jacket, and stand there with him for a moment, watching the gathering darkness and the lights coming up on the West Side. But something about his solitary stance deters her, and instead she sits in one of the twin sofas under the lamplight.

"What did Horowitz want?"

There is an unpleasant inflection, she thinks, in the way he pronounces the word "Horowitz," almost making it "Horrorwitz," as she has heard Michael's detractors pronounce his name before.

"The thing is, he can actually be very sweet," she says. "There's a kind of little-boy quality about him that's kind of endearing—a guilelessness. He's very persuasive."

"That's why he's a good salesman. What did your Granny Flo say about him? That he could sell umbrellas in the Gobi Desert? The guy could sell condoms on the front steps of the Vatican."

Condoms, she thinks. *"Like one of your used condoms."* She says, "Do you realize how much I've got at stake in this launch party, Brad?"

"A lot, I'm sure. A lot."

"Fifty million dollars."

"That's a lot."

"The party's on the seventeenth, Brad. That's next Thursday. Will you be coming?"

"I'm going to try."

"A funny thing happened in my office the other day. We were going over the plans for the party, and Mark Segal, our ad director, was showing us some of the press releases he's prepared. In one of them, it says that you and I will be co-hosts for the evening. I mentioned that you might not be able to make it, and Mark said, 'Well, it doesn't matter.' I realize that sounds a little insensitive, but remember that all Mark thinks about is publicity. I just wanted to tell you that it *does* matter, Brad. It matters a great deal, to me. I want terribly to have you there."

"Well, I'm certainly going to try."

Then she says, "It's a woman who's been calling."

"A woman?"

"The person I told you about, who calls and then hangs up. I answered a call the other day, when you were in Minneapolis. I identified myself. There was a little gasp at the other end of the line. It was a woman's gasp. Then she hung up."

"I see."

"Do you have any idea who would be doing this to us, Brad?"

Still facing the window, he says, "Yes, I do."

He turns, but his face is in shadow, and she cannot read his expression. "Have you ever made a mistake, Mimi?" he asks her.

"Of course I have."

"Well, I made one about three months ago. I got involved with a woman. She's a secretary in the office of one of our clients. Her name is—"

"Please," she says quickly, "I don't want to know her name. Have you been having an affair with her, Brad?"

"I did. It was very brief, and I've tried telling her that it's over, but she's become very demanding. She wants me to marry her. She's been telephoning me at the office. She's telephoned me here. She's even come to the office. She's threatened to come here. The other day, she was waiting for me outside my building and tried to force her way into a taxi with me. Sometimes she sits on a bench across the street and watches this building. Actually, I was just looking out the window now to see if she was there again tonight."

"Is she?"

"No, thank God."

"Do you love her, Brad?"

"No. If I ever thought I did, I certainly don't now."

"Is she . . . pregnant?"

"She says she is. I'm sure she's lying. We always took . . . precautions. I'm positive she's lying."

"Still," Mimi says, trying to keep her composure, trying to keep her poise, even though she feels herself about to be blown away, "how very unpleasant for you, darling!"

"Yes." Then he says, "Look, Mimi. It was a mistake; I admit that. I've told her that. I've told her that I'm not going to marry her. I've told her I never want to see her again. I've told her I love my wife. I've told her I don't want a divorce—unless you want one, Mimi, now that you know about this. I've told her that if she can produce a letter from her doctor, certifying that she's pregnant, I'll pay for an abortion. She hasn't produced any such letter, which is why I'm sure she's lying. But I've told her that this is absolutely as far as I intend to go. Beyond that, she is out of my life as far as I'm concerned. But she still refuses to give up."

"I see," she says. She stands up quickly and runs her fingers through her hair. "I see that you've thought this whole thing through very carefully," she says. "You've covered every point in your usual thorough, lawyer's way. You've thought of everything—including a letter from her *doctor!* You've thought of everything, except how I might feel. That somehow didn't enter your head—how I might feel about this! And do you know how I feel? I feel like used goods, that's how I feel! I feel dirty and abused and used and damaged, but perhaps to convince you of how I feel I should get a letter from *my* doctor certifying that! I hate you."

"Have you ever thought about how I might feel?" he says quietly.

"How *you* might feel! *I* haven't been running off and cheating on you, and telling lies about where I had lunch—telling me you had your partners' lunch downtown, when I saw the two of you together at a table at Le Cirque! Do you think I'm *stupid?* I even found a letter from her, you know."

"A letter?"

"Electric blue stationery. Monogrammed *R.* With a lot of silly yellow daisies on the border. Sound familiar? It was in the pocket of a suit you were sending to the cleaner's. Do you think I haven't known what's been going on? 'You said you had an unhappy marriage,' she wrote. 'You told me you loved me.' But I suppose you thought you were handling things very cleverly —until she decided to put the screws on you, if you'll pardon the expression, when she decided that you might be getting a little tired of screwing her!"

"I admit I've tried to let her down as gently as possible."

"Oh, of *course!* We wouldn't want her to make a *scene,* would we? That wouldn't *do.* We wouldn't want her to make any sort of *fuss,* would we? Like a lawsuit, or a scandal, or publicity—because how would that look to the commission up in Albany that's considering you to fill out Senator Miller's term? Anything like that would put the kibosh on *that,* wouldn't it? Tut, tut. 'Senate Appointee Accused of Marital Infidelity.' That just would not do! That's all you thought about, that's all you cared about: covering your ass! You never thought about how I might feel at all!"

"I'm not talking about that," he says. "I'm talking about how I've felt for the past two years."

"Two *years?* I thought you said it started three months ago. Or was that another lie?"

"Two years—while I've been trying to have a marriage, and all you've thought about, or talked about, is a new perfume."

Felix appears at the doorway again. "Dinner is served, ma'am," he says.

"Excuse me," she says, "but I'm feeling a little grippy tonight. I'm going upstairs to bed. Mr. Moore will be dining alone tonight, Felix."

Felix nods, and lowers his eyes.

Upstairs in her bedroom, Mimi turns the key in her lock and flings herself, face forward, across her bed, dry-eyed. I am not crying, she thinks. I am not going to cry. She turns her head a little to one side, and lying still, the thoughts rush through her head. I made a scene, she thinks. I promised myself I would never make a scene, but then I went ahead and made one anyway. But what the hell. It was the rotten timing he chose to tell me this, even though I knew about it anyway. And I let him hurt me, even though I promised I would never let anyone hurt me that way again. I let him hurt me and, even worse, I let him know he hurt me. Yes, you picked a swell time to tell me this, you bastard. The words from a Kenny Rogers song flash by. *You picked a fine time to leave me, Lucille. Three hungry children and the crops in the field . . .* You picked a fine time to tell me, you heel. A fine time to tell me, schlemiel. Edwee and a pornographic videotape. Condoms. Abortions. Filth, trash, sluttish women, filth and more filth. Candied Apple, rotten apples, filth rotting maggoty in a warehouse cellar, Mother, Daddy, Me, Badger, a man with a false scar, and a man with foolish dimples and a smile, and a line that is probably also false and rotten to the core. What if I were to tell you that Badger is not your child, but his, that I'm sure of this now? What if I were to tell you that Badger is a bastard? In England, they call it a love child. But I must not think about these things, she tells herself.

I must think about the party, I must think about launching "Mireille" on the seventeenth, the fragrance that is on my throat and behind my earlobes and between my breasts and on my wrists right now, this lovely and intoxicating and exciting fragrance that bears my name, and the lovely and intoxicating and exciting party that is going to introduce "Mireille" to the world. That is all that matters now, the party. That is the single most important thing in my life right now, the party; the absolutely single most important thing in the entire world. It begins with a *P*. It is a party with a capital *P*, and a party is gaiety and laughter, champagne in silver coolers, caviar in ice-sculpted bowls, beautiful men and beautiful women in their most beautiful dresses, lipstick-red roses scattered across white tablecloths, a full-ounce bottle of "Mireille" at each place setting (Mark wanted five-ounce bottles, but I said "Too show-offy"), and waiters in lipstick-red mess jackets, especially dyed to match my "Brandy by Firelight," that wonderful amber-crimson shade, red-gold, and gold epaulettes on their shoulders, a party to end all parties, champagne at sunset, not a bad name for a nail shade. Beauty. That is my business: Beauty. Perfume.

And she thinks: Did I just think that? That the only thing that matters to me right now is a party? Beauty? Perfume?

At the party, she will decide. At the party, she will make her choice. If Brad doesn't come to her party, that will be a signal. If Michael comes, and behaves as sweetly as he has promised to behave, that will be her second signal. These signals, omens, will point the way. It will be a beautiful way.

With one eye, she sees one of the buttons on her bedside phone light up, indicating a ring. It lights again, and then a third time. Obviously, someone has been instructed not to answer. She watches the blinking button, and presently she is counting the yellow blinks, the way one might try counting sheep before falling off to sleep. Thirty-six, she counts, thirty-seven, thirty-eight, thirty-nine . . .

The phone will ring all night.

Suddenly she picks up the receiver and shouts, "Leave us alone, you filthy whore!"

Then she breaks the connection with her fingertip and leaves the receiver off the hook.

She prays that she will not have the dream tonight. Then it comes: the shadow flying across the windshield, her mother's scream. Only she is not dreaming now. She is wide awake.

26

"*YOUR FATHER* is dead," her mother said on the telephone, and her voice was strangely calm, detached and dispassionate, as though she were making some not particularly interesting observation about the weather. This had been in April of 1962.

"*Dead?*" she had cried. "What happened?" Immediately she assumed that the stresses he had been under must have caused a heart attack.

"I'm not sure of all the details," her mother said in that same distant voice. "The police are there now. Will you go over to the apartment and see what has to be done?"

"The *police!*"

"They're there. At the apartment. I tried to call him there, and a policeman answered the phone. They'd just found him. Can you go over? I'll get there as soon as I can."

"Where are *you*, Mother?"

"I'm here—I'm in the Adirondacks. Or is it the Alleghenies? I came here yesterday—no, it was two days ago, on the train. It's a place called—" and she heard her mother call out to someone, "What's the name of this town? Oh, yes. It's a place called Cohoes, New York," she said. "It's not far from Saratoga. I'm at a pay phone. There's no phone in my motel room. Can you help me, Mimi?"

"What are you doing *there*, Mother?"

"We had a . . . a little disagreement the other night, your father and I. I had to get away. I had to find a little peace. And quiet. I went to Grand Central. I got on a train. I got off at the first town that looked pretty. And peaceful. I came here, to the mountains, to be alone for a little bit. And now it's snowing outside. . . ."

"Have you been drinking, Mother?"

"A little—a little liquid courage. Mimi, didn't you hear what I said? *Your father's dead!*" It was the first time her voice seemed to register any emotion. "Please go up to the apartment and see what it is the police want. They were asking me all sorts of awful questions. I'll be home as soon as I can. There's supposed to be a train at—" But the rest was incoherent.

When she arrived at her parents' apartment, she was met at the door by a young police officer who looked barely old enough to shave.

"You a relative of the deceased?" he asked her.

"I'm his daughter. Please let me see him."

"Afraid you can't. Besides, you wouldn't want to, ma'am."

"What do you mean?"

"Put a bullet through his head. Blew his brains out, ma'am."

She felt her body sag against the door.

"It looks like a clear case of suicide," he said. "He appears to have been alone here. No sign of forced entry, no signs of an intruder, no indication that a burglary was being perpetrated. A neighbor heard the shot and called the precinct. We've taken the deceased to the police morgue, where they need to perform a few more tests. Then we'll release the body to Frank Campbell's. Your mother specified Frank Campbell's, ma'am."

"Where was he?"

"You want to see where we found him, ma'am?"

She nodded.

"I warn you, there's pretty much a lot of blood."

She followed the young officer down the front hall toward the bathroom at the end.

"You sure you want to go in there, ma'am?" he said, looking at her uncertainly. "It smells kind of bad in there, too."

She nodded again.

He held open the bathroom door for her. "We found him there." He pointed. "In the tub."

She took one brief look, then turned quickly away, feeling ill. "A little disagreement," her mother had said. Had that been enough to cause him to do this dreadful thing?

"This was a considerate suicide," he said. "He chose the bathtub—he was fully clothed, by the way—to minimize the mess."

"Considerate," she whispered.

"The lethal weapon was found there," he said, and pointed to a section of the white-tiled floor beside the tub where the outline of a pistol was traced in black Magic Marker. "Smith and Wesson, forty-four," he said. Then he sat down hard on the toilet seat.

She noticed for the first time how pale he was. Beads of perspiration glistened on his forehead, though the apartment was quite cool, and there was a white, cakey substance at the corners of his mouth. "Sorry, ma'am," he said. "This is my first one of these."

"You poor thing," she heard herself saying. "This must be awful for you."

He cleared his throat. "They say you get used to it, ma'am," he said. "That's what they tell us."

"Let's go into another room," she said.

Outside in the hall again, she said, "I'm sorry, I didn't get your name."

"O'Connell, ma'am. Detective Kevin O'Connell, nineteenth precinct."

"How long do you have to stay here, Kevin?"

"Until I hear from the forensic guys. Till they're sure they've got the— you know, all the things they need."

They moved toward the living room, and she noticed that his hand was moving inside the pocket of his uniform jacket, and she realized that he was fingering his rosary beads. "Was there any sort of message? Any note?" she asked him.

"Not that we've been able to turn up. Like I said, he was considerate. Most suicides who leave notes are sado-masochistic manipulative personalities with persecution complexes and private agendas to work through. That's what they taught us at the police academy, anyway. It means, like, they want to get back at somebody. This deceased was a considerate personality, in my opinion."

"Yes."

"Do you know of any reason, ma'am, why your father would have chosen to take his own life? Any enemies?"

"No. Yes. I really don't know."

"Business pressures?"

"Oh, yes. Many of those. Do you need me for anything else, Kevin?"

"We may ask you to come down to the morgue to identify the deceased. When we've cleaned him up a bit, that is. The widow, I gather, is out of town."

"My mother's on her way back to New York."

"Meanwhile, you have my sincerest sympathies, ma'am, in your bereavement."

"Thank you, Kevin. Or I should say, thank you, lieutenant."

"Not lieutenant, ma'am. Detective. O'Connell. Nineteenth precinct."

"And I hope they don't make you wait here too much longer."

"I'll be okay, ma'am. It was just that this was my first of these. I mean, I've seen stiffs before, but not like this."

He was still fingering the rosary beads in his pocket. She could hear the beads' soft *chink* as they fell together from between his fingers.

"Say a bead for me," she said, and let herself out the door.

It was not until she reached the elevator that her father began to die for her, and he died again when she opened the front door of the building and stepped out into the bright sunlight of the street, and yet again when she raised her arm to hail a taxi, and again and again, all the way home.

That night, as she lay in her husband's arms, she said to him, "Was there something I could have done? Was there some signal I didn't see? Did I spend so much time worrying about what was happening to Mother that I ignored what he was going through, that I became blind to what was happening to him? Have I spent too much time caring for Badger, and you, and not enough time trying to understand the hell that the rest of my family was going through? And that time, two years ago, when you tried to tell me how terribly wrong things were becoming, and I became so angry with you, and let you . . . let you move out on me: should I have used that time to be with Mother and Daddy, to try to help them, instead of . . . instead of . . . nothing? Oh, why have I been so selfish, Brad? Why didn't someone —you—someone—tell me, show me, how selfish I was being, thinking only of myself? My comfort, my pleasure. You don't deserve someone as selfish as me. I don't deserve you. How could I have ever called you selfish, when I've been the only selfish one, the only selfish one, the only one."

"You mustn't think thoughts like these, Mimi," he said. "You mustn't let yourself. There's nothing you or I could have done that would have made things any different. Nothing either of us could have done differently would have changed anything."

"Oh, yes," she sobbed. "I think there was."

A crack of light appeared in their bedroom doorway, and then the silhouette of the toddler Badger appeared in the frame of light from the hallway outside. Rubbing his eyes, he said, "Mommy? Daddy?"

"Come here, Badger," Brad said, patting the bed. "Everything's all right." He reached out and lifted the little boy into the bed beside them. "Everything's all right," he said again. "Would you like to sleep in our bed tonight, Badger-buddy? Your Mommy and Daddy love you very much, Badger-buddy, and every day we love you more and more, Badger-buddy, yes we do. . . ."

And so, four days later, her father's simplest of funerals behind them, the little family group had met again in George Wardell's office in the Lincoln Building. This time, there were only five of them: Mimi and Brad, Nonie and Edwee, and Alice. Granny Flo had not been able to bring herself to attend, nor had she attended the funeral. She had been too devastated by the loss of her firstborn, and best-loved, child. Our little group, Mimi remembers thinking, grows smaller and smaller.

The will was read. Like the funeral service, it was simple and brief, barely one page in length. Her father had rewritten it, it seemed, simplifying everything, just a month before his death. A third of Henry Myerson's estate was left to his widow, and two thirds were bequeathed to Mimi. There were no other special bequests.

"Of course," George Wardell said with a deep sigh when he finished reading it, "there are many problems that I'm sure you are aware of. Everything, at the moment, is entailed by various lawsuits that have been instituted by certain of your cousins. We can expect Henry's estate to be in litigation for some time to come. The question becomes: What is to become of the Miray Company, which now, unfortunately, has no one to run it? Most unfortunate."

At first, none of them said anything.

"Mr. Moore," George Wardell said, "have you any suggestions?" Clearly, George Wardell had selected Brad as the one most capable of assuming any sort of mantle of family leadership.

Brad whistled softly. "Is it . . . Chapter Eleven?" he said at last.

"Yes, most unfortunately, yes," George Wardell said. "That is exactly what I have been thinking. I can see no other solution, I'm afraid. Therefore, with all of your permissions, I would like to institute bankruptcy proceedings on the part of Miray. Very sad, but there isn't a man in this country who would want to try to run this company now."

"Not a man in the country?" Mimi said.

"Well, perhaps that's putting it a little strongly," George Wardell said. "Let me say that no man in his right mind would want to take over the burden of this company in its present financial state."

"What about a woman?" Mimi said quietly.

"What?" said her aunt Nonie sharply. "What are you talking about, Mimi? *What* woman?" Nonie was still all in black, her face heavily veiled.

"Me," Mimi said.

"Don't be absurd," Nonie said. "You don't know anything about business. Besides, you have a baby."

"Now, wait a minute," Brad said, sitting forward in his chair. "Let's hear what Mimi has to say." He then began firing questions at her, and though they were difficult questions, she would always be grateful to him for asking them, because he had been the first one to take her seriously.

"Tell me," he said, "what's the first thing you'd do if you had the company—the very first thing?"

"I'd reposition the products back into an upscale market, back into the boutiques and specialty stores."

"But the name Miray is now associated with dime stores and supermarkets. How would you bring such a change about?"

"I'd change the name. I'd change it to 'Mireille,' spelled the way I spell my name."

"But yours is an unusual name. French. Most people wouldn't know how to pronounce it."

"I'd use television. The beauty industry hasn't really explored television yet. We've stayed pretty much with the fashion and shelter magazines. But when they hear the name on television, and see it on the screen, they'll know how to pronounce it soon enough. You see," she went on eagerly, sitting forward in her chair, "I haven't just been sitting around idly doing nothing while my father ran this company. I've been studying this business and doing a lot of reading and research. This is essentially a fashion business, and things go in and out of fashion. Just as there always has to be something new in fashion, there also has to be something new in cosmetics. Remember leg makeup? That was big a few years ago, but hardly anybody uses it now. With each new fashion season, there's got to be a new makeup fashion. One year, the emphasis may be on lips. The next year it could be eyes, the next year hair colorings. You see, I've got lots of ideas that I'd like to try out."

"And how would you propose to finance all this?" Brad asked her.

"I'd go down to Wall Street. I'd find some young and hungry and ambitious investment banking firm who'd be willing to underwrite us, and take our stock public. I'd raise the money that way."

"And *then* what would you do?" her husband asked her. "What would you do next?"

"Then," Mimi said, "I'd go out and call on the stores. I'd butter up the buyers. I'd try to get them to let me set up my displays in whatever little corner of the store they can give me. I'd walk up and down the aisles myself, with my little tray of samples, passing them out to customers. I've also had another idea: a free gift for every purchase. With every purchase of a ten-dollar lipstick, the customer gets a coordinated bottle of polish—or eye shadow or eyeliner—free. No one's ever done that before. It's just a new wrinkle on the old practice of *sampling*, of course, but it's *new*, because the customer first has to buy something before she gets the free sample. And I think it would work. The buyers and the merchandise managers will like it because it will bring traffic into their departments. It will build goodwill for the stores. Gradually, they'll repay me with bigger and better display space, and I'll repay them with gift samples for their wives and girlfriends. In my display space, I'll give beauty demonstrations: doing customer's makeup, free, telling her what shades suit her coloring and complexion best, and so on. In other words, I'd work hard, damn hard, until I got to the point that when a woman thinks of cosmetics, she'll think of Mireille."

"And *then* what would you do?" Brad had persisted.

"Then," she said with a smile, "I'd just keep on doing new things—new products, new product *areas*. This is a business where *new* is everything—new, new, new!"

"This is all too absurd," Nonie said. "Do you mean to say you'd abandon your darling little baby boy to do all that? It's absurd. Alice, she wants to abandon your only grandchild!"

"Badger won't be abandoned, Nonie," Brad snapped. And then, "I say let's give her a chance."

"Yes, a chance," she said. "Give me a year. Just see what I'll do in a year." And that was how it all began.

From Philip Dougherty's column in the *New York Times*, June 3, 1962:

GIFT-FOR-PURCHASE NOTION IS A HIT

Little knots of customers gathered around a particular cosmetics counter at Saks Fifth Avenue today. This was where the newly christened Mireille line of beauty products was displayed, and where the shopper discovered that for every Mireille product she purchased, she could take home another—free. This innovation in the time-worn practice of "sampling" in the beauty industry was unique in another way. The free sample was not a tiny miniature containing enough of a particular elixir for one or two applications. It was a full-size tube, or jar, or bottle of the elixir itself.

"Mireille," a homophone for Miray (its maker), is also the name of Miray's new president, Mireille "Mimi" Myerson, granddaughter of the company's founder. The Saks shoppers were doubly pleased today—not only with their free gifts, but with a chance to meet and visit with the lovely 24-year-old lady executive herself. Miss Myerson, it should be noted, provides an excellent walking advertisement for the efficacy of her various beauty and skin-care products.

"Have *you* always used these products?" a shopper asked her. "Ever since I was tall enough to see into a mirror," Miss Myerson replied with a laugh.

Mireille, Mireille, on the wall, who is fairest of us all? Saks shoppers seemed to have decided today.

"Something for your wife or a special woman friend?" she said to the dark-suited man who approached her counter at the crowded store.

"I have no wife, but there is a special woman," he said.

"What's her coloring?"

"Blond," he said.

"Then I'm sure she'll love this shade," she began, reaching for a lipstick.

"Like you. Polished-silver eyes."

She looked up at him and realized it was Michael.

"You're blushing, kiddo," he said, and winked at her.

"I'm sure all this publicity creates goodwill," she said to Brad that evening at the dinner table, "but the problem is still cash flow. After all, every free gift we give away represents a lost sale."

"What about your idea of making a public offering of stock in the company?"

"Are my figures good enough to appeal to an underwriter?"

"There's always commercial paper," he said.

"Commercial paper?"

"Commercial paper is like a promissory note," he said. "Think of it as a post-dated check. If you were to write a check for a hundred dollars, dated six months from now, you'd have trouble getting a hundred dollars for it today. But you might find somebody who'd give you ninety dollars for it. On the gamble that, in six months, you'd have the money in the bank to cover it. Of course, it's risky, but there are investment houses who specialize in commercial paper issues. Right now, commercial paper is being discounted at between eight and ten percent. You might think of going the commercial paper route."

"Hmm," she said thoughtfully, "it does sound risky."

"The underwriter who gives you ninety dollars for your check hopes he can find somebody who'll give him ninety-two dollars for it, and so on. Everybody's betting on the possibility that you'll have the cash by the time the note comes due. Don't try this with personal checks, by the way. It's against the law. But in banking it's done all the time."

"*Very* interesting," she said.

"If you decide to go that route, talk to Goldman, Sachs. They're tops when it comes to trading commercial paper."

"Do you know anybody there, Brad?"

"Not a soul, I'm afraid. But I do know that old Laz Goldman still calls all the shots down there. He's well into his seventies, but he's still very much in charge. Why not talk to him?"

"Yes," she said quietly. "Yes."

"The only other thing I know about him is that he's the most bereaved widower in the world. His wife died a couple of years ago, and he's been building shrines to her memory ever since."

* * *

That night, she had pulled Brad's copy of *Who's Who in America* from the bookshelf and read:

GOLDMAN, LAZARUS, inv. banker; b. N.Y.C.,
Aug. 20, 1889; s. Marcus and Esther (Loeb) G.;
B.A. Harvard Univ. 1910; m. Fannie Beer (dec.),
June 12, 1918 . . .

The biographical sketch continued with the names of the couple's five children, Mr. Goldman's various awards and achievements, the list of his clubs and affiliations, and concluded with the notation: "Donor (1960) of The Fannie Beer Goldman Memorial Pavilion, Mt. Sinai Hospital, N.Y.C." This, clearly, was one of the shrines Mr. Goldman had erected to his dead wife.

And suddenly, from some small niche in her memory, something floated into her mind, and she read through the paragraph carefully again. In 1955, in honor of her grandparents' fortieth wedding anniversary, her grandfather had privately published a volume of their wedding photographs, and everyone in the family had been given a copy. She had never done more than give this album a casual glance. Now she searched the shelves eagerly for her copy. Finding it, she lifted it carefully out, a heavy volume, bound richly in white Morocco, embossed in gold:

OUR WEDDING BOOK

Adolph Myerson

and

Fleurette Guggenheim Myerson

January 5, 1915–January 5, 1955

She flipped quickly through the pages. First were photographs of "Our Parents," her diminutive great-grandfather Myerson, looking frightened behind thick glasses and a walrus moustache, and his equally diminutive wife, wearing what was obviously her "best" dress; and the imposing senior Guggenheims, he in a Prince Albert frock coat, and she all in lace with her considerable poitrine slung with ropes of pearls. Then there were photographs of the bride and groom, stiffly posed, he with his familiar Van Dyke, and Granny Flo, looking incredibly young—almost childlike—in her veil and wedding gown, low-bodiced, surpliced, decorated with appliquéd roses and ribbon bows, its long train swirled at her ankles.

Next came a section titled "Our Groomsmen"—more serious-looking men in morning coats and high, stiff collars. Then came photographs of "Our Bridesmaids," and Mimi found what she wanted.

Now she was seated in the office of the great Mr. Lazarus Goldman himself at 43 Exchange Place, where he sat in a swivel chair behind an old-fashioned rolltop desk. He was in his shirtsleeves, wearing sleeve garters, and from the ceiling a green-shaded hanging lamp shone down on his round bald head. His office smelled of dust and old documents and looked as though nothing had been changed in it for at least fifty years. Even his telephone was of the old-fashioned upright variety, and a ticker-tape machine, of approximately the same vintage, burst into periodic clatter in one corner. His face remained expressionless as Mimi delivered her presentation.

"And finally," she said, "I plan to develop a line of men's toiletries. I firmly believe that cosmetics for men, since we are becoming such a youth-oriented culture, are going to be a part of the wave of the future. Traditionally, of course, it has always been assumed that the only men who used cosmetics and scents were homosexuals."

"You mean pansies?" he said.

"Well, yes. And, by tradition, the only fragrance a man would buy in, say, an after-shave, was something called Old Hemlock, or English Leather, or Woodspice. A whole mythology has developed over which fragrances are masculine and which are feminine. Piney and spicy fragrances are masculine, but floral scents are feminine. But it makes no sense. Why should both lemon and lime be considered masculine scents, while orange is considered feminine? Meanwhile, even the best men's after-shaves are ninety-six percent alcohol and only four percent perfume. That's why they sting, and the stinging is supposed to be good for the skin because the skin feels so good when the stinging stops!" She paused to see whether he would chuckle over this anomaly, but he did not. "But our research has shown that more and more men—masculine, nonhomosexual men—are dabbing themselves with a bit of their wives' perfume after they apply their after-shave or talc—just to make themselves smell a little better. Secretly, men *want* more fragrance in the products they use. Therefore, my idea is to develop a fragrance with a non-sexually-oriented name that would appeal to men. Naturally, a man would hesitate before buying, or using, an after-shave called Apple Blossom. But if it had a name such as Persuasion, or Undercurrent, which had no particular sexual connotation, and if it smelled just wonderful—even of apple blossoms—the name could be sold to the ruggedest of he-men. The market is out there, Mr. Goldman, and I'll leave you with one last thought. Though the market for scented beauty products has never been greater, only fifty-six percent of the male population buys any beauty products at all. The other forty-four percent is what I'm going after."

Making a steeple of his fingers, he tipped his chair backward and stared upward into the green-shaded ceiling lamp. For several minutes he said nothing. Then he said, "How old are you?"

"Twenty-seven," she said, lying a little.

"And you say all men are secretly pansies."

"I didn't say that, Mr. Goldman. I'm just saying that my research shows that men want more fragrance in the products they use, and will buy them if they're given more generic, non-sexually-associated names."

He waved his hand. "We have recently, successfully, underwritten an issue such as you suggest for the General Motors Corporation," he said. "However, I think you will agree with me, Miss Myerson, that your company is a far cry from General Motors. A far cry."

"My company has great promise, Mr. Goldman."

"Does it? What makes you think so? You are in the cosmetics business, a business subject to the whims of fashion. No matter what this year's fashions are, Americans will always purchase automobiles."

"Americans will always purchase cosmetics," she said.

"Yours is also a highly competitive business. There are only four major manufacturers of motor cars in America. But there are dozens and dozens of little cosmetics firms like yours."

"Miray was big once. I'm going to make it big again."

"Are you? What makes you think so?"

"Because, Mr. Goldman, I happen to think I've got what it takes!" She leaned forward in her chair for emphasis.

"Do you? What makes you think that?" He shook his head slowly back and forth. "No," he said. "I think not. You see, Miss Myerson, your enterprise is saddled with several factors which mitigate against its chances for success. To begin with, by your own admission, your capital structure, your capital foundation, is weak."

"That's why I'm here to see you—to help me build a strong capital base."

He held up his hand. "Please let me finish," he said. "There are at least three other factors, three other mitigating factors. Let me name them for you. One, you are young. Two, you are inexperienced. And three, you are a woman. All three factors combine to indicate to me that you are ill-equipped to compete in the dog-eat-dog world of the American cosmetics industry."

"Then your answer is no," she said.

His bald head nodded in the lamplight. "My answer," he said, "is no."

"Well, then," she said, reaching for the briefcase and purse beside her feet, "there's no point in my taking up any more of your time. I'm disappointed, of course, and I think you're making a mistake, but I'm not going to argue with you. But I did bring one thing with me that I'd like you to have, anyway." She placed her briefcase on her lap, snapped it open, and withdrew a manila envelope. "I thought you might like to have this."

Lazarus Goldman accepted the envelope, opened it, and slid its contents out onto the desk in front of him. For a long moment, he stared at the sepia photograph. Then he whispered, "My God . . . Fannie. *Fannie*. Where did you get this?"

"Your late wife was a bridesmaid in my grandmother's wedding," she said. "In nineteen fifteen."

"Nineteen fifteen . . . the year I met her," he said, and in the lamplight, she thought she saw tears glistening in his eyes. "My God, she was beautiful."

"Yes," she said. "Very beautiful. That's why I thought you might like to have the photograph. She was an extraordinarily beautiful young woman. And I feel I can speak with some authority about beautiful women, because that's the business I'm in, Mr. Goldman—beauty." She sat back in her chair again.

From the *Wall Street Journal*, August 24, 1962:

PUBLIC OFFERING OF MIRAY
STOCK IS ANNOUNCED

The Miray Corporation, a family-held company since 1912, will make its first public offering of stock next month, it was announced today. The offering is to be underwritten by Goldman, Sachs & Co.

Miray, long a respected name in the cosmetics business, manufactures a long line of hair, nail-care, and other beauty products. In recent years, however, sales have turned sluggish. This has been attributed to the marketing philosophy of the company's late president, Henry Myerson, who died earlier this year, who tried to reposition Miray in the mass market. Previously, Miray products had been sold only in select specialty stores. Mr. Myerson's attempt, a cause of some controversy in the industry at the time it was announced, has been deemed a failure.

Miray, with plant and inventory assets estimated in excess of $30,000,000, has also found itself saddled with a debt that industry leaders consider "worrisome." This has led, within the last two years, to layoffs and firings within the company. That the company has not yet managed to struggle out from under this debt has been laid to Henry Myerson's "lackluster" leadership.

But the company's fortunes may be headed for an upturn under the stewardship of its new president, Mireille ("Mimi") Myerson, 24, who assumed the presidency following her father's death in April. Miss Myerson is described as a "dynamo," a "whiz kid," and "a real get-up-and-go-girl." Miss Myerson has announced her determination to reestablish Miray's products in an upscale market, under the new product banner "Mireille," and she is already responsible for several merchandising innovations that seem to be heading her toward her goal. Her ascendancy, and considerable marketing savvy, have caused the financial community to look at Miray with new interest and respect. Miss Myerson is the granddaughter of Adolph Myerson, the company's late founder.

No price has yet been announced for the new Miray offering, but it is expected to reach the market at approximately $25 a share. . . .

"You did it!" he cried. "By golly, you did it!" And he flung the newspaper into the air, pulled her from the chair she sat in, and began dancing her around their living room, crying, "You did it! You did it!"

"*We* did it," she said. "We did it together! I couldn't have done it if you hadn't told me what you did about Lazarus Goldman."

"But *you* charmed the old fart!"

"Now, please," she said, and I could imagine her laughing her throaty laugh when she told me this story. "Mr. Lazarus is *not* an old fart. He's a fine gentleman of the old school. And, inside, an old softie."

"Let's celebrate! Let's go out for dinner and dancing. Let's go to the Rainbow Room!"

"Not the Rainbow Room," she said quickly. "Too . . . touristy."

"Wherever you say," he said. "This is your night!"

That was the night when they decided that Mimi's new line of scented toiletries for men—the after-shave, the talc, the shampoo and conditioner, the soap—could only, appropriately, be called Persuasion . . . by Mireille.

From Philip Dougherty's column, September 10, 1962:

COLOR TV DRAWS
NEW ADVERTISING CATEGORIES

With color television in more American homes than ever before, with constantly improving quality of color transmission and reception, and with no end in sight, advertising categories that have long shunned TV are now turning to color TV with enthusiasm. Two of these categories are the food and cosmetics industries.

"We avoided television because, in black and white, all food looked blah," says George Kalisher, spokesman for General Foods. "But with improved color transmission, food can be made to look appetizing, with very little doctoring." Similarly, the cosmetics industry until recently felt more comfortable in the glossy pages of the print media, where, it was felt, color accuracy was most important. But improved TV color quality is changing all that. Revlon, for instance, has become the new sponsor of *Catch Me If You Can*, the popular quiz show, and NBC-TV has hired quiz ace Prince Fritzi von Maulsen as a special $50,000-a-year quiz consultant. Von Maulsen will also appear regularly as a contestant on *Catch Me If You Can*. Also in the forefront of new cosmetics advertisers, with its brand-new line of "Mireille" products, including toiletries for men, is the Miray Corporation. Its fall schedule of TV commercials will air in 212 separate markets nationwide. . . .

From *Mother Hall's Chickens*, the Alumnae Magazine of Miss Hall's School for Girls, Fall/Winter issue, 1962:

CLASS NOTES '56

by

Barbara Badminton Bakely,

Class Secretary

Well, who'd a thunk it! Does anybody remember li'l ole Mimi Myerson? I mean, does *anybody???* Well, she was that shy little wallflower who used to lean on her mop in Main, and never had a date, much less a debut, dahlings. Well, that li'l gal we all thought was *least* likely to succeed is now all over the N'Yawk papers as the hot new lady exec!!!! She's, yup, prexy of the Miray Corp., hard as it may seem to believe, and now when yer readin' 'bout Mireille ("Mimi") Myerson in the tabs and the gabs, just pinch yourself and say, yep, that's our own little Me-Me Mouseburger. Will wondahs nevah cease???? Nevah, dahlings, nevah!!!!

Classmately,

B.B.B.

$$27$$

IT WOULD BE PRETTY to suppose that it had happened quite that fast, or that it had all been quite that easy. In those days, following Adolph Myerson's death, three giants had emerged in the cosmetics industry. These were Elizabeth Arden, Helena Rubinstein, and Charles Revson. It was my privilege (if privilege is the right word) to have known all three of these individuals. In temperament and demeanor, the three could not have been less alike. Miss Arden, as she was always called, was an ageless, creamy-skinned beauty who affected the manners and speech of a lady born to ancient wealth, though everything about her marbled persona was of her own manufacture.

Born in the Canadian outback as Florence Graham, she had concocted her name from two of her favorite works of fiction, *Elizabeth and Her German Garden* and *Enoch Arden*. After failing to complete a nurse's training course, she had borrowed $6,000 from a brother (a loan that, rumor had it, was never actually repaid) and come to New York to open a beauty salon. "If I couldn't make people healthy, I would at least make them beautiful," she once said. She had entered the world of American high society through the sport of kings, with her Blue Grass Stable and her racehorses, which she insisted be rubbed down daily with her Ardena skin cream. She survived, as did her horses, on a peculiar diet of wheat germ, honey, blackstrap molasses, and vinegar. Bowlsful of these comestibles were ceremoniously presented to her in silver vessels at the best tables of such bygone restaurants as The Colony and Le Pavillon. For all her patrician bearing and *Social Register* accent, she was known to turn into a screeching harridan at the sight of red ink in her daily sales figures.

Helena Rubinstein, who was always called "Madame," was an altogether different sort. Short, plump, and heavily Polish-accented, she had somehow managed to make her way out of the Krakow ghetto at some indeterminate point in the nineteenth century and come, by way of Australia, Paris, and London, to New York shortly before World War I as an enormously rich woman. Because she distrusted banks, the fat black pocketbook she always carried was always stuffed with wads of currency, the separate denominations of bills rolled together and secured with rubber bands. When the board of the co-op at 625 Park Avenue, where she wanted to buy the triplex penthouse, demurred because it did not wish to have a Jewish tenant, Madame Rubinstein simply bought the entire building, paying cash for it. At her dinner parties, she fretted that her guests did not eat enough. Crying "Eat, eat," she would scrape food from her own plate onto my own. She would also, I happened to notice, use the corner of her Porthault tablecloth to blow her nose.

Then there was Mr. Revson.

One afternoon in the early spring of 1963, the telephone rang in Mimi's office. And, because she answered her own calls then, she reached for the receiver and picked it up. "Mimi?" a man's hoarse voice said. "It's Charlie."

"Charlie?"

"Charlie Revson."

"Oh, yes, Mr. Revson," Mimi said.

"It's Charlie," he barked. "All my friends call me Charlie. Call me Charlie. Listen, sweetheart, you and I have got a problem. We need to talk."

"Certainly," Mimi said.

"First of all, sweetheart, you got to realize that this company of mine is my entire life, and my entire life is this company. I built this company from scratch, starting with three hundred bucks and working out of a garage in Boston. Everything I've done for Revlon I've done myself. Understand? I didn't get my company handed to me on a silver platter by my old man."

"Well, as a matter of fact, neither did I," Mimi said.

"Yeah. Well, like I said, sweetheart, I've worked hard for my own little piece of the action in this game, and now it looks like you're trying to muscle in on my turf. And that ain't okay. Understand?"

"Not exactly," Mimi said, although she was fairly sure she did.

"I'm talking territory, toots. Saks is Revlon territory these days, toots. So is Bloomingdale's. So is Bendel, and so is Magnin's. I fought hard to get that territory, toots, and I'm going to fight hard to keep it. Understand? That territory is *mine*."

"Well, we both work in a free enterprise system," Mimi began.

"Shit. Don't give me no free enterprise shit. Ever hear that it's the early bird that gets the worm? Well, in this case, I'm the early bird, and Saks and Bloomie's and Bendel's and Magnin's is all my worms, understand? I was there first, sweetheart. I staked my claim with those outlets before you was even born. Shit, I staked that territory before your old man could even get a hard-on."

"I'm sorry, Mr. Revson, but—"

"It's Charlie, I told you. Listen, just move out of my territory, and we'll be pals."

"I'm sorry, but if Saks wants to buy my products, I intend to sell to them."

"Listen," he said, "nobody fucks around with Charlie. Understand? If you think I'm going to sit on my ass and let some fucking debutante bimbo move in on my territory, you've got another fucking think coming, sweetheart."

"I was never a debutante, Mr. Revson," she said.

"Listen," he said. "I haven't got all day to shoot the breeze with some bimbo. Let's get down to brass tacks. How much do you want for your company?"

"I'm sorry. My company is not for sale."

"Don't hand me that shit. I'm asking you to name your price."

"I have no price."

"Everybody's got a price. Name yours."

"I'm sorry. I have none."

There was a silence. Then he said, "Okay, twat, then listen to me. There isn't room enough in this town for you and me both. Understand? I made a friendly offer, and you turned it down. Well, if you're turning a friendly offer into a fight, you know who's going to win? Me, that's who. Because Charlie Revson isn't going to let some little broad bitch move into *his market*. So you know what I'm going to do, twat? *I'm going to ruin you*. Wait and see. When I get through with you, you won't know your asshole from the Grand Canyon. I'll mop up the streets with you, bimbo, because nobody fucks around with Charlie. You're going to regret we had this conversation, twat."

"I believe," Mimi said evenly, "that it was you who made this call." Then she hung up, shaking with anger.

Then, as she recovered from the shock of her first encounter with the famously despotic Charles Revson, a dim memory floated into Mimi's mind. She let it hang there for a moment or two, savoring it, testing it, trying it on, as it were, for size. Then she picked up the telephone again and called the executive offices of Revlon.

After making her way through a considerable battery of receptionists and secretaries, with each of whom she had to identify herself and answer the questions, "What is the name of your company? Will Mr. Revson know the nature of your business with him? Will he know the purpose of this call?" she finally got the great man on the line.

"Yeah?" he said.

"Charlie, it's Mimi," she said.

"Yeah. You've changed your mind. You're wising up."

"Not exactly," she said. "But I did want to remind you of something."

"Yeah?"

"That quiz show you're sponsoring called *Catch Me If You Can*. With Prince Fritzi von Maulsen as one of your contestants, and NBC's quiz consultant."

"Yeah, what about it?"

"Wouldn't it look rather awkward for Revlon if it came out that His Royal Highness gets the answers to his questions fed to him ahead of time? I want you to know I'm worried for you, Charlie."

There was a prolonged silence, and for a moment Mimi thought the connection had been broken. Then Charles Revson said, "*Cunt!*"

Mimi hung up the phone again, deeply satisfied.

Her next call was to Washington. Old Senator Willoughby had been a good friend of her grandfather's. "Uncle Bucky?" she said when she reached him at the Senate Office Building. "I'll tell you why I'm calling. There's been talk that some of these big-money quiz shows on television are rigged, and that the public is being deceived. It occurred to me that this is something Congress might want to look into. It could be a lively issue for you, Uncle Bucky, since I know you'll be running for reelection in the fall. . . ."

That night when she came home, Brad noticed the expression on her face. "You're grinning like a Cheshire cat," he said. "That's a real ear-to-ear grin. What's up?"

She laughed her ripply laugh and told him about her conversations with Charlie Revson.

He whistled softly. "Do you know something?" he said. "I think you're really going to be good at this business."

"And do you know something else?" she said. "I think so, too. And for the first time since Daddy died, I think I'm going to be successful!"

"But I always knew that," he said.

Meanwhile, in the Willoughby Committee investigations of rigged TV quiz programs that followed later that year, a disgraced and shamefaced Prince Fritzi von Maulsen admitted that many of his answers to the more obscure questions were given to him before the show went on the air, and that the appealing grimacings and furrowings of his handsome brow as he appeared to be struggling to come up with answers were all carefully rehearsed beforehand, with the help of a television acting coach. At the time, the executives of the sponsoring Revlon company did their best to distance themselves from the day-to-day production details that went into the show. They had no knowledge, they insisted, of what went on backstage. But they all, including Mr. Revson, appeared deeply embarrassed by the committee's findings, and took *Catch Me If You Can* off the air.

And Prince Fritzi was fired from his $50,000-a-year job.

As I mentioned earlier, Mimi has been called a "visionary" in the cosmetics industry. But it would be wrong to assume that she, or anyone else in the business for that matter, is somehow endowed with powers of clairvoyance. Rather, the innovations in cosmetics fashion that she has brought about have been the result of much careful thought and no small amount of research. For instance, in October of 1963, when she had been head of Miray for a little more than a year, she prepared the first of her famous interoffice memos, proposing a new direction for the company.

MIRAY CORPORATION

Interoffice Memorandum

TO: All employees
FROM: MM
SUBJECT: Eyes

I remember my grandfather saying that this is a business that can't exist without news. "If a manufacturer has to *pretend* that there's news, he's in trouble," he said. And right now I think I have spotted a trend that is going to be big news.

As you know, my grandfather started in this business with nail polish. He then moved on into coordinated lipstick shades, and then into face and hair-care products. Last year, the "pale look," with pale makeup and white lipstick, enjoyed a mercifully brief period of popularity. Right now, I have reason to believe, the pendulum is beginning to swing in the opposite direction. Over at Revlon, I have heard, they are developing something called the "Toasty Look," a brownish lipstick accompanied by pale brown makeup, and from Paris I have heard rumors that a French manufacturer is about to spring a lipstick shade called "Cafe Noir," a black-coffee color with a coffee taste as well. But I don't think the trend toward darker shades is going to end with lipsticks. I think it is going to move upward on a woman's face—to the *eyes*.

Specifically, I have been studying photographs of the actress Brigitte

Bardot, as she has been evolving into a major film star. Bardot's principal beauty flaw is that she has too-large lips. In order to draw attention away from this flaw, she—or, more likely, those who supervise her makeup— have chosen to increasingly emphasize her eyes. Furthermore, though eye shadow has been traditionally used only to cover the upper eyelid, Bardot is now shading her eyes all the way up to her brows. At a fashion show in Los Angeles the other day, a model came down the ramp wearing black eye shadow above and *below* her eyes. A few minutes later, another appeared wearing red shadow above and below, and, on top of that, a third model appeared with one eye done in shades of green and blue and the other in shades of violet and navy. This is just gimmicky stuff, of course, but my feeling is that the eyes are going to provide women with their chief beauty focus for at least the next few years.

I am asking our lab technicians to develop a complete line of eye makeup products—pencils, eyeshadows, eye "glitter," mascara, false lashes, etc. I am also offering a prize of $10,000 to any employee who can come up with a device that will make the application of mascara easier— instead of the current, messy way, involving the mascara "cake" and brush.

Eye Makeup: A Brief History

Women—and men, too—have been making up their eyes for at least 6,000 years, in ancient Egypt, Rome, throughout India and the Near East, and in Europe. According to folklore, the eyes were shaded in order to ward off the "evil eye." If you look directly into another person's eyes, your own tiny image will appear reflected in the dark of the other person's pupil. In fact, the word *pupil* comes from the Latin *pupilla*, meaning "little doll." To the superstitious, this indicated that some sort of transference could take place—that one person could capture another by staring directly into his eyes. But darkly painted circles around the eyes absorb sunlight and consequently minimize reflected glare into the eye. Ever wonder why football and baseball players smear black grease under their eyes before games? That's why.

By 4000 B.C., the Egyptians had zeroed in on the eye as the chief focus for facial makeup. They preferred green eye shadow, made from pow- dered malachite, a green copper ore, and they applied this heavily to both the upper and the lower eyelids. Outlining the eyes and darkening the lashes and eyebrows were achieved with a black paste called kohl, made from powdered antimony, burnt almonds, black copper oxide, and brown clay ocher. Scores of jars of kohl have been unearthed in archaeological digs, their contents intact and still usable!

Fashionable Egyptian men and women also wore history's first *eye glitter*. In a mortar, they crushed the iridescent shells of beetles into a coarse powder, then mixed it with their malachite eye shadow, using a little spit!

My lab technicians assure me that modern science has synthesized some more appetizing ingredients for eye makeup!

It was this memo that launched Miray into eye products in the 1960s. And it was the idea for an automatic, roll-on mascara, which Mimi christened "Mas-Carismatic," that launched the career of Mark Segal in the company. At the time, he was working in the mailroom (where he was first to read this memo), and now, of course, he is the advertising director of Miray.

And this memo was the first of many "Mimi Memos," which, over the years, would make her as famous in the beauty business for writing long, detailed memos as David O. Selznick was in Hollywood.

✑

28

*A*ND NOW, sitting in a corner of Mimi's office, in the shipping carton in which they were delivered this morning, are her grandfather's diaries: thirty-one years' worth of daybooks, in as many neatly numbered volumes, beginning in 1910 and ending, somewhat abruptly, in October of 1941. Why did he suddenly stop making entries? she has asked herself. He did not die until eighteen years later.

She has obviously not had time to read through all of them, which she feels she must do before turning them over to Jim Greenway, but she has scanned through enough of them to ascertain that they are, indeed, written in her grandfather's spidery, but legible, European copybook hand.

Most of the entries she has read so far—she has to agree with Michael on this—have not been terribly interesting. In most of the earliest ones, for instance, her grandfather spent a great deal of time complaining about his younger brother. Sample: the entry dated July 4, 1910:

National holiday! Great Parade in New York, led by Mayor. But had to work today, painting house at 5570 Mosholu Pkway. Leo kvetched all day —wanted day off. A raise he even asked for yet! He is impossible to work with. All he does is kvetch and krechtz. . . .

July 10, 1910
More kvetching from Leo. I told him he is the number one World Champion kvetcher in the United States . . . Leo is stupid . . . Leo is lazy . . . Leo is nothing but a golem . . .

Out of curiosity, wondering what her grandfather's reaction had been to her birth, she had flipped forward to the year 1938, to see what he had entered for May 24.

Alice had the baby today. It is a girl. Very difficult labor for Alice, Henry says. Doctor tells them that they should have no more. When he married her, I told Henry that Alice did not look too good for childbearing—too weak-looking, pelvic structure too small, and I was right. Baby is very sickly and runtish, only 5 lbs. 6 oz. Now I shall have to count on Edwin to give me the grandsons I want. They have named it Marie.

He did not even get my name right, Mimi thinks.
She then flipped back to 1916 to see how her father's birth had been heralded.

July 17, 1916
My first son is born, the first of many I know, and I am a man blessed by God! A fine, fat, healthy, happy baby, weight 8 lbs. 14 oz. Flo doing fine, nursing, with milk to spare. I was right in my estimation of her capacity for childbearing, fine strong hips, broad pelvic structure are what one must look for in a woman. We have named him Henry, in honor of my father Hermann, may God bless his memory. . . .

She had moved further backward to learn what she could of her grandparents' courtship and marriage.

May 10, 1914
I have joined Temple Emanu-El, where all the uptown swells belong, where it is so grand that they do not even call it a shul! The bankers Schiff, Seligman, Loeb, Warburg and Lehman are all members, and a Lehman is its President. They will begin to take me seriously in New York now, for now I am one of them. This is a momentous day for me. . . .

July 19, 1914
There is a pretty little blue-eyed girl who sits in the pew just in front of mine at temple. Sometimes she turns and smiles at me. Today, she dropped her prayer book, and I reached down and fetched it for her. She thanked me in the prettiest way, just with her eyes, which are the prettiest blue for a Jewish girl.

August 10, 1914

I have just learned the identity of the little blue-eyed girl at temple. She is Fleurette Guggenheim, of the smelting family, and the man who sits beside her is her father, the great Morris Guggenheim, and the other men in the pew are his brothers. They are Swiss Jews, which explains the blue eyes, fair hair, and they are very rich—richer even than Rockefeller! This means that I will have no chance with her. Still, it is pleasant when she turns and sees me there, and smiles at me with those eyes. In French her name means "a little flower." That is the perfect description for her. . . .

August 17, 1914

Today we spoke for the first time, just a pleasant "Hello, how are you?" "I am fine, and you?" after the temple services. I really think she begins to like me. Is it possible? Should I ask her if I can walk her home? Should I ask her if I could pay a call? This will be very difficult, because she is always surrounded by her father, and all those powerful-looking uncles, who are very protective of her, which of course is as it should be. . . .

September 12, 1914

Fleurette, Fleurette—oh, my fragrant little summer flower! Summer is fading now, and so are all my hopes, for you are forever unattainable. Yet you are forever with me, in my thoughts and in my dreams, in my heart and in my soul—your sweet and gentle voice, your gentle eyes, my gentle Fleurette. Do you ever think of me? Do you sometimes dream of me as I dream of you? There is a song they're playing everywhere—"You're the Only Girl for Me"—and that is the song I hum in my head when I think of you, which is always, and yet it is never to be. Oh, Fleurette, my love, my love. This diary today sends only sweet thoughts to you. . . .

October 9, 1914

I cannot believe my good fortune! I think I must be dreaming! The Guggenheims have offered Fleurette to me! It is their proposal! They asked me today if I would consider taking Fleurette's hand in marriage! It is beyond my wildest hopes and dreams, that they should think that I am good enough for their Fleurette. Surely God has made me the most blessed of men. . . .

November 12, 1914

The wedding date has been chosen, January 5 of next year, and the rabbi has been retained. It seems an eternity from now, but they say that there are many things that must be done in preparation, and of course they are right. She asks that I call her Flo, which is what her family calls her. Flo. Flow. Yes, you make my blood flow stronger, my little Flo.

January 5, 1915

My wedding day! And today, if that were not enough, Flo's father and her uncles presented me with their wedding gift—her dowry of one million dollars! I am sitting here, staring at the cheque, and cannot believe my eyes. I am already rich, but now I am three times rich—rich in happiness, in health, and in wealth as well. Surely goodness and mercy shall follow me all of the days of my life, and I shall dwell in the House of the Lord forever.

Mimi had then flipped further backward, to the year 1912, the year that the momentous event that had changed all their lives had happened.

March 16, 1912

Stupid Leo! Poured too much coagulant into the red paint for Mrs. Spitzberg's kitchen. So viscid that it dries practically on the brush. Ruined, Leo said, wanted to throw it all out—two dollars' worth! Wait, I said. Idea! Sell it as paint for ladies' fingernails!

March 20, 1912

Bought case of nail polish bottles at Manufacturer's closeout. Investment: $10. Will fill all bottles from our 5-gallon drum, label each bottle "Three Alarm Quick-Drying Nail Polish," sell up and down the street at 10¢ each —should be a nice profit!

April 3, 1912

Mrs. Feldman, 3065 Grand Concourse, loves "Three Alarm." Wants more for her daughter in Canarsie—our first reorder!

May 7, 1912

Levy's drugstore wants to stock "Three Alarm." Thinks we should raise the price to 15¢ per bottle. Ordered more bottles today. Mixing new batch. . . .

July 6, 1912
That Leo! He's telling everybody he "invented" Quick-Drying Polish!
Him we're calling an inventor now! What a gonef!

She couldn't help wondering what he would have written in his diary about that visit of hers to his office in the spring of 1957, when she told him that she wanted to marry Michael. But of course the diaries did not go that far ahead in time. She did, however, as she flipped randomly through the volumes, find an entry for April of 1941 that reflected how he must have felt. The page bore the heading:

Inappropriate Members of This Family
1. Leo
2. Nate
3. Alice!!!!
4. Naomi (sometimes)
5. Other son (alas)

Though cannot truly say that Yrs. Truly has no faults, think it safe to say that Yrs. Truly has never done anything that was inappropriate, unsuitable, undignified. Proud of that. Must make sure that new little granddaughter marries well, someone appropriate, suitable. Never too soon to plan appropriate husband for her. Reminder: Keep eyes open for Right Man for her as years go by. Husbands, etc., must be suitable, no matter how many hearts are broken in the process. Are there worse things in life than broken hearts? Yes. Broken promises.

"Love is a test," he had written to her that summer in Europe.
Finally, she had turned to some of the diaries' most recent entries for 1941. She had read:

August 1, 1941
Leo knows where I keep these diaries. I must find a better hiding place, for he could use them against us! Where? Leo has got to go! Must put final plans into execution to drive him OUT! NOW!

Then she had turned to the last entry of them all, which was also in some ways the most mystifying.

October 10, 1941

Henry has been "borrowing" money from Flo! Found out about it going through her canceled checks. $50 thou. she gave him! Why? What for? Henry earns PLENTY! What is the reason? Not Leo. Leo has been PAID OFF! Nate? Is Henry that STUPID? All evidence has been destroyed! *Have had a word about this with Flo this evening. Flo is too soft-hearted with him—and too soft-hearted where $$$ is concerned. Will have a word with Henry about this in the morning. This has got to STOP! That damned Alice!*

On that note, her grandfather's diaries ended. There are, of course, many thousands of more words that she has yet to read, but now it is time for her appointment with her aunt Nonie, which is much more important. She will get back to the diaries later.

"Miss Naomi Myerson is here," her secretary says.

"Good. Please show her in," Mimi says.

"Mimi, *darling*," Nonie says, sweeping into the room in a red Trigère suit. "How wonderful to see you!" Mimi rises, and the two women greet each other with little pecks on the cheek.

"You're looking well, Aunt Nonie," Mimi says, trying to keep her tone casual and family-friendly. This will not be an easy feat for her—nor will this be an easy interview—because, try as she may, she has never really been able to *like* her father's younger sister. For this reason, because of the possibility of tension between the two women, Mimi has asked that I not be present at this meeting, promising to tell me all about it later on.

"*Thank* you," Nonie says, touching the collar of her jacket. "I picked this color just for you: lipstick red. Where shall I sit? Oh, not there—I'll clash. How about here on the sofa?" She seats herself and begins removing her matching red gloves, finger by finger. Then she crosses her knees, letting the heel of one red patent pump dangle fashionably from her toe so that the Delman label on the instep shows. "It seems ages since I've seen you, Mimi, dear," she says. "Not since that night at your house, when your mother made that . . . rather unfortunate scene. Oh, well. By the way, how is darling Alice?"

"Very well," Mimi says easily, and perches herself on the corner of her desk, deciding that this informal pose will seem less lady-executive than if she had seated herself behind the desk.

"Oh, that's *wonderful*," Nonie says, a trifle too effusively. "It's a pity that Alice and I have never been really . . . *close*. The great difference in our ages, I suppose."

Mimi smiles, thinking that her mother and her aunt are almost exactly the same age. And you've never been close, she thinks, because you've been taught for years to despise my mother because neither she nor anyone else would have ever been good enough for your parents' treasured Henry. "I suppose that's it," she says. "I wanted to see you, Aunt Nonie, because—"

"So this is the way you've redone Daddy's office," Nonie says, looking around. "I *like* it, I really do. It's very 'in,' isn't it? I'd heard that chintz is coming back. What are those?" she says, pointing to the stack of diaries.

"Oh, just some old books I'm thinking of buying."

"Are you and Brad into collecting old books now? I thought it was Chelsea plates. Well, I suppose you can afford to collect whatever you want, you have the money. Me, I've always been the poor relation, as you know."

"As a matter of fact, that's one reason why I wanted to talk with you, Aunt Nonie," Mimi says, trying to begin the meeting again.

Nonie tilts her chin in the air as though balancing a feather on the tip of her nose. "And you know," she says, "I've always thought that I could be sitting at that desk where you sit now. And I could be—if I'd been quick enough to grab the opportunity, before you pounced on it."

Mimi decides to let this comment pass with an easy laugh.

"I'm not joking. I could have run this company."

"I'm sure you could have, Aunt Nonie. But would you have wanted to? There are such a lot of headaches. For instance, right now—"

"But meanwhile, darling, I'm quite desperately looking forward to your launch party on the seventeenth. I'll quite definitely be there, and so, believe it or not, will Mother. She's even bringing her friend Rose Perlman. I said to her, 'Mother, all they're going to be doing is airing a couple of Mimi's new little television commercials; you won't be able to *see* them.' She said, 'Well, I can *hear* them, can't I? I watch television all the time, just by listening to it.' Isn't she a sketch?"

"She certainly is. Now what I—"

"And do you know what else she does? She turns off the television whenever she gets undressed to put on her nightie. She thinks the people on television can see her."

"My, my. Well—"

"But, darling, you must have had a more important reason for wanting to see me than just to talk about Mother. Really, it's such an honor for me, the perennial poor relation, to be invited to the executive offices of the Miray Corporation! Little me, invited down here by the great Mimi Myerson! Surely you don't want *my* advice on anything, darling."

"Not so much your advice," Mimi says, leaning forward eagerly. "Your support, Aunt Nonie. I'm going to ask you for your help."

"Oh, my goodness. Well, surprise, surprise. Well, tell me what I can do for you, darling. I'm putty in your hands."

"I've been meeting with all the members of the family," Mimi says. "All the family members who own Miray shares, including the Leo cousins, whom I'd never met before."

"Most unattractive people, so I've been told."

"Well, some are more attractive than others," Mimi says with a little shrug. "But the thing is, what I'm trying to get is a consensus—a unanimous consensus of family approval of a plan Badger and I are working on, which will affect all of us."

"I see," Nonie says guardedly.

"What we suspect is that we've become the object of an unfriendly takeover. We're quite sure we know who's after us. It's Michael Horowitz. He owns more than four percent of us already, and he's already approached the Leo cousins and made attractive offers for their shares."

"I see," Nonie says, again guardedly.

"The plan—and this is Badger's plan, actually—is that we would take the company private again. If we were to go private, that would leave Mr. Horowitz out in the cold. We'd become a family-owned company again."

"And how, pray, would you manage to accomplish this?"

"Going private is the exact opposite of what I did after Daddy died when I took the company public—but with a difference. Instead of a buyback of publicly held shares, which would cost us millions, we would telescope the stock. It's called a reverse split. For every thousand shares of old stock, for instance, we'd issue one share of new stock. Holders of less than a thousand shares would be paid for their stock in cash. There's another advantage to this. If we can do this, we figure we can reduce the number of Miray shareholders to less than three hundred, which means we would no longer be subject to SEC regulation. That in itself would save us a lot of money annually. Those savings could go into new-product development, as well as increased dividends to the remaining shareholders. Do you follow me, Aunt Nonie?"

"Well, what good are increased dividends to me?" Nonie says. "Everything that I own is in that damned trust. I can never get my hands on any of the principal. Even if you doubled the dividends, which I'm sure you wouldn't, I'd still be the poor relation, wouldn't I? How many shares does my trust own, anyway? I've never bothered to look at the statements, since they're quite meaningless to me."

"Approximately two hundred and fifty thousand shares."

"So, if you do this reverse split you're talking about, instead of having two hundred and fifty *thousand* shares, I'd wind up with a measly two hundred and *fifty* shares. That hardly sounds like a good deal to me, Mimi."

"Your shares would have the same monetary value, Aunt Nonie."

"Well, I don't like the sound of it," Nonie says. "No, I'm opposed to it.

I'm unalterably opposed to it, Mimi, and if you want unanimous family backing of this scheme, you'll have to count me out."

"Really, Aunt Nonie? Why?"

"On general principles," she says, crossing her knees in the opposite direction and letting the other red pump swing from her toe. "Because it doesn't sound fair. Because nothing this company has ever done to me has ever been fair. Because I know my big brother Henry would have been opposed to it. Henry was horrified, absolutely horrified, at the way I was treated in our father's will."

"Your big brother Henry was also my father," Mimi says.

"Well, I knew him a lot longer than you did, and a lot better. I know he'd be horrified with this scheme of yours. Or, I should say, this scheme of Badger's. I'm surprised you even listen to Badger, Mimi. He's not a real Myerson."

"Now, Aunt Nonie—that's not fair."

"His name is Moore, isn't it? He doesn't have our family's best interests at heart, if you ask me."

"Well," Mimi says quickly, "I happen to disagree. But there's another thing you might consider."

"What's that?"

"If we do this, we in effect would be reorganizing the entire company. We would even adopt a whole new corporate name—Miracorp, Inc., for instance, or something like that. And issuing an entirely new issue of stock, in an entirely new company—I've checked with our lawyers about this—would also have the effect of dissolving Grandpa's trusts."

Nonie sits forward in the sofa. "Dissolving his trusts?" she says.

"Yes. The trust he set up for you, for instance, applies only to stock in the company that existed then. The stock you'd acquire in the new company would have to move out of the trust."

"Out of the trust? You mean it could be *mine?* Free and clear?"

"Absolutely."

"How much would it be worth?"

"Roughly twelve and a half million dollars," Mimi says.

"To do with what I *want?*"

"Well, we'd hope you wouldn't turn around and sell it to Michael Horowitz," Mimi says with a little laugh. "But, yes, it would move into your personal portfolio."

"Well, in that case . . . well, that puts a different light on it, doesn't it? With twelve and a half million, I could—I'd be—"

"Free from Grandpa's trust."

"Free! Free at last!" Then she says, "What does Edwee think?"

"I haven't approached Edwee yet. I'm seeing Edwee on Monday. I wanted to know what you thought, first."

"Well, if it will dissolve that damned trust, I'm all for it!" Nonie says. "But don't expect me to try to talk Edwee into it, Mimi. Edwee and I are . . . a little on the outs at the moment. Edwee is being incommunicado to me right now."

"Oh? What's that all about?"

"Edwee wanted something, and I helped him try to get it. But now he can't get it, and his nose is out of joint."

"Does this have something to do with Granny's Goya?" Mimi asks quietly.

Nonie is silent for a moment. Then she says, "All I can tell you right now is that Edwee and I had a contract—a legal contract, with a witness. It should stand up in a court of law, if I decide to take it there. I held up my end of the deal, but now Edwee is trying to welsh on his end. We'll just see what happens next."

"Well, I suppose that's a matter between the two of you," she says, deciding, probably wisely, she thinks, to let the subject rest at that.

"But if this plan of yours goes through, it won't matter! I'll have all the money I need. How long will it take, do you think, before I get the money?"

"It won't be money, Aunt Nonie. Remember that it will be stock. And remember that it's more difficult to sell stock in a private company than it is in a public one."

"But I can use my stock as collateral for a loan, can't I? With twelve and a half million in stock, I could borrow . . . five million, couldn't I?"

"I see no reason why not. Why not? The stock will be yours."

"That's all I need. When will I get it?"

"After the launch party, there'll be a stockholders' meeting. We'll notify each of you. We'll take a vote."

"Well, you can count on *my* vote," Nonie says. "I'm all for it *now*—now that you've explained it all to me. Just think, a whole new company! Miracorp, Inc.—I like the name, Mimi. Just think, I'll be a first-class stockholder of Miracorp, Inc.!"

"Just please keep all this confidential, Aunt Nonie. We're not ready for news of this to reach the street."

"Oh, I *will!* As you know, I'm a woman of my word. But, Mimi, there's just one thing."

"What's that?"

She hesitates. It kills her to ask a favor of Mimi, and she is certain that Mimi knows it kills her. She has always known that Mimi never liked her very much. Perhaps, Nonie sometimes thinks, it is because she and Mimi are so much alike. Both are ambitious, driven women. Both are clever, both are smart, both are beautiful. Both have inherited the genes of Adolph Myerson and, with them, his keen business sense, his astuteness, his intuitive know-how, his stamina and guts, his courage and integrity, and his charismatic flair. All that is from Myerson genes. The only difference between them is that Mimi has been lucky, and Nonie has not. In life, and in everything one encounters in life, luck is everything. Every success, every failure, is a matter of luck. Mimi has had all the luck; Nonie has had none of it. But now Nonie's luck is beginning to change. She can feel it beginning to change.

"Do you think," Nonie begins, "that after you've gone private, and after the new company is organized—do you think I could be on the board of directors of Miracorp, Inc.?"

"Why, I think that's a lovely idea, Aunt Nonie," Mimi says. "I've always thought that there should be women on our board."

Nonie claps her hands. "Oh, Mimi," she cries. "I always thought you were a darling girl! And Badger too! And brilliant! Both of you—just brilliant!"

Mimi hops down from her desktop perch, steps toward her aunt, and clasps her hand in hers, her eyes shining. "Do you know something, Aunt Nonie?" she says. "I've just had the craziest idea!"

"What's that, darling?"

"I think that, after all these years, you and I could actually be *friends!* Is that possible?"

"I'm losing her, Flo," he says to her. "I can feel it. I'm losing her."

"Losing who, Bradley?" Granny Flo asks her visitor. Granny Flo has always had trouble with Brad Moore's name, sometimes calling him "Bradley" and sometimes confusing his name with his son's nickname, calling him "Bradger."

"Mimi," he says. "I wanted you to be the first to know, in case something happens between us. I've always suspected, you see, that it was you, and not Mimi's grandfather, who was behind that trip to Europe, where Mimi and I met. If it hadn't been for you—"

"Well, you're right about that one," Granny Flo says. "That trip was my idea, but I let Adolph take the credit for it. She was so brokenhearted, you know, when that romance with the other one, that what's-his-name, didn't work out. I've never seen a girl so brokenhearted. My own heart just went out to her, back then."

"Well, it's beginning to look as though our marriage may not be working out, I'm sorry to say. And I felt I owed it to you to warn you."

For several moments Granny sits in her chair, saying nothing, her mouth working, her eyes staring vacantly into the distance. Then she says, "Well, it won't be the first divorce in this family, if that's what's worrying you. Look at Nonie. Do you still love her, Bradger?"

"Oh, yes."

"You haven't been fooling around, have you?"

He studies the backs of his hands. "Yes," he says quietly.

"Well, there you go," she says. "That's the thing of it. A woman like Mimi won't put up with a man who has mistresses. That's one thing I can say about my Adolph. He never had mistresses. Or, if he did have, he was smart enough not to let me find out about it. That's the other thing about it. A woman doesn't mind if her husband has mistresses, as long as she doesn't know about it. Like they say, what a person doesn't know won't hurt her. But if she finds out—watch out! Particularly a girl like Mimi. The finding out is the part that hurts."

He nods his head silently.

"Do you want to keep her?"

"Yes," he says.

"Then tell me something," she says. "Did you ever meet my friend Dr. Sigmund Freud?"

"No, I didn't."

"He's actually some sort of relative of ours," she says. "He's related to us, by marriage, through the Bernays family. He used to stay with Adolph and me when he came to America giving his lectures. But I think he's back living somewhere in Europe now."

"I think Sigmund Freud has been dead for a number of years, Flo," he says gently.

"Is that so? Cousin Sigmund's dead? Why didn't Cousin Nettie write and tell me, I wonder? Well, anyway, he was supposed to be so smart. He was supposed to know all about the brain, you know, and all about the whatchamacallits, the emotions. But if you ask me, Bradley, that man wasn't as smart as he was cracked up to be."

"Why do you say that, Flo?"

"I'll tell you why. Exactly. He was staying with us, with Adolph and me, when we had the house on Madison Avenue, and he was here to give those lectures, or whatever it was, which were to tell everybody who'd listen to him how smart he was. And one night after dinner, I said to him, 'Cousin Sig, if you're supposed to be so smart, then suppose you tell me what *love* is.' He looked at me with that kind of stupid look of his, and he said, 'Flo, there *is* no definition of love.' What do you think of that?"

"Well," he says cautiously, "is there a definition of love?"

Granny Flo slaps her knee and says, "Of *course* there is, and I told him so. I said, 'Love is *sacrifice*—that's all it is, sacrifice.' "

"But," he begins, "doesn't the sacrifice have to be . . . mutual? On the part of both the people involved?"

"Nonsense! When you start thinking like that, that's when you're in trouble. Sacrifice is what it is—just that, sacrifice. It means giving up something for another person. It doesn't have to be tit for tat, if you'll pardon my French. In fact, when you make it tit for tat, that's when you're in trouble again. Sacrifice is giving up something *you* care about, for the person you love. It's something *you* do—never mind what the other person does. Sacrifice means personal. It means *individual.* If you give up something you care about, and then expect the other person to give up something she cares about, then it's not a sacrifice. That's called a trade-off, and that won't work. It's as simple as that."

'Sacrifice," he says.

"Just keep that word in mind if you really love Mimi, Bradley, and if you really want to keep her. The word is sacrifice. Even the great Dr. Sigmund Freud didn't know what to say when I told him that. Just gave me that stupid look of his." Then she says, "But remember, it doesn't have to be a big sacrifice. Nine times out of ten, a little one will do."

29

*C*AN WE TALK a little?" Brad asks her. "Can we talk a little about what's going to happen to you and me, about the future?" It is Sunday morning, and they are sitting at their breakfast table at 1107 Fifth Avenue. It is the first time they have spoken to one another in two days.

"Yes, I suppose it's time we talked," she says, setting down her grapefruit spoon into a Chelsea plate with a raised border of hand-painted grapefruit sections. "Yes, I guess it's time."

"No tempers this time? Just two middle-aged married people who are supposed to be intelligent? Just two mature adults?"

"Goodness, are we middle-aged? I guess you're right. Maybe that's part of the trouble."

"I'll start with a grown-up question," he says. "You've been locking me out of your bedroom. Is that intended to tell me something? Is it . . . divorce?"

She studies the border of the plate. "Frankly, I'm not *think*ing about divorce right now," she says. "Or at least I'm trying not to. I'm thinking of a dozen different things right now, but not divorce. Not now. Not yet."

"Tell me what you're thinking about, Mimi."

"Oh, I'm thinking about these Chelsea plates," she says absently. "When we bought them. That little place on Lexington Avenue. You spotted them first."

"I remember the shop. I think it was I who spotted the shop. You spotted these plates."

"No, it was—" She sighs. "It doesn't matter. They're pretty, aren't they?

But that's the thing about divorce, isn't it? Things get broken up. We'll have to divide the collection."

"No, it's your collection, Mimi. I'd want you to have it all."

"But I don't think I'd want it. It was something we did together. Do you remember that hotel in the south of France?"

"What hotel?"

"Outside Béziers. The dresser in our bedroom had five drawers. We each insisted that the other one had to take the fifth drawer. We got into such an argument that we wouldn't speak to each other all through dinner, though I remember the wine was nice. Somehow, this discussion reminds me of that. But we're supposed to be talking about the future, and here we are talking about the past."

Now there is silence between them for several minutes, and a breeze from Central Park through one of the partly opened windows blows a strand of Mimi's loose hair across her face, and she brushes it aside with one hand. She rises slowly and walks to the mantel where the pair of pink Sèvres vases stand. With a fingertip, she traces the tiny cat-scratch markings where the glaze has been repaired. "And these vases," she says. "Who'll get the one that Badger broke?"

"What else are you thinking about?" he says. "You said there were a dozen things."

"Oh, and I'm thinking about how I loved to go to those windows there, and look out at the park, and the lake. But now I can't, because I'm afraid I'll see her sitting there, watching this apartment."

"I think she's finally gotten my message," he says. "It's been three days now, and I've heard nothing. No telephone calls, no threats. No more signs of sidewalk vigils from across the street."

"But how can you be sure she won't come back?"

"I can't, of course," he says.

"And so how can I walk out of this building without keeping my eyes on the ground, without looking up or around, without diving into my car as fast as I can so I won't catch sight of her? I feel right now like some sort of strange prisoner in my own house, that my freedom has been usurped by her, that I'm under some strange sort of house arrest—that I don't own myself anymore, that part of me is owned by her. I'm thinking that."

"And what else?" he persists.

"And I'm thinking how hurt I was the other night—when you said you'd spent the past two years trying to have a marriage, while I'd spent the time creating a new perfume. That hurt, Brad. Years ago, I swore I'd never let a man hurt me like that again, but that did hurt."

He says nothing.

"Because, you see, I also think you don't understand what I've tried to do with this business, and that also hurts—hurts more than anything that's happened between us."

"That's not true, Mimi. I've always admired your ambition."

"Ambition?" she says, studying the network of cracks in the vase. "I've never thought of it as ambition. I think of ambition as wanting money, or power, or fame. But that's not really what I ever wanted, though I suppose I've been able to achieve some of those things."

"What was it you wanted, then?"

"I guess I've always thought of myself as Little Miss Fix-It," she says quietly. "I'm always trying to set things to rights. As a little girl, I was always thinking of ways I could make my parents' marriage better. When Daddy died, I wanted to take over his company in order to vindicate his memory. People were saying that he'd taken an ailing company and run it into the ground. I wanted to prove that he'd left something that was salvageable. I also wanted to do right by Mother, since when he died he left her in a worse state than ever, and what would have become of her if we'd let Miray go into bankruptcy? I wanted to do right by Granny Flo. Grandpa had pirated her trusts, and I wanted to see to it that she got those funds back. I wanted to do right by Nonie, who was always bitter about how she'd been treated in Grandpa's will. I even wanted to do right by Edwee, I suppose. I wanted to do right by the *family*."

"And you've done all those things," he says.

"And now I want to do right by Badger. He'll take the company over someday, and I want to hand it over to him in the best possible shape. And now we have this—this perfume that you mentioned. Yes, it's only perfume. And when we started developing this product two years ago, it was more like fun and games. But suddenly it's become terribly important, Brad. Everything hangs or falls, depending on the success of this little scent. And the ad campaign—the man with the scar—it's a terribly risky thing we're doing. If the public doesn't buy it, and the scent fails . . . well, if that fails, Badger's privatization plan could also fail. If that fails, we remain a takeover target, and if we lose the company, that's the end of it for me, and for Badger, and for everybody we've worked with, and of everything we've worked for, for twenty-five years. Do you see why what happens Thursday night at the Pierre, and in the weeks that follow, is suddenly, all at once, so terribly important for me, and for Badger, and for all the rest of us? Our competition would like to see us fail. But we—we're simply desperate for success!"

"I can understand all that," he says. "But I guess what I don't quite see is how I fit into all of this."

She hesitates. "You fit," she says. "Or at least I thought you did. I thought I needed you for balance. For balance and sanity and solidity. For your logical lawyer's mind. For ballast. Mine *is* a crazy business. There's no logic to it at all. It's all nonsense and fairy tales, when you get right down to it. I used to think it was nice, at the end of the day, to leave that crazy business and come home to you, to a world where there were real causes and effects and explanations, and to get my balance back. That's why I thought ours was a good marriage. My business was all Las Vegas chaos. Yours was about order, sequence, and precedence. In our lives, we seemed to balance each other out. And we were both successful, and hardly competitive. And I thought that was . . . kind of nice. But now I'm not so sure."

"Because of what I've done, you mean."

"No, not because of that. I've known about your woman friend for some time. What hurts much more than that is what you said the other night. Because, you see, Brad, I think you find this business that I'm in a little bit . . . frivolous. A little bit superficial. Not quite classy enough for your taste. After all, you're a prominent Wall Street lawyer, with your eye on the Senate, and then maybe the Supreme Court. And I . . . well, it said it on the cover of *Time*, didn't it? 'Beauty Queen.' Is a Beauty Queen the right sort of wife for a senator, or a Supreme Court justice? I think that's what you've begun to wonder lately. This business of mine is too . . . too *Jewish*, maybe? After all, with the exception of the late Miss Arden, it is pretty much a Jewish business. And I'm not even sure about Arden. After all, she changed her name from Graham to Arden, and she could have changed it to Graham from Goldstone. That's what hurts the most, Brad: to think that my success has made you a little bit ashamed—no, not ashamed, perhaps, but a little bit embarrassed by me."

His look at her now is hard and level. "That," he says, "is horseshit. That is absolute horseshit. You're the woman I married, and the woman I love. I wouldn't love you any differently, or any less, if you drove a garbage truck."

She looks at him briefly, then returns her gaze to the pink Sèvres vase, tracing its cracks again with her fingertip.

"And I think you know it's horseshit," he says. Then he says, "Were you ever unfaithful to me, Mimi?"

She says nothing, but her scrutiny of the cracked vase grows more intense.

"Who was he, Mimi?"

"It doesn't matter," she says. "It was a long time ago, and the circumstances were quite different." But even as she says this, she realizes that neither the time gone by, nor the different circumstances, have much bearing on the matter.

"Why were the circumstances different?"

"You'd moved out on me, moved to the Harvard Club. My father was having terrible problems. My mother was drunk all the time. The emotional center seemed to have dropped out of my life. I was scared. I had nowhere to turn. I needed someone to lean on."

"You called me and asked me to come back. You said you needed me."

"I did."

"The other night you said you needed me at your launch party. If you still need me, I'll be there."

"Thank you, Brad. It's only for appearances, I know, but in this business appearances are everything."

"It was Michael Horowitz, wasn't it?" he says.

She closes her eyes, and two tears squeeze out.

"I forgave you long ago," he says.

Now it is Monday, and her uncle Edwee is in her office, and she has been trying to demonstrate the advantages of privatization to him, but Edwee, it seems, has an entirely different agenda. She had been shocked, first off, by his appearance. When he walked in her office door, she hardly recognized him. His long mane of silver hair, usually so impeccably blow-dried, combed, and sprayed, is a tangled and disheveled mass. He is unshaven and looks as though he needs a bath. His silk Sulka shirt is open at the collar, and his necktie is askew. He is wearing one of his bespoke Savile Row suits, but it is so rumpled that he might have slept in it. Even the signature red carnation in his buttonhole looks many days old. His socks sag at the ankles, and one of his shoelaces is undone. At first, she thought that Brad had been right, that he was undergoing some sort of breakdown. She also thought that he might have been drinking, or that he might be under the influence of some sort of drug. She also wondered whether he might be delivering some sort of theatrical performance and had dressed, rather carefully, for the part. As he speaks, his come-and-go stammer is more pronounced than ever.

"I don't c-c-c-c-care what you do with your damned c-c-c-company," he shouts, pounding his fist on her desk. "All I want to know is what's become of my m-m-m-m-m-mother's Goya!"

"Edwee, dear," she says gently, trying to calm him, "I have no idea what she's done with it. Why would I know anything about that?"

"I'm telling you I want you to f-f-f-find out!"

"Why don't you just ask her, Edwee?"

"I've tried that. She just pulls her senile act on me. It's all an act, you know. It's like her blind act. She can see just as well as you and I. I want you to go up to the Carlyle, M-M-Mimi, and find out what she's done with it."

"Why me? I have nothing to do with her art collection."

"You're the only one who has any influ-flu-flu-fluence on her. You're Henry's daughter. He was always her favorite child."

"Perhaps she gave it to the Prado in Madrid. I remember, several years ago, she had some correspondence with them about it. Perhaps she's loaned it to an exhibition. You see, Edwee, the point is that it's her painting. She's free to do with it whatever she wishes. It's hardly up to me to interfere with whatever it is your mother wants to do."

"She's not f-f-f-free! If nobody else wants it, it could be given to me. Nonie doesn't want it. De M-M-M-Montebello doesn't want it."

"Which really astonishes me," Mimi says. "I thought he'd had his eye on that painting for years—and I know Granny was prepared to offer it to the museum as an outright gift."

"He doesn't want it because it's a f-f-f-fake! He wrote me a letter and told me so."

"Really, Edwee? Well, if it's a fake, then what's all the fuss about? Why do you care so much what happens to a fake Goya?"

"Because I w-w-w-want it! Because I've always wanted it. There's a space on the wall of my study that's been waiting for it!"

"Then why don't you go out and commission somebody to do another fake? That shouldn't cost much."

"I don't want *another* fake! I want *that fake!*"

"Really, Edwee, I think that this is a matter that will have to be sorted out between you and Granny. I don't want to get involved in it."

"You mean, you refuse?"

"Yes. I just don't have the time to get involved in this."

He sits in the chair opposite her desk for a long time, glaring at her, saying nothing.

"And if that's all, Edwee . . . ," she begins.

He looks away from her. "Have you talked to Brad lately?" he says.

"My husband? Of course. I talk to him every day."

"Did he tell you what I have in my possession?"

"He mentioned something, yes," she says easily. "Some sort of film. I didn't pay too much attention."

"What I have," he says, "is a videotape. It features your young male model, Mr. Gordon. It depicts him performing fellatio, and frontal and anal intercourse, with a woman . . . and another man."

"Oh, dear," she says. "Isn't it sad? These young models in New York— they often have to do that sort of thing in order to earn enough to eat. It's so hard getting started on a modeling career in this town."

"But couldn't that be a little . . . embarrassing . . . to your new ad campaign? Your Mireille Man, involved in something like this? If I were to release this?"

"Oh, it could be, I suppose," she says, tapping a pencil lightly on her desktop. "I'd have to see what's on the tape in order to decide."

"You'll see it, all right! Aren't you planning to show him in your new commercials at your party Thursday night? It said so in the invitation."

"That's correct."

"What if I were to release the tape before the party? What if word of it got to the press?"

"Well, if worse came to worst, we might have to shoot some new commercials, using another model. Male models, unfortunately, are a dime a dozen. This man was only one of several finalists for the job. But that would be a worst-case scenario."

"Won't that cost you a lot of money? Didn't I read in the *Times* that it costs nearly a million dollars to produce a thirty-second television spot?"

"Something like that. But it's only money. And, if I have to skip a dividend or two—"

"Skip a *dividend*! But that's all we have to live on is our dividends! You wouldn't dare do that."

"Wouldn't I?" she says with a smile. "You seem to forget that I am the president of this company, Edwee, dear."

"You wouldn't dare! As a stockholder, I—we—"

She laughs. "Don't worry, Edwee, dear. I was really only teasing you. You won't lose any of your precious dividends. It won't cost the company anything to reshoot a few commercials. We have insurance for this sort of thing."

"Insurance?"

"Of course. With something called a morals clause. If Mr. Gordon has violated the morals clause in his contract, as it sounds as though he may have done, our insurance will cover everything. A morals clause is standard in all film and television contracts for performers. So don't worry about that, Edwee."

"Worry? *Me? You're* the one who should be worried, Mimi! What about this videotape of mine?"

"Well, as I believe my husband told you, we refuse to take this threat of yours seriously until we've seen the alleged tape. Why don't you bring it around sometime? We have plenty of facilities here for screening videotapes. Actually, if it's as juicy as you say it is, there are some people here in the office who would probably get a kick out of seeing it!"

He jumps to his feet. "Damn it, Mimi," he shouts. "You'll pay for this! You'll see! You'll pay for this! You'll be sorry when I'm through with you! If you don't find my mother's Goya for me before your party Thursday night, you'll be sorry!"

"And do me a favor, Edwee, dear," she says. "That suit of yours needs pressing badly. And do something about your hair and fingernails. That messy, mousey look went out in the sixties."

He charges across her office toward the door.

"Love to little Gloria!" she calls after him as he stalks out the door and slams it hard behind him.

And Mimi takes a deep breath.

30

*N*OW IT IS SIX O'CLOCK on Monday evening, her secretary has left for the night, and Mimi sits alone in her office, reading her grandfather's diaries. In some ways, as she reads, she recognizes the stern old man she remembers from years ago, but in other ways he emerges as a stranger. For example:

> *January 7, 1940*
> *Problem with Edwin at his school in Florida. Man named Collier—a whole string of young schoolboys Edwin's age! Worse than Fagin in Oliver Twist! Why do they not arrest this man Collier? No solid Evidence, they say. Edwin much too young to understand this sort of thing. School has him safely back, will keep an eye on him.*

> *January 18, 1940*
> *Edwin run away from school again! Authorities found him with Collier again. What does this scum of the earth do to keep himself out of prison? Corrupt Florida police, I know. Thank God no publicity. Edwin still a minor, but publicity of this nature could ruin Edwin's Presidential chances later on. Was Edwin too young to send away to boarding school? Have found new school for him in Massachusetts. Closer to home, away from Collier influences. Damn Collier! If I were there I'd strangle the scum with my bare hands. . . .*

January 23, 1940
Have straightened out Naomi's problem with Bloomingdale's. Store satis-
fied, store security people satisfied. No publicity. Naomi's Dr. says she only
does these things when she finds herself in stressful circumstances. Blames
Naomi's recent sudden marriage, and even more recent sudden divorce.
Damn it, if Naomi would just marry a decent husband, and stay married to
him, and start giving me grandsons I need to carry on, there wouldn't be
any "stressful circumstances"!

January 26, 1940
More trouble with Edwin at his new school in Mass. Ran away, took bus
to Florida. Found with Collier again! Would start legal proceedings
against Collier, but what about publicity? Oh, Edwin, what is wrong with
you? I begin to despair. Edwin being returned to N.Y. on train tonight.
Must find new school for him with greater discipline. School in Mass.
doesn't want him back—disruptive influence. Had words with Flo last
night. Blame her for making him a "Mama's boy."

Also, beginning in the late 1930s, Mimi has found entries referring to
certain shadowy figures, working either within or outside the company, who
seemed to have been engaged, without her grandfather's approval, by his
younger brother. In the diaries, these people are semi-cryptically identified
as "Leo's friends," and the diaries become increasingly peppered with the
phrase "GET LEO OUT," or "LEO MUST GO," as in the following
series of entries over a two-and-a-half-year period:

February 5, 1939
Damned Leo! Had him on the carpet today about friends he is still using
to "help" our business. Leo just laughed in my face and said this is all part
of the normal cost of doing business. Everybody does it. The fool! These
people are nothing but animals, no respect for human life. These friends of
his could ruin us if any of this got out. Must begin working out careful
plan to get Leo OUT—and his friends.

May 27, 1939
Guess what! Leo came in today to ask for promotion for his son Nate!
Wants Nate promoted over Henry, because Nate is a few years older. Told
Leo to go to hell. Leo is a schmuck, but Nate is a worse schmuck. Leo
said, "Where would you be if I hadn't added quick-drying chemical to
paint?" I said, "Where would you be if I hadn't figured out a way to sell

it? You wanted to throw it all out—schmuck!" Work on ways to get Leo out.

September 12, 1940

Now it's Alice who's telling me how to run my business! Damn Alice! She came in to see me today, drunk of course. She tells me all the things I know already about Leo and his friends. Is Henry a fool? He was a fool to tell Alice about any of this, because when Alice is drunk she runs off at the mouth. A woman has no business interfering with her husband's business. Told her that. A woman has no business coming to her husband's place of business and demanding this & that. Why doesn't Alice stay home and take care of her baby? Told her all this. Told her she is nothing but a yenta and a troublemaker. I told Henry when he married her that I saw nothing but trouble ahead with her, and I was right. Told her to get out. Told her I never wanted to lay eyes on her again. Too harsh? Henry didn't seem to think so when I told him what had happened. Just looked sheepish. . . . Alice puts him through holy hell, I know. . . .

October 2, 1940

Started work today on a plan to GET LEO OUT. It must be very careful, very detailed, and foolproof because even though Leo is stupid he can be a tough cookie. . . .

November 27, 1940

PLAN TO GET LEO OUT

Step 1: Stop office memos coming to him. Let time pass to let it sink in to Leo what is happening.

Step 2: Disconnect all Leo phone lines but one. Ditto about letting time pass. Tell switchboard to direct all his calls to me.

Step 3: Get his office repainted some ugly color while he's out of it. "Vomit green." Ditto re time.

Step 4: Remove nameplate from his door. Hide it. Make door of steel so he can't screw new one on. Ditto re time, but time gets shorter now between Steps.

Step 5: Fire his secretary. Disconnect final phone line same day. Instruct switchboard to say, "Mr. Leopold Myerson is no longer with us."

Step 6: Have him painted out of "Founders Portrait."

Start date for plan: January 2, 1941.

Read plan to Flo last night before dinner. She likes it. Added a few touches of her own (nameplate, e.g.).

There follow entries for the dates that each step of the plan was carried out.

January 7, 1941
Took Leo a week to figure out something's going on, why he's getting no interoffice memos, he's so stupid. Now he runs up and down office corridors after mailroom boys, trying to snatch memos from their stacks! Told Flo about this last night. She laughed and laughed. . . .

March 1, 1941
All Leo's extra phone lines cut off today. Took him most of the day to realize it. He's hopping mad! Tried to get in to see me, but Jonesy won't let him. Using private elevator direct to car to avoid him. Others in the office now realize something's going on, and they're getting a big kick out of it because all of them hate Leo, too. I think Henry knows something's going on, too, though I haven't told him about my Plan. Henry's in a much better mood these days, cheerier, more compliant. Think maybe my tough talk with Alice has paid off. Maybe she's nagging and henpecking him less. . . . Thank God for Henry! I despair of the other one. . . .

April 4, 1941
Step 3 carried out last night, after hours! Had his office repainted last night, ugliest puke color I could find. For good measure, had his carpet torn up and one large sofa removed, and had Clorox poured into the pots of all his precious plants! It will be fun when they begin to die! Painters still at work when he came in this morning. Leo started screaming like a banshee, yelling, "Who ordered this?" Painters just said, "Company orders, sir," and went on painting. Now he is running up and down the corridors, screaming and yelling at everybody, making everybody crazy,

but everybody really getting a big kick out of what is going on. He keeps trying to get me on the phone or get into my office, but can't. Ha, ha, ha.

April 9, 1941

Leo wailing and kvetching, "What's the matter with my plants?" Making his secretary crazy. Hope I can get to Step 5 before she quits on him, he's making her so crazy. . . . He runs around like a chicken with its head cut off, trying to get in to see me. Not yet!

May 5, 1941

Had his office door replaced with steel one yesterday. "Fire regulations," he was told. His nameplate "lost" in process. He went out and ordered a new one, and spent an hour this morning trying to hammer his new name-plate onto the steel door, while nails kept bending and Leo cursing and screaming and banging his thumb with hammer. Wish I could have been there to see this! What a schmuck!

May 17, 1941

Had Personnel Dept. give Miss Applegate, his secretary, her walking pa-pers last night. They say she cried a lot, but then she said she was thinking of quitting anyway, he was making her so crazy. Also had his last phone line disconnected. Leo strangely silent today. Not a peep from him all day long. They say he just sits in his office, staring into space. Is he planning something? Or have I finally "broken the camel's back"? I hope so. Any-way, I think I'll hold off my final move for a while, and let him settle into this silent state of his before I deliver the "coupé de grace"!

Now, as Mimi turns the pages of the daybook for the year 1941, she encounters an entry that is not an entry at all, but a yellowed clipping from the *New York Times*, dated June 4, 1941, and affixed to the pages of the diary with dried and crumbling Scotch tape.

HIT-AND-RUN DRIVER KILLS
PEDESTRIAN ON FIFTH AVE.

Early afternoon shoppers on Fifth Avenue looked on in horror yester-day as an automobile, ignoring a red light, tore across the intersection of 54th Street, striking a male pedestrian who was crossing the Avenue from west to east and injuring several others. The victim, whose identity is not yet known, was pronounced dead upon arrival at Roosevelt Hospital. While bystanders rushed to the victim's assistance, the driver of the vehicle, which did not stop at the time of the accident, sped northward and was quickly lost in uptown traffic.

Several other pedestrians received bruises and minor injuries as they rushed, or were pushed, out of the path of the speeding car.

Though there were literally scores of witnesses to the accident, it was difficult for police to get consistent descriptions of either the car or its driver. Most, however, maintained that the automobile was a black Lincoln Zephyr sedan, of the year model 1939 or 1940. Others, however, claimed that the car was dark blue or dark green. There appeared to be a consensus among witnesses that the driver of the car was a young woman between the ages of 25 and 30, wearing a white sailor-type hat. Others claimed to have seen a small child in the front seat beside her.

Several bystanders attempted to note the license number of the car. According to one witness, the license number was KLG-130, while another claimed to remember it as HJG-030. Still others claimed that the automobile was moving too fast to note the license. All agreed that the car bore New York plates.

"What we're looking for," said Police Chief Walter O'Malley, "is a dark Lincoln Zephyr sedan, 1939 or 1940 model, with a license plate containing at least one G as its third letter, and one three, and at least one zero. This will narrow our search considerably."

The accident occurred at approximately 2:45 P.M. yesterday. A four square block area immediately surrounding the scene was cordoned off by police for about one hour to allow access to ambulance and other emergency equipment.

The next day's entry was a second clipping, from the *Times* of the following day:

HIT-AND-RUN VICTIM'S
IDENTITY LEARNED

The identity of the pedestrian killed on Fifth Avenue Tuesday afternoon by a hit-and-run driver was revealed by police today. He was Larry J. Elkins, 39, of Utica, N.Y. Mr. Elkins, a teacher in the Utica public school system, was vacationing in New York with his wife. Mrs. Elkins, who was not with her husband at the time of the accident, was waiting for him to return from a short shopping errand in the couple's room at the Gotham Hotel. The Elkinses have two children, aged 13 and 9. Mrs. Elkins returned to Utica with her husband's body today.

No arrest has yet been made in the case. However, according to Police Chief Walter O'Malley, "We have narrowed this down and have several very strong leads that we're pursuing. We are confident that an arrest will be made in the very near future."

The driver of the car that fled the scene of the accident at the corner of Fifth Avenue and 54th Street has been described as a young woman in her mid-twenties or early thirties, wearing a white hat and driving a dark (black, dark green, or dark blue, according to various witnesses) 1939 or 1940 model Lincoln Zephyr sedan, with New York license plates.

The entry for the following day was once again in her grandfather's hand, and his words were especially terse.

June 6, 1941
My suspicions confirmed. Henry came into my office this morning. Told
him I will handle everything. Alice leaves for Bar Harbor immediately.
Servants there have their instructions. Everything else to be taken care of.
Alice! She is Henry's nemesis, his bane, his curse, his bad penny. Told
Henry that. Also told him that this is the last time we will be using his
uncle Leo's friends. For ANYTHING.

What had her grandmother said that night at the dinner table? "She killed a man once, you know. It was all in Adolph's diary." With a feeling of despair, Mimi thinks: This was the man she killed, the man Granny meant, not Daddy. Oh, Mother, Mother, she thinks—was that you? The pretty lady in the big white hat? Was the white hat ever a part of her dream? She cannot remember, but this man was the dark shape flying across the windshield of the car, and those screams were perhaps not her mother's screams but his screams, or the screams of the onlookers standing at the intersection or trying to cross the street. Slowly, all the pieces of the puzzle now are tumbling into place: Why she could never tell her grandparents about her scholarship, why there was never enough money, why her mother and father exchanged those dark, secret looks, why her parents fought all the time, why there was always the hidden threat of tension and misery in the air on 97th Street. Why her mother drank. As Granny Flo said, it was all in Adolph's diary.

She turns the page to find another clipping from the *Times*.

5TH AVE. HIT-AND-RUN VEHICLE
BELIEVED FOUND

June 8. The automobile involved in the vehicular homicide which occurred on Fifth Avenue at 54th Street Tuesday afternoon has been found, police officials say. The accident, from which car and driver fled the scene, left one man dead and others slightly injured, while creating pandemonium and disrupting midtown traffic for nearly an hour.

The automobile, a black 1940 Lincoln Zephyr sedan, was found abandoned on the street in the docks area at the foot of West 23rd Street. The car matched eyewitnesses' descriptions of the death vehicle. Its hood and right front fender were deeply dented, police say, and tests showed that spatters of dried blood on the hood and windshield matched the blood type of the victim, Larry J. Elkins, 39, a schoolteacher from Utica, N.Y.

The car bore painted-over license plates with the numbers HLG-031, which also closely correspond with eyewitness accounts. This license number, however, corresponds with no known owner of record in New York State. Under the painted-over plates, police were able to identify the luxury vehicle as one reported stolen from a Brooklyn garage in April of this year. Tests of the car's interior revealed no fingerprints.

"The fact that the vehicle was stolen hamstrings our investigations somewhat," Police Chief Walter O'Malley told the Times today. "But we are determined to find the perpetrator of this homicide and are actively pursuing various leads."

Now Mimi is puzzled. Would her mother have been driving a stolen car with painted-over plates? It makes no sense. The driver must have been an entirely different person. And yet why would her grandfather have devoted so much space and attention to this accident in his diary? She turns the pages slowly now but finds no more reference to the accident in the weeks that follow. Then, under the date of August 9, she finds the following:

Executed final phase of Step 6 today. Summoned Leo to my office. Have refused to see or speak to him since Step 1. Jonesy, all smiles, showed him in (she knows what's up!). Leo looked thinner, paler. Held out his hand to shake mine, then noticed portrait of "Our Founders," which has been significantly altered. Portrait now titled "Our Founder." They say, "I hate to see a grown man cry." I didn't. I liked it. Leo blubbered like a baby, said, "How can you treat your own brother this way?" I said, or in words to this effect, "Face it, Leo, you're through in this company. I have no further

*use for you. This company has no further use for you. You've had it, you're
finished, you're through, you're out. Now go back to your office, clean out
your desk, get out of here and never come back. I have the goods on you,
you know. I know all about your dealings with those friends of yours. It's
all on record, it's all written down. Now get out." After he left, Jonesy
stepped in and gave me a saucy little wink. She's kind of cute. Tonight,
Flo and I to celebrate with dinner at "21."*

But then, a week later, on August 15, he still seemed to be worried about
Leo.

*Could Leo sneak back and find these diaries? Too dangerous. Ordered
locks changed on all doors—closets, too. Consider ordering wall safe with
combination lock to keep these in.*

And then, on August 27, she finds another entry that seems to allude to
the accident, and to the fact that, even though Leo was now out of the
company, her grandfather still feared him and his mysterious friends, and
that Leo still wielded some ominous power over the family.

*Leo has put 2&2 together re Alice—or thinks he has. Has approached
Henry with threat. Wouldn't dare approach me! Henry in to see me this
morning, very frightened. Wrote Henry cheque for $100,000, which is
what Leo wants. Worth it, I guess, to shut Leo up. But told Henry this is
the end of it. No more where this came from! Besides, Leo has no evidence, only guesswork. Police have closed case. End of this.*

There are only one or two other entries of interest.

September 20, 1941
*Ordered combination wall safe today. Mosler people here to measure.
Delivery: one month.*

Then she has come, again, to the final entry of all, the one dated October
10, about her father borrowing money from his mother. But now, as she flips
absently through the blank pages, she discovers a loose piece of paper placed
between two of these. It is a letter, and she removes it and reads it. It is
typed on a letterhead that rings only a faint bell in her memory.

THE KETTERING PLAY SCHOOL
24 East 39th Street
New York 16, N.Y.

Nathan Myerson, Esq.   *June 20, 1941*
1 West 72nd Street
New York 23, N.Y.

Dear Mr. Myerson:
Thank you for your interest in the attendance record of your niece, Mireille, at our School. Our records show that little Mireille spent a normal, happy day at School on June 3, and was collected promptly by her mother at 2:30 P.M. to be driven home.

Sincerely,

Edith Kettering
Headmistress

June third, of course, was the date of the accident, which had occurred at 2:45 P.M.

Suddenly Mimi realizes she is not alone in the room, and she looks up, startled.

"Hi, kiddo," he says.

"How did you get in?" she cries.

"Just walked in off the elevator," he says. "Nobody's here but you, but the place is wide open. I guess they were counting on you to lock up the store."

"How did you know I was here?"

"Walking down the street and saw the lights on in your corner office. Figured you might be here, reading the diaries."

"How very strange."

"What's strange?"

"Brad's girlfriend has been watching our building from across the street, and now you're watching my office."

"Not watching, really. Just glanced up and saw lights on. I'm not as bad as our friend Mrs. Robinson, kiddo."

"Is that her name?"

"Rita Robinson. Just like the song. 'God bless you, please, Mrs. Robinson, heaven holds a place for those who pray, ay-ay-ay.' "

"She's married, then."

"Separated. I gather she thinks she can land a bigger fish with Mr. Bradford Moore. Mind if I sit down?" He flops in her sofa without waiting for a reply, kicks off his Gucci loafers, and, lying back, stretches out on the sofa, his stockinged feet up on the arm. He glances at the stack of diaries on her desk. "Well, what did you think? Did you get through all of it?"

"Yes."

"I warned you that there'd be some unpleasant things there, but you insisted."

"But I don't understand it all, Michael. For instance, what was Nate Myerson's role?"

"Can't you fit the pieces together, Mimi? Nate was Leo's son. Both of them, *père et fils*, were probably pretty bitter about the way your grandfather was treating Leo. But Leo wasn't the real blackmailer. The real villain of this story was Nate."

"But what did Nate know?"

"Look," he says, staring up at the ceiling from his sprawled position on the sofa, "this is what I figure must have happened. Your mother drove a black nineteen forty Lincoln Zephyr in those days, with a license number pretty close to the one those witnesses remembered. She picked you up at your nursery school that day. You were—how old? Three? Would you remember any of this? Probably not."

"There's a dream I sometimes have. It involves a car, my mother screaming, a dark shape across the windshield."

"She picked you up at that school, headed uptown, and had the accident. Maybe she was drunk. Anyway, she left the scene, which is a bad no-no. I figure the first one to put two and two together was your father—with the license plate. And one look at the condition of his car would have told him something bad had happened. Maybe he confronted your mother, and she confessed and begged him to help her. Maybe the police had already called them for questioning. Anyway, your father was pretty scared and went to see his father the following day. The diary says he did."

"Yes."

"Your grandfather came to your mother's rescue, in the only way he knew how: using those people he refers to as 'Leo's friends.' A plan was worked out. Your mother was shipped off to Bar Harbor, where the servants were instructed to say that she'd been there for several days, maybe weeks, and was hundreds of miles away from New York at the time of the accident. Meanwhile, those friends of Leo's went to work for your grandfather. A new pair of painted-over plates was slapped on the car, taken from a similar Lincoln that had been stolen in Brooklyn. The car was then driven to the West Side and abandoned, for the police to find it."

"But how did Nate get involved in all of this?"

"I figure the second person to put two and two together was Nate. Nate and Leo then put their little heads together. Both Nate and Leo would have known what kind of car your parents drove, and either one of them, or both of them, could have recognized the license plate. The first one to put the screws on your father was Leo. He got his hundred thousand. But Nate had the foresight to write a letter to your nursery school and got exactly what he wanted: proof that your mother *was* in New York that day, and in fact had been just a handful of blocks away fifteen minutes before the accident happened. Using that letter, Nate was able to bleed your father for the next twenty years."

She shivers. "And I was a part of it, too, wasn't I? I, or at least my nursery school, was part of a scheme to destroy my father. They used me, too. And —oh, my God, I've just remembered something else."

"What's that?"

"How old was I then? A little over three? And yet I can remember someone—one of Granny's servants, perhaps, someone who was taking care of me—saying to me, over and over again, 'If anyone asks you how long you've been in Maine, you're to say, "Mama and I have been here since my birthday party."' I remember being made to repeat those words again and again, 'Mama and I have been here at Granny's house ever since my birthday party.' My birthday is May twenty-fourth. It must have been that summer, and it must have been to help her establish—"

"Her alibi."

"Yes. So I was part of the cover-up, *too!*"

"So it seems. *Did* anyone ask you how long you'd been in Maine?"

"I don't remember. I just remember being made to memorize that line. But if anyone had asked me, I know I'd have said what I was told to say. I was always the sort of little girl who did what she was told. Oh, Michael, this is all so awful."

"Well, I warned you," he says.

"But how could Nate go on doing this? It said the case was closed. Isn't there something called the statute of limitations?"

"There is no statute of limitations in a criminal manslaughter case, Mimi. That case could have been reopened at any time. Nate knew this, and he must have made it very clear to your father."

"You mean the case could be reopened . . . even now?"

Still staring at the ceiling, he says, "Even now. Forty-six years later."

"Oh, God," she says.

He glances in her direction. "Look," he says, "I don't think it's very likely. The prosecutor's office would have a hard time rounding up any witnesses after all these years. Most of the original witnesses are probably dead by now, or disappeared. But, technically, it could be reopened—the whole can of worms."

"My mother could never be put through such a thing. Not at this point, Michael."

"Meanwhile, Nate or Leo, or the two of them, got hold of your grandfather's diaries, with all the other very incriminating stuff in them—the date of your mother's departure for Bar Harbor, and all. The diaries turned up in Nate's daughter's house."

"How did they get hold of them?"

"That I don't know. But they obviously got them in the fall of nineteen forty-one. There are lots of ways they could have got them: bribed a security guard, bribed one of the building's cleaning staff. There are lots of ways to burglarize an office building. Look at Watergate."

"Has Louise Bernhardt ever read these, do you think?"

"That I don't know, either. But I do think one thing."

"What's that?"

"That your father had her father killed."

"*What?*"

"Remember that day in nineteen sixty-one—the day we drove to East Orange to see my new house? The day I'd been to see your father at his office, to see if there was some way I could help him save the company? I didn't tell you the complete truth of what happened in your father's office that day. He asked me if, through the building trades, I had any contacts with the Mafia. There was a man he wanted killed, he said. The man's name was Nathan Myerson. Your father was very serious—desperate, in fact. I told him there was nothing I could do to help him. But I think by nineteen sixty-two, when Nate's body was found in the Saw Mill River, he'd found somebody willing to do it for him."

"Oh, my God," she says.

"And then less than one week after Nate was murdered, your father shot himself."

"Do you think there was a connection?"

"Probably, yes."

"But *why?* Oh, it just gets worse and worse, doesn't it? But still—*why?* Even if he'd just had that horrible thing done, that desperate thing done, why would he then kill himself? Why would he come home to that empty apartment, lie down in a bathtub, and put a bullet through his head?"

"Who knows how he felt? Guilty conscience, perhaps. His cousin's blood was on his hands, and maybe he couldn't live with that. Maybe it was that, and a combination of other pressures. You have to admit he was under a lot of different pressures. Probably only your mother knows the real reasons now."

"My mother was out of town when it happened. She said she had to get away, to find some peace."

"Yes, I imagine she'd have been looking for a little peace at that point. At least, when your grandfather was alive, he did what he could to try to help her—even though, as you can tell, his opinion of her wasn't the highest. When the chips were down, the old man did what he could to help his family. That's when I began to revise my opinion of him. He wasn't *all* bad. He had a side that cared about all of you."

She is silent for a moment. Then she says, "But a lot of this that you've just told me—it's just conjecture, isn't it? We don't really know—"

"Well, this much isn't conjecture," he says. "Just to be sure, I had one of my guys go down to the Motor Vehicle Department and look up the old records. In the year nineteen forty-one, a nineteen forty Lincoln Zephyr sedan, color black, was registered in the name of Alice Myerson, Eleven East Sixty-sixth Street. License number: KIG-013—awfully close to the plates the witnesses remembered. So it's a good shot to guess that the police were close to an arrest before you and she left for Maine. And here's another thing we found. Later that summer, she registered another Lincoln Zephyr in New York. It had been previously registered in the state of Maine. Your grandfather went to a lot of trouble, and must have spent a lot of money, to save your mother's skin and cover her tracks. The only thing he hadn't foreseen was Nate."

"But that's not the worst part, is it? The worst part is Mother and Daddy, and what they did to each other. I used to think it was all my grandparents' fault—that they were to blame for everything, that they destroyed my father and my mother. But now . . . it's clear, isn't it? Mother and Daddy destroyed each other. When I was old enough to know, couldn't one of them have told me? I might have done something to help. Just sharing what happened with me might have helped them. Now it's all too late."

"We turned up one other thing," he says. "And this may make you feel a little better." He reaches in his pocket and hands her a photocopy of a newspaper clipping. "It's from the *Utica Gazette*, dated October fifteenth, nineteen forty-one."

She reads:

ANONYMOUS BENEFACTOR
REMEMBERS WIDOW, KIDS

Betty Lee Elkins of 37 Oak Street, Utica, received a Postal Money Order in the amount of $50,000 today from an anonymous benefactor in New York City. Mrs. Elkins is the widow of Larry J. Elkins, the popular Utica High School math teacher who was slain June 3 by a hit-and-run driver on New York's Fifth Avenue, and the mother of the couple's two children, Mark, 13, and Justin, 9.

In a letter accompanying the gift, the donor said, "I have read of your recent, terrible bereavement, and wish to extend my sympathy. As a parent myself, and aware of the cost of educating children, I have calculated the size of this gift to provide a college education for your two little boys. You, of course, are free to use this money in any way you see fit." The letter, which bore a Manhattan postmark, was unsigned.

"I'm absolutely overwhelmed," Mrs. Elkins told the Gazette today. "Everyone in town has been so wonderful—with cards, condolence letters, gifts and flowers. I can't express my gratitude. But this, coming out of the blue—so unexpected—words simply fail me at this point."

Mrs. Elkins told the Gazette that she plans to place the funds in a special savings account in her sons' names, to be used for the purpose requested by her mystery benefactor: their college educations.

"I'm sure that the benefactor was your father," Michael says, "and the sum matches the amount he borrowed from your grandmother that month. He did what he could to try to make it right."

"Well," she says quietly. "What to do now? Destroy all these books, I suppose. I know I can never confront my mother with any of this."

"Do now?" he says, still stretched on his back on her sofa. "Well, I have one suggestion. First of all, you've got an important party to get through on Thursday night. Still want me to come? Because I'm planning to be there. Then, on Friday, we'll fly to Palm Beach. Don't start shaking your head, kiddo; listen to me. We'll fly down on my jet for the weekend. Have you ever been in Palm Beach in September? It's the best time, absolutely the best. The season hasn't started yet; we'd have the place to ourselves. You won't believe how peaceful it is there right now, before the usual zoo arrives after Christmas. That's what you need right now: peace, and quiet, and nothing to do but slather suntan oil on each other and lie in the sun. I'll take you sailing on the lake. We can water-ski. Or we can just sit on the terrace and listen to the palm trees rustle and smell the jasmine flowers. You need to get away from all this, Mimi. You've had too much shit thrown at you recently. What have you got here? A husband who's been cheating on you, and you sure as hell don't think that this is the first time he's done it, do you? Or that it will be the last time? I'll tell you one thing, if you'd marry me I'd never cheat on you."

"Are you suggesting that I divorce Brad and marry you?"

"He's offered you a divorce, hasn't he? I want you, Mimi. You see, I have everything in the world I've ever wanted—except you. I told you I wanted to be the richest guy in New York, and now people say I am. Who knows? But the one thing I always wanted was you."

She studies him thoughtfully. "There was a time, years ago, when I was ready to say yes," she says. "Do you remember that day in East Orange? You hurt me terribly then. I don't think I've ever felt so hurt, so rejected, as I did that afternoon. Can you ever expect me to forget that kind of hurt? Every time I look at you, I remember that hurt."

"It was all different then," he says. "Everything was against us then—your family, your father's situation. Now that's all changed. We're two different people now. We're rich. We're independent. We're free, and we still love each other. You needed Brad then, and you don't now. So come to Palm Beach with me, Mimi. Just for a few days. The main thing is, we could get to know each other again—get to know these two new people we now are. That's the main thing. Letting ourselves feel together again. There's a lot we can talk about. There are lots of things, secret things, that we share, that no one else knows about. Do you remember how I said I wanted you to have towers—towers, and mosques, and minarets, and waterfalls? Well, my house in Palm Beach has towers, and minarets, and even a waterfall. Come to Palm Beach, and I'll place you in a fairy tower, and every night I'll climb up a golden stair to see you." He smiles. "Or we can even talk a little business, if we feel like it—family business, like Badger's plan to take your company private again."

"What?" she cries. "How do you know about that?"

"I've said this before, Mimi. New York is a village. People talk."

"Do you know *everything* about me?"

"I sort of make it a point to," he says.

"Now wait a minute," she says angrily. "Now I see. Now I see what this is all about. You're planning to use these diaries and that letter against me, aren't you? You've probably got all this Xeroxed! You'd even use my mother, my poor seventy-year-old mother, who's going through the most difficult period of her entire life right now—use her, to blackmail *me*, in order to get what you want. That's it, isn't it? I should have guessed this all along! Of course! You'd stop at *nothing*—and to think I was about to say yes, I'd go to Palm Beach with you!"

He sits up, a little wearily, swings his long legs over the side of the sofa, and plants his stockinged feet on the floor. "Oh, Mimi, Mimi," he says. "Look at what this has done to you. Listen to what you're saying. You're saying you don't trust anybody. You're saying everybody in the world is gunning for you. You can't go through life like this, Mimi. Everybody in this life has to have *some*body he can trust. What's happened to you, Mimi? What's happened to the little girl with the broken skate lace? Has this business turned you into some kind of monster?"

She says nothing, but stares at him defiantly from behind her desk.

He pats the seat of the sofa beside him. "Come," he says. "Come sit beside me for a minute. Let's see a little of the old Mimi with the polished-silver eyes. The lady executive is done for the day, isn't she? Come on, Mimi. I won't hurt you. Come. Come sit by Papa, and let me tell you my plan."

Reluctantly, she rises and moves to the long sofa and takes a seat a little distance from him. "I'm very tired," she says.

"Of course you are. But this is better, isn't it? Maybe I'm a chauvinist, but I can never talk seriously to a woman when there's a desk between us. Now let me tell you what we're going to do. There are monsters in those diaries there. There are demons that have got to be exorcised, and there's only one way to be rid of them. We're going to destroy those little devils. We're going to carry those books out of here and place them, one by one, in the incinerator. This building has an incinerator, doesn't it? Most buildings do. It's usually in a closet near the elevator bank, and that will be the end of the demons. Exorcism by fire. But first—"

"First?"

"Give me your hand." She extends her hand. "No, the other one," he says. "First, we're going to turn back the clock, back to a time when we didn't know about the demons. Remember how they used to do it in the movies? The calendar pages flipping backward across the screen, leaves falling, then snow blowing, back to the humble little cottage where it all began." Slowly, he begins twisting the rings from her ring finger.

"Please don't," she says, trying to withdraw her hand.

"Just for a little while," he says, and gently but firmly he removes the rings—the emerald-cut ruby engagement ring, the ruby-and-diamond wedding band, and the two smaller ruby-and-diamond guard rings—and places them on the coffee table in front of him. "Now you're naked," he says. "If I had your real engagement ring, I'd put it on your finger now. Where is it, Mimi?"

"At home . . . in my jewelry case."

"Then this will have to do instead," he says, and he lifts her bare finger to his lips and kisses it. "Oh, my God, Mimi," he says, "I love you so. I've tried so hard to forget you. Nothing works."

"We mustn't—" she begins.

"We must."

"No, no," she repeats, even as she feels the room around her seem to turn into a kind of sea, and herself caught in an undertow, a warm, dark tide of loneliness and desire. His lips find her mouth now, and then the hollow between her breasts, and his hands move expertly in all the tender, special places. "*Michael!*" she suddenly cries out because, with no more than that, she has felt the first wild burst of orgasm.

"Oh, my," he says. "You see? It was meant to be this way from the beginning." And then, "No, don't turn out the light yet. First, I want to see all of you, all over. I want to look at all of you. Oh, my, this is going to be so fine . . . so fine."

When it is over, he says, "White stars."

"White . . . stars. Whave have we done, Michael?"

"Done? Just exactly what we should have been doing all these years, that's all. Did you see them, too?"

"See them?"

"The white stars flashing? Was it just as wonderful for you as it always was?"

"Mm," she says drowsily. "Mm."

"Is that a yes 'Mm,' or a no 'Mm'?"

"Mm," she says again, and she thinks, wonderful, wonderful. As it always was, as it always will be, always. Her mind and her body were provided with wings, and they were stretched and arched and flying. There. For a moment she was there. But now the wings have begun to fold, and she is here again, back in this room, and her rings are in a little row on the coffee table.

"Let me hear you say it."

But how can she tell him that it was not the same, not really, because how can anything ever seem as wonderful as it once did? Nothing is ever quite the same, nor is anything ever quite so wonderful, even if one could turn back the clock, after the years have reaped their haphazard harvest. "Brad knows about us," she says.

"Good."

"Good?"

"That will make it easier when you tell him you're leaving him to marry me."

"Is that what I'm going to do?"

"Yes."

"Oh, Michael—"

"Of course. All the obstacles that stood in our way are gone now."

"Obstacles . . ."

"First your grandfather. Then your parents' problems. Then the man you married. They're all gone."

"Brad is . . . gone?"

"He's got another ladyfriend, hasn't he? He has no more claim on you. Now we're free to do what we've always wanted to do. Which is just this." He is gently stroking her nipples, and, against her thigh, she feels his erection swelling again. "Oh, my, so much catching up to do," he says, and enters her smoothly and easily again. "Tell me," he whispers, pushing himself more deeply and with greater urgency into her, "did he ever make you feel this way? Was it ever like this with him? Did he ever make you feel as good as this? Tell me . . . tell me, Mimi. Tell me what I've always wanted to hear you say. Say the words I've waited half my life to hear. Tell me you never loved him, Mimi. You *never* loved him! Let me hear you say it! Say it! *Tell me!*"

But all at once tears come, and she sobs against the body pressed so insistently against her own. "I can't," she sobs. "Please don't make me say that, Michael! I can't say that. I can't, I can't, I can't."

Or at least that is what I imagine must have happened that night when he let himself into her office. How else to explain the four jeweled rings that were still on her coffee table the next morning, and her flustered look when she saw them there and hastily scooped them up and replaced them on the third finger of her left hand?

And the guilty look when she glanced at the photographs in the silver frames on her desk: Brad in his Bachrach portrait and Badger in tennis whites, looking as though he had just aced a serve.

That same night, I learned later, Granny Flo Myerson was busy on the telephone. "Alice?" she said to her startled daughter-in-law, who, in the twenty-five years since Henry's death, had not had a telephone call from Granny Flo more than once a year, on Henry's birthday, to remind her to decorate Henry's grave at Salem Fields. "Alice?"

"Yes, Flo. What can I do for you?"

"Alice, I think it's high time you and I buried the hatchet, and I'll tell you why. There's two reasons, and they've both got to do with Mimi. We've got to stand behind her, Alice, the both of us, and here's why. That nice Mr. Greenway, you know, he tells me things, and so I know more than meets the eye, even if I happen to be blind. We talk about the stock market. I don't like the boom that's going on in the stock market. It doesn't smell right, and I don't think it's going to last. I think there's going to be a big crash, like 'twenty-nine, and I think it could happen within four or five weeks. That soon. By the middle of October, and Mr. Greenway thinks I might be right. Now the reason why that's important is that Mimi has this plan. She calls it taking the company private, and I think we should stand behind her. If we stay a public company, we could all be hurt when this crash comes. But if we go private, the way Mimi wants, we'd hardly feel it. We'd be out of the stock market. We'd be off the Big Board, or whatever they call it. But we've got to be fast. We've got to all vote the way Mimi wants us to, for going private. Mimi doesn't know it, but I know the names of all the Leo cousins, and I'm going to call them all and tell them the same thing. Mr. Greenway thinks I'm right, and Mr. Greenway ought to know. He works for *Fortune,* which is all about money and the stock market.

"That's the first thing I called to tell you. The second is more personal. There's another man in Mimi's life. How do I know? Let's just say I smell another man. Since I've lost my eyesight, I can smell things better, and I can also smell *situations,* not just things. I smell another man in her life right now. In fact, there's always been another man, but now he's come back, and he's sniffing around her again. I can smell this happening right now as I talk to you, it's as plain as the nose on my face. She's going to have to make a choice, and you and I are going to have to stand behind her and make sure she makes the right one. After all, she's your flesh and blood, and she's mine, too. So we've got to put up a united front, and see that she makes the right choice. United we stand, divided we fall—right? So let's you and I bury the hatchet, Alice, and make sure Mimi chooses right. A family should stick together. What holds a family together is its blood, not flour-and-water paste. . . ."

Now it is Tuesday morning, and the office is hectic with last-minute details and preparations for Thursday night's launch party, and everyone, right down to the boys in the mailroom, is feverish with excitement. People dash in and out of Mimi's office, each person presenting some tiny new crisis.

"Here's a sample of the roses. Are they the right color?"

"The caterer can't find wild strawberries. Will you settle for California jumbos?"

"I *told* the banquet manager you wanted gold bunting on the ceiling! They're tacking up *silver!*"

"It's Liz Taylor's agent! She has a temperature of a hundred and two!"

"Your grandmother's on the phone! Line three!"

"My grandmother?" Mimi picks up the phone. "Yes, Granny Flo?" she says.

"Look," her grandmother says, "you're probably pretty busy, what with getting ready for your party and all, but this is pretty important, and I thought I ought to talk to you."

"Yes, Granny."

"I understand that you and Bradley are having your little difficulties," she says.

"Why, Granny, whatever gave you that idea?"

"Let's just say a little bird told me," Granny Flo says. "And the same little bird told me that Bradger has been cheating on you. That won't do, Mimi."

"Granny, right now I have a—"

"Now wait a minute. Hear me out. A woman can't put up with a husband who cheats on her. I never would have done, and you can't, either. It's just too *embarrassing* to a woman, Mimi, to have a husband who cheats on her. So if you'll take my advice, Mimi, dump him. Take an old woman's advice and dump him. Don't tell me you always trusted him. He couldn't cheat on you if you didn't trust him! Dump him is the only thing you can do to save your face. Dump that Bradger, Mimi; he's just plain no good. He's certainly not good enough for you, a man who cheats. My Adolph would never have *dared* to cheat on me, because he knew I'd have dumped him faster than you can shake a stick at if he tried. And he couldn't afford to have me dump him, because he needed my money. But you don't need this Bradley's money, Mimi. So dump him, and go out and look for Mr. Right. And I also have a suggestion for a Mr. Right who'd be just right for you. Remember that Horowitz fellow you were so in love with him? Marry him! He's never married . . . and he's rich! I guess you knew he's bought my old Palm Beach place, and if he can keep up a place like that, he's got to be rich! Why not marry him? He'd snap you up in a second, I bet. Besides, I think he's awfully cute-looking—those dimples and that smile. At least, I used to think he was cute-looking when I still had my eyesight, and he can't have changed that much. So dump that cheating Bradley and snap up Horowitz. He's the best around, Mimi, and you deserve the best. That Horowitz— why, he's like champagne! Why should you settle for *vin ordinaire,* like that cheat Bradger? Well, at least I've given you something to think about, haven't I?"

"Why, Flo, I'm actually shocked at you," Rose Perlman says when Granny Flo reports this conversation to her friend. "Telling Mimi to dump that nice husband of hers they say is being considered to run for Senator Miller's unexpired term! Yes, I'm shocked at you!"

"And I'm shocked at *you,* Rose," Granny Flo says. "You—with a high school education, and all that! Didn't they ever teach you anything about human nature? What I'm talking about is human nature. Don't you know what happens when a woman tells another woman what to do? Especially a woman like me telling a woman like Mimi what to do? Nine times out of ten, she'll do just the opposite of what she's told to do. That's just human nature."

"Well, I hope you're right," Rose Perlman says, sounding unconvinced.

"Of course I'm right. Mimi thinks I'm gaga. But there are times when it pays to let people think you're gaga."

31

I DON'T MUCH CARE for the headline," Mimi says to Mark Segal. It is Wednesday, the day before the launch party for her Mireille fragrance, they are in her office, and the headline—from the Advertising column of this morning's *Times*—which Mimi doesn't much care for, reads, "Is BEAUTY QUEEN IN THE 'UGLIFICATION' BUSINESS?"

"Listen, all publicity is good publicity," Mark says. "It's a grabby headline, and his story's cute. Read it."

Mimi reads:

Remember the Man with the Eyepatch who plugged so long for Hathaway Shirts? Remember "Does she—or doesn't she?" for Clairol? Remember "Which twin has the Toni?" Well, in a new wrinkle on that theme, Madison Avenue is asking today, Who is the mysterious Man with a Scar who will make his debut in print and television advertising later this week for "Mireille," the new and pricey fragrance from Miray?

And, just as the advertising community—and the public—spent months wondering whether Baron George Wrangel, Hathaway's model, really *needed* his eyepatch (he didn't), now publishers and TV producers who will be running the ads and airing the commercials are wondering about the authenticity of the Mireille Man's scar. The rugged good looks of the blond male model are marred by a nasty-looking scar across his left cheek, leaving the question: Was his scar legitimately acquired in a duel or some other romantic feat of derring-do? Or has his face been deliberately "uglified" through the artful application of cosmetics, something Miray knows more than a little about?

For the moment, Mireille ("Mimi") Myerson, Miray's beauteous President and CEO, is being very close-mouthed on the subject. Nor will she reveal her male model's name. All she will say is that guests at her Thursday night launch party for "Mireille" will be "introduced" to the Mireille Man. (But don't count on getting all the answers even there, insiders say.)

The sold-out party at the Pierre will be another of those push-me-pull-you affairs of which New Yorkers never seem to tire. On the one hand, it is clearly a commercial event designed to promote a new perfume, and is being completely underwritten by Miray. On the other hand, it is also a "social" affair by virtue of being a benefit for a Worthy Cause, the cause in this case being the New Books Fund for the Public Library. Proceeds from the sale of tickets (which start at $500 each) will benefit the library. Thus, once again, members of the beauty and fashion press, department store buyers, and other working stiffs will have an opportunity to rub shoulders with the likes of Brooke Astor and Jacqueline Onassis.

"Are we really sold out, Mark?"

"Yup."

"What about Elizabeth Taylor?"

"If she shows up, I kinda think we'll be able to make room for her—don't you?"

"I still haven't decided what I'm going to wear," she says.

"A suggestion," he says. "Wear red—lipstick red. Lipstick red has always been our signature color, the color of our logo. And something by an American designer, I think, don't you? I think an American designer just makes for good P.R."

"When I first met you," she told him years ago, "I had just almost—almost, but not quite—got over being in love with another man, just as you were getting over being in love with another girl. It wasn't a physical affair, as yours was, but still it was very strong, very powerful. That first love made me feel weak, almost ill. It made me feel powerless to act, as though I had no will of my own. I felt helpless and weak, unable to think clearly, as though some force outside my life were in control of my body and my mind. The love I feel for you is very strong, too, and yet it's different—a different kind of love that makes me feel strong, and powerful, and forceful, and in control of what I do. You've given me something to hang on to, something tangible and real. It's just a different kind of love. Better, I think."

They lay in the sun, on the sand at the beach at St.-Jean-de-Luz. It was their wedding trip.

"Are there different kinds of love? Of course there are. You can love people in so many different ways. Even though I was in love with this boy, there was always something about him that I couldn't quite be sure of, and it made my feelings for him so confused and uncertain. I don't think it would have made a good marriage. It wasn't just that my family disapproved of him. There was something a little wild about the boy, something brash and headstrong. He was always headed into the fast lane, almost frighteningly ambitious. Maybe it was his drive that made me feel powerless and ineffectual. I mean, he was the kind of boy who, when he walked out of a room, I could never be certain that he'd return, that he wouldn't turn up someone better while he was gone. With you, when you leave the room, I just think to myself: He'll be back before you know it. Or maybe it's just that I was younger then, and couldn't believe that someone as damned self-confident and cocky as he was could really and truly be in love with someone like me. With you, there's never been any question in my mind that you could love me. You make me believe in *me*, somehow. Do you see what I mean?

"I'll tell you what it's like. When I was a little girl, and we lived in the apartment on Ninety-seventh Street, there was a tree that grew in an air shaft outside my bedroom window—a locust tree. A locust is a junk tree, a weed tree. It will grow anywhere, in any climate. You can't kill it: you can cut it down to the stump, and it will grow up again. Someone told me once that if you cut a locust tree up into fence posts, you have to be sure to plant the fence posts upside down, or else instead of fence posts you'll have a row of locust trees. It's a messy tree. It has tiny, feathery leaves, and in the fall they all come down. I had to keep my window closed, or else my room would be full of falling locust leaves. But every winter, I noticed, there was always one little locust leaf that refused to fall. It was always in the same place, and it managed to cling to its stem all winter long. That's the way you make me feel—that you're my strong, tough stem, and I'm your determined little leaf, refusing to let go. Do you feel that way too, Brad? That we need to cling to each other, stick to each other, like a leaf fitted into its stem, refusing to be torn apart by any winter storm?"

She can't remember what his answer was as she lay in the sun, and he began covering her body with soft little mounds of warm sand.

And now, the picture of domesticity, she turns her back to him to let him raise the zipper on the back of her red dress.

"How do you feel about this evening?" he asks her. "Excited? Nervous?"

"Terrified," she says. "Absolutely terrified. I had a dream last night, and it was all about Candied Apple. Oh, I almost forgot my superstition, Brad—a kiss on the left shoulder, please. For luck."

He brushes her shoulder with his lips and touches her bare elbow. Then he looks up, and his eyes meet hers briefly in her mirror.

"Well, what do you think?" she asks him as she studies her reflection in the glass. Her crimson silk-and-cashmere dress falls in a series of little swirls about her upper body, and in more swirls down the slightly pegged, mid-calf skirt. For tonight, Howard Barr of Cloutier has taken her trademark simple ponytail and plaited it into a single, silvery braid, and, since tonight's theme flowers are roses, he has woven dozens of tiny red tearose buds into the plait. With the flowers in her braid, she has decided on very little jewelry: just two small ruby earclips, and the ruby-and-diamond rings on her left hand.

"You are too beautiful," he says.

As the guests begin to gather in the ballroom of the Hotel Pierre, I can't help noticing how easily Mimi conducts herself. If there is terror here, it certainly doesn't show. She manages, as she moves among her guests in her red dress, to hold the center of the stage and to find, as they say in the theatre, the key light. At the same time, she manages to draw the focus of attention to the guests themselves, making them seem to shine—as shine they must, for many of them are greater media stars than she is.

It is hard to believe, watching Mimi move easily among her arriving guests, that this evening's party is the culmination of two years' worth of work and planning. And now all that work has been done, and the fragrance —"Mireille"—is here in this room, tonight, its final formula a secret, its suggested retail price a hundred and eighty dollars the ounce.

All the members of the fashion press are here, the writers from *Vogue* and *Harper's Bazaar*, the reporters from *Women's Wear*, the *Post*, the *Times*, the *Daily News*, and *New York Newsday*, busily scribbling in their notebooks, noting who is here, and who is wearing what.

"Whose dress is that, Mrs. Astor?"

"This is Adolfo," Brooke Astor says, touching her pale blue ruffled organza skirt. "I think it's awfully pretty."

Guests have begun unstoppering their gift bottles of Mireille now and are dabbing it on their wrists. "There's something almost *feral* about the scent," Diana Vreeland is saying to Mimi, "something a little *wild* and *primitive*. It makes me think of mountain *tarns*, and jungle *pools*, and swaying *liana* vines, and *sarongs*, and—yes—*volcanoes!*"

"Thank you, Diana, dear."

All this is nonsense, of course, and Mimi knows it. No one can judge a perfume in a crowded room like this, filled as it is with other odors: the red roses on the tables, other women's scents, the smells of food as the red-coated waiters move among the guests with trays of canapés, the smells of liquor from the two bars, and cigarette smoke. The real judgment of the success of the fragrance will come later, but the success of the launching of the fragrance will depend only on the success of this evening, and how much the guests end up enjoying the party. Still, everyone ventures an opinion.

"Mmm. Sexy!"

"A bit too floral maybe? Of course I've personally never cared for floral scents, being from California."

"California is all floral, isn't it."

"Totally. That's why I moved to River House."

The room is a sea of moving people now, and the waiters move in and out adroitly between little knots of groups, and groups within groups, with their laden trays.

"That's Alice Myerson over there—in the green. Mimi's mother."

"I must say she looks better than she's looked in a long *time*. She used to be the most awful drunk, you know."

Her friend taps her champagne glass significantly. "Betty Ford Center is what *I* heard."

"They say she's into est."

"Who is?"

"Annette Reed."

There is suddenly a little flurry of activity at the entrance to the ballroom now, and a volley of flashbulbs explodes, as Jacqueline Onassis glides in, in a pouf of red and black. In an incidence of poor timing, Gloria Vanderbilt follows her through the door on the arm of Bobby Short—who will play later—and almost goes unnoticed as the reporters fire questions at Mrs. Onassis.

"What's your favorite scent, Mrs. Onassis?"

"Actually, I have several favorites."

"What are you wearing now?"

"Actually, I don't remember."

A whisper: "It's a Valentino. I've seen her wearing that dress before."

The champagne flows, and the noise level in the room rises.

Seated at her table in a corner of the room with her friend Rose Perlman, Granny Flo Myerson says, "Is that Edwee over there? What's he doing?"

"Yes, that's him." And then, startled, "Why, Flo! Is your eyesight improving?"

"Of course not. I can't see him. I can smell him. I know all my children by their smell."

"He seems to be having some sort of discussion with the what-do-you-call-it. The man who's going to run the film. The projectionist."

"Well, don't let Edwee get near me. I don't want to talk to him."

In another part of the room, Blaine Trump is saying, "You don't spend fifteen thousand on a Christian Lacroix and expect to see another woman walk into the room wearing the same dress! As far as I'm concerned, he's already one of yesterday's designers. I'll never buy a dress from him again."

Moving about the room, Mimi suddenly finds herself face to face with the woman she saw Brad lunching with at Le Cirque. She extends her hand. "Good evening, I'm Mimi Myerson."

"I'm Rita Robinson."

"Oh, yes. My husband's told me about you."

The other woman eyes her narrowly. "You think you've won, don't you?"

"Won? I didn't know we were fighting over anything. But I will say this: you're very pretty. I can see why he was attracted to you."

"Was? What if he still is?"

"And I must say you don't *look* pregnant, dear."

The two women move apart.

"She's here," Mimi whispers to Brad.

"I know," he says grimly.

"Did you know she was coming?"

"Of course not. Does this upset you?"

"I told her she was very pretty. You have good taste, Brad."

"How did you know that was her?"

But Lily Auchincloss has moved in to join them and wants to talk about Cancun. "It's an entire new *city!*" she exclaims.

Now there is another flurry of activity at the door, and more flashbulbs go off, as Elizabeth Taylor makes her entrance, looking radiant, a rope of diamonds plaited through her hair.

"It's something of a surprise to see you here, Miss Taylor," a reporter says.

Elizabeth, well rehearsed as always, replies brightly, "I had to sniff out the competition, didn't I?"

There is polite laughter because everyone agrees that Elizabeth is a damned good sport to make an appearance at Mimi's party.

Now Edwee Myerson has joined his wife at their table, and as his sister, Nonie, passes, he reaches out and seizes her arm. "Where is the Goya?" he hisses.

"And where is my money?"

"I know you had something to do with this!"

"And speaking of that, how much do you know about the science of encausticology, Edwee?" she says.

"What's that?"

"Encaustics—ink analysis. It's something I picked up from my days as a magazine publisher. There are certain tests that have been developed by the

FBI. There are X-ray fluorescence tests, and there's something called the Mossbauer Test, which is a test for moisture. Using these tests, the age of any mark in ink can be determined with great accuracy—even something as small as, say, a question mark."

"Just tell me where it is and you'll get your money."

"And when are you two leaving for Belize? I thought you'd be gone by now. Or is it Biafra? I never can keep those places straight."

He glares at her.

"Excuse me," she says. "I want to say hello to Elizabeth. I taught her to ride, you know, for *National Velvet.*"

"Are you that *old,* Nonie?" Gloria says.

His sister moves away, and Edwee grabs Gloria's wrist beneath the table and squeezes it hard in his fist.

"Ouch, Edwee," she says. "What was she talking about, ink?"

"Did you tell her about Belize, you little slut?"

"Ouch!" she cries. "She knew already. *Ouch!* Edwee! You're hurting me!"

The conversation moves in swirls and eddies as new guests enter the room and old friends greet each other and as, with little gestures, the rich and famous recognize each other and congratulate each other on being rich and famous together.

"I've heard that some gay men make marvelous lovers," someone is saying to Barbara Walters.

"I'd have to disagree," Miss Walters says. "Most of the gay married men I know are very cruel to their wives."

"I didn't say *husbands,* darling," the other woman says.

Greeting Mimi with an upraised champagne glass, Michael Horowitz whispers just two words. "Palm Beach."

Promptly at seven-thirty, Mark Segal gives Mimi the nod, and she mounts the steps to the small stage and moves to the microphone. The lights in the room dim slightly, and a pink spot falls on her. The voices hush.

"I promise you there aren't going to be any speeches," she begins, "but I just want to tell you all how happy I am that you all could come. This evening is a happy occasion for me for several reasons: First, and most important, because we've been able to raise slightly over seven hundred and twenty-five thousand dollars for the public library tonight." (There is a round of applause.) "This money will go to the library's Book Purchase Fund. I'm also happy because all of you people who did this will be the first to sample my new perfume—of which, understandably, I'm just a little bit proud." (More applause, and calls of "Hear, hear!") "But tonight I'm happiest of all for a very special, very personal reason. As some of you may know, this company was founded in nineteen twelve by my grandfather, Adolph

Myerson, whose widow, Fleurette Myerson—Granny, will you please stand up?" (Granny Flo stands, and bows) "—is right over there, and his brother, Leopold Myerson. Years ago, as some of you may also know, the two brothers had a famous falling-out—though what it was all about nobody really remembers." (Laughter.)

"It was about women!" Granny Flo says in a strong voice. (More laughter erupts all over the room over this.)

"Anyway," Mimi continues, when the laughter finally subsides, "this falling-out created, sadly, a deep rift between the two branches of the family—the children and grandchildren of Leopold Myerson and what I guess you'd call my line." (Laughter.) "But tonight, I'm happy to say, for the first time in almost fifty years, all my Myerson cousins and second cousins—all of whom I've gotten to know only recently—are here with us. We're a united family again." (Strong applause.) "Now, as I call their names, I'd like each of my cousins to step forward and be introduced to all of you. First, my cousin Louise Myerson Bernhardt, and her husband, Dick . . ."

One by one, as she calls their names, the Leo cousins step forward until they form a small semi-circle in front of the stage.

"Thank you all for coming," Mimi says.

"I never thought I'd live to see this," Granny Flo says in her loud voice. "And I had to live to be eighty-nine to do it." (Laughter.) "And now that it's happened, I can't even see it. Blind as a bat." (Sympathetic, light laughter.)

"There are a few other, very special people that I'd like to thank," she continues. "First, my advertising director, Mark Segal, who has prepared the short—very short, I promise you—presentation that you're about to see." She gestures in Mark's direction. "Next, my son, Brad Moore, junior, our director of sales. And finally, my wonderful husband, Brad Moore, senior." Both Brad and Badger step forward and take small bows, to applause. "We're all here," Mimi says. "Together—one big happy family. Thank you all." Mimi smiles, leaves the microphone, and moves quickly off the stage amid more applause.

Now the lights dim further, and the big screen descends from the ceiling. The lights dim altogether, and the screen comes to life with the sting of music and diamond flashes of sunlight on the water of Long Island Sound outside the Seawanhaka Yacht Club. The girl in the white dress waves as the yawl-rigged sailboat moves into view with a blond young man at the tiller.

THE GIRL: You're late!

THE BOY: Tricky winds!

The boy turns his head just slightly toward her to reveal the jagged, uneven scar that mars his perfect handsomeness, and there is a collective gasp from the audience in the Pierre ballroom. The boy secures the boat to the dock, reaches up for the girl, and lifts her down to the deck of the boat with him.

THE BOY: You smell brand-new!

And the commercial continues, concluding with the line that travels across the screen against the sunlit water: *Mireille . . . at last the miracle fragrance!*

Next comes the second commercial, a hunting scene filmed in the horse country of northern Westchester, in which the boy reaches down from horseback and lifts the girl lightly up into the saddle with him. Once again, there is the shock as he turns to reveal the harsh scar.

At her shoulder, Dan Rather whispers to Mimi, 'I don't know a thing about perfume, but you've got a hell of an ad campaign."

The third commercial uses an interior setting, and the Mireille Couple encounter each other on the huge, curved staircase of a manor house, she ascending and he descending from the shadows above to meet her.

During the applause that follows, Mimi steps to the microphone again. "And now," she says, "I'd like to introduce you to two people you'll be seeing a good deal of in the coming months: the Mireille Woman and the Mireille Man." The Mireille theme music comes up on cue.

Mimi returns to her seat, and from stage left, Sherrill Shearson emerges, wearing the white gown from the final commercial. She moves to center stage, into the spotlight, and performs a deep curtsy (executing it perfectly, to Mimi's relief) and then, after a spin or two, exits into the wings on the side where she entered.

Now the Mireille theme music increases a bit, and the Mireille Man appears from stage right in a dinner jacket, and as the spotlight catches him, the shock of canary-colored hair is unmistakable, but so is the mask from *Phantom of the Opera*—that eerie white mask that was the show's signature, the mask that gazed balefully from the marquee of the Majestic Theatre and from posters advertising the show, which decorated, it seemed, every outdoor advertising space in New York that year, from the sides of Fifth Avenue buses to public telephone booths.

As Dirk takes his bow, the Mireille theme dissolves into the theme from *Phantom.*

There is applause, of course, but there are also, inevitably, some groans, and cries of "No fair!" and "Take off the mask!" But after his bow, Dirk Gordon exits, stage right, still wearing the mask.

At this point, the lights are supposed to come up, but instead, the pink spot fades and the screen flickers to life again. Mark Segal sits forward in his chair. "What's going on!" he whispers. "That's the show! It's over!"

Slowly, on the screen, vague images appear. The quality of the film is grainy, and the lighting is poor, but figures can be made out, unclothed figures, twisting and writhing together in silent contortions, as though involved in some sort of coupling. Nothing is clear, not even faces, but there seem to be three people, two men and a woman, although one of the male figures, with long silver hair, could also be a woman. Arms and hands reach out in what could be caresses; the figures disappear then reappear out of focus. One of the male figures, Mimi realizes, could possibly be Dirk Gordon, while the silver-haired one, she sees with a gasp, could be Edwee himself—and the woman could be his wife, Gloria! "Brad," she says urgently, "we've got to stop this!"

"Hold on," Brad says quietly.

The dimly lit, out-of-focus figures continue to writhe and undulate together for another moment or two. Then the screen goes blank, and the confused audience sits in total silence, obviously unsure of what it has just witnessed.

Brad Moore steps quickly to the microphone and, with a broad smile, says, "And that, ladies and gentlemen, is my wife's way of saying, 'so much for Calvin Klein. So much for Obsession.'"

The first to see the joke, inside joke though it is, is Calvin Klein himself, who laughs and claps his hands and cries, "I love it, Mimi! My ad people and Helmut Newton never did better."

And now Mimi moves to the microphone. "One thing my husband didn't mention," she says, "Is that I love *you,* Calvin. Look: I'm wearing one of your dresses! Nothing comes between me and my Calvin."

Now the whole room is laughing and cheering and shouting. The lights come up, and Bobby Short dives at his keyboard with the fast opening bars of "Anything Goes." In this jubilant mood, the red-jacketed waiters swiftly resume their rounds, refilling glasses with champagne. The room swells with sound.

> In olden days, a glimpse of stockin'
> Was looked on as somethin' shockin' . . .

"Thank you, darling," Mimi whispers to Brad. "How did you ever—"

"One thing I've learned about your business," he says. "It pays to be quick on your feet."

But there is no time to say more, for Mimi suddenly finds herself in the center of a growing rush of people, all trying either to take her hand or to kiss her all at once, all mouthing incoherent words of congratulations and praise. She recognizes one of these as the cosmetics buyer from Bergdorf's, who is begging her to let him have a six-month exclusive franchise on

Mireille for the Fifth Avenue store. "Just six months, Mimi—exclusive in New York," he is imploring her.

"Will you give my wife a window?" Brad is saying. "On the Fifth Avenue side?"

"Why, Brad—you really do care about this business!" she says.

Now the photographers and reporters from the fashion press are crowding around her. Microphones are being thrust in front of her face, and flash-bulbs are popping everywhere.

"Smile, Miss Myerson. . . ."

"Over here, Miss Myerson. . . ."

"What does your husband think of it, Miss Myerson?"

"Who did your hair, Miss Myerson?"

"Will you be touring with this, Miss Myerson, the way Elizabeth did with Passion?"

"What is the secret ingredient? Just give us a hint."

"Is it some special rose attar? I've never seen so many roses in one room!"

"And roses in her hair, too!"

"What's next from Miray, Miss Myerson?"

And as the noise level in the room rises around her, and Bobby Short cooperatively segues into "Rose of Washington Square," Mimi realizes, at last, that her launch party is a success.

From Suzy Knickerbocker's column in the *New York Post* the following day:

AN EVENING OF FUN . . .
AND SURPRISES

"Frolicsome" was the word **Diana Vreeland** used to describe last night's wingding at the Hotel Pierre to introduce "Mireille," that much-talked-about new fragrance from Miray Corp. And if the great D.V. says it was frolicsome, then it was, darlings. Added the Oracle, "The scent of 'Mireille' is scandalously serious. But the mood of the evening was positively larky."

Five hundred members of New York's glitter set sipped champagne and made little piggies of themselves on caviar, while aaaahing and oooohing over "Mireille," including **Brooke Astor, Jacqueline Onassis, Annette Reed,** the **Saul P. Steinbergs, Blaine** and **Robert Trump,** Gloria Vanderbilt, Mica** and **Ahmet Ertegun, Ricky** and **Ralph Lauren, Bill Blass, Ann** and **Gordon Getty,** and on and on and on. You get the picture.

It was also an evening punctuated with a series of little surprises.

Surprise No. 1: The appearance, in a cloud of white chiffon, of **Elizabeth Taylor,** just back from a national tour pushing "Passion," a perfume of her own. What caused Queen Liz to set foot in a party that was plugging her competition? "I wanted to sniff this one out," said she. Could H.R.H. still sniff under the weight of all those diamonds? Well, she tried.

Surprise No. 2: The preview of three TV commercials for "Mireille" that will begin airing cross-country next week. The gasp in these commercials comes when the otherwise hunky male model turns his head to reveal a nasty scar along one side of his face. The burning question industry insiders have been asking is: Is this model a guy with a real scar, or is the "scar" a cosmetic concoction, courtesy of Miray? Guests at last night's gala were promised that they'd be introduced to the real "man with a scar," and see for themselves.

Surprise No. 3: They were, but they didn't. The Mystery Model made an appearance, all right, but was wearing the famous spooky white mask which **Michael Crawford** wears in "Phantom of the Opera." So the question still burns. For this, we hear, Mr. X is being paid in seven figures.

Surprise No. 4 brought the house down. The house lights dimmed, and the audience was treated to a hilarious parody of **Calvin Klein**'s famously naughty ads for "Obsession," in which birthday-suited boys and girls seem to be carrying on in oh-such-kinky-looking sexual hijinks. The parody was cleverly shot in soft focus and with home-movie graininess, which left partygoers wondering not only who was doing what and with which and to whom, but also who was who. Or whom.

It was all pretty daring, come to think of it, what with Calvin and Kelly Klein right there in the audience. He stopped pouting, though, when Miray's president, **Mimi Myerson,** stepped to the microphone and pointed out that her smashing tea-length gown was by (but you guessed it) Calvin Klein.

And let's nominate Calvin for Good Sport of the Year. "Mireille is a wonderful fragrance," he said. "Perhaps not quite as exciting as Obsession—but close." And this, of course, was surprise No. 5. For the first time in the recorded history of the meow-meow beauty business, we had bitter rivals actually saying nice things about each other! What's the world coming to?

All this went nicely with the surprise that rounded off the night's surprises to an even half-dozen. Long before you were born, darlings, the two brothers who founded Miray, **Adolph** and **Leopold Myerson,** had a famous pffft over business philosophy. (Mimi's Adolph's granddaughter, so that's how long ago it was.) Ever since, the Myersons have been a house divided. But last night, under the influence of "Mireille, the Miracle Fragrance," as it's being billed, Mimi brought off another miracle of her own: a massive family hatchet-burying. All the scattered members of the clan were there, all smiles and kisses, after something like fifty years of battling. Surprised? Of course you are.

"My God, she gave us her whole column!" Mark Segal says.

"Well, it looks as though Mimi has another hit on her hands," Granny Flo Myerson says to her friend Rose Perlman, after Mrs. Perlman has finished reading the *Post* story to her. The two have met for lunch at what is their favorite meeting place, the top-floor Charleston Gardens coffee shop at B. Altman & Company. "I'm going to have the tomato surprise," she says. "That's always good here. Of course, nothing can ever replace Schrafft's, but this is next best."

"That's with tuna, isn't it?" Rose Perlman says. "I think I'll have the same."

"Actually," Granny Flo says, "I didn't think those naked people in the film were all that unrecognizable. I could have sworn that one of those men was Edwee."

"Why, Flo!" Rose Perlman says, putting down the newspaper. "Your eyesight *is* getting better! How could you have recognized *any*body in that film?"

"I didn't *see* him," Granny Flo says impatiently. "I *smelled* him, the way I always can."

"You can even smell him in a film?"

"Certainly. Why not? He's always smelled the same—a kind of vegetable-soupy smell. My little Henny-Penny, on the other hand—he was the sweetest-smelling baby on the whole East Side. Just thinking of him, I can remember how he smelled."

"Really, Flo, you are remarkable!"

"It's what happens when you lose your eyesight. All your other senses get better. My hearing, for instance. Did you hear that?" She points. "I just heard someone drop something. It sounded like a napkin."

Rose Perlman follows the direction of Granny's pointed finger and sees another diner at a nearby table reach down and retrieve a napkin from the floor. "Amazing!" she says.

Their waitress arrives to take their order. "We don't want to be *too* surprised by the tomato surprise," Granny Flo says. "It is with tuna, isn't it?"

"Yes, ma'am. . . ."

"Speaking of Edwee," Rose Perlman says when the waitress has departed, "what *did* you do with your Goya?"

"I gave it to Nonie."

"Really, Flo?"

"Yes. When Nonie told me what Edwee was up to, trying to have that painting declared a fake when it's not a fake, I decided Nonie should have it."

"And Edwee wanted that painting so badly."

"Well, that's just hard cheese on Edwee, isn't it? You see, poor Nonie really was stiffed by Adolph in his will. He really stiffed her, Rose, and I really wanted to right that wrong. Of course, if Mimi's plan to take the company private goes through, Nonie will finally have some money of her own. But having . . . sponsored, I guess, is the word—having sponsored Nonie in some of her other business ventures, I'm a little worried about this new one of hers, and I didn't like the smell of that man she's going into it with. She's always been unlucky in business, and unlucky with men. I'm afraid she's going to lose her shirt again, but I know there's no stopping Nonie when she decides she wants to do something. Meanwhile, that painting is worth a lot of money. When I gave it to Nonie, I said to her, 'This is for your insurance. If this new business of yours fails, Nonie, the Goya will be your insurance.' "

"I wish I could say I thought you'd done the right thing, Flo," Rose Perlman says.

"Why not?"

"There's so much bad feeling between Edwee and his sister already. Won't this just make everything that much worse?"

Granny Flo sighs. "Let me tell you something, Rose," she says. "Something that may help explain Edwee to you. Something I've never, never told anyone else before."

"What's that?"

"In my family, there's something called the bad Guggenheim gene. That bad gene pops up in every generation or so. My cousin Peggy had it. You know what a rip she was. She even wrote a book about it—about all her love affairs, and the illegitimate children she had by different men. She had so many lovers at one time that she had no idea who her children's fathers were! Peggy was crazy. Then there was Uncle Bob. Uncle Bob had the bad Guggenheim gene. He's the one who died of a heart attack getting out of his taxi in front of his mistress's house in Washington, D.C.—it was in all the papers at the time. He was *really* a rip. At dinner parties, he used to reach down inside the fronts of women's dresses and say, 'Just checking your cup size.' There was also Uncle Bill. William Guggenheim was crazy as a bedbug. He was two people—really! He had two names, and you never knew when you ran into him which one of his selves he was going to be. Some days he called himself William Guggenheim. Other times, he went by Gatenby Williams. When he was in his William Guggenheim phase, he was a very pious Jew who was studying to be a rabbi. When he turned into Gatenby Williams, he became an anti-Semite who claimed he'd come up with the Final Solution for Hitler! He wrote a book, too. His book was written by his Gatenby Williams self, but it was a book about his William Guggenheim self—all about how his William Guggenheim self, and all the other wealthy Jews, were plotting to take over the world and then exterminate all the Christians. I mean, he was really crazy, Rose. So you see, even though the family had a lot of money, there was always that bad Guggenheim gene that kept popping up and spoiling things for everybody. And that's how I've always explained Edwee:—it's the bad Guggenheim gene again, and there's nothing he can do about it. Of course, in a way, I have to blame myself for it: it came down to him, from me, in my family bloodline."

Rose Perlman studies her old friend's face quietly for a moment. Then she says softly, "You know, you said that Edwee was in your apartment when your poor little Itty-Bitty had her . . . accident. You don't suppose, do you, that Edwee—"

Granny Flo's fingers fly to her throat. "Oh, no," she cries. "Don't say that! Oh, I've thought of it, yes, but I can't let myself think that! I can't let myself think that my own son, one of my own flesh and blood, would ever do a thing like that—harm a poor little innocent animal who never would have hurt anyone, who never had anything but loving, gentle thoughts for everyone. I just couldn't bear to go on living if I let myself think a thought like that. I think I'd die if I believed that! Besides, I have a new Itty-Bitty now, you know. You've got to come by and meet my new Itty-Bitty. She's so adorable, so cute and cuddly and fun-loving and sweet and playful. She has a little rubber ball, and I toss it to her, and she fetches it and brings it back and drops it in my hand. So sweet! You see, Rose, that's what we have to remember. We have to replace the things we loved and lost as quickly as possible—the way you did with your little Fluffy, remember? We have to remember, always, that everything we're given in this life is replaceable— everything. Everything in our lives is replaceable, Rose, except our lives themselves, and God takes care of that. Next time we have lunch, I want you to come to my apartment and meet my new Itty-Bitty. We'll have a nice room service lunch."

"I'd love that, Flo," Rose Perlman says.

"And as for what happened to the other Itty-Bitty, I have a theory. To begin with, the day was warm, and all the windows in my sitting room were open, and there was a little slipper chair that I'd moved close to the window so I could sit in the breeze. Edwee came and started to carry on. He carried on, carried on, and Itty-Bitty was barking at him—Itty-Bitty never really liked Edwee—and finally Edwee was carrying on so much that I marched into my bedroom and closed the door and turned the bolt. Edwee kept carrying on, pounding on my door, and Itty-Bitty was still barking. Then Edwee's carrying-on stopped, and the barking stopped, and I waited in the bedroom for a few minutes to make sure that Edwee was gone. Then, when I came out, Edwee was gone, and Itty-Bitty was nowhere to be found. But there was that little slipper chair, too close to the open window. I think what happened was that after Edwee left, and Itty-Bitty was all alone in the room, she thought she'd been abandoned. She thought I'd abandoned her, since I was nowhere in sight, behind a locked bedroom door. She thought I'd locked her out—locked her out of my life. All alone there, like that, feeling she'd been abandoned by the one person she loved the most, she became terribly depressed. She saw the little slipper chair, hopped up on it, saw the open window . . . and jumped. At least that's what I believe is what must have happened. Oh," she says, patting the tabletop in front of her, "I just heard someone set a plate down in front of me, and I can smell tuna. It smells like Chicken of the Sea. This must be our tomato surprise."

From the *New York Times*, two days later:

FIRST: A "MYSTERY" MODEL . . .
NOW A "MYSTERY" VIDEOTAPE

The cosmetics industry, long fraught with secrecy and intrigue, has a new and intriguing riddle on its hands. First, there was the secret identity of the mysterious "Man with the Scar" who makes his elusive debut in a series of arresting and industry-acclaimed print ads and television commercials this week for "Mireille," a new fragrance from the Miray Corporation. Guests at a gala benefit Thursday night to launch the scent were promised they would "meet" the mystery "Mireille Man." They did, sort of. But when the blond male model made his appearance on stage, he was wearing the now-familiar chalk-white mask that Michael Crawford, the actor, wears in "Phantom of the Opera," the Broadway musical hit from London.

Now a second mystery has evolved. The capstone of the evening's festivities at the Hotel Pierre was the screening of a short videotape, a parody of the sexually suggestive advertising campaign that was used to promote Calvin Klein's perfume "Obsession." Diane Sawyer, the television personality, who was a guest at the launching party, pronounced the videotape "the cleverest, wittiest send-up of a competitor's advertising I've ever seen." And, the following evening, Dan Rather, another guest, made a humorous reference to the tape on the CBS Evening News, calling it a "must see."

Meanwhile, what amounts to a celebrity guessing game has begun among New Yorkers fortunate enough to have viewed the tape. Several guests at the "Mireille" launch claim to have been able to identify the unclad participants in the mock commercial as men and women prominent in New York's business, social, and artistic communities. The "commercial," those who have seen it told the Times, featured three people, a younger, fair-haired man, an older man with silver hair, and a young blond or red-headed woman, and a number of people at the party insist they know exactly who those three people are. The only problem: no one quite agrees with anyone else.

The younger man, for instance, has been variously "positively" identified as the film and rock star Sting; as rock star David Bowie; and as either singer Billy Joel or rock star Mick Jagger "with a wig." As for the young woman, a number of votes have been cast for Ivana Trump, the wife of Donald J. Trump, the real-estate developer and casino owner. Others, however, are casting their ballots in favor of Mrs. Trump's sister-in-law, Blaine Trump, who is married to Donald Trump's brother Robert. Other prominent New York women who are suspected of playing the "role" include Tina Brown, editor of Vanity Fair, Grace Mirabella of Vogue, and New York mega-editor Fredi Friedman. Fran Lebowitz, who was at the Pierre party, told the Times, "I know it was either Susan Gutfreund or Gayfryd Steinberg, unless Susan Gutfreund and Gayfryd Steinberg are the same person, which is a possibility."

There are nearly as many candidates who might have played the role of the older man as there are for the young woman. "It was definitely Felix Rohatyn," says Helen Gurley Brown, another guest. "Even though you could only see the back of his head, I recognized Felix's curls." Others insist that the older man was portrayed by Senator Patrick Moynihan. Since the event on Thursday benefited the New York Public Library, a number of guests believe that the man in question was the library's director, Vartan Gregorian. Mr. Gregorian roared with laughter when the question was put to him on the telephone today.

All this has created something of a popular demand for copies of the videotape. But the mystery has deepened, and the question now is: Where is it? At the Miray Corporation, no one is saying. Mark Segal, the company's advertising director, is insisting that he knows nothing about it. "It was as much of a surprise to me as it was to everybody else," Mr. Segal told the Times, managing to keep a straight face as he did so.

Meanwhile, Jeffrey Jones, the projectionist who screened the film at the Pierre, and who is not employed by Miray, says only that "a Miray executive" collected the tape from him after it was screened. Miray's president and chief executive officer, Mimi Myerson, could not be reached for comment, and repeated telephone calls to her office were not returned.

But Miss Myerson's husband, Bradford Moore, a prominent New York attorney, did come to the phone at his Wall Street office and provided an answer of sorts. "My wife's business," he told the Times, "is a business of unknowns. Mystery is always a part of it. The word *cosmetics* comes from the Greek *kosmetikos*, meaning arrangement, or adornment, through artifice. What are cosmetics, after all, but beautiful disguises, gentle deceptions, creating illusions by changing appearances to obscure and soften realities? Mystery is part of the fun—you know, does she, or doesn't she? Cosmetics are about how human beings change, and rearrange, their senses and feelings about one another. But I'll tell you one thing, since I was there Thursday night. My wife was as taken by surprise as everyone else when that little gem flashed on the screen, and so, to me, this narrows the maker of this tape down to a field of one: our son, Brad Jr., who's Miray's Director of Sales.

"Brad's nickname is Badger," Mr. Moore went on. "The badger is a very sturdy, industrious, and resourceful little animal, with more tricks up his sleeve than most people give him credit for. I suggest that if you want to get to the bottom of this, you should try tracking the badger to his lair."

The younger Mr. Moore was in Tulsa today at a Miray sales conference and could not be reached for comment.

Meanwhile, the plot thickens. Stay tuned.

"Mark?" Mimi says, when she reaches him on the intercom. "Have you *read* this? Isn't it *wonderful*? Didn't you love what Brad said—giving all the credit to Badger? We could never buy publicity like this!"

"Listen, I've got both *Time* and *Newsweek* on the phone," he says.

"Have you been following me?" she asks him. She has just looked up to see him standing beside her, waiting for the light to change at the corner of Fifth Avenue and 59th Street.

"Of course," he says.

"I often walk home on nights like this."

"I know that."

"Do you always know everything?"

"Of course."

The light changes, and they start across the street. "When I didn't hear any more about Palm Beach, I thought I'd give it one more try," he says.

They continue walking northward on Fifth Avenue.

"We're almost there," he says.

"Almost where?"

"The skating pond . . . remember?"

"Oh, yes."

"Shall we go and take a look at it?"

"All right."

At the next light, they cross the avenue and move into the park.

"It was right there," he says. "That bench, there."

"Are you sure? Wasn't it—?"

"I'm positive. It was this one."

"It has a broken back."

"We can sit on this end. Shall we sit here for just a minute?"

"All right."

The skating pond is just a pond again, its surface riffled by a westerly breeze and scattered with a few early-falling autumn leaves. Two gulls settle on the water, arching their wings and nestling their bills into their wing-blades' cavities, probing and preening. The gulls move like a pair of plows across the water.

"That means a storm's coming," she says. "Whenever a storm's coming, the seagulls fly in from the Atlantic. The gulls are a barometer. It's nice to be reminded that we live in a seaport. Did you feel the wind change just then?"

"Yes."

"And look: a rabbit."

"Where?"

"Over there." She points.

"Oh, yes. You know, I've always thought it was too bad this park can't be developed. High-rises, garden apartments. A guy could make a fortune."

She looks at him briefly, just to be sure he isn't being serious.

"Well," he says at last, "I guess I know what your answer is."

"Yes, I think you do, Michael."

"Just tell me one thing," he says. "Did you ever love me?"

"Oh, yes. Terribly. Didn't you know that? Unbearably. And . . ."

"And what?"

"And in some ways, I still do. And probably always will. But there are different kinds of love, Michael, you know that."

"You're saying you love him more."

"It's not a question of degree. It's not a question of quantity. It's more a question of quality, I guess."

"His love is better, then."

"No, not even that. It's just . . . I mean, look at us, sitting here, two middle-aged people—"

"You still look eighteen years old to me."

"I told you I was nineteen."

"You were lying."

"You knew that?"

"Of course."

"And you look just the same to me, too," she says. "But underneath, we're not the same. I think you know that. And for me—I just don't think I could bear it, to go back to the kind of love I felt for you. It was too . . . grueling, I guess the word is. I'm not saying I regret any of it, because I don't."

The wind picks up, and there is definitely the smell of rain in the air. "Let me tell you what it was like," she says. "Three winters ago, Brad and I went on a horse safari in Africa. Ten days on horseback through the Masai Mara. Eight, nine hours a day of hard, rough riding, across rivers and mountains and rock slides, in the most uncomfortable Australian saddle I've ever sat on. It was wonderful, out there in the middle of the herds of animals, but by the third day I wondered if I'd ever walk again without a limp! I wouldn't trade that experience for anything, but nothing could persuade me to live through it again. It's the same with you. I don't want to repeat the experience, even though I know I could, because I've felt perilously close to it in the past few weeks."

"Have you?"

"Oh, yes. But I've had to force myself to think the way Brad thinks, the way a lawyer thinks. You know, 'on the one hand, . . . but then, on the other hand . . .'"

"A cold-blooded way of thinking."

"No, not cold-blooded. Not at all. But I've thought, on the one hand, there's the danger, and excitement, of running off into uncharted territory with a man I loved desperately years ago, but really never knew too well. And, on the other hand, there's the comradeship I have with my husband. That's what we have, Michael: comradeship. We've been through a lot together, he and I. I've invested twenty-nine years in my marriage—that's nearly half a lifetime. That's a very valuable investment to me, Michael, and I don't want to let it go. I'll fight very hard to keep that investment, and that's not cold-blooded because it's an investment in a marriage, and in love. Do you understand what I'm saying, Michael?"

"I suppose so," he says. And then, "But let me just tell you one thing, since you say you never knew me very well. When I started buying shares in your company, it wasn't because I wanted to take it over. It was because I wanted you."

She laughs softly. "You chose an odd way to go about it."

"It got your attention, didn't it?"

"Oh, yes. But are you sure there wasn't a little motive of revenge in it as well? Over the way Grandpa treated you years ago?"

"Well, perhaps, a little," he admits, studying the backs of his hands. "But I'll tell you one thing: your idea of taking your company private is a good one. Right now, Miray is a sitting duck as a takeover target. If I were you, I'd go for privatization. Then nobody could touch you."

"It's Badger's idea, not mine."

"But all I really wanted was you," he says. "And Badger."

"I don't want to discuss Badger with you now. Badger's a grown man, with big, strong shoulders, who can pretty much tackle anything. I'll just say this much: you may be Badger's father, but Badger will always be Brad Moore's son, if you can see that subtle difference."

"Yes, I suppose I can."

"And if you ever say anything otherwise to anyone, I'll deny it to my dying day."

"I'd never say anything otherwise to anyone, Mimi."

"Good. Then—" Other gulls have joined the pair on the skating pond, and the late-afternoon sunshine, filtered through the turning leaves, dapples the surface of the water.

"I guess you don't know me very well," he says, "if you think I'd ever make that sort of claim. I don't think you've ever trusted me."

"Perhaps that's true."

"Like a rough ride across Africa. I was that rough on you?"

"Yes, dear heart, you were." Still are, she thinks.

He looks out. "But I have a broken skate lace to remember you by," he says.

"And I have a ring."

"You cried when I gave you that ring."

"I cried because it was the most beautiful ring I'd ever seen. It still is."

"Will I ever see your tears again? Tears in your silver eyes?" He stands up, raising his arms high in the air, crossed at the wrists, his fists clenched, and takes a deep breath. "I'll walk you back to the street," he says, and she also rises.

When they reach the street, he says simply, "Good-bye. Just don't forget me."

"You told me once I never would. I won't."

"Well, see you around, kiddo," he says, and he gives her a little wink.

See you around, kiddo, she thinks. And she thinks too: Is this parting going to be as matter-of-fact as this? Is this all there was to it for him, just a *so long,* and a *see you around?* Is that all it was for him? Then she remembers that this, after all, is Michael, and there has always been something a little careless about him, a little oh, well, so what. This is a man who asked her to marry him before he remembered to tell her he loved her. This is a man who stuffed his socks every which way into a drawer, who chucked his dirty laundry under his bed, who stored his fireplace logs behind the skirts of a sofa, and who hung up his neckties without bothering to unknot them. He is careless about women, too, treating the hundreds who have wandered in and out of his life over the years as though they were no more important than properties on a Monopoly board, acquiring them and disposing of them as casually as he acquired and disposed of condominiums. All he is doing now is wandering off from her, off into his vast carelessness.

"It wouldn't have worked out for us," she says, realizing that this is not a great last line. "It wouldn't, because we never took the trouble to think things through."

He merely shrugs, then turns and begins walking south. After a moment, she also turns, slowly, and starts walking northward.

Oh, yes, she thinks. Even our parting seems careless. But he remembered my tears that afternoon. And he remembered my James Robinson silver eyes. And he remembered, oh, I know he remembered, how I loved him. She feels the first drop of rain on her cheek. It is a raindrop, she will always swear it, not a tear.

Have I let him hurt me again, she asks herself? Dear God, if there is a God, I swore, I will never let him hurt me again. Yet this cannot be a hurt, this time, because this was my choice, my decision. And yet, dear God, if there is a God, will I always miss that hurting? Of course I will.

She continues walking northward.

Then, after a few steps, she stops and turns back to watch his retreating figure. There is very little pedestrian traffic on upper Fifth Avenue at this time of day, and the two of them are alone on this stretch of shaded, darkening sidewalk. Something is missing, she thinks, something is wrong. Shouldn't he have kissed me good-bye? Don't I deserve at least that much? Shouldn't he turn, right now, and see my eyes following him, and turn back to me for that? If this were a movie, there would be that obligatory turn. She can see the scene on the screen. He turns, sees her standing there, watching him walk away, and the lovers run toward each other under the trees, in that mottled, late-afternoon fall sunlight, for that final kiss, with the cool wind from the sea as a benediction. But that doesn't happen, and he doesn't turn, and he isn't going to turn.

Stop, she commands him with her eyes. *Stop, look back at me. I am one of the most famous women in New York right now, and I was ready to give myself to you. I deserve this much. Stop, look back at me.*

But he refuses to obey her and is walking, instead, steadily away from her, his hands in his trousers pockets, walking with what she has always called his pugilist's walk, bouncing slightly on the balls of his feet, like a winning prizefighter returning triumphant to his corner of the ring.

Then she sees that it is not a pugilist's walk, but more of an aerialist's walk, as though his feet were bouncing on a high, taut wire. She thinks: Ah, we are both successful aerialists, two tightrope walkers who approached each other along the high wire, our balancing poles poised, who met, performed a brief duet above the circus crowd, and then retreated. He is a true *Luftmensch,* she thinks, a man who lives on, and in, the air, for aren't making big deals and money and getting rich all things that are as flimsy and transitory and invisible as the thin air itself? Ah, but the difference between this pair of aerialists is that he always spurns the net. She always makes certain that the safety net is securely set beneath her. It is there in place underneath her now. She sees him toss that wayward lock of sandy hair back across his forehead, sees him jut out that purposeful lower jaw. But when her vision clears and her eyes refocus, she sees that the sidewalk is empty now, and he is gone. She turns northward again, toward home.

Of course, all that was nearly a year and a half ago. The privatization plan went smoothly, with a majority of Miray's stockholders voting in favor of it, including the Leo cousins and Michael Horowitz, who did not attend the meeting but voted by proxy. Miracorp came officially into existence on October 15, 1987, just days before the crash that Granny had predicted. As a private company—as Granny had foreseen—it was scarcely affected by the market's collapse.

Nonie, with her own money now, has set up shop as a currency trader—a foreign exchange, or FX, as they call it, specialist, with her partner, Roger Williams. They have opened an office on Pine Street, with a small cadre of employees, and their firm, Myerson & Lahniers, appears to be doing very well, even in these uncertain financial times. It should be pointed out that there is no one named Lahniers in the firm, but that is not uncommon. There was no one named Rhoades in Loeb, Rhoades & Company. The name was added for cachet, which Nonie has done, picking the name at random out of the telephone book. It is often useful, in a firm like this, to append one Christian-sounding name, and Lahniers had that right, Christian-sounding ring. For some reason, Roger Williams did not want his name on the firm's masthead, even though he is the mastermind behind the firm's success. There are rumors, to be sure—nothing specific—that there is something shady about Roger Williams's past, even rumors that Roger Williams is not his real name. It is not that this Roger Williams is an Ivan Boesky—not in that league at all. Just a lot of questions about where he came from and who he really is. There is nothing at all illegal about what firms like Myerson & Lahniers do. There are dozens of firms like theirs in the city. It is fast-paced, nerve-wracking work, but spot traders' desks can often show a net profit of between $150,000 and $200,000 a day. Not quite $8,000 a minute, perhaps, but O.K.

There are also rumors that Roger Williams and Nonie may marry, despite the marked difference in their ages. But, to this, rumors that Roger Williams already has a wife somewhere have been added. Oklahoma City has been mentioned, but I am only repeating gossip. It is a little odd that Roger Williams will not be interviewed and refuses to be photographed. But Nonie, who enjoys high visibility, handles the press.

The mystery of the identity of the Mireille Man, and the authenticity of his scar, was kept alive almost to the end of the ad campaign. Then, just when the public was beginning to lose interest anyway, Mark Segal released the news of the model's name and the fact that the scar was another example of the cosmetician's art. This produced a nice final flurry of publicity for Mireille, which, as you know, is now firmly established in the pantheon of fine American fragrances.

Meanwhile, the formula for Mireille remains a secret, locked in a vault in Mimi's office, known only to Mimi, Badger, and one or two of their top, most trusted chemists. Using what are known as gas chromatography tests, competitors have tried to "fingerprint" its essence, but so far they have been unsuccessful. But I suspect that one of its key ingredients is Bulgarian rose absolute, don't you? I know that when I splash it on my face I envision Bulgarian peasant maidens, in long dirndl skirts and babushkas, or whatever it is that Bulgarian peasant maidens wear, gathering rose petals at dawn in the foothills of the Balkan Mountains overlooking the Black Sea. Foothills facing east, toward the rising sun.

In any case, by the campaign's end, both models' careers were finished—the victims of overexposure, as anyone could have told them. Perhaps someone did tell them, but people usually only listen to what they want to hear. Oddly enough, of the two, Sherrill Shearson was the more clever in terms of managing the money she earned. She invested shrewdly in East Bronx real estate, and though it would be unfair to call her a slum lord, the East Bronx is the East Bronx, and the income from her rentals has made her a reasonably rich woman. In January, she married a dentist from Forest Hills, and they are now a part of the country club set out there.

Dirk Gordon was less fortunate, despite his suavely knowing and worldly persona. Having read somewhere that the most likely places for singles to meet one another were bars and Laundromats, he and a friend decided to put all their money into a bar-cum-Laundromat on Second Avenue. It was to be called The Laundry Bag, and its slogan was "We Do Your Thing." It failed miserably, and Dirk lost all his money in the venture. When last I heard, he was working as a salesman for Coca-Cola, or perhaps it was Pepsi-Cola. He is still occasionally recognized, and since I like to imagine such encounters, I imagine someone saying to him: "Hey, didn't you use to be big in TV commercials?" And his reply: "I'm still big. It's the commercials that got small."

Granny Flo died at Christmastime, and you may have seen the headline in the *Times:*

MYERSON CLAN LOSES ITS
BELOVED MATRIARCH AT 90

Beloved? Well, by some, I suppose . . . but matriarch, certainly. She was found in her chair in her sitting room by Harry, her favorite night bellman, when he came up to tune in Lawrence Welk for her on television. At first he thought she was asleep, but when he couldn't awaken her, he phoned down to George at the front desk to say, "Mrs. Myerson won't wake up!" Nor did she. Itty-Bitty was sitting on her lap, guarding her protectively. In fact, the hotel staff had quite a struggle with the little dog to get her to relinquish her place on Granny's lap so that Granny's body could be removed. Rose Perlman is very lonely now, having lost her last contemporary friend, but she does have the companionship of a new Fluffy.

The turnout for Granny Flo's funeral was enormous, nearly filling the main sanctuary at Temple Emanu-El. No one had realized that she had so many friends and admirers. The family was all there, in the front pews: Mimi and Brad and Badger, seated together; Edwee Myerson, a few seats away, his face expressionless; Nonie, weeping quietly, clutching the arm of her friend and partner, Mr. Williams; her contemporary, Alice, dry-eyed and with what even seemed to me a quiet smile of triumph hovering about her lips; and the Leo cousins. All told, as I counted them, four generations of the Myerson clan were represented there—five, if you counted the old lady who had been wheeled down the center aisle in her coffin.

The entire staff of the Hotel Carlyle, just up the street, had been given two hours off to attend the services, and they were all there, along with scores of others who, though they might have known Granny Flo only slightly, had been recipients of her benefactions, large and small, over the years.

During the eulogy, Mimi stood up and said a few words. "Though she lacked a formal education," I heard her say, "she possessed a great store of what I can only call natural wisdom."

Rabbi Sobel delivered the final eulogy. "Though small in stature," we heard him say, "Fleurette Myerson was large in spirit, large in heart and giving, large in the spirit of *zedakah*, of righteousness, large in wit and humor and courage. Though the last years were handicapped by near-blindness, this daughter of Israel bore her affliction with grit and without complaint. Her life . . ."

As the rabbi spoke, a small, dark object made its way out of one of the back pews and scuttled down the center aisle of the temple, toward the ark and the bier on which Granny's flower-blanketed coffin lay. It was Itty-Bitty, who had been smuggled into the sanctuary by Harry, Granny's favorite night porter, underneath his jacket, and who had been released, either by accident or design—no one ever knew—at just that point in the service. There was a collective gasp in the temple when the mourners realized what had happened.

Itty-Bitty proceeded briskly toward the coffin, her toenails clicking on the polished marble floor; and when she reached the bier, she sniffed it once or twice, then lay down beside it, whimpering softly.

From the pulpit, Rabbi Sobel saw what was happening and paused briefly. Then he continued, "Her life touched hearts large and small." And there was a ripple of soft laughter from the mourners.

Itty-Bitty now resides with Badger and his lovely new wife, Connie. Yes, Badger was married about six months ago, to a girl he had been seeing quietly for some time. Badger's announcement came as quite a surprise to Mimi, but Mimi and Connie get on famously. Badger and Connie are expecting a baby in the fall. Will this mean that there will be a fifth-generation Myerson to run Miray? No one has a crystal ball, of course, and such occurrences within a family company are pretty rare. But they have happened.

On the other side of the matrimonial coin, Edwee and Gloria were divorced not long after our story ended. At first, Edwee tried to fight it, but when Gloria threatened to expose some of his more bizarre sexual experiments, Edwee backed down, and Gloria ended up with a nice settlement. Also, Gloria was clever enough to have her bruises photographed in the aftermath of what happened at home that night following the Mireille party at the Pierre. "Always have your bruises photographed," she now counsels friends who find themselves in similar situations. "And always have it done, in color of course, on the second day after he beats you up, 'cause that's when they look the worst. I'll give you the name of the most marvelous little man, who does fabulous color work, who used to work for Bachrach."

I've seen very little of Mimi lately. In recent months, she has been turn-

ing more and more of the control of her company over to Badger, in preparation, perhaps, for her retirement or, more likely, for her assumption of the
role of sort of an elder stateswoman at Miray. And now, of course, as a
Senate wife, she spends much of her time in Washington, though she is far
from retired at Miracorp.

The choice to see little of Mimi has been partly my own, for my own
peace of mind, you might say. Because, you see, at the time when I thought
that Mimi might be going to leave Brad, I had the crazy notion that she and
I might—but no, I think I'd rather not go into that at this point.

During congressional recesses, she and Brad usually travel, and from time
to time she remembers me with a postcard from one exotic place or another,
such as one I received a few weeks ago from St.-Jean-de-Luz in the south of
France. I knew, of course, that this was where she and Brad had spent their
honeymoon in the autumn of 1958. She wrote:

> *We refuse to call this a* second *honeymoon, despite what you'll think. Just*
> *visiting special places, doing touristy things, visiting museums, cathedrals,*
> *shopping, eating too much. Cheers!*
> ### XXXX & OOOO
> *Brad & Mimi*

Then, just the other day, I ran into her on 57th Street, coming out of one
of those china shops just east of Park. She had just been looking at a set of
Chelseaware plates decorated with lobster claws, she said. Brad's birthday
was coming up, the double-five. She asked me how my book was coming.
"Moving along," I told her.

"Just don't forget the lesson of the Sèvres vase," she said. "Things are
more interesting when they've earned a few battle scars," and she laughed
that special pebbly, thrilling laugh of hers.

Then she was off, blowing me a kiss. She was still a woman whom, if you
saw her on the street, you would look at twice, whether it was her posture, or
her sense of style, or her loose and bouncing blond hair, or her extraordinary
eyes, and as she walked quickly away from me down 57th Street, I saw
various heads turn—both men's and women's—for a second look.

For a moment I wondered what she meant by her parting piece of advice.
Then I decided that I knew. She was telling me that a damaged marriage,
like a broken piece of porcelain, can be redeemed through love and caring.

Meanwhile, the acquisitive Mrs. Rita Robinson has abandoned her quest
and, I understand, has moved on in search of other prey. In New York,
perhaps more so than in other places, life goes on.

As for Michael Horowitz, from what I read in the papers, he just goes on making money, and with each successful deal, the more grandiose grow his future plans. Right now, he has unveiled a scheme to turn a tract of abandoned railroad yards on the Upper West Side into a whole new city within a city: theatres, shopping malls, a sports arena, high-rise luxury apartment and office towers, and, for good measure, a structure that will be the tallest building in the world with views from here to Philadelphia. Sometimes I think that with men like Michael money and deal-making become a narcotic, and that the more money he makes the more he needs to feed his habit. Certainly he has more money now than he could ever possibly spend. And sometimes I wonder, too, whether his coming back to pursue Mimi after all those years was because she represented, to him, one deal that he had never quite been able to pull off. But I also wonder—since he doesn't seem to be the kind of man cut out for marriage—whether, when they said good-bye, he was bitterly resigned to his loss, or whether he was secretly a little bit relieved. Perhaps he always knew that he was someone who could provide a certain summer to her heart, but not the full four seasons of the year. Who knows?

Meanwhile, his enemies—and he has many—and his competitors, all those people who call him "Michael Horror-witz," predict that he is riding for a fall. So far, this hasn't happened, and he climbs on, higher and higher, toward the center of the Big Top, and when he reaches that . . . But in the meantime he must climb on, higher, faster, toward whatever dizzy goal remains.

His friends say that he will never marry.

Michael Horowitz and Badger finally met for the first time just two months ago. Their meeting was quite accidental. They met—almost literally bumped into one another, in fact—as they were stepping out of their respective shower stalls in the men's locker room at the Century Country Club in Westchester County. Toweling his hair dry, the younger man stepped out of his shower and turned right. The older man, doing the same thing, stepped out and turned left. Thus, each other's bare shoulders and elbows barely missed colliding in the process.

"Oops. Sorry."

"Sorry."

Stepping back, it was Badger who first realized who the older man was. "You're Michael Horowitz," said Badger.

"Yes."

"Badger Moore."

The two nude and dripping men shook hands with one another as formally as was possible under the circumstances, though neither man could avoid casting his eyes briefly downward to see how the other was hung. Then both quietly slung their towels around their middles.

Both are well-muscled and flat-bellied, and there is even a certain physical resemblance between the two of them, though Badger Moore is an inch or two taller than the older man.

"I didn't realize you were a member of this club," Badger said, immediately realizing that this sounded snotty. He hadn't meant it to sound that way.

"Yes. They're letting in quite a few of my element these days."

"Beg your pardon?"

"Never mind. It's a long story." Then Michael said, "By the way, I really wasn't trying to take over your company, you know."

"Well, it doesn't matter now, does it?"

"No hard feelings, then?"

"None."

"Good," Michael said. Then he said a strange thing. "I'd really like to get to know you better," he said. "I'd like us to be friends."

For a moment Badger wondered whether Michael Horowitz might be gay. But he quickly dismissed this thought as both unworthy and unbecoming. "Sure," he said pleasantly. "Let's have lunch someday."

"I'd like that."

"Give me a call."

"Call you."

The two shook hands again, and then each man headed for his respective locker—Badger's being number 24, and Michael's being 316, in the opposite direction—to dress.

To my knowledge, that lunch has yet to take place.

The only person I feared hurting with the diaries that Mimi turned over to me was her mother. I finally decided to approach Alice Myerson directly with what I knew and to ask her what I ought to do.

She said, "It was the most terrible moment of my life, beyond question. I hid the car in the garage that night, thinking that the nightmare of what happened that afternoon would go away if I could just hide the car. But Henry read the account of what happened in the newspaper the next morning, and that night he went down to look at the car. He came upstairs and said to me, 'Did you do this?' And I said, 'Yes—oh, yes, oh, Henry, help me!' And the next day Henry went to his father, and his father went to work to fix things up, using those friends of Uncle Leo's. I was sent to Maine, and the servants were told to say I'd been there all summer, since Mimi's birthday, to give me an alibi. People were paid off, license plates were switched, cars were switched, and everything was supposed to be fixed up.

"But then Leo became suspicious, and I'm certain Leo stole the diaries, though how he did it I don't know. Then Leo started blackmailing Henry, and then Leo's son Nate took over. He had some sort of letter proving that I wasn't in Maine but was in New York at the time. For years, Leo and Nate bled us. At first, it wasn't for too much, but it kept getting worse. It got worse and worse as the years went by, and once we had started it there was no stopping it. Nate said to Henry, 'The fact that you're paying us is proof that she's guilty, isn't it?' Then Leo died, and Nate took over single-handedly, and it was worse than ever. He bled us and bled us until it seemed there was no blood left in us. There was no stopping it.

"Then, one night in nineteen sixty-two, Henry came home and said to me, 'I've gotten rid of Nate. We're free,' or something like that, and I said, 'What do you mean?' And he said, 'I've done it—I've had him killed.' And I screamed—I was drunk, but I can remember everything I said. I screamed, 'I can't live like this! I can't live with a man who'd do this sort of thing to me! Because you blame *me*, don't you! You're saying I have one man's blood on my hands already, and now I have another's. You blame *me*. You've always blamed *me* for everything, you and your family.' And I ran out of the house, with only my purse, and I ran . . . ran all the way to Grand Central Station, fifty blocks, and got on a train. I didn't even know where the train was going. I found the bar car, and I drank and drank, and finally I remember thinking it was time to get off. And when I got off, there was a motel, and it had a bar. And I didn't even know where I was, but I stayed. I don't know how long I stayed there, but it was while I was gone that Henry did what he did. And of course he did it just to place more blame on me."

"Could that old case be reopened?" I asked her.

She smiled, and it was almost a defiant smile. "Do you know something?" she said. "I don't even care. Because that was a different woman who did all those things. I don't know her, don't even recognize her anymore. It's as though she died, even though I know she didn't die. The statute of limitations may not have run out, but that woman's statute of limitations has run out."

I asked her what she meant by that.

"The limitations that limited that woman are gone," she said. "That other, that terribly limited other woman, was a woman who couldn't face the truth, couldn't face reality. I can face reality now, and knowing that I can face reality—any reality, even the reality of this—makes me even stronger, more sure of myself. Because the reality is that I was *not* to blame. I was not to blame for any of it. I am without guilt. Part of the blame lies with Adolph and Flo, for the way they treated Henry and the way they treated me. But that was only part of it. The real villain was alcohol. It wasn't me driving the car that afternoon, it was alcohol. So you see, if that case is ever opened up again, I have my iron-clad defense. Not guilty, Your Honor! I even have witnesses. Dr. Bergler, my therapist, has told me that I'm guilty of nothing—no crime, no felony, not even the tiniest little misdemeanor. The members of the support group that I go to—they'll all take the stand and swear that I did nothing wrong, that the criminal was not even me. It was alcohol. And if you put that in your story, and I hope and pray you will, maybe it will help Mimi realize who the real criminal was, and help her understand me a little better, and appreciate me a little more, because Mimi has never really appreciated me. The real me."

And of course I did not write my story for *Fortune.* Or, to be more honest and exact, I did not write the story their editors wanted. They wanted a story about corporate muscle, about fiscal derring-do in a glamour industry; a story that told of how old Adolph Myerson launched each new nail polish and lipstick shade by turning the Miray offices into the equivalent of the War Room in the Pentagon, in contrast with Mimi's more limber and upbeat and personal style. I see that, instead, what I have written is a love story, about different kinds of love: of Adolph's love for Flo and, in his fashion, his children; of Granny's love for Henry, and her long line of Itty-Bittys; of Henry's love for Alice; of Nonie's love of money and power; of Edwee's love for Goya's Duchess of Osuna; of Mimi's love for Brad and Badger, and her love for Michael, and Michael's love for her. And if there is one connective theme uniting all these different kinds of love, it is that if life is a tree, as someone else has said, then love is the power that holds the leaf to the stem.

There is a favorite bar I sometimes drop in at, on Columbus Avenue just north of 72nd Street. My father used to say, "All bars are alike, but it's the personality of the bartender that makes the difference." That's what I like about this particular bar. The bartender's name is Alejandro, but everybody calls him Al, a fat, jovial Hispanic whose belly bounces when he laughs. I dropped in there the other day and was sitting at the bar, sipping a Scotch and swapping stories with Al, and I said, "Let me ask you something, Al. Booze is your livelihood. Are the distillers of America to blame for alcoholics?"

He laughed. "I tell you some-sing," he said. "Ze alcoholics is ze biggest liars in ze world." He placed his large palms flat on the bar. "And I tell you some-sing else," he said. "When zey are a-sober, zey are ze even bigger liars."

We both laughed.

Al's bar, mind you, is not the sort of bar, nor is Al the sort of bartender, that anyone would associate with anything remotely connected with the Myersons. But as I sat there, I became aware of two older people seated at a table in the far corner of the room. They were holding hands and looking deeply into each other's eyes, and at first, I thought that these were two elderly lovers meeting for a secret tryst, and the scene was not without its certain charm and poignancy. One is never too old to fall in love, I thought, and I said the same to Al, who'd also noticed them. Then, as my eyes grew more accustomed to the certain gloom of the place, I realized that what I had mistaken for elderly lovers were, in fact, Nonie Myerson and her brother Edwee. I stepped over to their table to speak to them.

What had happened, I learned, and what accounted for the expressions of rapture on both their faces, was that Nonie had just given Edwee her Goya. She had never been interested in art, she explained, and had never really cared for eighteenth-century *anything*. The eighteenth century hardly went well with her hard-edge, high-tech, contemporary decor. She had not even hung Osuna but had kept her, with her face to the wall, in the back of her refrigerated cedar closet where she stored her winter furs. Furthermore, now that her Pine Street firm was prospering so nicely, Nonie no longer felt any need for the kind of insurance her mother had intended the painting to be. Now it was his, and she felt much better about the whole thing.

I was so surprised by Nonie's news that I never did find out why she had chosen a place like Al's bar to announce her decision. But, considering everything Edwee had put her through, I could only conclude that it was a gesture on her part that was—well, magnificent.